PRAISE

'Pat Black has breathed n
To Pay the Ferryman, the
highly entertaining series'
Mark Sanderson, *The Times*

'Arresting writing . . . the art theme works very well, and the villain is a surprise'
Jeremy Black, *The Critic*

'With a well-worked plot and credible, sympathetic characters, this is an enjoyable slice of tartan noir'
Allan Massie, *The Scotsman*

'Plenty of Scottish police humour, awful coffee, and a most dramatic ending'
Daily Mirror

'A gripping, multi-faceted mystery with a cast of engaging characters and a delicious dose of camaraderie spiced with dark humour'
Sally McDonald, *Sunday Post*

'There's a dark sense of humour that bubbles away nicely beneath the grisly plot, and Black's writing style is hypnotically succinct'
Scottish Field

'A classic murder mystery . . . laced with Scottish humour. Glasgow-born Pat Black is the author of several thrillers and this is a fine addition to his expert storytelling'
Ella Walker, *Irish News*

'A smartly-written thriller'
Alastair Mabbott, *The Herald*

'Packed with urgency and threat, and ultimately satisfying'
Jen Med Book Reviews

A note on the author

Pat Black lives in Yorkshire with his wife and children. He will always belong to Glasgow.

Jack-in-the-Box

PAT BLACK

Polygon

First published in 2026 by Polygon, an imprint of Birlinn Ltd.

Birlinn Ltd
West Newington House
10 Newington Road
Edinburgh
EH9 1QS

www.polygonbooks.co.uk

1

ISBN 978 1 84697 717 6
eBook ISBN 978 1 78885 823 6

British Library Cataloguing-in-Publication Data
A catalogue record for this book is available on request from the British Library.

Typeset by 3btype, Edinburgh.

Printed and bound by CPI Group (UK) Ltd

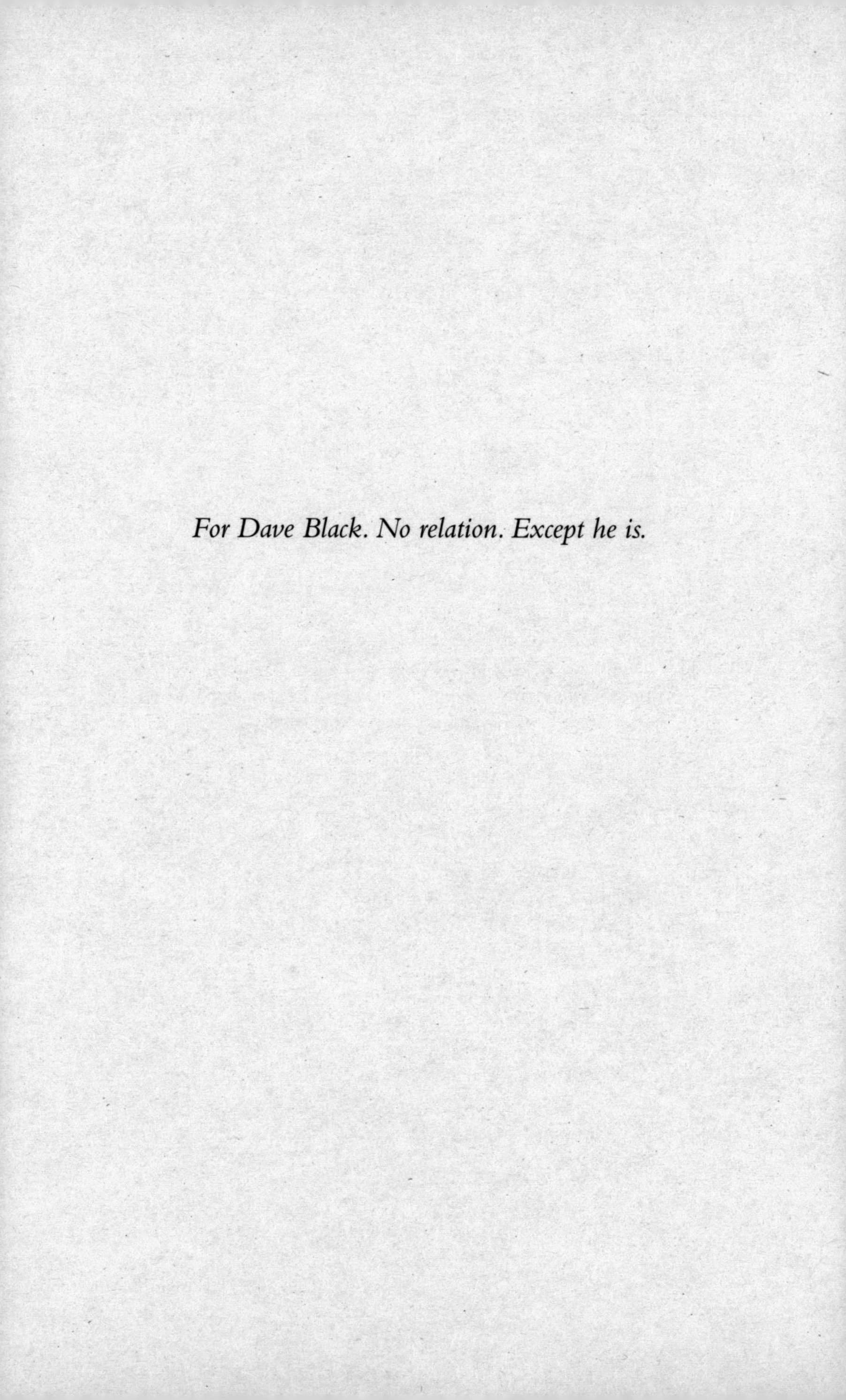

For Dave Black. No relation. Except he is.

1

Kath had a mother hen moment as Beatrice waved goodbye.

It might have been the falling snow, the leaden skies, or just January in general. A need to stay close to the little one, to keep her safe. Kath remembered her own mother had once declared a snow day, when she was about the same age as Beatrice, without any warning other than a few thick flakes of snow. They'd had a wonderful time away from the school. Tea and toast, and the radio; felt-tip pens and colouring books, and even a cake after lunch. Just for a moment, at the bus stop, Kath had considered doing the same. *Might be nice.*

But the moment was lost for ever upon sight of the bus's yellow and green livery. The little girl in pigtails turned to wave before she hopped up to take the seat beside Jessica, her best friend.

'Have a good day, sweetheart!' Kath cried, loud enough for Beatrice to hear through the glass. Absurdly, she felt on the verge of tears. Beatrice waved and smiled, oblivious.

She'd been jumpy all morning. Ed was gone for a few days – some jolly in Amsterdam: eyebrows raised, uneasy smiles, work, of course – and while she wasn't worried about what he got up to over there, she had a childish habit of not being able to sleep while he was gone. Lights on and everything. Something she'd have scolded Beatrice about. Kath still saw monsters in corners. Unblinking yellow eyes under the bed. She reproved herself for these childish fancies, but she couldn't stop them. As she checked inside the hall cupboard for the second time, she thought, *I'll do this until my dying day.*

There were some odd moments as the morning wore on. The snow had stopped minutes after it started, and it even grew mild outside. Kath decided to give some bedsheets an airing after the washing-machine cycle finished, not liking the fusty smell that hung around house-dried laundry, usually a necessity given the time of year.

She'd been happy to see two foxes playing in the frost-covered wasteground as she pegged out the sheets. But only an hour later, when the blue skies had given way to grey cloud, they were gone. The only warm-blooded life out there was a dirty great crow squatting in one of the trees that obscured the houses backing onto the garden. The wind was bitter, and Kath wondered if more snow was on the way.

Worried that the bedding would freeze with the sharp drop in temperature, she gathered the sheets and spaced them out on the clothes rack in the utility room. They flapped and billowed like grasping hands, and Kath felt a brief panic as the white fabric twisted around her – echoes of ghosts wreathed in sheets with scissored eyes. Jittery as a kitten, she closed the windows, locked the patio doors and then, on an impulse, checked the security cameras monitor. Nothing, of course. Nothing in front of the house, nothing in the garden, nothing in the garage, nothing down the side where the bins lived, in front of the padlocked gate . . .

Kath called her mother on the landline, but there was no reply. Neither the computer's humming solace nor the cosy DJ she favoured after lunchtime could shake that feeling of isolation that came during quiet afternoons alone in the house. The snow was turning to slush on the patio, frosting the trees beyond the fence. Kath didn't want to look too closely. She always imagined that someone might be hiding there.

Despite the ticking of the radiators and the warmth they exuded, she decided to have a bath. *Warm those bones. Nice and cosy.* Her shoulder muscles unbunched at the thought.

Lying back in the intense fog from the churning water,

Kath kept one eye on the bathroom door. No snib lock. Ed had wanted one, but Kath was against it. *What if Beatrice got locked in*?

So, even when the door crept open and the dressing gown hanging from the peg swung towards her, blurred through the shower screen, Kath's mind rationalised the situation. A window left open, surely. A sudden gust of midwinter wind pushing the bathroom door open.

And then the door closed.

Someone was standing there.

2

Corinne said cheerio to Mrs Gleniffer outside Grazers and Blazers. After a good two hours inside, this should only have taken a minute or so, but Corinne managed to extend it to at least five. Even Mrs Glennifer was turning a little bit twitchy, especially with that cold wind in her face. Sliced right through you, that, Corinne thought, turning her back on the sleety gusts and tucking her ears inside her hat.

'Oh, my Brian's back,' Mrs Gleniffer announced, brandishing the phone screen towards Corinne, far too fast for her to focus on. 'I'd best get home or he'll get some daft ideas in him. Start thinking he can make the dinner!'

'God forbid!' Corinne said, laughing, and the farewells were made at last. As she turned into the high street, wincing as a snowflake landed plum on the point of her nose, she thought her Brian would die before he boiled a bloody egg. Must be desperate to be rid of me, or something. Mind you, they'd been in Grazers and Blazers a while. Nice selection they had there. Good vanilla slice. You didn't often get one, these days – usually muffins and brownies. They could be a bit much.

Corinne had made it to the shelter of the supermarket entrance, right beside the strange pet shop, inside which she had never seen any customers, nor members of staff either, although the squeezy toys and bird tables and a dog bowl filled with water for passing trade – buffed up better than the silver service in her own house, she had to admit – were left outside the entrance as ever. She was thinking about Mrs Gleniffer and wondering if the phone was new, or just the case – Mrs

Gleniffer was forever dropping her bloody phones, or maybe firing them off Brian's head, which would make sense – when she realised she hadn't checked her own phone in a while. Reaching into her bag, her fingers curled around it. It was quivering and purring.

Corinne saw that she had missed twenty-six calls. She'd put the phone on silent in order to talk to Mrs Glennifer in Grazers and Blazers. She'd only meant to be in there an hour at most. New place, crafty stuff for sale, but none of your rubbish, mind . . .

Twenty-six calls. Suddenly she understood. She peeled off her gloves, the better to skate across the surface, but her fingers had forgotten how to operate.

She tried to swallow, but a hand seemed to be clamped round her throat, jamming the mechanism. She said 'Ach' instead, not the lament, or the exasperated version, just a click. Not even a human sound. It was, she would recall much later, exactly the same as she'd made when the phone went thirty years previously and her Gordon's site manager was on the line, struggling to tell her the news.

The first of the missed calls was from Kath. Then followed three from an unknown number. Then twenty-two from Ed. Ed was away in Amsterdam.

Corinne triangulated. She moved her fingers to trigger Kath's number first. The phone buzzed in her hands, confusing her. She was swaying in the wind, trying to remember what to do, what button to press. Her thoughts were spilling out like pennies from a smashed piggy bank. Somehow she put it together that someone was calling her. It was Ed's name, Ed's slightly sardonic smile in the wee photie; green was go. Corinne responded.

'What is it, Ed?' she said. 'What's happening? Tell me it's not Bea?'

'What are you talking about?' He was angry, not scared. 'What's happening there?'

'I don't know what you mean, Ed. I was out for the afternoon. There's no signal down at the Plaza Centre, you know how it gets in there—'

'Have you spoken to Kath today?'

His tone was so sharp, so savage, that she started to cry. He had a temper, did Ed. 'I've not spoken to her since Sunday, Ed, when you were round for your dinner. Is everything—'

'Right, never mind. Corinne, I need you to go to the school. Beatrice is there. Kath hasn't shown up. She was supposed to get her after her piano class at after-school club. She didn't show. Beatrice is waiting at the school with her teacher.'

'I've got a bag of messages here, Ed. What's happening with Kath?'

She could hear him grinding his teeth. It was a good connection. 'One thing at a time, Corinne. Go to the school. Pick up Beatrice. Don't frighten her. I can't get hold of Kath. The neighbour says the car is still at the house, but there's no answer at the door. So I need you to pick up Beatrice at the school. Take her back to the house, and use your key to get in.'

'Oh, son! What's going on?'

'Probably nothing,' Ed said. 'She did this once before, when Beatrice was going for gymnastics. Got her dates mixed up. It happens. Don't panic, Corinne, and don't frighten the wee one. Pick her up, take her home, and let yourself in. Give Kath a call yourself, when you can. It's probably nothing.'

3

It was a street that a lot of learner drivers were taken down to practise U-turns. A glorified cul-de-sac – that had annoyed Ed, when Corinne had said it; it was out of her mouth before she could think about it, really – a dead end, just a crescent where the houses arced round, backing onto some trees and the scrubland. Corinne usually parked outside the house rather than going onto the drive, but she went right in this time, parking up beside Kath's 4x4.

Beatrice knew something was wrong, all right. How could it not be?

'Where's she gone, Nana?' she said from the seat in the back, fidgeting with something in her hand that caught the corner of Corinne's eye while she was trying to straighten up in the driveway.

'What have you got there? Stop fidgeting.' Then Corinne saw what it was in the girl's hand. Her rosary beads. Pale blue, and blessed at Lourdes, no less.

'She's never usually late, Nana.'

'It's a cold day – maybe she had things to do and ran out of time. She probably thought you were getting the bus, and forgot it was your piano lesson today.'

Beatrice's lip trembled. So did the tips of her pigtails.

Corinne unclipped her belt and turned round. Her gloved hands covered the girl's. Even through the material Corinne felt the chill of her fingers. She cursed herself for not thinking. 'Now don't you worry,' she said, in a light tone that grew brittle before she had finished the sentence. 'It'll be fine. She's just forgotten. It's easy done, sweetheart. Now, you'll wait in here, OK?'

'It's dark, Nana. I'm scared.'

'Oh, don't you be scared.' Corinne coughed to hide the tremor in her voice. She clasped Beatrice's hands tighter. 'I'll be back in two minutes. Anything happens, you just beep that horn, right?'

Beatrice nodded. Corinne got out – cold wind immediately slapping her cheeks and forehead, threatening to tear her hat off. She locked the car, waved to Beatrice, then tried the door. Locked. She hit the doorbell, courtesy really, and the dull, emotionless tones were still ringing out when she put her key in the lock.

There was already a key in the lock – or something in the lock, at any rate. Corinne grunted as she tried the key again. It would not go all the way in. She extricated it gently. Her heart had surely never been this loud, her blood in revolt against the chill. She moved back and scanned the windows. There was a suggestion of a light on in the front room. Nothing upstairs. She slipped as she followed the path round to the side gate, her footsteps gouging weeping prints into the slush. She steadied herself, took a breath and turned to wave at Beatrice. With the glare of the streetlights, she couldn't really see if she was there or not. It was bloody dark too.

The gate creaked open. The swing set and slide bolted to the ground. Wee one was too old for them, really. Ed should get rid of them. Lawn was like a pudding itself, come to think of it. No footprints, she remembered later. She was quite firm on that point.

The patio door was open a crack.

'Kath?' She slid it open. Much warmer through the threshold; heating was on. Kitchen tidy. Clock ticking. Glowing red script on the oven not reset since the clocks went back. Bloody Ed again. 'Kath? Where are you, pet?'

Water on the laminate flooring catching the light. Footprints, it seemed. Bit of a mess. God, had she slipped?

'Kath? What's going on? It's me!'

She didn't get much further into the kitchen before it fell into place in her mind, the way it was meant to. Exactly how it had been planned. The kitchen had a play area with a big toybox in it – crammed full, it was an old-style wooden thing painted with animals and dinosaurs on the front. Beatrice was a lovely girl, bless her, but they'd got her too much stuff. Spoiled rotten at Christmas. She didn't believe in Santa, really, but she'd gone along with it one more time, so as not to upset her mummy or daddy, or her nana. That was the kind of girl she was, nice like that.

Corinne saw that the box was ajar, just a wee bit. And out of place – it had been moved from the corner where it fitted snugly beside the wall units and dragged into the middle of the room.

But that wasn't the first thing Corinne noticed. The first thing she noticed was the red scarf, dangling from the box lid like a tongue. It had been pulled straight, and was snagged on something inside. Something was stopping it from closing properly. It invited you to open it, and Corinne did. And then just covered her eyes, and screamed.

4

Detective Inspector Lomond switched off the car stereo, then slowed to a crawl. The snow had come on a lot thicker since he'd set off from the house, and even having the wipers on double-time couldn't clear it off the windscreen fast enough. Lomond spotted DS Slater's long, somewhat spindly form in the distance, saw what it was wearing and promptly discounted the evidence. Must be Malcolm's doppelgänger, he thought. Surely that's not him.

He sped up and had almost driven past Slater, who was standing in a bus shelter just before the crossroads that would take them deeper into the Southside, before a frantic arm gesture brought him to a sudden halt. Lomond eyed with some astonishment the figure that got into the car.

'What?' Slater said innocently.

'Malcolm.' Lomond was as grave as a father who has been specifically told by his wife to bollock a child. 'What in God's name are you wearing?'

'What d'you mean?' Slater glanced down at his coat, tugging the collar.

'I mean . . . did you inherit that jacket?'

'As it happens, it's vintage, gaffer.' Slater frowned, but one corner of his mouth twitched in a smile.

'Vintage? Vintage what, curtains?' To Lomond's eyes, Slater's jacket looked more like an analogue television tuned to static, a black-and-white monstrosity.

'It's style. Distinctive. And you'd think it was brand new. Never been worn, they said.'

'Aye, there's a reason for that.'

'It was featured in a Sunday supplement, apparently.'

'You say "apparently",' Lomond said in a flash. 'Meaning someone told you about it. Meaning this wasn't your idea.'

'Maybe that's what I'm saying, maybe it isn't.'

'Meaning it was Meghan's idea.'

'Hey, you've been dressed by your missus since you were sixteen, so–'

'Sixteen and a half.'

'So give me peace.'

'You're about to talk to traumatised people tonight,' Lomond said, indicating and pulling out. 'Last thing I want to do is make it even worse for them.'

'Well . . . at least it's warm.'

'Give you that one.'

'What's the damage, then? I had a look at the notes. Bad one?'

'Bad one,' Lomond agreed. 'Kathryn Symes, known as Kath, thirty-six years old. Waved her daughter off at the bus stop this morning – that was the last time she was seen alive. Lives at one of the big houses in Fairham.'

'Fairham? What part of town is that?'

'New builds. Or new-ish. They just gave it a name, not even sure it means anything. I think it was called Renfrewshire when I was a boy.'

'It was probably called Rome when you were a boy.'

Lomond ignored this as they waited at a red light. 'Daughter didn't find her, thank God – that was her mother. Corinne Bruce, seventy-seven years auld. Went to pick up the wee girl after the victim was a no-show at school.'

'Husband?' Slater asked.

Lomond cleared his throat. 'Away on business. Amsterdam.'

'Oh aye.'

'What do you mean, "oh aye"?'

'You been to Amsterdam?'

'No.'

'You planning to?'

'No. Why would I?'

'Bit defensive.'

'Anyway. He was in Amsterdam. Clear as you can get. He got the call from the school first, to say his wife hadn't showed up. He brought in her mother to go and pick up the girl and make a check on the house. She let herself in. Found the body, rang him back and told him to come home.'

Slater sucked his teeth. 'She bearing up?'

'Haven't heard.'

'Not good. Just . . . please tell me the daughter didn't see it?'

'The daughter didn't see it.'

'That's something.'

'Life's wrecked as it is, anyway,' Lomond mused. He listened to the soft brushstrokes of the snow on the car for a bit.

'Details?' Slater said.

'Minchin won't say much. You know what that means.'

'Aye. A weird one.'

Slater shook his head. 'We were saying that the other day, were we not? Haven't had a serious one for a while. Couple of open goals – like that boy getting the pool cue in his eye socket. But nothing random.'

'We might be lucky,' Lomond said.

'When are we ever lucky, gaffer?'

'Fingers crossed this is the first time.'

'Suppose the snow's lucky.'

'How's that?'

'The forensics' friend. Footprints.'

'We'll soon find out.'

Slater peered through the windscreen as Lomond crept around a bus pulled over by the side of the road with its hazards on. There seemed to be no one inside, and the lights were off. 'Fair way out, isn't it?'

'I'd have been there already if I hadn't had to swing by and get you,' Lomond said tersely.

'Motor's off the road.' Slater sniffed. 'I did offer to get a taxi.'

'Never mind,' Lomond said irritably.

After a silence, Slater ventured: 'Mind if I stick the radio on? I like to take my mind off it for a bit before I have to get my head into it, if you know what I mean.'

'Aye, whatever.' Lomond's head was into it already. Roads, routes in and out, neighbours. Vantage points. Map of the estate. 'Hey, wait . . .'

But Slater had already touched the on switch, and what Lomond had been listening to came on loud, mid-song. Lomond used the control built into his steering wheel to bring down the volume. He said nothing more as the song played on.

Slater was silent, resting his elbow on the car door, chin in his hand. Without turning round, he said, 'This isn't the radio, is it?'

Lomond shrugged.

'This is a playlist, in't it? This is . . . *your* playlist.'

'So?'

'I mean, nothing wrong with this song, is there? Nothing at all.'

'It's just a song.'

'Uh huh. That's fine.'

'What makes you say that, Malcolm?'

'Oh, no reason, gaffer,' Slater said, not quite expressionlessly.

5

Lomond hated the ghostie suits – they made him sweat, and the tight band that compressed the brow and jaw clearly illustrated that he was fleshier around the eyes and cheeks than the fresh-faced uniform polis of his first warrant card. Slater knew this, of course, and while they had an unwritten code not to crack jokes of any kind at crime scenes – well, crime scenes where they met other officers of the forensics team, at any rate – the razor's edge sparkle of the DS's eyes told the story of his amusement.

'You lost weight, gaffer?' he said, innocently enough.

'Not really, Malcolm. You grown a fringe?'

As he adjusted the hood over his shaven-to-exorcise-male-pattern-baldness head, Slater's eyes lost a little of their malevolence.

The houses in the crescent were two-storeyed and broad. The snow fell steadily, blanketing the dark slate roofs.

'Don't look like new-builds,' Lomond said. 'When did these go up? Can't be long.'

'I checked just after we pulled in,' Slater said smugly. 'Sixteen-odd years ago.'

'What? Financial crash? Someone was confident.'

'Some bugger's always got the money. Good investment, as well.'

'They look OK, decent big houses – kind of an oppressive street, though.'

'Aye.' Slater frowned. 'Reminds me of a nick, I dunno why. Maybe the circle . . . what d'you call it?'

'Crescent. Myrtlewood Crescent.'

Most of the neighbours seemed to be watching – couldn't help that, of course, with the glowering evidence tent, the uniforms and, worst of all, the masked, white-suited forensics team hunched over in the falling snow. The photographer had already been in and out, and the media had decamped. Just about everyone in the crescent had been spoken to already. You had to imagine it, Lomond thought. The knock at the door, the shock and confusion. Then you had to imagine the worst thing, the one that would linger. The idea that a couple of doors away from you – or even next door – something terrible had happened. Something that might have happened to you, given a different set of circumstances: a change in the weather; a simple whim indulged. In another universe, it was you. Kath was answering her door to the police, aghast, and you . . .

'Where's the husband now?' Slater asked, scrolling through his phone.

'Got him at the station. He's in a bad way. Someone was saying they might have to take the mother to hospital,' Lomond said.

'Christ. How about the daughter?'

'She's with an auntie. Husband's sister. She drove through from Coatbridge and collected her.'

Slater sighed. 'Best get in there, then.'

*

Lomond and Slater entered through the front door. Somehow the coverings on their feet were apt in the spotless hallway, which stretched a good distance past the carpeted stairway angled up the western wall. The flooring looked and felt like real oak, and the carefully placed lamps lent the space a warm, burnished look. The upper-storey landing led off to three bedrooms and a main bathroom.

'I've stayed in flats that would fit in this hallway,' Slater remarked. 'Kitchen and bathroom, the lot.'

'Place looks clean,' Lomond said.

'What you reckon? Tidied up after himself?'

'Maybe.'

Anita Khavari was the senior pathologist on the scene. Her striking good looks and height were neutralised by the ghostie suit, but her voice was clear and distinctive enough from the bottom of the hallway. 'Through here, gents.'

The hallway opened into a spotlit kitchen, almost too bright to look at. Khavari had already laid out the path the two men should take; one or two forensic officers remained on site, photographing the worktop and the breakfast bar at the back of the room. Strong portable lights bleached the whole scene.

Lomond narrowed his eyes; he could feel the beginnings of a headache spreading from his neck to his temples in dull waves. 'Much to say about the scene? Footprints, specifically?'

Under the glare, Khavari's eyes were difficult to read behind glasses. She bit the side of her mouth and shook her head. 'Nothing that we can see.'

'Did he clean up after himself? Any mops around?'

'It doesn't seem like it. It looks like she was in the bath. There was a struggle in the bathroom, lots of water on the floor and the mat, even on the walls. We think he killed her up there, then dragged her down the stairs.'

'How?'

'Smothered her,' Khavari said. 'Used one of the bath towels.'

'She fight him?'

'She's broken some nails – we'll have to examine what's underneath them.'

Slater cleared his throat and asked, 'Sexual assault?'

Khavari gazed at him. 'Nothing to suggest it so far. It's possible, but there's no indication of it.'

'He panic?' Slater asked. 'Lose his nerve?'

'I don't . . .' Khavari hesitated. 'It's a strange one. I'm not going to speculate. But you'll see.'

'He had to have dragged her down here for a reason,' Slater said. 'Is it the extra space? The light?' He stared at the high ceiling.

As well as the portable lights, Lomond noticed that the wall was studded with small, circular spotlights – all of them functioning.

'When you get those wee fancy lights, they always conk out, I find,' he said. 'My wife hates them. I don't like them either, for that reason. You're always up and down the steps, replacing them. It's a well-kept house. What did she do?'

'No job,' Khavari said. 'She looked after her daughter. Hadn't worked since maternity leave. Paralegal.'

Lomond and Slater came to the kitchen table, beyond which were the patio doors. The view outside was even harder to look at than what was inside the kitchen: flooded with white light, glaring off the fresh-fallen snow.

'Footprints outside, surely?' Lomond said.

Khavari shook her head. 'No. He was lucky. We think he might have come down the side of the garden path – you see that area shaded over by the trees, the conifers? He came down there. We think, going by some of the neighbours' door cameras and other security equipment, he got in and out just before the heavier stuff came down. We've photographed every inch of it, been out with the thermal cameras, but there's nothing.'

'Any chance he got in from the front? Or a window?'

'It's possible but unlikely.' Khavari gestured. 'You'll see it better in daylight, or if you look at the survey map. This is the perfect way to get in. It's not overlooked at all – the gardens were designed that way. Wasteland out the back. There's every chance he sneaked in, then sneaked out. That would be my guess, except there's a problem with that too.'

Slater was ahead of her. He pointed towards a console set in the wall, with an LED digital face that was so quaint Lomond supposed it was retro-styled. 'That a security camera system?' Slater asked.

'Yes. The camera was switched on all afternoon.'

Lomond turned to the pathologist. 'But she was here, wasn't she?'

Khavari nodded. 'Hadn't left the house since seeing the daughter off to school.'

'But she put on the security system?' Lomond flipped open his notebook, writing in his indecipherable scrawl. 'While she was inside?'

'She'd gone for a bath,' Slater reminded him.

'Even so.' He drew a line in his book. 'So . . . there are cameras? Outside?'

'Yes.' Khavari sounded weary.

'And they got something, right?' Slater asked.

'No.'

'No?'

'We're analysing the recordings, but they didn't get anything out in the garden.'

'So he didn't get in that way,' Lomond said.

'We can't be sure. One of the cameras was out. Again, our man could be lucky. Or he could have knocked it out. It would have shown him coming off the side of the path and along the patio.'

'Don't like the sound of this,' Slater said, tutting. 'We're well into the stalker zone here.'

Lomond frowned. 'But the weather's been crap all day, right? Sleet before it turned cold, then snow. So there must have been some water down here?'

'Just what was left behind when he dragged her in from the staircase.' Khavari indicated a track on the floor, marked out with fluorescent numbered signs, showing the meandering path of the body from the bottom of the stairs towards the box. 'Nothing that showed footprints.'

'Nah, this isn't good,' Lomond said. He nodded towards the red scarf, still dangling out of the toybox. 'OK,' he sighed. 'Let's get it over with. Is she over there?'

6

The two crime scene investigators who lifted the lid were slightly pissy about it. Lomond wondered if they'd had to do it a few times that day. It was one of those grim things rendered comical by repetition, though no one was laughing at this point.

'How high do you want it?' said one – short, pugnacious, with a lot of chin jutting out of his white suit.

'You being smart, son?'

The man shrugged. He didn't look away either. 'Up or down? Let me know.'

Lomond turned to Khavari. 'This boy on his first day here?'

'It's been a long day,' Khavari said, glaring at the CSI over her glasses.

He sighed and lifted the lid.

Slater flinched at what was underneath, far more sharply than Lomond did. 'What in the name of God's going on with that?' he said, turning to the pathologist.

'I can't answer that. I was hoping you could tell me.'

'He's done that for shock,' Slater said. 'Hasn't he?'

Lomond nodded. 'That's a display. Her poor mum.'

'Assuming that's who it was left for.'

The face was turned up towards the onlookers, though only the top of the head from the eyes upwards was protruding from the lip of the toybox. The hair was black, tightly curled and matted along one side. Seeing this, Lomond had a flashback to his own daughter. He had once been stretched for time while putting her to bed. He had to go out on a job that night and had been waiting on Maureen to come off shift so he could leave. He didn't have time to carry out the full salon-style hair dryer and brush job – which Siobhan had borne with a stoicism that Lomond had found hilarious. He had made do with an undignified buffeting with a towel and sent Siobhan to bed without telling his wife as he left. After Amy Winehouse had lurched out of bed the next morning, there was a full and frank exchange of views. The hair had been so bad, Maureen had taken a photo and threatened to send it to social services.

Something in the texture of the hair and the untreated way it had been left reminded Lomond of that night. The comparison disgusted him, which meant he should make a note, and he did. It was black hair, possibly curls that had been tamed through prolonged use of straighteners, perhaps over decades, and there was no sign of silver in the roots.

The eyes were the main thing. Wide open, as if glaring at the viewer, the expression was baleful rather than horror-struck or simply blank. Lomond had seen victims of suffocation several times before, and the signs of petechial haemorrhage were obvious. Purple patches on the glassy whites, almost entirely covering the right eye. Insult to injury: even more of a horror movie. As if she wanted to weep blood but couldn't.

These blemishes and purplish starbursts were dotted around the face and head, particularly on the cheeks. She had a natural beauty spot on one, parallel with the underside of her left ear, almost obliterated by the livid haemorrhage line. The rest of the skin was that awful blue colour, a repulsion of life and lividity.

The nose was bloodied, perhaps broken. Lomond noted that the hexagons of dried blood his keen eyes picked out stopped abruptly at the nostrils. He wrote on his pad, *Nose wiped post-mortem?*

The mouth was closed, the chin almost defiantly thrust upwards. The mouth should have been hanging open from that position. It wasn't, because something was holding it closed: her feet, crossed over, placed at roughly forty-five-degree angles. One big toe was turned up, the way a toff might turn up their pinkie while drinking tea. The veins in the feet were horribly blue, the rest of the skin white. The blood had not settled there.

The head nestled between the shins. These had surely been shaved recently, a sheen under the punishing lights; perhaps in the bath, moments before the arrival of the person who killed her. Visible beyond tufted black hair pooled behind the head, her knees. It was a grotesque contortionist's act, the kind you might see at random on your phone or on a TV show, and automatically wince.

'The legs been severed?' Lomond asked.

Khavari shook her head. 'No. Dislocated at the hip.'

'She's been bent over backwards.'

'Looks that way. We'll take it from the top.' Khavari pointed a silver object at the face and clicked it; an even stronger beam spotlit the mouth. 'You see the foam at the mouth, just here? You might have to bend down to get a better look, just at the right-hand corner, here?'

Lomond did so. Bringing his own face so close to that of death brought the first waves of nausea. You never, ever get used to this, he thought. 'I see it.'

'Suffocation, something placed over the face. If you look up at the nose, right there on the nostrils, you'll probably see some fibres.'

The spotlight washed over the nose, washing the skin clean except for where the blood clung. It was dried, but still rich in red. 'I see it,' Lomond said. 'Fibres. Fluff. New bath towel?'

'Spot on,' Khavari said. 'Having had a look inside, we think it's underneath her, beneath the abdomen – like a mat she'd been laid on.'

'What's the score with the legs?' Slater said, in a choked voice. 'I can see it's a display, but how'd he manage that?'

'All done post-mortem – like, immediately post-mortem. I'll have to wait until we get her onto the table before I know for sure, but so far as I can tell, she was dragged downstairs feet first, then he emptied out the toybox and placed her inside. Carefully. He meant to do it.'

'But the bones, the joints . . . was this lady an acrobat or a contortionist?'

'No – she was slim and kept fit. There's a gym upstairs,

looks like for her use mainly. That would have made it easier for him to fold her up. Look at the placement of the feet. This wasn't an accident.'

'How did he do it?'

'Immediately after she was gone, I'd say he bent her into that shape, cool as you like. Popped out the hip joints, gave the base of the spine one hell of a kick and folded her in, like you'd fold some clothes.'

'Planned it like that.' Lomond turned to Slater. He was dying to be rid of the suit. The elastic was pinching his face, a headache pinching his skull. Even to be out in the cold and the snow would be the purest relief from the oppression, the heat of the lights, the restriction. 'We've got someone here who plans. Nothing random about this.'

Slater merely nodded. 'No doubt about it. None.'

The cheeky forensics officer cleared his throat.

'Yes, you can lower the lid,' Lomond said.

'And make sure you're not so wide, in future,' Slater snapped, before he could reply.

7

He'd found a flight fast enough. Direct from Amsterdam. Even at that stage, in that scenario, Slater had made a joke or two about the fact of Edward Symes' absence. Lomond had told him off for it, wearily.

Symes himself even allowed room for it, as soon as he'd made contact with Police Scotland upon his return, then been ushered into a squad car and driven from Glasgow airport to Govan. 'I actually was on business. No one believed me. You should've seen my mother-in-law's face.'

Joking aside, Edward Symes – 'it's Ed' – had been sober, horribly so, perhaps as sober as he would ever be. There was an edge to his voice, even when he laughed, which he did surprisingly often. Lomond had seen plenty of examples of this. It could go any way, really. Someone going monkey tits was a possibility. Monkey tits was one of a million crudities an old sergeant from back in Lomond's uniform days had used: something else he wished he could forget, and never would. They might cry. Or, worst of all, they might withdraw. Twin receding points of light in the eyes, like an old analogue telly settling itself from static to silence. Lomond wasn't quite sure how far Symes would go.

He had taken it upon himself to bring a lawyer, which wasn't necessary but was entertaining. Friend of the family. Lomond had never met him. His face resembled a shirt front struggling to contain a big belly: huge mouth, huge lips, red cheeks. Ed Symes was sober, but Lomond wondered about his brief.

'My client would like to make it clear that he was out of the country when this terrible incident happened. However it came about, he has no knowledge of it, nor did he have any active part in it . . .'

Lomond raised a hand. 'Please, settle down there. We know he didn't do anything. We know where he's been. We just want to have a conversation to see if he can provide us with anything that could steer us in the right direction. It's important we move fast. I know you'll want to see a quick result, Ed.'

Symes sat back. He was holding his hands in a strange way. Later, Lomond would liken it to someone grappling with an invisible Rubik's Cube.

'It's fine,' Symes said. He took a breath. It was a bad place to be chatting to him. The lighting, the desk, the recording equipment, and Lomond and Slater – everything had the appearance of an arrest, an accusation. The lawyer didn't help.

'If you'd like a tea or something?' This wasn't the first time Lomond had asked.

'No, I'm fine.'

'A smoke, then.'

Bingo. 'Yes – is there a smoker's area somewhere?'

'There is. We usually have to put a ball and chain on folk, though. Stop them jumping over the walls.' When Symes didn't smile, Lomond added quickly, 'I'll take you outside.'

'I'll come with you,' said the lawyer, scraping his seat back.

'No, that'll be OK, Bennett,' said Symes.

'Keep the lawyer company, please, Malcolm,' Lomond said, patting Slater on the shoulder. Slater looked at the red-faced man for a moment, then folded his arms, a disgruntled teenager.

Outside, Lomond, who detested smoking, stood far enough away to keep his expression and manner neutral as Symes burned a cigarette down to the filter in seconds. 'Sorry. Nerves going crazy.'

Lomond coughed. 'Anyway. First question, how are you bearing up?'

'I'm not,' Symes said quietly. He was a tall man with a kind face, prominent cheekbones and thick, prematurely grey hair, somewhat unruly and all the better for it. He was someone who had aged well. Him and Kath would have made a fine, striking pair. 'I'm all over the place.'

'All I can say is – take things at your own pace. I don't want to waste your time. And I definitely don't want you to feel as if you're being interrogated or anything.'

Symes raised a hand. 'It was my call to come here. I thought it was the best thing . . . Can I be honest with you?'

'Course you can.'

'I wanted to get out of my sister's house. Total, sheer madness. I didn't want more police in there. Beatrice was sleeping. She just missed it, you know. Kath's mother is a royal pain in the arse, but she had the foresight to keep her in the car. Imagine if she'd come in and seen it.'

He might have cried then. He took a long draw, composed himself and said, 'Do you know if it was quick?'

'I think it was reasonably quick, Mr Symes.'

'Reasonably. Interesting word, that.'

'That's off the record. The forensic report isn't in yet. I can't officially comment in any way until the pathologist tells me what happened.'

'Was she cut up? Was she . . . anything else?'

'Again, off the record, it seems she was smothered. There is nothing else I can say.'

'God.' He shook his head. 'How did it happen? The cameras must have caught it.'

'From what we've seen so far and the information you've given us, one of the cameras had a fault.' Lomond kept his tone conversational. 'We're looking into what that was. Had you had any problems with the camera system?'

'Absolutely not. I was paranoid about it. Well, that's maybe not the right word to use,' Symes added, seeing some subtle change in Lomond's expression. 'I wasn't paranoid about the situation. We only moved into that house about a year ago. Before last Christmas. An Avalon King house. Rock-solid build.

Good rep. And they had all these extra security features on them. I was obsessed with making sure it was all working. Like a new toy, I suppose. I remember we caught a jackdaw one morning, perched on the edge of a camera. Screengrabbed it – I think Kath used it as her screensaver for a wee while.'

'So you knew how to use the system?'

'Yep – and one thing about it, if there's any issue, it tips you off, as well. Any break in the chain and a light flashes up.'

'This is obvious?'

'Aye – red light on the console. It happened when one of the cameras wasn't picking anything up.'

'When was this?'

'Six or seven weeks ago . . . Halloween time? Turned out a wood pigeon had shat on it One of the problems with having woods out the back. One of the blessings, as well.' He searched in his pocket for a fresh cigarette.

Lomond felt the drifting flakes settle on the back of his neck and find their way through his hair to his scalp. 'And everything was working when you left?'

'Yep – I remember showing Beatrice the basics, in case the alarm ever went off for some reason. It happened when Kath was out sorting something in the car one day.' He paused, placing the cigarette between his lips, lighter poised. 'You're asking me this . . . surely the cameras must have picked something up?'

Lomond didn't take long to weigh up how much he should say. 'Like I said, it seems there's a fault somewhere with one of the cameras.'

'Which one? I know where they are.'

'The one that covered the lawn.'

'And that's how he got in? The garden?'

Lomond shook his head. 'We don't think so – there had been snow, thicker than this, and it had landed. There would have been footprints. But there was nothing. It's possible he came in another way, around the side of the shed, an area where he wouldn't have left footprints. But–'

‘That would mean someone knew there was a weakness in the system. The cameras didn’t cover all the angles. Not every direction. There’s a blind spot.’

‘Who else would have known about your camera system, Ed?’

‘No one.’ Symes shook his head determinedly. ‘All watertight. Beatrice didn’t know the code, and we were damned careful about it all. Kath wouldn’t have . . .’

‘And your mother-in-law?’

‘She knew the code. And she’s a gasbag.’

‘No one else?’

Symes frowned. ‘How did this happen? Cameras everywhere, and there must have been footprints somewhere!’

‘We’ve got dozens of officers out there, knocking on doors, checking for footprints, the whole street. Don’t you worry about that,’ Lomond said.

‘Unbelievable!’

He was on the verge of losing it, Lomond thought. He said quickly, ‘How about grudges, anything like that? Anyone you know with a problem?’

‘Well. Closest thing we’ve had to that for a while is the guy at the top of the crescent. Vincent Finch. Think he actually worked on these houses, owned a few nearby. Liked what he saw, obviously. He’s wanting to build an extension, but it’ll block out a lot of light, so the rest of the street told him to bugger off. Cheeky bastard. He took a spite against most of us for that. Me in particular.’

‘You say “for a while”,’ Lomond said, his notebook appearing in his hand without Symes noticing. ‘Have you had problems with anyone before? Friend or business partner you fell out with, someone from the past?’

‘Aye,’ Symes said, with an almost comically venomous edge to his voice. ‘Just the one, you could say. That bastard comedian.’

8

Cara Smythe had sleep in her eyes, but she hadn't slept. This was a new one. She rubbed it away, then flipped open her compact. Dark shadows under the eyes, and those lines around her mouth. She didn't have time to do anything about either. She dry-swallowed a couple of ibuprofen; they fought her all the way down. Time to get on, she thought.

Out of the cubicle, Cara fixed her shirt collar, then smoothed down the lapels of her jacket, straightened her back, and – holy cow, Batman – just like that she was DS Smythe. She appraised her reflection as she crossed over to the sinks. In the mirror, even in the stark lighting, Smythe wasn't looking too bad, provided she didn't try to smile. Smythe had learned that it was better not to. Not that the old headmistress death-stare was without problems. You got looks in return, sometimes comments. The worst of these were at weddings.

'You know, you'd be a lovely lassie if you smiled a bit more.'

'And you'd be a lovely auntie if you breathed a bit less.'

Had she actually said that, at the last wedding? She had.

Into the briefing room, and there he was, the wee Buddha himself, preparing to present, all five feet eight of the good stuff. Inspector Lomond was the SIO, and people would bitch about it, but there was a reason he got these jobs. To his credit, Lomond sometimes couldn't believe it either. He had lost a little weight since the Ferryman carry-on, but he still looked like you could punch him in the belly all day and neither of you would feel anything. Cara saw his brown eyes narrow in annoyance as he spotted Slater strolling into the room, a folder under his arm. The slightly nettled daddy. Smythe smiled for the first time that day.

Slater nodded as he sat beside her, and she felt a stab of irritation to go with the throbbing cramps in her abdomen. Slater had a puckish charm – 'more front than Blackpool', it had been said more than once – at odds with his gym-pinched features and close-shaven head. Smythe had worked with him for so long she had developed a liking, and then a disliking, for him.

'Here we go again, eh?' was his opening line.

'What d'you mean?'

'Another serial job.'

'Let's hope not, eh?'

'Goes without saying,' Slater muttered, annoyed.

Lomond said, 'I'll make this as brief as I can. Victim is Kath Symes. Thirty-six. On her own at home in Fairham. New estate, big house. She was found yesterday afternoon by her mother, after waving her daughter, Beatrice, off to school in the morning. She'd been dragged out of the bath, we reckon just after lunchtime, smothered, then stuffed into a toybox in the kitchen. You'll see here the position of the body, and you'll note in the other photos the placing of the scarf. Not to get too psychological about it, that's as close as the guy who did it can get to drawing a big red arrow pointing to where the victim was put. Her mother followed it, and found the body. The wee girl, thankfully, was out in the car.'

Lomond let the briefing room, a dozen plainclothes officers, absorb the pictures as he clicked through them. The bluish face, the jemmied-open eyes. The red scarf, white tiling. The only sound aside from the click of the tablet Lomond used to control the images on the screen was the hum of the lights.

'No sign she was sexually assaulted, though she was subject to some violence. If it was a single killer – and we can't be sure about that – then it was someone strong and able. She died on the bathroom floor, then she was dragged down the stairs, feet first. The killer took his time to fold her into the toybox – if I can call this neat, then he . . .' Lomond caught himself. 'The killer was neat.'

The image changed again. The snow-dusted garden, like icing on a Stollen cake. 'Here's the garden,' Lomond said. 'Not overlooked, which gives us a problem. We've got no witnesses. The way the houses are built, these gardens look onto waste-land at the back: quite a few conifers, a path taken by dog walkers. As you can see, this image looks onto the garden. Going by other security systems and doorbell cameras on the rest of the street, it doesn't look like our killer got in through the front door. But here's the tricky bit: he didn't get in through the back door either. Not that we can see.'

'There're no footprints? Along that path or on the lawn? In that snow?' Smythe hadn't meant to say this out loud. One or two tuts from the rows behind her; Smythe knew she was known as a bit of a school swot, because she was.

'I was coming to that,' Lomond said dryly. 'No – there were no footprints. The way the snow fell was odd – there was a dusting in the morning, it melted, then a bit more in late afternoon, right as Kath was killed. It could be that her killer was lucky – got in and out of the back door when it had melted, got to the bottom of the garden and went out via the snib-lock gate opening onto the back that you can see here.'

'Cameras?' Smythe fought the urge to look round. She knew that voice, coming from the back of the room: self-consciously raspy, over-confident.

'There's a security system attached to the house,' Lomond said. 'A good one. Cameras, multiple spots. The connecting wire for one of them was damaged, and it seems damaged that day. That's the one covering the western edge of the lawn. You can see here the pine trees at the edge of the western wall – they might have provided some cover for the killer. The wire had been cut recently. But if that was the case, then the killer would have left footprints, some kind of evidence, in the soil underneath the trees. The ground was nice and soft. There were no new footprints that anyone could see.'

'Any other way in?' Slater asked.

'It doesn't look like anyone could have got in through any of the windows at the side – they're overlooked, and covered by some of the neighbours' security systems. And there's nothing to suggest he got in through the attic or the roof – the snow dusted the slating, as we can see here. No one had disturbed that.'

This time Smythe remembered to put up her hand.

'Yes, Cara.'

'So this woman was killed by an intruder, but there's nothing to suggest how they got in or out?'

'Correct. They did get in, obviously. And they got out again without being seen – that means the back of the house. But the rest of it's a blank. All we know is it wasn't the husband.'

'Hitman?' Myles Tait again.

'Doubt it,' Lomond said. 'We'll check it out, but it's highly unlikely. Everything about this – the fact the husband was away, that she was alone in the house – points to it being planned. Someone stalked this woman, sneaked in without being seen, killed her, then sneaked out again. And if they've done it once, they'll probably do it again.'

9

Lomond held Slater, Smythe and Tait behind in the briefing room. The trio waited for him to gather his notes, which he pinched between thumb and forefinger before pausing in the act of flipping them over, his attention distracted by something he read there. He was sipping water from a polystyrene cup in his other hand, and there was something painterly in his demeanour, offset as it was by the dust motes chasing each other through the light above his head.

'The dream team,' Slater said, rubbing his hands. 'Wonder who's Team A and who's Team B?'

'We know you'll be Team A, teacher's pet,' Tait said tartly. 'Or maybe he'll shock us.'

Tait had put on a bit of weight, Slater decided, with no little satisfaction, now that he was close up. Previously Tait had had that 'rugger bugger but svelte' look to him – all sculpted sideburns and nary a hair out of place, with the accent to match. He'd grown a little jowlier and had taken to wearing glasses, although they were far too small for his beefy features. The fat of comfort, thought Slater: new girlfriend, maybe. He was vain, though, and wouldn't have meant to put on any weight.

Lomond snapped back to it, slid his paperwork into a folder and tucked it under his arm.

'I won't take up much more of your time,' he said, as he stepped away from the lectern. 'What I didn't share with the rest of the squad is the jobs we're going after right now, based on a couple of tips we got from Edward Symes.'

All three visibly straightened up. Slater wanted to yawn;

instead he bit his lip. Already they were tired. This would become the norm.

'First, he mentioned someone he had a dispute with, east side of the estate, a Mr Vincent Finch. There was some problem with a planning application, and I think it went as far as the court. Mr Finch wanted to build an extension; the rest of the street didn't like the idea. He lost, and we gather he's not happy about it.'

'Spoken to him already, sir?' Smythe asked.

Lomond nodded. 'Couple of officers in uniform asked where he was. Apparently home alone at the time of the killing. His wife and daughter were out at . . . Rainbows. Is that like the Guides?'

'Aye – sort of feeder club for the Guides,' Slater said. Noting the expressions of the other three, he added, 'My niece goes. Has her wee uniform and a badge.' He shrugged, colouring.

'Aye, so, he was on his own,' Lomond continued. 'There was one line in the notes I was curious about. *Didn't like him.*'

'Who was the uniform? Who wrote that, I mean?'

'Moira Duncan. Don't know her but it struck me as an odd thing to write. She said it wasn't for any good reason, nothing openly dodgy. Just a hunch. And a hunch is good. Plus we don't know exactly where he was. So I'd like him to talk us through it. The other tip I got was what Mr Symes called "that bastard comedian".'

'Not Benny Kettles, was it?' Slater snorted.

'Aye.' Lomond frowned. 'How did you know that?'

'It has to be Benny Kettles, with that description,' Slater said. He grinned at the confusion. 'None of you seen him?'

'I've read something on social media. Usually slagging him off,' Tait offered. 'Haven't had time to check him out yet.'

'He's' – Slater struggled for the right expression – 'sort of funny.'

'Ringing endorsement,' Tait muttered.

'He's nasty with it, though. Makes Frankie Boyle and Jerry

Sadowitz look like those comics you remember your granny liking.'

'I thought the shock jock thing was dying out a bit,' Tait mused. 'People have gone back the way – gentler comedy. Less swearing. Less filth. So you quite like him, then?'

Slater shrugged. 'An acquired taste.'

'I think I remember something,' Smythe said. 'Was there not footage of him getting punched? Some girl about half his size letting him have it onstage.'

'That's right!' Slater was delighted. 'One of many times he's been panelled on a stage. He has a "Greatest Hits" playlist on YouTube. Badge of honour.'

'What's the link?' Smythe asked.

'Well, it's difficult to say. Mr Symes didn't get along with him – had words not long ago – but apparently Benny Kettles and Mrs Symes were friends.'

'*Friends*,' Tait said, lip curling. 'Friends how exactly?'

'All he said was "friends", but let's find out a wee bit more,' Lomond said. 'We're looking at the emails and social media to see if there's anything in it, without bothering Mr Symes. It looks like they were pals at university, possibly boyfriend and girlfriend, but there's no way of knowing for sure yet.'

'Is it possible they are just friends?' Smythe asked, destressing the word, the opposite of Tait's meaning.

'That's what I'm hoping you'll find out for us,' Lomond said. 'Now, the interesting bit is, we can't actually locate Benny Kettles at the moment. No contact on the phone, and his agent was cagey. She said he was in Glasgow, but wasn't sure where. Doesn't seem that switched on for a showbiz agent.'

'Which is a bit suspicious,' Slater remarked.

Lomond ignored this. 'So first of all I need Kettles traced, then spoken to. Might be nothing. Might just be ticking him off the sheet.'

'But you've got a hunch, all the same, gaffer,' Slater said, grinning. 'Kettles is my bag. I'll find him. He plays gigs all the time. Open mics all over Glasgow. Famous for it. Tests out new material everywhere. I saw him at the Stand years ago. I'd be happy to talk to him.'

'I think Cara and Myles will take this one,' Lomond said. 'I don't want you doing a fanboy thing while we're out on a job. Asking him to sign DVDs or something.'

'DVDs?' Slater scoffed. 'What is this, the dark ages?'

'Anyway,' Tait said, 'you look too much like a polis. I don't know a comedian yet who liked the polis. Maybe Jim Davidson.' Tait winked at Lomond. 'Can you send us the numbers, sir?'

'Already with you both,' Lomond said. 'Let me know if you trace him. If there's nothing, get back to me straight away. Malcolm, you and me will take Mr Finch and his many grievances.'

Slater nodded. Then he called out to Tait: 'Here hang on! What d'you mean by I "look like a polis"?'

10

The club reminded Smythe of a place she'd gone to when she was way, way too young to be going anywhere of the sort. Fresh as a daisy, tall as a sunflower, in what passed for the height of summer in Glasgow, and fuelled by Canadian Club, fifteen-year-old Cara had whooped, leapt, hopped and skipped. She had a clear memory of pressing her hand against the ceiling. It hadn't just felt damp, it had felt pliant. A disturbingly sensuous experience, like diving into a full skip. The men hadn't been too predatory, but predatory enough, and Smythe cringed to look back on it. Not at the nerve of the clothes she had worn, the brass neck of her friends, the drunken state they'd all been in by three a.m. when the place tipped out into chaotic taxi queues – not even the guy, maybe in his mid-twenties, maybe even older, who had come very close to breaking the law with her in the lane beside the pizza shop – but the risk. The ways it might have gone wrong. The ways Smythe had seen it go wrong, in stricken, bloated, battered, misshapen faces over the years, every one of them a keeper, every one of them with its own space in her head.

So: low ceilings, a pit space in a basement, decent fire escape fore and aft, a good long bar at the back. It became a club after the comedy show ended. Smythe and Tait perched themselves on stools at the back of the hall. The clientele was spread a good few years either side of Smythe and Tait's well-kempt thirties bandwidth, with a few outliers into their fifties and beyond. Smythe's attention was arrested by one jolly-looking fellow with an immense belly under a heavy metal T-shirt and a beer in each hand. He laughed louder than anyone and seemed to know many of the punchlines before they landed. His girlfriend was blonde, short and beautiful, and Smythe envied him and his life at that moment.

'Reminds me of Fury's,' Tait said at her ear, as they waited for the compere to return. 'You remember Fury's? Probably a bit before your time.'

'Well before my time. It reminds me of one near Finnieston.'

'Fury Murray's was further up. Great place to go when you're young.'

'That where you spent your salad days?' Smythe grinned. 'Sweaty basements don't seem your style. I had you down as an Art School kind of boy.'

Tait snorted. 'Arches, if you please. Sub Club if I'm on my best behaviour. But Fury Murray's was for slumming it on a Sunday night. I had some fun in there.' He stood up from the stool and touched the ceiling. 'Bet it sweats in here.'

'When was the last time you were in a nightclub?'

'Not for a while. Passed out of that phase, really. Comes a point you get ID'd going into clubs for the opposite reason you got ID'd before. In fact, the last time, I think they asked me point blank if I was in the polis.'

'Did you lie to get in?'

'Showed them my warrant card. Should have seen their faces.' He grinned at the memory. 'How about you?'

'What? When did I last get ID'd?'

'No, when were you last in a nightclub?'

'Put it this way, it was at Christmas, and I fell asleep for totally the wrong reasons.'

'Meaning you were knackered.' Tait nodded. 'Job does that.'

'It does.'

'I don't get out much, if I'm honest. Sophs likes to go out for a nice dinner. I'm in that zone now. Struggle to drink beer any more. Glass of wine, maybe a dessert, that'll do.'

Sophs? This was new. Smythe had wondered, without prejudice, whether Tait was even into women. His private-school-winner veneer and arch manner could veer into camp at times. Not that it mattered. We all wear a mask, Smythe thought.

'So is Sophs OK with you going out to a club with another woman?'

'We're working, DI Smythe,' Tait said, mock-soberly. 'Try to restrain yourself.'

Smythe snorted into her soda water and lime and gestured towards the stage. 'Maybe you should be up there instead.'

'Maybe I should. Maybe this'll be the night it changes. My career. My life. I reckon I could do it–'

Whatever sarcasm Smythe was about to unleash was drowned out by the lights dimming and the compere bounding onto the stage. He was a muscle-bound fellow, tight polo shirt, veins threading up his neck and arms. 'All right then, how's it going? We're on to the main event now, so if any of you fancy a pee, you're too late. Because you absolutely dare not fucking move when this next man takes the stage. Let's have a warm hand – two warm hands, in fact, smashed together at high speed . . . that's it . . . c'mon, folks, that's it! Applause! You get it! C'mon! And, yes, even the two off-duty polis at the back of the room! Yes, I can see you! Hands together!'

Tait and Smythe grinned like a pair of waxworks. But their hands worked well enough.

'Ha ha,' said Smythe.

'Ha ha,' said Tait.

'And now, the one you've all been waiting for . . . the man who makes you glad to be alive the minute you flee this place, screaming and crying for your maw . . . It's the one and only . . . *Benny Kettles*!'

11

Benny Kettles, in a suit the colour of mustard gas, was already sweating by the time he bounced on stage. His butterbean face was oddly cherubic, and he might have been at one point, and perhaps might still be, a good-looking man. His oatmeal-coloured hair was styled into an absurd kiss curl, not unlike Superman's, and it bobbed around in front of his face like a lure with a hook hidden inside.

'Evening then!' he said, his accent strangely high-pitched. 'By God, I thought I'd seen some ugly audiences, but you people take the urinal cake, let me tell you! Yes, that's right, whoop, clap, cheer, laugh, the torture will never stop.' He froze in the spotlight, glaring at some undefined point at the end of the room. 'Never, ever stop. Yes, I'm Benny Kettles, hello, good evening and go fuck yourselves.'

It went on like this for five or six minutes, and Smythe was snagged in the hysteria that rippled through the audience. She turned to check out Tait. His expression was unreadable. He took tiny sips of his pint of fresh orange and lemonade and kept his gaze fixed on Kettles.

He had been filthy but amusing, and his patter was propulsive, but that changed in an instant when one hardy soul got out of his seat in the middle of a huge laugh about a member of the royal family and a colostomy bag. The man – Smythe never did see his face properly – was seated dead centre of the audience and as he moved between the tables he created a huge silhouette.

Freeze frame: Kettles glowering at the retreating figure blocking out the light, hand shielding his face from the glare, wide blue eyes tracking the man's progress. 'Where are you going?' The high-pitched tone became a growl, so loud that it obliterated the question mark.

'Just the toilet,' was the tragic response.

'Get back,' Kettles commanded, stabbing a finger at the empty seat. 'Get out of my light, prick, and get back over there.'

A tense exhalation among the crowd. Smythe sat up in her chair. The hapless man said something inaudible and waved a hand at Kettles. But that was not the end of the exchange. Kettles spluttered, as if a bucket of water had been emptied over his head, then collapsed to the floor, arms and legs splayed. The wave of unease turned into gasps of shock. One or two people even stood up at the sudden drop, and one of them was Smythe.

Tait took her by the elbow, gently, and shook his head. 'Wait.'

Kettles then spun with a breakdancer's rubber-jointed sinuousness that completely belied his frame, not to mention his clothing. Soon he was literally bent over backwards – both hands planted on the stage, upside down, his sweat dripping to the floor, shoulders quivering with the effort, and his legs bent back at the knees. In a contortionist, this pose would have been credible, but in someone of Kettles' girth it was more like a special effect or a video game.

The upside-down crab began to walk – fast. 'Come back here!' Kettles said. He scuttled sideways. His shirt popped open, displaying an expanse of pink flesh with a hairy dimple in the middle that might have contained a belly button. 'You've spoiled my concentration! I'll have to do the whole show like this now! Back, I say, back!'

There was a smattering of applause. Kettles, who had regained his footing with the same deceptive twirl of the hips, smiled and waved as if he'd been given a standing ovation. He unbuckled his belt, tongue protruding from the side of his mouth, and Smythe feared even more of an outrage. But he was simply tucking his shirt back in before fastening the buckle with a flourish.

'Gets the blood going, that does. Do not try this at home, though. Unless I don't like you, in which case, wire in.'

'Looked painful, that,' Tait said. 'Joke or no joke.'

'Looked bloody fatal is what it looked like,' Smythe replied. 'Nimble for a big lad.'

'Ah, I'm just messing with you, pal,' Kettles said, his voice back into its high-pitched register, as he waved towards the interrupter retreating to the toilets. 'Pee away, mate, pee away. Oh, hey, darling, how's it going?' Kettles sprang off the stage, mic in hand, and made his way through the crowd to the chair the man had vacated. He sat down and batted his eyes at the man's companion date as she giggled and covered her face. 'Mind if I move in here? Not for you, girl. I mean your boyfriend's wallet. Is it in there? Here we go . . . it is, inside pocket, blue ball, first shot! Let's see what he's packing . . . You haven't been going out long, have you? Nah, didn't think so. I can tell, you see. It's a gift. Some people read palms, some people speak to the dead. I work out virgins. No, not you, darling.' Of course I don't mean you.'

Tait turned to Smythe. 'How long till the intermission?'

'Why? Have you got to go?'

'And who have we here?' Kettles' voice and face changed again. He stood up, dropping the absent man's wallet onto the table, where his girlfriend stretched to stop it careering onto the floor. 'Jim, can we . . . Yeah, those two at the back. Stick the spotlight on Mr and Mrs, will you? Bit to the left. Oh, there we are. Ladies and gentlemen, let's have a big hand for Presbyterian Scotland!'

Smythe and Tait flinched as the spotlight washed over them, bright and brutal as sunburn.

12

Tait and Smythe were unaware of it, but their smiles were identical – taut, and seemingly painted on by a toddler trying very hard to stay within the lines.

'Now then,' Kettles said, making his way to the back of the room. 'Let's get a good look at these two. I will try to link minds with them . . . round about now.' He gripped his large, sweaty forehead underneath the kiss curl, eyes drawn tight in concentration. 'OK. I think I've got them, ladies and gentlemen. I'm going to go for . . . out on a date. Right? By some horrible mistake, you're out on a date.'

'Don't say anything,' Smythe said – too late to stop Tait from declaring in his loud policeman's voice: 'No, we are not.'

Kettles clapped his hands together, almost dropping the mic. A shriek of feedback accompanied the impact. '*No, we are not.*' Kettles mimicked, in a bloodcurdling growl. 'Well, you are one hundred per cent not shagging, that's for sure – but does one of you want to? That's the question.'

Smythe smiled on. Tait rolled his eyes.

'I think we've got a performer here, ladies and gentlemen. That's right, Mr Midnight Blue Suit. Good god, you're smartly dressed for this dive. Did you come here by accident? That's a serious question.'

'Sadly not,' Tait replied. If Smythe could have cringed any further, she'd have absorbed herself. Arse first.

'*Sadly not!*' Kettles repeated, in a pompous Kelvinside accent. 'The young master here has found himself in this cradle of iniquity! Here he was, putting a move on this deputy head-mistress . . . No, don't laugh! That's a good job, that is! Great holidays! And you know as well as I do that anyone who signs up to be a teacher and isn't doing it for the holidays is fucking lying, right?' Kettles waggled his eyebrows. 'So what's the script? First date? C'mon, you clearly don't know anybody here.'

'Here on business,' Smythe said, coughing nervously.

'Oh, I see,' Kettles said, allowing the laughter to build at the implication of his tone of voice. 'Well, I'd better move on here, folks. But, hey . . . remember that painting? The old American couple? Dungarees and a pitch fork? I'm just saying, if there was a way of making that image even more miserable, aside from painting it in Glasgow . . .' Kettles aimed two fingers at Smythe and Tait. 'Either that or you're a pair of off-duty polis. Right, where were we? That's the torture over and done with. Time I told you jokes or something . . .' He hurried back to the stage.

'*Farmer with Pitchfork and Wife*,' Tait said, once the spotlight had swung away from them.

Smythe tugged at her collar. 'What?'

'That's what the painting was called. The one he was talking about.'

*

At the intermission, Smythe and Tait followed Kettles as he trooped off the stage to sustained applause. A female bouncer handed him a bouquet of flowers, and he pursed his lips and clenched them tight in his hands like a beauty queen. Then he bit the head off the foremost carnation, spitting out the petals as he descended the steps to the backstage area.

A giant with a hand like a baseball mitt barred Tait's way. 'Behave yourself, pal,' he said. 'I know he slagged you off, but you can take a joke, eh?'

'I'm very well behaved.' Tait showed him the warrant card which he had wisely kept handy as he approached the stage. 'And hopefully you will be too. We need to talk to your man for a couple of minutes.'

The bouncer stared from one face to the next, then made great play of scratching his head.

'Right now,' Tait insisted, shifting his stance. For one absurd moment, Smythe thought he was going to get into some sort of scuffle with the big-bellied, bearded man. But the bouncer relented. 'Make it quick,' he said to their backs.

'Shut up,' Tait said, striding along the corridor. The female bouncer who had presented the flowers was less of a hindrance, knocking the dressing-room door and showing them in.

The room was a tarted-up cupboard, hardly big enough to stretch out in. It had a table and a chair, with a mirror in front – though there were no lightbulbs surrounding the fixture, disappointingly. Kettles seemed to be in a weird half-trance, gazing into his own eyes, the small lips moving as he mumbled to himself. He'd taken off his suit jacket and hung it up on a hook by the door. His white shirt was pink with sweat patches, but he'd thankfully towelled off the worst of the perspiration on his face and neck. He looked oddly shrunken, sitting in his seat, less corpulent. Again, Smythe was struck by how striking his looks were, devoid of stage mannerisms and gurning.

Without looking up at the two detectives, or moving his lips too much more, Kettles said, 'You'll have to bear with me. Just doing the old mantra. Mind-clearing exercise. Just a few more seconds . . .' He blinked. 'OK. In you come. Bugger me, you actually are two off-duty polis after all, eh? My agent warned me someone might appear tonight.'

'In fact we're on-duty,' Smythe said.

'We're here to talk about a very serious matter,' Tait added, as they both held up their warrant cards. 'I take it your agent told you what it was about?'

'Actually, no, she doesn't want to bother me before a show.' Away from the stage, Kettles' voice had lost some of its camp quality. 'I know it seems chaotic, but I really do have to get into focus beforehand. Lots of preparation, lots of rehearsals. Plus . . . do you know how many death threats I've had?'

Smythe frowned. 'Someone's threatened you?'

'Not lately. But I've had them all. Jewish people and Muslims, Catholics and Protestants, and they're your starter for ten . . . Trans and terfs, gays and straights, you name it, they've wanted to kill me. So when I hear someone's looking for me, I lie low. No offence.'

'This might be something you'll want to listen to,' Tait said. 'Did your agent mention we're here in connection with a murder inquiry?'

'No, she didn't.' Kettles' eyes flicked from one to the other.

Smythe caught Tait's eye. He nodded at her and looked away. She asked Kettles, 'Are you acquainted with someone called Kath Symes?'

'Is this a joke?'

'No. Her maiden name was Bruce. We understand you knew her quite well?'

'She's my best friend.' He stood up. 'What's happened?'

'I'm afraid she was found dead in her house yesterday.'

For the second time that night, Kettles hit the floor. For a moment, gazing at the crumpled figure at her feet, Smythe was sure he was dead.

13

Smythe couldn't help noticing that the bouncer's arm, brandishing a bottle of orange juice, was the colour of a Lorne sausage. Benny Kettles gulped from the bottle like – there was no avoiding the comparison – like a newborn on the boob, eyes intent. He had regained some colour. When he had first opened his eyes again, he had gone a sort of pistachio green. Smythe was sure he hadn't faked it, and a glance at Tait reassured her he was thinking the same.

Once the bouncer – who had flown in at the sound of a commotion, shouldering Smythe and Tait aside as they prepared to give first aid – had established Kettles was all right, she left them to it. 'Any problems, we get an ambulance in,' she said.

'Yeah, we're actually in charge here,' Tait said, rising to it. 'Don't disturb us, please.'

As she took her leave, she scowled like a teenager – probably because she was a teenager, Smythe thought.

'Ach, Pauline's a good 'un,' Kettles said, rubbing his eyes. 'Don't be mean. Not the first time she's had to look after me when I take a wee turn. And she'd tie you in knots for your cheek, so, you know . . .'

'She'll keep her distance and not get wide,' Tait said. Smythe wanted to elbow him, but Kettles didn't seem to have heard.

'Last time she woke me up on the dressing-room floor, I'd peed myself. Christ, I haven't peed myself, have I?' Kettles gazed at his crotch in horror. 'Some nights it's hard to tell.'

'You'll have to be the judge of that,' Smythe said. She leaned against the table, back to the mirror, the better to avoid her own face. 'These "wee turns", you call them . . . you had them checked out?'

'It's a mystery. It could be one for Police Scotland's finest, in fact.' He tapped his head. 'Not a tumour – they did all the scans. They established I have a brain, though, so there's that. One in the eye for Mr McYule, modern studies, who said I didn't have one.'

'That isn't what happened on stage, was it?'

'Nah, that was a good old pratfall. I'm not bad at them. Practise and everything. Regular Charlie Chaplin, me. Stan Laurel. But this was the real thing.'

'Does it just happen at random? When you're driving, say? That's scary,' Smythe said gently.

'I don't drive because of it. I can't. Nobody knows what it is. If I went private, I might get it sorted, but they might be just as stumped. It might be that thing when it's something in your mind rather than your body that causes it. What is it, again?' He clicked his fingers rapidly. 'Psycho . . . psychical . . .'

'Psychosomatic?' Tait offered.

'No. Gay, that's it.' He giggled at his own joke.

'That's not very funny, Benny,' Tait said.

'Ach, it was a bit. But, no, I'm not diabetic . . . it's not a blood-sugar thing. All normal. Pancreas and kidneys working away like happy wee soldiers.' His voice broke on the last two words and he covered his face with his hands. His shoulders shook. Tait squared his and stayed back, remaining silent. Instinctively Smythe touched Kettles' back.

'It's my pal, you know?' Tears like a kid's marbles spilled down his cheeks. 'My best pal. You've got to be fuckin' *joking*.'

'I'm so sorry,' Smythe said. When he took a breath, she felt it rattle through his chest, transmitted to her fingers. 'It's a shock. You take your time.'

'Murdered? Please, God, not a pervert.'

'We can't share any details at the moment, because we don't

know,' Tait said. 'I'm sure you understand . . .'

'A pervert, then. She was beautiful.' He shook his head, then beat his temple with a fist, an alarmingly powerful blow. 'Scum. Absolute scum.'

'Take it easy.' Smythe increased the pressure on his back, just a little.

'I can't.'

'How long did you know her for?' she ventured gently.

'From uni. We were sat beside each other, first year, Glasgow Uni. One of those where the guy at the introductory talk says, "Turn around and talk to the person next to you." So this gorgeous thing turns round and is confronted with . . . Kate.' He snorted, a sound like a sob tripping over itself to leave. 'I was thinner then, shy with it, but I'm one of these people, when I start gibbering, I can't stop . . .'

'You don't say.' Tait raised his eyebrows.

'She wasn't from Glasgow. I was. Well, Rutherglen. Near as damn it. She was from Pittenweem, originally, East Neuk, or her dad was. I think the family moved to Glasgow when she was five or something. We spent the lunch break together. It sounds weird, but she was one of the first people I made laugh.' He stabbed a finger at Tait. 'Your next line is "She's the only one".'

'Saying nothing,' Tait muttered, shaking his head. 'Absolutely nothing.'

'We just hit it off. And it went from there, you know. Pals right through uni. You're going to ask me something kind of leading and borderline offensive, now, to find out if we slept together. So which one of you's coming out with it?'

Smythe drew back a little and shrugged. 'Don't think either of us was gearing up for that one, Benny, but, answer it for us, if you would.'

'Yeah, we slept together. Absolutely. By that, I mean passed out in the same bed. Lodges out Loch Lomond way, youth hostels, and once, after the grad ball, a beautiful night in a four-poster. But it was a marriage of convenience. Slept together but never shagged. We thought about sleeping together again on the night before her wedding, but that might have been pushing a flirtation too far. She was a *mate*.' He took a deep breath, then another. Something faded from his eyes then. 'And you're asking me this for a reason. What is it?'

Tait said, without a pause, 'What was your relationship like with Edward Symes?'

'Darling Eddie. Did he do it?' The stage stare was back again, and it ricocheted between Smythe and Tait.

'Edward Symes was away on a business trip. When he found out about his wife's death, he was in Amsterdam.'

'Amsterdam! I wouldn't trust Eddie in Amsterdam.' He raised a hand. 'That was unkind, sorry. There's no reason for saying that.'

'A personal reason, maybe?' Smythe asked.

'Well, he's a dickhead. Not good enough for her. She could have done so much better. Now I know what you're thinking. When someone says, "Hey, you know, she could do so much better than him," what they're really saying is . . .' He jabbed a finger towards his crotch. 'But, no, I mean it straight up. She could have done better. Something uptight about him, from the very start. He couldn't handle our relationship. Jealous Ellis was my name for him.'

'Was that an unreasonable thing for Edward to think?' Smythe asked. 'You and Kate were obviously close.'

'It doesn't matter what he thinks. We were pals; nothing he says or does gets in the way of that. We came through a lot together, all the way through uni, all the relationships and splits . . . Her mum always wondered why we never got together. Used to say it openly.'

Tait wrote something in his notebook. 'Edward Symes says you had a falling-out recently.'

'Does he now?'

Tait nodded. 'Said you came over and said a lot of nasty things. To him and to Kate.'

'Well, we had a disagreement. It was nothing to do with Kate, though.'

'He says it was.'

'No, it wasn't.' The stare returned but only fleetingly. 'If you must know, it was about property. Investments he was looking into. That's his line of business. He wants to buy up flats and turn them into property leases. Short-term lets, holiday cottages. He wants to branch out, start a property rental company. Students, young couples. Standard rip-off. He wanted me to invest in it. He actually thinks I've got money! We had a free and fair exchange of insults.'

'What kind of insults?'

'OK, I said he was a big Tory-voting profiteering bastard, and he said I was a . . . let me think now, it was quite inventive for him . . . a mithering ponce. I dunno how he came up with any of those, or how they apply to me.'

'He asked you for money?' Smythe asked.

'Not exactly. He's a businessman. But that's what he wanted. He wants to invest in a place called Gillman Flats. It isn't actually flats, it's a piece of land, near the Campsies. He wants to build a holiday village or something. I told him where to go. Which was, to fuck. But it wasn't really the thing to say to Kate. Well, in front of the kid, anyway.'

'And what happened then?'

'I left, standing on my hands.'

Tait frowned. 'You mean that? We need you to be serious.'

'I mean it. It's my party trick. Which you saw on the stage.'

'And when was this?'

'Four nights ago.'

Smythe said, 'And we have to ask you – where were you between nine a.m. and five p.m. yesterday?'

'In the flat. Shawlands. Tinkering with my material. Lana Tully was with me for the early part of that, until she had to go and start a shift at the baker's.'

'Lana Tully is your . . . ?'

'Lana Tully is not my anything. A friend.'

'She lives at your flat?'

'No. Stays over. Slept in my bed, in fact . . . You don't seriously think I have anything to do with what happened to Kate, do you?'

'We don't think anything,' Tait said. 'We just want to hear what you've got to say.'

'We'll be back in touch,' Smythe said. 'I know it's a shock. I'll leave you with a number in case you want to talk it over with someone. If you remember anything at all you think might help us, please call us straight away.'

'You got someone with you tonight?' Tait asked.

'I think Pauline might be staying over,' Kettles said. He indicated the door, which had opened silently to admit the bouncer. She folded her arms and gazed balefully at the far wall.

'Take care, Benny,' Smythe said, passing him a card.

'Sure,' he said. And even as Tait and Smythe went out of the door, Smythe fancied she saw him deflate, his head sinking towards the floor.

14

Slater hung the scarf around his neck, made a loop, and pulled it tight, arranging the material until it was just so. 'Every time I see you with those wellies, gaffer,' he said, with some bitterness, 'I open my mouth to give you a slagging. Then I remember: I've forgotten mine. Every single time.'

'You're a slow learner,' Lomond said, throwing his shoes into the boot. 'Once you go for the wellies, I'm telling you, you never go back. But . . . see that feeling you get when your trousers bunch up a bit and you have to poke them down? The way it felt when you were five? You never, ever get used to that.'

'Walk it off, gaffer,' Slater suggested. 'It'll right itself in a minute.'

They were parked near an electricity substation fence, which bore a sign warning them not to. Lomond noticed that the sign was more prominent, colourful and threatening than the one that promised instant death should anyone attempt to gain access to the humming structure itself.

'Odds-on we get clamped,' Slater complained, looking as ill at ease as a newborn foal as they turned down the slushy track. 'We take your car, flights of angels sing it to its parking space. But whenever it's mine, tickets, clamps, blowouts, bomb scares, lunatics shooting at us . . . practically guaranteed.'

Behind the substation was a patch of waste ground that stretched for maybe a quarter of a mile towards the rear of the new-build houses, hemmed in by crash barriers and wild, scrubby bushes and trees, winter-bare. It was early evening that same day, after some food and a cup of tea at the canteen and a quick change of clothes, while Smythe and Tait were prettying themselves up for their date with Benny Kettles.

'Anything we want to see here that forensics haven't seen yet?' Slater said.

'Not exactly. Just looking.'

'It's dark, gaffer.'

'That's the idea.' Lomond smiled.

'That means we won't see anything.'

'Yes, we will.'

'I like the suspense,' Slater said, peering into the slush and mud of the path. 'No, seriously. Totally fine with it.'

The lights outside the substation and the other industrial units faded to a faint orange glow through the trees. Lomond fitted a head torch and clicked it on, the blue beam creeping along wet, leafless boughs.

Slater snorted laughter.

Lomond turned towards the DS, dazzling him. 'After tonight you'll want one. That's a promise.'

'Who says I don't have one? Maybe when I go out cycling.'

'You don't go out cycling, Malcolm. You just look like you do.'

The path was soon hemmed in by the bare branches, a gloomy hollow that was uncomfortably like a phalanx of spider legs, all seeming to move in the thin but piercing blue beam. Lomond moved the light over anything that might conceal a track of some kind.

'Needle in a haystack stuff,' Slater grumbled. 'Waste of time. And, Christ, I wish I had a coffee here.'

'You don't like the cold?' Lomond asked sharply.

'I don't mind the cold. I can deal with sleet and drizzle. I can handle a bit of wind, but not all at once.'

'We won't be long,' Lomond said. 'We just need to get to the end of the path that backs onto the houses.'

'Want to give me a clue? Or will I guess?' Slater thrust his hands into his overcoat pockets. 'OK. I'll say . . . you're looking for a vantage point. You think she was stalked.'

'Spot on.'

'But surely we've had uniforms out looking? They've combed over this place the day. Dogs, helicopters, hands, knees and boomps-a-daisy, the lot.'

'We won't find any evidence,' Lomond scoffed. 'We're not that lucky.'

'Then what is it you're looking for?'

'A nice spot.' Lomond pointed to a gap between the trees, the bark silvery under the ray of light. 'That one'll do it.'

'It's muddy . . . ach!' Slater's boots slurped in accompaniment with Lomond's wellies, but only the inspector walked with any confidence until Slater saw what he was getting at. 'Right you are. I see what you mean now.'

They had followed a narrow path that became as tight as a top button as they squeezed between the branches, but when they reached the point where the blazing lights and church-like glow denoting the evidence tents surrounding the Symes' home appeared they had a clear view of the property, albeit through a loose tangle of beech trees.

'You do reckon he stalked her, then?'

'Better than average chance of it,' Lomond said. 'Husband away . . . left on her own in the house . . . no plans for the day. She was usually a busy woman.'

'That's my top theory. I'd say it was bang on . . . but you aren't saying that.' Slater shivered. 'What's your other theory?'

'OK.' Lomond cleared his throat. 'How the husband did it. Go.'

'You're joking. He's out the frame, gaffer.'

'Let's think about it while we're here. If the husband did it, what's the score?'

Slater paced up and down the uneven terrain, the surviving brown detritus of autumn shot through with forlorn grasses. 'First. Contract killer.'

'Not out of the question. No one's mentioned marital problems or anything, though.'

'Doesn't matter, gaffer. Money. She was insured, I bet. Motive? What else do you need? Money gets mentioned, that's the trigger for some. Seen it *loads*.'

'That's a point for you. Go on.'

'OK. If it's a contract killer, then he was helluva messy with it. Face to face, smothering her like that . . . you'd think they'd want something cleaner, something with a bit of distance. But if he just had her shot or poisoned, then it'd be obvious it was to order. So maybe it *is* a contract killer, with instructions to make it look like a pervert.'

'Again, point to you.'

'But that seems pretty complicated. So I'll go with "lone maniac". And if it was the husband . . . There's a window, isn't there?'

'He left Glasgow for Amsterdam on the morning of the day before. So that's plenty of time to double back – although he was seen at several business meetings on the afternoon she was found,' Lomond said. 'But there is a window in the morning, which he had free to explore the city. He didn't. He said he stayed in his hotel. CCTV will clear him, you'd think. Plus his phone and Passport Control. But let's say he used that window to sneak back. How does he do it?'

'Hires a double? Leaves his phone with the double?' Slater bunched his shoulders as a wind threaded through the trees and tickled his chin. 'Flies back on a fake passport? Do the flight times tie up? There and back?'

'They do,' Lomond said. 'It's tight, but it could be done.'

'Nah,' Slater said. 'I mean we'll check it, like, but nah. Lone maniac, for me. Stalked her. Waited till she was on her own. Got into the house. Did it.'

'The house is another thing that bothers me, but we'll come to that. Anyway . . . reckon you could climb up that?' Lomond nodded towards an oak tree, a good age, its bark reptilian in Lomond's torchlight.

'What . . . now?'

'I'm sure it's not a problem for a strapping young man such as yourself, Malcolm.'

Slater spluttered, 'Climb a tree? In these clothes? In this light?'

'I reckon you could get up there. And our boy could, as well. And . . .'

Lomond's silence went on several beats too long. Slater drew breath to speak, but Lomond silenced him with a wave of the hand, then flicked off the torch. A rustle answered them, somewhere off to the right.

'Out you come,' Lomond said, into the gloom. 'It's all right. Let us see you.'

15

'Out you come,' Lomond repeated, peaceably enough.

The man who emerged from the branches was wearing dark clothing, except for fluorescent stripes around his collar and sleeves, snow-glare-white under Lomond's headtorch. He was about medium height, and had a lupine look familiar to Lomond from squaddies, or even young lads who'd joined the force. He had looked like that himself, once. A grimy look around the eyes and sunken cheekbones told of an even harder lot in this case. The man had sheathed his skull in a tight beanie, and it was quite impossible to tell his age.

'What are you pair doing?' he asked, utterly unabashed.

'Investigating a murder,' Slater said, taking a couple of steps forward. 'Your turn.'

The man frowned, but there was no outward change in his demeanour. 'I can tell you exactly where I was today, and the day before that,' he said.

'We'll get to that. How about a name, first?' Lomond asked.

His name was Daniel Laybourn, with a y, and he told them that he'd been out in his van delivering parcels so many times that Lomond had to tell him to stop.

'And I'm hardly going to be creeping around with this gear on, am I?' he said, flexing his shoulders, making the reflective material wriggle.

'That's why we didn't lift you straight away,' Slater told him.

'What's your story, mate?' Lomond said. 'This is still a crime scene.'

'Shocking what happened to that lassie,' Laybourn said. He chewed the side of his mouth as if it was his only nourishment. Lomond had a flashback to the kids on his housing scheme when he was younger.

'What did happen to that lassie?' Lomond asked.

'Cut her head off, I heard,' he said. 'Place was like a butcher's. Shocking people about, man. Whoever done it.'

'Whereabouts do you live?'

'Here,' the man said. 'Top of the drive.'

'Near the substation?'

'Aye, the flats at the top. Springley Drive.'

Lomond nodded. Technically a different postal district and parliamentary constituency, and plenty more besides, yet only a band of woodland separating the two. 'And why are you out here now, Daniel?'

'Carrying out my own enquiries,' Laybourn said. He turned towards one of the thicker trees. 'And gathering a wee bit of firewood.' He reached towards his pocket, and Slater caught him in half a second, stopping the arm as it folded over into the dark jacket. 'Here!'

'What have you got there, Daniel?' Slater said. 'Slowly, mate. Don't do anything daft.'

Lomond was expecting a surprise: a bunch of flowers, perhaps, or a rabbit, or the ace of spades. What Laybourn brought out was indeed a knife. A Swiss army-style pocket knife, of course, but nonetheless a knife.

'Christ's sake. It's legal. Less than three inches.'

'That what your dad said to your ma?' Slater said.

'I take offence at that. So would my dad, probably.' He allowed Slater to look at the knife, dangling it from the loose key ring attached to the end. 'Can I have it back, or are you taking it as evidence? Can hardly cut anybody's head off with that, can I?'

'You'd be surprised. What exactly were you going to cut with it?' Lomond asked, as Slater handed the knife back to him.

'Wood. I just told you. Wood. From the woods.'

'For what?'

'What do you think? A fire. I've got a burner out the back. Neighbours hate it. Couple of them complained. Couple of them came round for a beer. That's how it goes, eh?'

'What kind of wood can you cut with that?' Slater asked, genuinely amazed. 'Doesn't have a wee portable chainsaw there, does it?'

'Watch and learn, son,' Laybourn said. He withdrew a thin blade, with diamond-pattern serrations at the end. 'I'm not here for logs or that, just for kindling. Get the fire going. Cheaper than buying it at the garage.' Laybourn approached one of the low-hanging branches, knobbled and bulging like an old lady's hands, and began to saw. In Lomond's torchlight, the stripped-back bark glowed. He winced at the flaying: daft, he knew. He glanced around the other trees, noticing the stark nubbins where other branches would have been until recently. 'You do this quite a lot, Daniel?'

'Oh aye. Good thick woods here.'

'You know them well?' Lomond asked.

'Aye. Lived here all my life. Or hereabouts, anyway. Used to be a Scout hall there.' He indicated the windows, visible through the trees.

'I think I remember that, from old photos of the place,' Lomond said. 'Have you taken down any larger branches lately, Daniel? Round about this wee bit?'

'Definitely. I gathered some logs and took down some of the dead trees. Ash dieback here, y'know? Gathering fuel. Not illegal, is it?'

'I couldn't tell you off the top of my head,' Slater said. 'We'll let it go tonight, anyway.'

'I did take down some bigger branches.'

'Where? Can you remember?'

'Just about here, in fact. There. Look.'

Laybourn indicated a sharp, splintered end on an oak tree.

At first glance you would not have known, even under a spotlight, that a healthy limb had ever been there, owing to the corkscrewed bark. But upon closer inspection, it was clear it had been recently cut.

'Gave me a bit of bother at the end. Bit of push and pull.'

'Got you,' Lomond said. 'Quite a thick branch, aye?'

'Oh, definitely. Could've done pull-ups on it. Well, I could've in my army days.'

'You see anybody round about here the past few nights?' Slater asked.

'Nobody. Well, up on the main path you get dog walkers. And a couple of times the young team have been up at the clearing, setting off fireworks. Bonfire night. Before they got chased, anyway. But not in here, where it's thick.'

'No signs of anyone? Cans of juice, cigarette ends, that kind of thing?' Lomond said. 'Empty bottles? Drink?'

Laybourn shook his head.

'And did you know the woman, Daniel? The one who was killed?'

'No . . .' He straightened up, and in a firmer voice said, 'I did know her to see her.'

'To see her?'

'Aye. Out and about, like.'

'Out here?' Slater asked.

'No, not out here. Just up by the scheme. Well, the street with the big houses. She went running, that kind of thing.'

There was silence for a moment. Lomond and Slater said nothing, did nothing.

'I wasn't spying on her,' Laybourn said, his Adam's apple bobbing. 'You can hardly see anything out here. I come here cos it's quiet. Nobody sees me; I can't see them.'

'That's OK, Daniel. We'll take your name and your details, though.' Slater took out his notebook.

'What you're telling us is important,' Lomond said, in a friendly tone.

'All right. I wasn't going to bring it up, but with what happened to the lassie, you know . . .' He snapped off a branch, then paused.

'Know what?' Slater asked.

'Well, as I said, I've been carrying out my own investigations.'

'Aye?' Lomond said.

'Aye. Strange things happen out here, mate. Late at night, early in the morning. Weird things.'

'What like?'

'You'll laugh,' Laybourn said, grinning ruefully.

'Promise we won't,' Lomond said. Not being close enough to elbow Slater, he shot him a glance, the headtorch temporarily blinding the DS – a death ray.

'Well,' Laybourn said. 'Basically . . . UFOs.'

16

The thing to notice about Vincent Finch was . . . well, there were lots of things, really, Lomond reflected later. There was the fact that he had either started getting undressed or had been in that state for his whole day. Sartorially, the look was purest jakey, the kind who often found a liquid lunch had turned into an entire evening, and probably another morning too. Lomond was just old enough to remember the final days of such characters in the former Strathclyde Police. Finch's tie was undone to the nipples. His shirt had gone further than that, unbuttoned to the navel. The observer's eye was biased, and expected to see uncouth colouring, stains and patches down that shirt, and yet it was crisp white. Similarly, Finch's face was clear and unblemished, with a fine straight jawline that was surely a stranger to hops and grapes. In terms of the shape of the skull and jaw, the hollowed regions that could have done with some feeding, Finch had a similar look to Slater, cycling-obsessive slim, with the only outlier on an otherwise angular face being a bulbous nose that instantly reminded Lomond of the actor Karl Malden. Finch was fifty-one, and you had to look closely before you saw that he did look his age; a greying fringe snaked across one eyebrow, but the parting revealed a hairline that had crept back some distance. Bizarrely, his trousers looked as if they wanted to run off after his shirt and tie, with an unbuckled belt swaying between his knees like a power cable.

The next thing to notice was how quickly Finch's eyes dodged from Lomond and Slater's gazes, looking off somewhere to their left.

'I've already given you a statement,' was his opener.

Lomond and Slater hadn't so much as reached into their pockets for their cards. 'I'm sorry?' Lomond said.

'I said, I've already given you a statement. You're police, right?'

'That's right. I'm Detective Inspector Lomond, and this is Detective Sergeant—'

'I've nothing more to say.'

'We'd just like to take you through one or two things, Mr Finch. We're sorry to disturb you.'

'You off out somewhere?' Slater asked, pointing at the loosened belt.

'No,' Finch mumbled, the voice gravelly. 'I was taking my work gear off. Had to work late. Your officers took up a lot of my time earlier. Nice lassie, mind.'

'Sure,' Lomond said. 'We had to ask you a few questions. You're aware that Mrs Symes was killed yesterday?'

'Killed. All I knew was she was dead. I didn't credit all I heard, but I put two and two together, like . . . I mean, you don't put out a tent like that for nothing, do you?'

'Maybe we could come in for a wee bit?' Lomond suggested.

Finch pondered this a moment, then without replying moved aside to let the policemen in.

⋆

Instead of doing his belt up, Finch seemed to grow angry at it, unlooping the leather and tossing it onto a table in the hall. The belt slithered off and clattered onto the chequerboard-tiled floor. Finch ignored it. His trousers clung for dear life to the slim hips. 'Kitchen's through here,' he said.

Lomond and Slater exchanged raised eyebrows behind him as they followed Finch down the arched hallway. The dimensions of the house were identical to the Symes' place, though the décor was utterly different. Framed children's artworks covered the wall opposite the staircase, ranging from nursery spots and splotches to some fairly sophisticated drawings of horses in flight. The kitchen was the same as the one that had contained the corpse a few doors down, even in terms of the unforgiving overhead lighting. But this was more of a working space, Lomond might have said. 'Mess' was another way of putting it. Paper, loose pens, pencils, crayons and felt-tips. Fine paintbrush heads clustered in jars and glasses on the mantelpiece near the patio door, the water of the darkest purple. The white walls were stained here and there, and freshly too, going by the bright yellow, orange and red scarring.

A girl of ten or eleven sat in the corner before an easel, drawing with pastel crayons. Lomond discerned lilac and pale blue lines, running diagonally, cutting across a fine black line-drawing of a stallion, face on, charging towards the viewer.

'Those your drawings, sweetheart?' he asked, nodding towards more of the paintings and sketches hung haphazardly around every surface.

The girl, who did not have her father's skittish eyes but did have his pallid, flawless complexion, nodded slowly.

'You're really good at that. I can't draw a bath.'

'This is my daughter, Kay,' Finch said, standing a little proprietorially between the two men and his daughter. 'Art, that's all she does. You might have, ah, guessed.'

'Mind if we borrow your daddy for a wee minute?' Lomond asked.

The girl looked to her father, who said, 'In the living room, please, pet. Five minutes.' He looked at Lomond. 'That OK?'

'Five minutes will do it,' Lomond said. The girl slid off the artist's chair – slightly too big for her, Lomond thought, though that'd change soon enough. She did not look at anyone's face as she left. Spooky kid, Lomond thought.

'Nice kid,' Slater remarked. 'Very polite.'

Finch ignored him, turning to Lomond. 'What else was it you wanted to know?'

'It's about the Symes, Mr Finch. We understand there was a dispute between you and them recently?'

Finch took a sharp breath through his nose. 'That was dealt with in the courts – as I'm sure you know.'

'I've read the judgment. I just want to know what went on.'

Finch folded his arms. On doing so, he became aware of the change in texture, and hastily buttoned his shirt. He said, in far from the assertive tone he'd intended, 'You think I killed her.'

'We've just asked you about the dispute,' Slater said. 'Let's not leap to any conclusions.'

Lomond sniffed. 'Something burning, Mr Finch?'

'Aye.' Finch nodded out to the patio. 'We've got a chiminea.'

'A what?' Slater said.

'A chiminea. A wood burner. Out in the garden. The snow's off . . . if it's cold and clear, me and the other half go out with a glass of wine on a Thursday night. We sit with the fleeces on.'

'Mind if I take a look?' Slater already had his hand on the patio door handle.

'Eh, sure. Why not? You can just about see the flames flickering . . . Turn right as you go out. We've got a wee nook built at the side wall, there. Nice and private.'

While Slater followed these directions, taking care not to slip on the decking, Lomond said, 'I understand the problem was with an extension, Mr Finch?'

'Yes,' Finch said, back straightening. 'Simple matter, really. And it was all him.'

'Him who?' Lomond asked.

'Symes, Ed, Eddie, whatever they call him. No one else objected to the plans until he did – at the last minute. After that, everyone piled in.' Suddenly, Finch remembered himself. 'Sorry. His wife's dead. That was thoughtless. Last thing I want to be talking about.'

'That's all right,' Lomond said equably.

'It's just . . . I had a suspicion about him.'

'Oh aye?'

'Yeah, he's just . . . always on at you, you know? One of those people. Your bin, it doesn't go there, he tells me. Knocked on my door, day after we moved in. It was on the pavement outside my house. I asked him what he was talking about. He says eventually, "My bin goes there – if you put yours there, the binmen might forget to take mine." You know the type.'

Lomond said nothing.

'Anyway. From there it's "Don't block my light at the front, if you have too many people round". I wanted to tell him to piss off.'

'Did you?'

'No. I'm not a sociopath – you've got to live in the same street, even if the houses are this big.' He paused a moment. 'But I didn't like the guy. His wee girl and mine, they're of an age, but they don't play together.'

'Why is that?'

'Beats me. Belinda, my other half, she sees the wee lassie and says, "Oh, that's nice, a pal for you," but that wee girl doesn't give Kay the time of day. Didn't even knock our door at Halloween, so there you are.'

Lomond noted this down. 'And how did the extension thing come about?'

'At the absolute last minute.' Finch looked like he wanted to spit. 'Got all the plans. Said nothing. It wasn't overlooking his property. There may have been a slight issue with the setting sun, but nothing you'd notice. On the final day of the consultation among the neighbours, he knocks the door to let me know – we've all banded together, he says, and we reject your proposal. Then we're going to court, I says. You're out of order. He just laughs at me, sets the papers down on my doorstep and off he goes.'

'And what happened then?'

'Well, you tell me. Court decides in his favour. Well, his and the neighbours'. But it was down to him. Clennehan, up the street – he was out with his dog – told me one night, "He talked the rest of them into it. I didn't agree, didn't put my name to it." Symes wanted to put my nose out of joint. Why? I honestly don't know. Dominance. Being the big dog. Insecurity. Christ knows.'

'And you hadn't had a row, or anything? A falling-out?'

'Nothing. That's the only contact. We don't go out, you know? We don't have parties. We don't play loud music. We've had one barbecue – that's the one he complained about: too many folk parking and blocking his light, he said. That was it. You'd have to ask him what the problem is.'

Lomond spotted Slater poking around in the garden and looked away, keen not to draw Finch's attention. 'And is your wife around, Mr Finch?'

'She's gone out – over-fifties aqua-aerobics. She'll be back in tonight.'

'We'll probably want to speak to her.'

Slater knocked on the patio door and came back inside, shivering. 'Getting frosty out there,' he remarked.

'What were you looking for? Burned clothes and such?' Finch said.

Slater was startled for a second. It did not happen often. 'As a matter of fact I was admiring your – what did you call it? Chiminea? My old dear would love something like that.'

'We have it on all the time. Summer, winter. Like an open fire, you know?'

'It's a cracker,' Slater remarked.

'Do you ever see anything weird out there?' Lomond asked, remembering Daniel Laybourn's dramatic announcement.

Finch tried to suppress a laugh, and failed. 'What . . . you mean, like, killers roaming the forest at the back?'

'I would hope you'd've already told us if that was the case.'

'I've told you in some detail what I saw,' Finch returned,

sobering. 'Which was nothing.'

'How about anything really odd or unusual?'

'Like . . . shooting stars? You see them, usually in August. Perseids. Some crackers last year, in fact. Got some good shots.'

'Yeah, anything of that nature,' Lomond said. 'Anything strange at all.'

'Next you'll be asking me if I've seen wee green men in flying saucers.'

Lomond smiled benignly. 'Just on the off chance. Every little detail can help. Speaking of which – do you mind if I talk to your daughter for a second?'

Finch shrugged. 'Go ahead. Living room, first on your left there.'

*

The girl was on a mobile phone, to Lomond's surprise, when he knocked and entered the living room. This was more of an adult's space, cluttered with large untidy bookshelves and CD towers whose contents threatened to spill over into each other's territory. Lomond was amused to see a wall of ancient VHS cassettes, and even more amused to see one spine denoted *Close Encounters of the Third Kind*, the black night on the box cover faded to denim blue in the sunlight, but the stars just as bright.

The girl didn't look up as Lomond entered.

'Hiya – Kay, is it?'

She didn't say anything, or even acknowledge him. She blew her fringe away from her face, and her fingers and thumbs worked hard at the keypad. Lomond was reminded of a rat's paws, and winced at the comparison. 'Hope I'm not interrupting.'

'I'm just speaking to my friend. She's a bit freaked out.'

'Oh?'

'Just to do with a test. Well. Maybe she wants to know what's been happening here.'

'What did you tell her?'

'Nosy.' She smiled, and her face was transformed. That grin couldn't have come from her father, Lomond thought.

'It's bad,' he said. 'Something very bad happened.'

'I'm not a baby,' Kay said.

'I know. That's why I want to ask you a grown-up question.'

Now he had her attention. She laid the phone aside. 'OK.'

'Have you ever seen anything like flying saucers outside?'

She shook her head slowly from side to side, maintaining eye contact with eerie equanimity. Then she chuckled. 'You're messing with me!'

'I'm not. Anything like that? Anything unusual, especially out at the back of the house?'

The girl shook her head, then giggled again. Her cheeks were bright pink. 'You're going to think I'm messing with you!'

'Ah, that's my job in life, love,' Lomond said, grinning. 'My wife and my daughter – she's about twice your age – that's all they do. Mess with their poor old da. What's on your mind, Kay? You know, what you tell me could be really important.'

'It's daft. In fact, it's fine. I was getting mixed up. There's nothing to say.'

'Hey . . . that's weird,' Lomond said. He touched the back of his head.

'What is?'

'I could have sworn I buttoned up the back, here.'

'Get away!'

'Ah, c'mon now. You want to tell me something. You can tell me. I want to know about it.'

She covered her face. 'It's daft.'

'I bet it isn't. And, you know, things that seem daft can be really important later on. It's true. That one wee detail can help crack a case.'

'You catch murderers?'

Lomond nodded. 'A few. I know what I'm talking about. So, c'mon – spill the beans. What is it you were going to say?'

She took a deep breath. 'I haven't seen UFOs. But I have seen a ghost.'

'A ghost?' Lomond raised his eyebrows.

'You're laughing at me!'

'I absolutely am not. Lots of people think they've seen ghosts. What did it look like?'

'It was kind of all weird.'

The light blinked on above Lomond's head, far too late, really. 'You could draw it, I bet.'

'Oh, yeah. That's a good idea.'

17

'What the hell is that?' Slater said, holding the A4 sheet up to the car's interior light.

'A ghost, I'm told.' The last time Lomond had seen Slater look that disgusted, he had just dropped a full fern cake on the street. This included times Slater had seen dead bodies.

'A ghost? It looks worse than a ghost. Can something be worse than a ghost?'

'She's quite good, isn't she?'

'What, the wife drew it?'

'Nah, the daughter. Kay.'

'Wowsers.' Slater paused. 'I mean, it's good, you know. Call the school counsellor now, like, but she's got some talent.'

The ghost had been sketched, freehand, with an HB pencil. Lomond hadn't seen one of those since primary school. The girl had carefully selected it, and begun to draw with enviable control and economy. She'd made no amendments, had never once reached for the eraser, never expressed any frustration or started again. With her lips compressed and her eyes focused, she had transposed what she'd seen onto a page. She was a leftie, Lomond noticed. He'd read somewhere that left-handedness corresponded to a greater facility with art, though he expected there were all kinds of biases built into such studies.

He supposed the figure, and its clothing, had a lot to do with the somewhat airy style of the composition. It wore something like a poncho, draped over thin shoulders, and the arms were outstretched. The girl was good at drawing people: the joints, the Vitruvian proportions. 'Have you been taking classes?' Lomond had asked her. She had. Mummy had taken her.

The edges of whatever the figure was wearing were ragged, as if the fabric had been cut via shark bite. The face was nondescript, part of the effect, with no discernible eyes.

'And she really saw this?' Slater asked.

'So she said.'

'Whenabouts?'

'Well, here's the first Moment of Doubt. She says she first saw it at Halloween.'

Slater let the page fall with a theatrical pause; Lomond caught it before he did. 'That'll be that, then.'

'Not so fast. She said she saw it again a week or two later, a wee bit after Bonfire Night. She was looking out for it at Christmas time, but no dice.'

'She see it from her window?'

Lomond peered at the drawing again. 'She said she saw it while she was playing in the woods. Alone.'

'Vivid imagination.'

'That's what I thought.'

Slater gestured over his shoulder towards the crescent of houses. 'This estate . . . it's all very gate and fence, you know?'

'I don't know what you mean at all, Malcolm.'

'I mean, there's no kids out playing. And I don't think it's just to do with what happened at the top of the road. It's not the sort of place where the kids are out playing football on a patch of grass. Mind you, I'm not even sure kids do that these days. They get ferried to soft play and whatnot by their folks.'

'I think it can depend on how many kids you get on an estate, and how close they are in age. They'll play together, usually, when the weather's good.'

'All I'm saying is . . . well, would you have let your daughter out to play by herself in the big scary woods when it was dark?'

'You've got a point.'

'So I reckon the junior artist has a vivid imagination.'

'You're probably right. I'll ask about it, though. It's incredibly detailed. You'd think someone else who lived here would have remembered a big scary ghost like that roaming about after dark, maybe called it in. Another kid. So far as we know, the only other wee lassie about Kay's age is the victim's daughter. According to the dad, they don't play together, owing to the feud over the extension.'

'Suppose we can ask. Looks like Mr Redley McHerring to me, though.'

'We'll see. Other thing is UFOs, according to Laybourn.'

Slater chuckled. 'Aye, strange lights in the skies. Weird machines piloted by weird gadgies.'

'IFOs, you mean.'

'IFOs?'

'Aye. Identified Flying Objects.'

'Drones, you mean?'

'Got it in one. We need to ask if anyone's seen anything out there. Our man might have stalked Mrs Symes from on high.'

'Maybe Laybourn was right,' Slater said. 'And maybe the thing Kay drew wasn't a ghost. Maybe it was the pilot.'

'Intergalactic or not, I want to know everything about Laybourn,' Lomond said. 'The full bhoona.'

'No obvious suspects here,' Slater said, suppressing a yawn. 'No obvious evidence, either.'

Lomond said nothing. Outside, tiny flakes of snow began to fall. He checked his phone and grunted. 'Funny one,' he said, peering at the screen. 'When these homes were built, they all went to one private developer. They sold them on.'

'For a modest profit.'

'Looks like it.'

'What's the builder?' Slater asked.

'Avalon King.'

'Cracking name for a folk band. Mean anything to you, gaffer?'

'Got a good name, so far as I know. You'll have seen the signs, the logos. They usually turn round brownfield sites, put up poky wee houses and blocks of flats on top. But these ones look a cut above. No buy-to-lets on this road. I've heard the name mentioned. Read it in the paper. The same way people talk about single malts and fancy motors.'

'*Some* people, you mean.'

'Aye. The kind of folk who bang on about vintage gear. You know the type.'

Slater cinched the collar of his analogue-interference-screen jacket with an exaggerated prissiness. 'Some people just have no taste, gaffer. They're not connoisseurs.'

'They're not daft, either.'

'Who are we doing next, then?'

'We need to talk to the mum.'

'Going to be bad, eh?'

'It's going to be bad.'

18

Lomond took it like a boxer taking punches from a much younger, much faster opponent. You had to look carefully for an opening, and you also had to make sure that they played themselves out. That they'd slump, exhausted. At the moment, there was little chance of Corinne Bruce doing that.

'I mean, my Gordon, right, was a big man, strong; he could have done it. Bent iron bars with his hands. He did it one time, there was this guy who wouldn't move his car away from our house, and Gordon pulled him up for it, and he had this tyre iron, you know, for changing tyres, and–'

Slater got right out of his seat and stood up straight, hands raised, like Nosferatu sprung from the tomb. Lomond couldn't stop him. Slater said, in a very high register, 'That . . . is some view out this window, eh?'

'Aye, it is,' Mrs Bruce said, without pause, 'I don't like these windows, though . . . I reckon they have to do it to keep the heat in. A bit too warm . . . You'll be warm in that jacket, mind you.' Here she paused. 'Where did you get it? Looks like something you'd see at the Klondyke.'

Lomond coughed into his hand.

'Klondyke?' Slater said, examining himself. 'Goldminers and that? The wild west? Cold weather, I suppose. Keep you warm.'

'Nah, the Klondyke was a nightclub, son. I went to it when I was a lassie. That wasn't its real name, just what folk called it, cos . . . you know. Anyway. You used to see that kind of stuff on people then. Tartan ones as well – Bay City Rollers fans. I loved the Rollers. Everybody did. Didn't see bald folk so much back then, mind. People did what they could to hang on to their hair. Hard for the young ones, like you – they'd have combovers, remember them? Like they'd glued bootlaces to their heads. They just whip it off now, like you. Much better, you ask me. I think you'd suit a jacket like that if you were a bit hairier, say if you had sideburns and a bit longer on top, you know . . .'

Slater sat down again, seemingly unable to speak.

They were in a waiting room at the private hospital. Mrs Bruce had been sent there by her son-in-law – 'maybe he's got a season ticket', Slater had said – and checked over after taking what everyone had termed 'a funny turn'. Understandably. She had been given no medication so far as Lomond or Slater had been told. An experienced nurse with kind, if tired, eyes had waited with her until the detectives had arrived, and had left with remarkable haste when the interview began.

'I fancy another tea,' Lomond said. He turned to Slater.

Before he said another word, Slater nodded. 'That's a cracking idea, gaffer. You fancy another one, Corinne?'

'I will, son. Maybe put two sugars in it, give me a bit of pep.'

'Pep,' Slater said, blinking. He remembered to smile and withdrew about as fast as the kindly nurse.

'Nice lad,' Corinne said. 'Goes on a bit though, eh?'

'Can't shut him up at the best of times.' Lomond leaned closer. 'How are you feeling now, Corinne?'

'Good. Just want the paperwork signed and get up the road. Ed's sister's nice, met her a few times. But the wee yin needs to be with me, I think. I shouldn't be away from her.'

'You've done most of the heavy lifting today,' Lomond said. He put a hand on her back, instinctively, and then he saw it coming. Some change in her chemical constitution, it might have been; a solid form becoming liquid, impossible to contain or suppress. She sagged against him, wheezing. In some alarm, Lomond looked around for the emergency buzzer.

'It's fine, it's OK,' Corinne said. 'I just . . . it hit me, you know?'

'You just take your time there.'

'Why are you holding on to Ed? You don't think he had anything to do with it? He's a crabbit bugger but he wouldn't . . . he couldn't have . . .'

'We've got to ask him some questions – it's the last thing anyone wants, but it's important. We don't think he had anything to do with it.'

'No . . . unless he hired a hitman, obviously.' She straightened up.

'Well. We don't know about hitmen, but we want to know if anyone saw anything unusual. Those're the kind of questions we want to ask.'

'Or maybe it was a jealousy thing. My lassie was good-looking, you know. Got my Gordon's features – you can see it in Beatrice as well. Not saying I was walloped with the ugly stick or anything, but I married up the way.'

'Not at all. Your granddaughter's a lovely lassie. You've got a look of her.'

'You're a big flirt, you are.'

Lomond grinned. 'Don't tell the missus. But you mentioned a jealousy thing there?'

'Och, just speculating. Don't let me do your job for you.'

'Speculate away, Corinne. Send it over to us – anything you saw that was unusual. Anything Kath told you that stuck out or seemed odd.'

'Nah. Just that bugger across the way. The one who tried all that legal carry-on over his stupid extension.'

'I think I know the neighbour you mean.'

'Stuck-up git. The mad professor, I call him. Finch, his name is. I noticed he came over one Sunday when Ed and Beatrice were out. We'd been out the night before for a show at the Pavilion – musicals, you know. I like them. Ed took Beatrice to see *Walking With Dinosaurs* down in Manchester, live show – she likes that kind of thing. They stayed over, so I stayed at Kath's. And I noticed himself over the back fence, dodging about in the woods.'

'You could see him?'

'Just at one part of the fence – the part where he could see in, near one of the posts. He was out there spying, I reckon. They don't have a dog or anything. No reason for him to be out.'

'Can you remember when this was?'

'It was about last October – when we had that right cold spell, quite early on, I'd say. Leaves were just beginning to come down.'

'About Halloween time?'

'Could have been. Maybe a bit before – the October week holiday. I had Beatrice for a couple of days that week, so it might have been then.'

'What did Kath say about it?'

'Rolled her eyes. She thought he was an eejit. I reckon someone like that isn't right, you know.'

'In what way?'

'I mean, the state of him. Nice-looking man but his wife needs to be getting him some decent gear. He walks about wearing a dressing gown, flip-flops, Hawaiian shorts and some kind of vest, like he's Rambo. In fact he had a bloody headband like he was Rambo as well. Or that boxer, what was he called?'

'Rocky?'

'That was him. No, wait – Chris Eubank, I think he was called. Anyway, someone like that. He used to walk about the street like that, calling after their wee lassie.'

'And Kath wasn't wary of him? Did she mention he'd been round before?'

'Don't think so – think that was it. To be fair he could just have been out there minding his own business. But it was a bit weird.'

'How about anyone else on the estate?'

'Most of them keep themselves to themselves. Nice enough. You get a lot of delivery vans driving up and down. Use the crescent as a turning point. Gets annoying, after a while.'

'Delivery vans, you say?' Lomond made a note.

'Aye. And driving instructors. Tons of them. One the day before she died, I remember.'

'Right enough. I suppose they use the place for three-point turns and so on.'

'Aye. And there's a dual carriageway on the road in, long straight road, you know? Good practice for them. The house'll be dark now. Empty for a while. I wonder if Ed and Bea can ever go back there? I don't think I can. I just . . .'

This was the thought that finally shattered the facade. Over the woman's heaving shoulders, Lomond caught sight of Slater hesitating outside the frosted glass window, a smudged wraith bearing a tea tray. The figure withdrew, then mercifully returned a few moments later with a nurse to see to Corinne.

19

Maureen and Siobhan were still up when Slater dropped Lomond off, much later. Even from the driveway, with a miserly spoonful or two of snow after a fresh fall, Lomond could see the boxes piled up in the window of the vestibule. That was how it went, he supposed. It had been a while since his last house move, and he wasn't sure he was ever going to have another, but he remembered with a sudden pang the physical encapsulation of a life: all the possessions, the hard decisions made about what should be kept and what was heading for the skip. Lomond hated having his simple, orderly life at home disrupted, plus he was tired. He composed himself before sliding his key into the lock.

He was greeted by the sound of packing tape being dispensed and cut. Boxes lined the walls, an assault course for Lomond as he hung up his coat, looped his scarf round the peg and extricated his feet from his wellies. Feeling a little like Indiana Jones dodging traps in an ancient temple, though maybe with a little less speed, Lomond swivelled his hips around the teetering piles and into the kitchen.

His wife Maureen and their daughter Siobhan were sitting on the floor, the spotlights that Lomond hated bathing the scene. There was something about the sight of the pair of them with scissors and tape and boxes, as well as the empty bottle of wine on the counter, which reminded Lomond of Christmas.

'You had your tea?' Maureen said, without looking up. She was throwing paperback books into a box. Lomond spied mother-of-pearl spines, fairies in pale blue lace, unicorns – the stuff Siobhan had loved as a wee girl.

'Yeah, grabbed a couple of rolls. Be fine.'

‘Not a murder, was it?’ Siobhan drained the last of her glass of wine.

‘Afraid it was.’

There was a pause, then, between the three of them. The shadow of the Ferryman will always be hanging over us, Lomond had reflected more than once.

‘Bad?’

Lomond nodded.

‘Bad-nasty or bad-weird?’

‘Both.’ Lomond clicked on the kettle and opened the tin of zero-caffeine sleepy teas. As ever, he could not resist taking a good sniff at the opened container before sticking a bag in a mug. ‘Anyone for a cuppa?’

Maureen shook her head. ‘Sorry about the mess. Thought we’d have been finished by now.’

‘Always the same with flitting, isn’t it?’ Lomond said, perching on the kitchen counter. ‘Always another box to fill.’ He scratched his forehead. ‘Darling, I’m awful sorry, but I’ll need to be back on it early tomorrow. I won’t get the day off. I’m not going to be able to help you with moving in.’

‘Now that’s convenient,’ his wife said. A blank look came over Lomond’s face, and she knew the kinds of things that might have engaged his attention in the twenty-odd hours he’d been out of the house. She was sorry she’d said it, but she also knew there was no need to apologise to him.

‘Don’t worry – that’s why we hired the removal men,’ Siobhan said. ‘Unless you meant “moving in” as in “me taking a nosey at the flat and spying on the neighbours”.’

Lomond gazed at the ceiling with a sly little smile. ‘Oh, already done that, sweet pea. Two of your new neighbours, a retired pair of West Enders, didn’t pay their poll tax back in the day. Pleased as punch with it, as well.’

‘My kind of people. High five.’ Siobhan grinned.

‘And I think there’s a young man somewhere on the top floor who’s been done for breach of the peace. But who hasn’t?

A rammy on Sauchiehall Street at taxi queue time. But that's it. Quite a genteel wee block of flats you've got. Upwardly mobile young professionals. And no dogs. You're going up in the world.'

'One tries one's best. I've done well, given the start I had in life.' Siobhan stretched and yawned. 'You know, I think I'll turn in. Long day tomorrow.'

'You all about finished?' Lomond said, sounding a little more hopeful than he intended.

'That's it,' Maureen said, smoothing down a roll of tape along the closed flaps of a packing box. 'Just wee bits and pieces. We were wondering what stuff we should keep in the loft and what should go with Siobhan . . .'

'The bloody lot should go with Siobhan,' Lomond muttered.

'We were looking through some old stuff. Amazing the things you forget. Check this out.' Maureen raised a tiny pair of baby bootees, bright white, with a knitted image of an angel on the front surrounded by blocks of gold, blue and pink, like an ancient computer game.

Lomond chuckled. 'Those are from your first Christmas,' he said, coming forward to take the socks in his hands. 'Your granny McGrain knitted these for you. My God. Think you could still fit in to them?'

'I could have them for earrings?' Siobhan stood up. She was about as tall as Lomond – taller, in heels – and Lomond still had that feeling that she was stooping somewhat to give him a hug.

'What's that for?'

'Helping out. Putting me up while the flats got finished. Not taking any money for it either.'

Lomond hugged her close. 'You're still buying us pizza, though. Let's get that established.'

'On my honour.' She smiled. 'I think this lot belongs here,' she told her mother. 'If you don't mind.'

'We've got the room. Don't worry.' Maureen took a thick marker pen and wrote SIOBHAN'S STUFF/LOFT on the top of the packing box in slanted capitals.

Lomond watched his daughter head up the stairs, wearing what looked like her running gear, to get the things she was taking with her packed. She'd become willowy as her early twenties edged towards the middle but, from the back, with her dirty blonde hair in a ponytail, there was a glimpse of the tigerish wee football-playing tomboy she'd been for one summer between primary school and secondary. She had moved out once before, for her post-grad Year that Could Not Be Named, but she'd stayed at home to do her teacher training the year after that, and then a few months beyond that while she'd found a flat for herself as she'd got on with her first year teaching the wee ones at St Vincent's Primary. Lomond and Maureen had saved quite a bit for her, and helped out with the deposit – no option, it seemed, these days: your folks helped you, or you had an inheritance, or you won the lottery – and here, at last, was the final severance of life with her parents. Lomond had found it difficult when she moved into her student flat, and he hadn't quite got to grips with the fact that, apart from Christmas, this was probably it as far as her family home went. Lomond wondered what they'd do with the space. He felt a greater, cosmic horror at the idea of possibly moving somewhere else himself.

He swallowed it down with a nice sip of camomile and fennel and smiled at Maureen as she put away the scissors and tape. 'It's a hell of a job, that. Thanks,' he told her.

Maureen smiled. 'How about your hell of a job?'

Lomond sucked his teeth. 'Someone broke into a house. Locked door. Security camera. No footprints – even in the snow. Nobody saw anything. Got in, murdered a woman, got back out. Her mother found her.'

'Jesus.'

'We've got nothing. I'm hoping the SOCOs have found something, but now I need to sleep. Just for a bit.'

He collected his second cuddle of the night.

20

While Lomond lay in bed, staring into pools of shadow on the ceiling, about four and a half miles away on the other side of the river four faces lit up in the heat of orange flames.

These belonged to Chas, Del, Hannah and Stan. It would have been hard to pin down their ages in broad daylight, never mind in the shifting flares and gutterings of firelight. A cynic might have said that not one of them was over thirty, and would have been proven correct.

Outside, beyond the empty window frame, was a decent view of the city. The snow had laid off, replaced by a clear sky. The stars were an insult when you were out in the open. Chas had told them for days that the old Hazell Court wasn't being watched at night – that no one had been seen through the fencing, that no dogs had barked, and no torchlight had been visible through the fence. No one had believed him until the graffiti had begun to creep over the cladding tiles, like fruiting fungi.

'I'm telling you,' Chas had said, 'we can bunk in there, no danger.'

When the temperature dropped even more, four figures had crept in.

Someone had given Chas a battering a couple of days ago, and he hadn't been in the mood to talk about it. 'Polis,' had been his explanation, though most of them knew Chas had a mouth on him and a tendency to open it when it was least welcome. Chas had been known as the Human Pipecleaner when he was at school, and it could be said he had grown into the role. He was tall enough, but his shoulders drooped, to the extent that his social worker back in the day had wondered if this was caused by a deformity. Had Chas's mother had much to do with him after the event, she might have told him that his birth had been a difficult matter, but that was guesswork on everyone's part. The other three didn't take so well to how Chas spoke to them, but on this particular night he had the bollard-sized bottle and a willingness to share it.

Del and Hannah were a pair, though Chas and Stan had tried often to turn them into two separate units, a fact that Del ignored. He was handsome, which maybe had a lot to do with it, although his eyes were small and sunken beneath a heavy brow. Hannah was a pigeon of a girl with mousy roots in her black-dyed hair. They hadn't been on the streets very long, and there was talk of a room in a hostel, but they'd been driven out by a couple of psychos. There was always a couple of psychos. Hannah would snuggle into Del, her round pale face poking out from underneath his armpits, her arms clasped around his neck. Stan was long-haired and bearded, but looked the least like the kind of person who bunked up wherever he could. He had a leather jacket, and someone said they'd seen an Angels tattoo on his back. He also had a military-green bikers' backpack, covered in decals and band names the others had never heard of, the jagged lettering of the logos delicately stitched in red. The bands of old vinyl collections belonging to big brothers, in memory, the kind of stuff that ended up in house clearances after the older brothers died.

Piled-up ribbons of ancient vertical blinds were stripped from a pile of refuse, and despite an acrid stench they had burned easily enough. Del and Stan had made short work of a chest of drawers, and that had burned equally well, giving off a spectral green when it was added to the fire.

'They'll move us on,' Chas had said, as the flames grew brighter, all four of them with their hands outstretched. 'With the fire.'

'So,' Stan said, 'you going to crack open that bottle or what?'

Chas grumbled, but fair dues to him he did, and they began to drink, their shadows growing tails and horns and tentacles around the mould-flecked walls.

'I have to go,' Hannah announced.

Chas giggled. 'Well, go then.'

'Your en-suite bidet awaits,' Stan said, gesturing towards a dark, doorless portal over their shoulders.

'There's rats in there,' Hannah said, folding her arms and shivering. 'I can't go by myself if there's rats.'

She gazed pointedly at Del, but he was busy gulping down the cider. 'Not bad,' he remarked, to no one in particular. 'Could do with a toke, mind.'

'Tell you what,' Chas said. 'I'll head through with you. I'll keep an eye out for rats.'

'Aye,' Stan said, eyes glittering. 'Any long pink things appear, just give us a shout.'

Hannah shook her head, but she followed Chas into the next room.

Chas laid his hands on her shoulders, and she squirmed. 'Don't you worry, doll,' Chas told her, lips close to her ear. 'I'll stand over here, with my back turned, and keep an eye out for the rats.'

'You'll not laugh at me?'

'I promise,' Cham said, already trying not to snigger.

Hannah crouched close to a pile of rotting carpet tiles. Cham stood over by the door, a dignified distance away. He giggled as the sound of tinkling began.

'You said you wouldn't laugh,' Hannah hissed.

'Sorry. Honest, if there's rats in here, you'd have heard them.'

Shifting footsteps, right at that moment. The kind made by shoes, not ones that scuttled. Another door off to the left.

'Here!'

'What's happening?' Hannah said, panicking, struggling to fasten her jeans.

'Somebody there. Here, you! Come out!'

Something that might have been a shadow in the doorway. Chas strode towards it, careful to make lots of noise, though he stopped short of moving over the threshold.

A shadow scurried through a door on the other side, then there were louder footsteps as the hidden figure jumped down the stairs.

Chas made his way into the room. The wind reached its jagged fingers through a window with panes of smashed glass embedded in the frame like shark's teeth. The moon shone clean through, and the far wall glowed. As did the old fridge in the far corner.

'What's going on?' This was Stan, at Chas's shoulder, making him jump.

'Not the polis. Not a guard either. Some wide-o,' Chas said.

'Sounds like he got off his mark,' Stan said. The buttons and dangling zips on his leather jacket glittered in the milky light. He crossed over to the window and peered outside. 'Aye. Someone's running away across the court. Through the fence . . . and . . . *adios*.'

Chas turned towards the fridge. 'Hey. What's that sticking out of that thing?'

Stan scratched his beard. 'Looks like an old clothesline.'

Chas seized the plastic-coated line, which was jammed between the door and the frame, and pulled. The door opened as the fridge toppled sideways with a puff of dust. Then something fell out.

Behind him, Del and Hannah weren't sure which of them screamed. They didn't wait to find out, but scuttled back the way they had come, down the stairs and away through the fence.

21

Lomond was talking in his sleep, something about a canoe and a waterfall. He sounded untroubled, more curious than anything else. Maureen, giggling to herself, was in the middle of making a note of this before she forgot, so that she could wind him up later, when his phone detonated, startling them both.

'Right,' Lomond said, in the sudden businesslike tone of a drunk shaken awake before he falls off his bar stool. 'Yes. Hello.'

'Sir.' Smythe – the phone would have told him that, but Lomond's vision still swam. 'We got a tip in from a snout. It looks like there's another one.'

'You're joking!' He was out of bed, kicking off his shorts.

'It's complicated, sir. It's not exactly new.'

'Where?'

'Hazell Court. Old tower block.'

'They not coming down soon?'

'At some point. Been derelict eighteen months, maybe two years.'

'I'll be over in a minute . . . two minutes.'

Once he'd hung up and struggled out of his long-sleeved top and stumbled for the en-suite, Maureen said, 'Another one. Meaning another murder.'

'Aye.' Lomond mussed his hair.

'Feels like we only just got rid of the last one.'

'You're telling me.'

'I'm sorry.'

'Isn't your fault. Unless there's something you want to confess.'

'You'll be careful, though. Last time wasn't good.'

'I'll be careful,' he said soberly.

'I read things about that woman who was killed. I heard someone broke into her house. Middle of the day.'

'Nothing to worry about. No need to do anything out of the ordinary. Lock the doors, alarms on, be smart.'

'God, remember last time? The Ferryman protests? You almost got bloody killed.'

'Sullivan can handle that carry-on this time. I'm staying well out of it. I'll do the donkey work, nothing else. If it's a serial job, we'll catch him. They make mistakes without realising it. If he's from outer space, we'll catch him. If he travels through time, we'll catch him.'

Maureen frowned. 'What in God's name were you dreaming about?'

'An ice cream van. I think there was an ice cream van in it.' Lomond paused, frowning. 'Nah, it's gone.' Then he got in the shower.

*

Chick Minchin crept up on Lomond while he watched the remains being lifted onto the table.

'Jesus, Chick.'

'Sorry, Lomie.' Minchin wore a smart shirt and trousers as usual. Lomond thought he recognised the tie, a yellow and black chequerboard that reminded him of burnt cheese on toast. The pathologist uncoiled this from around his neck and laid it over a hook alongside his suit jacket. 'You got a coffee down you?'

Lomond tapped the paper cup on the table with the end of his finger. 'That's my third. It'll do for now.'

'We're into serious territory here, are we not?'

'We are,' Lomond said. He took up the empty cup for want of something to do with his hands. 'Soon as I saw the position of the legs, the hands, I knew it.'

Minchin nodded. 'Off the record, there's too much similarity to ignore.'

The stark white lighting, the shiny silver instruments and the bleached-clean surroundings made for a stunning contrast to the condition of the body. Even over and above what Lomond had seen so far in his career.

Beyond the observation window, Anita Khavari and a junior pathologist prepared for the post-mortem. Brown flesh, sightless eyes, denuded bones slipping through green-flecked black mould like a daring show of leg in a vaudeville show. Lomond could detect nothing from this position, but he knew the smell. Smythe had been on it when Lomond and Slater had arrived. She'd struggled to speak afterwards, which wasn't like her.

'Male or female?'

'I'd say male,' Minchin said, 'but we'll check to be sure.'

'Not so decomposed as you'd think. How long?'

'This is the thing – no insect activity, really. Not as much as I'd expect. And flies get in everywhere, as you'll know. Even given he's been stored in a fridge. I'd say he's been dead six weeks – done November, maybe. After the leaves turned, anyway.'

Lomond nodded. 'Any chance he was in a fridge that was switched on?'

'Then dumped? Aye, it's possible. We'll check, see if there's any sign the flesh has been frozen. Given he's not been totally skeletonised, that'll give us a chance to check one or two things. Body's a mess, but if it had been there for six months, say over the summer, it'd be worse.'

'Same deal as the other day, in Fairham,' Lomond said. 'This was left to be found.'

'Thing that strikes me, Lomie – the arms, elbows, knees, chin, all appeared to have been propped up on the stuff that fell out of the fridge with him. Old books and boxes. Whoever did it wanted to preserve the shape of the body. Compression. All folded in on itself.'

'And stuffed into a box,' Lomond said.

'The woman at Fairham was smothered,' Minchin said.

'Offer you evens it's the same.'

'That's a bet.'

Lomond nodded towards the tall, slender white-suited figure beyond the window. 'What d'you reckon to Anita, then?'

'Oh, she's a threat,' Minchin said, a little wide-eyed. 'Better than me by miles. Calm. Efficient. Gives you chapter and verse, studies, papers, forgets nothing. Great with her hands, on top of that. Plus, she takes a better photo than me.'

'Ach, you're not so bad yourself, Chick.'

'Stick her on the front of a Sunday supplement, she wouldn't look out of place. I mean that's just stating a fact, right? Not sexist.'

'Totally not sexist,' Lomond said, a tad hurriedly.

'She'll be running the place in five . . . maybe even three years. Game's a bogey, Lomie. I've had it.'

'So – this you checking up on the competition?'

'Yeah, something like that. Or call it professional interest.'

Lomond smiled. 'You're not retiring on me any time soon, are you?'

'Me? Christ, never. I'll be on the table over there before that. Besides, who else is going to bust your chops the same way I do?'

'Everyone else.'

'You'd better go in. This looks like a menthol job.'

'You're not kidding.' Lomond held up a tub of vapour jelly.

'I'd have given you a dod on the house. My own brand. Special reserve. The good stuff.'

Lomond unscrewed the cap of the tub. 'I should have brought the military issue.' Before they could continue, Khavari's muffled voice came through the speakers.

'Before we start, gents, you'd best take a look at this. We've found something in one of the hands.'

⋆

Later, Khavari wouldn't touch the tea and biscuits, Lomond noticed. Her long black hair was tied back. Close up, her eyes were startlingly black, stealing the light from every source.

'Well, the opinion was that this was a man in his late thirties, about five foot six inches tall. Stripped naked. Throttled, it looks like, going by a ligature wound deep in the neck.'

Lomond made notes. 'Seems like you were spot on.'

'I suppose it does help if you get a great big clue clutched in the dead man's hand.'

'Yeah. You didn't know about that right away, though.'

'I'll take that, all day long.' Khavari clicked on the screen, moving away from the close-up of the ghastly face. The flesh had slipped, revealing a grin that missed a tooth or two. The next image was of a slimy piece of card, which the pathologists had cleaned off. It had been lodged in the crook between the right thumb and forefinger. The embossed plastic revealed his name, and his face. A security pass, and a sun-bleached face, curly-haired, somewhat round-eyed and startled-looking, with a stubbly chin. William Ross.

'Makes our job easier, that's for sure.'

'Like everything else about this body in situ, it suggests it was posed, to me. With a bit of movement, and allowing for the body at the scene falling on the floor, this is exactly the same as the Fairham woman.'

'And he was killed nearly two months before.' Lomond tapped his notebook. 'Different sex, same method.'

'Not quite,' Khavari said. 'Throttled. Kathryn Symes was smothered.'

'He wasn't the biggest,' Lomond noted. 'But it would have taken a lot of effort to do either of them.'

'A strong man, to fold them up like that,' Khavari said.

'Not to mention the method.'

'Fridge man was throttled from behind. Harder to do than smothering someone. In theory. We'll see what the toxicology tests bring up.'

Lomond peered at the edge of the pass, where faded blue lettering fell in a vertical line. '"Avalon King" – that's a builder's,' Lomond said. 'Recognise the font.'

'Aye,' Minchin said from the far side of the room. 'They did some work on my extension. Few years ago now.'

'I'll make a couple of phone calls.' Lomond turned back to Khavari. 'It looks like we could have the same man. That's my feeling.'

She nodded. 'There are a lot of similarities between the way each body was posed. Too many to be a coincidence.'

'Except he did this one weeks ago. And it's not the same situation at all. So what's the link?'

22

When someone slid into the seat next to her, in the briefing room, Smythe jumped.

'Bad one?' There was nothing particularly offensive in Myles Tait's manner, voice, or expression, but something in him conveyed this anyway. Maybe Slater's right about him, Smythe thought.

'I don't know if it's the worst,' she said. 'When I was in uniform I saw an old lady in a flat. Neighbours had been complaining. The smell, you know? I thought I'd seen it before, but she was in an unbelievable state. I remember thinking it was like she was in a cocoon – she was turning into something else. Place was absolutely jumping with maggots. I don't think anything will top that, but this one . . . it was like something from a video game. The colour, that muddy brown. I'm not sure how to describe it. I want to say mummified.' She blinked. 'So, aye, it was bad, is what I'm saying.'

'Sorry.' Tait blew onto the surface of his tea. 'Same killer, eh? Another one. They must absolutely love this city.'

'Lucky for us, eh?'

'Love your work . . . hate your work.' He lowered his voice. 'Speaking of which . . . you going for it?'

She frowned. 'Going for what?'

'You not see it? It was posted today.'

'No. I haven't stopped, Myles.'

'DI.'

'Oh aye. Where?'

'Edinburgh.'

'That suit you?'

'Yes. Time for a change. And you? You'll go for it, surely?'

Slater appeared and sat down alongside Smythe, sparing her the need to answer. He nodded in Tait's direction. Slater being curt wasn't unusual when Tait was present, but it was usually spiced with the odd gag or flat-out insult. He tapped at his phone, then tucked it in his pocket.

'You in the mood for lunch after the PM?' Tait asked.

'What? No.' Slater crossed his arms and sat back, sighing. Tait shrugged at Smythe just as Lomond appeared in the room and laid down his folder.

'OK, folks, I won't take up too much time here. To confirm what you probably already know: we potentially have a second body courtesy of our friend from Fairham. Died before Kathryn Symes. We believe his name is William Ross, age thirty-seven, been off the system for three years. Last known working as a labourer at a building firm called Avalon King. He'd been there since school, until he got his P45. Since then, nothing much. Remaining family is his mother and an older brother, neither of whom sounded particularly cut up about it. No one reported him missing. Cara and Myles, I want you to get talking, find out anything you can about William Ross. Try the family again, see if you can dig out what happened.'

Tait lifted his hand. 'Any last known movements or contacts?'

'No, and that's bothering me. It's all far too vague. William Ross himself is far too vague. We'll put out some appeals in the press.'

Smythe asked, 'Does any of this tie in with Kathryn Symes?'

'We don't know how,' Lomond said, 'but it certainly looks like it.'

'Are we sure it's the same killer?' Smythe asked.

Lomond clicked on the link. There was the image Smythe had been confronted with that afternoon. Almost like muscle memory, her palate and gullet were in revolt, just for a second. Silence fell on the room at the sight, while the smattering of detectives and uniformed police collectively tried to process what they were seeing, and then instantly rejected it. It wasn't a gasp, or even an inhalation. It was an un-noise, an anti-flinch. 'What I want everyone to pay attention to is the position of the body. Head, arms, elbows, all stuffed into a tight space. William Ross was folded into a fridge, and the limbs were propped up with detritus – landfill, apparently – so that the body would retain its position.'

'That level of decomposition . . . when was he killed?' Tait asked. 'Meaning, was the body actually stored in the fridge before it was switched off and wheeled over to Hazell Court?'

'Anita and Chick are in agreement – the body was never refrigerated. But it had been enclosed for nearly two months.' Lomond hesitated. 'It may have been preserved in some way. Somewhere dry, maybe mummified. Even late October, early November, there should have been insect activity or at the very least a more advanced level of decomposition . . . Malcolm, you with us, son?'

Slater was on his phone. He glanced up at Lomond with a look that resembled hostility, Smythe was amazed to note. Without looking away, Slater clicked off his phone and tucked it in his coat pocket. Then he raised a hand, back in character. 'Sorry, gaffer.'

Lomond blinked, then continued. 'Malcolm, I want you and Lorna McGill to have a look through the CCTV at Hazell Court. It seems they were a bit lax over there with security – that's why folk were able to break in. It might be that they don't have any records, but something might show up. I'm thinking that William Ross's body was in storage somewhere, maybe an industrial unit, something like that. Then it was moved recently to the room in Hazell Court, for us to find. Or someone to find.'

'OK.' Slater caught the eye of the short, thick-set plain-clothes officer, who nodded in return.

'I'm going to speak to Avalon King, see what comes up,' Lomond went on. 'That's a link between Kathryn Symes and

William Ross. Avalon King built the Fairham estate where Kathryn Symes lived. I'll want to have a look at their security system set-up as well.

'That's all for today. Everyone else, I want all tips dealt with and followed up. And for the moment, we are not sharing with the press that the two cases may be linked. The state in which the bodies were discovered doesn't need a public airing just yet either. I'll look forward to your reports.'

Lomond remembered the ghastly images he'd left on the big screen just in time before he stepped away from the lectern. With one or two hasty clicks, they were gone.

'Georgia on your mind?' Tait said to Slater, grinning.

Slater was back on his phone. His reaction was delayed, but still faster than most. 'Your ma won't leave me alone, Myles. I want you to have a word.'

Tait snorted. 'My ma would never have sent you out the door looking like that. Care to explain the jacket?'

Slater extended a finger, nodded to Smythe, then caught up with McGill.

'Not like him,' Tait said, nodding towards Slater's back.

'Dodgy case, isn't it?' Smythe offered, zipping her notes up in her bag. 'It gets to you sometimes.'

23

Nicole Kingsley didn't move a muscle. She sat there at the centre of a huge black coat that seemed to double in size when she sat down. Her breath steamed up in the cool air, wisps of it trailing from her sharp nose. If she was impatient or bored, there was no outward sign of it. There was no outward sign of anything. She'd even let the tea grow cold, having sniffed, made a face and simply left it to die on the table after its delivery from the vending machine. A pretty face stared out from underneath long blonde hair that had taken a while to straighten that morning. Nicole believed in looking good while doing dirty work. She was forty-two, but she could have passed for at least a decade younger.

The sun was a welcome sight that morning after the snow, low and sickly as it was in early January. It bleached the wall of the Portacabin, casting long shadows on the tatty items pinned to the notice boards, the printouts and pictures excised from newspapers. Someone's got some Photoshop skills, Nicole noted.

At last, the door to the cabin opened. Nicole kept perfectly still, her hands folded. She'd kept her gloves on – pearl white, as was the pashmina draped around her shoulders. She regarded the big, bumptious man in the uniform with a look of open amusement. He carried a comically oversized travel mug in one hand, steaming hot.

Joe paused, as if caught doing something. 'Right,' he said, at last.

'Your shirt's . . . um . . . down there.' Nicole nodded towards him.

He felt each button before finally reaching the smooth point where the button had been dislodged by his belly. 'Right,' he said again, fixing it.

'You've had a busy time of it,' she said. 'Polis talking to you, eh, Joe?'

'Aye,' he said.

'Hell of a thing to see,' Nicole said. 'Sorry about that.'

'It's . . . it was bad,' Joe said.

'No one wants to see that.'

Joe shook his head. He moved towards the table. Before the mug could be placed on the lacquered surface, she said, 'Don't bother getting comfortable.'

'You what?'

'I said, don't bother getting comfortable. Definitely don't sit down.'

'What do you mean?'

'I heard funny things about the security on the site here, Joe. Apparently the cameras have been on the blink. That's your job. And you haven't told anyone.'

Joe blinked. 'I did tell someone. Someone on site mentioned there was something wrong with those cameras. I mentioned it to Alan when he came in to take over. Mind the cameras, I said.'

'Alan Pringle, you mean?' She still hadn't blinked. Or separated her hands. 'Alan Pringle's logged in every night, checked the cameras, and chased anyone who appeared on the site who shouldn't have been there. This is something that you didn't do, apparently. Now I have to hand over the CCTV footage we have of the building, and I find out that when you're on . . . there isn't any. That's not very good, Joe.'

He shrugged. Bluster, now. 'Not my fault if the equipment isn't working.'

'It's your fault that no one knows about it, though – if you're telling the truth. And then there's the type of people who were crawling around on the site . . . junkies and down-and-outs.

No suggestion of you taking backhanders to let them sleep there, was there?'

'No. God, no. I don't know how they got on site. It isn't my fault—'

'No, it's just your job. Or was your job.'

'You're giving me my jotters?'

'P45 will be with you very soon, Joe. Thanks for all your efforts.'

Joe stared into space for a second. 'That's out of order.'

'Can't have that kind of slacking, Joe.'

'I'll get on to the union.'

'Why, have you joined one? You paying their fees?'

'Twenty-six years . . .'

'We all need to move on to new projects, Joe. Oh, and when you try to get a job with Proudfoot . . . or Merrion Security . . . or even good old Henry Mulcalhy . . . don't bother, is what I'd say.'

'You can't do that to me,' he said. Visibly angry, now, not just indignant.

In a detached fashion, Nicole wondered if he might attack her. That would be kind of fascinating.

'I have and I will. Take your mug and go. Paperwork'll be sorted at head office. Have a nice day, Joe. There's probably decent casual work to be done somewhere. You're a big boy. You could lift parcels all day. I can see you doing that.'

'There was nowhere else for them to go,' Joe said, with a slow, terrible clarity. 'It was freezing cold. They die on the streets. It happened to my cousin.'

'Well, now they've got you, my angel,' Nicole said, 'they'll want for nothing.'

He swore at her, a single, terse word. She smiled sweetly at him for the first time, showing him her teeth. 'Get off my site, Joe. Don't let me see you on it again.'

He slammed the door behind him.

Nicole opened her phone and checked her face in the

mirror effect, turning her head left and right, licking her teeth, smelling her breath, checking her lipstick. Satisfied, she closed the phone and stood up, a shorter figure than might have been supposed when she was seated. Her heels clicked on the floor as she crossed to the door. The plastic cup with its vile vending machine tea was left to stew, for someone else to bin.

24

Lomond thought she was overdressed for a building site. The road was churned with tyre tracks, hardened with the overnight freeze and topped with the last of the snow. In the morning sunlight it had the look of a Christmas cake, and secretly delighted him. *Sparkles*, the child in him said.

Adding to the picture was the type of Portacabin that a child might draw if asked to create a house: a squat rectangle jammed in the mud. In the background, the outlines of homes had begun to appear. Soon roofs, red bricks, doors, finished articles would come to fruition. Lomond didn't like the look of the houses pictured on the display board at the entrance, but then, as he often reminded himself and other people, he'd been lucky to end up in the house he had.

Nicole Kingsley waited on the top step of the cabin, watching as Lomond struggled to park on the only serviceable piece of ground. The wheels growled as he swung round. When he got out and approached, she still hadn't moved. Lomond wondered if she was expecting him to carry her somewhere less muddy, and given the heels she had on he wouldn't have blamed her. His own shoes slithered a little as he came closer.

'Pratfalls and everything,' he said, smiling. 'DI Lomond.'

'Nicole.' Her handshake was light, the gloves smooth.

Lomond had an absurd notion he should bow. 'Thanks for your time.'

'Not a problem.' She smiled. 'Bear with me a second or two; there is a path through here. We can walk over to the site.'

'That'd be fine. It's a lovely morning.'

'Mmm, isn't it just? Cold, though.' She was standing before a shopping bag embossed with a name Lomond should probably have been aware of. She took out a pair of battered, steel-toecapped boots, and swapped her heels with little fuss or ceremony. She left the bag where it lay beside the step, and beckoned Lomond to follow her.

'Terrible thing,' she remarked to him, as they approached the new estate. 'We've been prepping the old Hazell Court site for demolition for a while – it's going ahead in April. I'm sorry to say security let us down, and a few undesirables got onto the site.'

'We're tracking them down,' Lomond said. 'It's unlikely they had much to do with it.'

'They'll be the people you want to speak to first.' This was not a question.

'Sure,' Lomond said. 'They'll turn up. We've got good CCTV networks.'

'About that. It seems one of the security guards had a very lax attitude to our own camera network.'

'What firm did he work for?'

'He's private to Avalon. Well, he was. We've had to let him go. Shame, he's been with us for a while. A nice guy, but nice guys maybe don't make great security guards.'

Lomond, who was probably never happier in his collar and tie than when he took time out to blether to lonely security guards and dead-of-morning cleaning crews, said nothing about that. 'You hire your own security?'

'Easier than going off-the-peg. We've had bad experiences. By and large we've got good guys. By and large.'

'Well, any CCTV you do have would be a help.'

'It was a fridge, wasn't it? They used a fridge? To store the body in.'

'I can't say anything on the record, but the body was found in some sort of refrigeration unit.'

'On the second floor of Hazell Court . . . must have been

more than one person involved, eh? Strong guy, lifting that all the way up the stairs. Lift had been out of commission for ages. Totally sealed off.'

'We've no idea. Hopefully we will, soon.'

'And do you have any idea when your officers will be off the site?'

Lomond glanced at her sharply. 'As long as it takes. We have to gather every bit of evidence we can, down to microscopic level. I'm sure you appreciate the need to be thorough, Mrs Kingsley.'

'Ms Kingsley. I hate Mrs.'

'Oh, I am sorry. I thought you were married?'

'Yeah, every now and again. This is my maiden name.'

'No relation to Raglan Kingsley, are you?'

Those tight nostrils fluttered. She glanced at him, a cheeky look on her face, Lomond thought. A very attractive woman. 'C'mon. You telling me you asked for a chat, on my own building site, and you didn't check those details out? You know I'm his daughter.'

'OK,' was all he could say.

'It's not a big secret. I don't have anything to do with my father's business dealings. Avalon King is my company. I built it from scratch.'

Lomond raised a hand. 'I'm not here to ask you about Raglan, though how's he doing, anyway?'

'You know him?'

'In passing,' Lomond said, after a careful pause. 'I don't think I've spoken to him directly.'

'He's in a nursing home. Has been for a while. Shame. He thinks he's in prison, sometimes. A couple of times they had to get him settled down. Took six of them, I heard. When I spoke to them about it, they told me it was actually seven of them, and another one trying to sedate him.'

'They actually do that to people? In this day and age?'

'You fancy fighting Raglan Kingsley on your own?'

'Not especially.'

'Well, then.' She had a look of pride on her face for the first time. Lomond glanced around the site, the builders and labourers moving around on scaffolding, the hammering, the sounds of activity, the chirruping of smart speakers, one lad with an incredible voice giving it laldy on Queen's 'I Want To Break Free'. When Lomond and Kingsley appeared and were noticed, all eyes were on the lady, not the policeman. A lot of the activity ceased. One or two actually touched their hard hats as she passed – that subservience thing, Lomond thought. Maybe it's built in. Maybe we're all mummy's boys.

'I'm not really here to ask about Hazell Court. Anything outstanding there is a matter for the SOCOs . . . sorry, I mean forensics. Scene of crime officers.'

'I'm aware of the term,' she said tartly.

'OK. So we know that your security was lacking and that someone took advantage of it, but there is another thing I'm interested in. I want to ask about Avalon King – and some of the other sites you're involved with.'

She stopped and folded her arms. 'Quick question – will I need a lawyer?'

Lomond couldn't help but laugh. 'No. Not unless you've got a confession to make.'

'I'm perfectly serious.'

'I'm sorry. No, of course not.'

'Only I'm very busy today. I can't be doing with trips to police stations.'

'It's only a couple of questions, Ms Kingsley.' He laboured the Ms part, and hated himself for doing so. 'It's really only to get a few things straight in my mind.'

'Straighten away, Inspector . . . what's your name?'

'Lomond.'

'As in the loch?'

'That's right.'

She pulled out her phone. As she did so, one side of her

mouth attempted to form a smile. She looked as if she was considering some sort of pun. Lomond had reached the stage in life where he had ceased to be exasperated by these, and genuinely looked forward to hearing a new one, somewhat like a weary gunfighter seeking a worthy opponent in a western. But she lost her train of thought. 'Oh, there you are. That's you.' She expanded a picture of Lomond, one that had been used in the papers in connection with a case a few years back. Lomond remembered hating how his face had looked in that photo for a long time. As so often happened, now he didn't mind it. There was a definition in his jawline that in real life had grown somewhat relaxed.

'That's me. Guilty.'

'So, Inspector Lomond, what would you like to know about my company?'

'Avalon King developed the plot at Myrtlewood Crescent, is that right?'

'Fairham.' She nodded. As if she'd been expecting it. 'That's where the woman was killed the other day.'

'That's correct.'

She shook her head. 'Terrible. How something like that could happen. And those houses have all bells and whistles when it comes to security. How did he get in, do you mind my asking? No, wait, I can't ask you that, can I?'

'You can ask me anything you like,' Lomond said pleasantly. 'I can't give you many answers at this stage. I'd like to. Security is what I want to ask you about, in fact. How involved were you in the process – design, finishing, and so forth?'

'I was all over it. So was my husband. He's my partner.'

'Ah.' Lomond pulled out his notebook. 'I'm sure we have this on file, but could I have a name, please?'

'Neil Glennie. An architect. Husband number three – he's the star player, so far.'

'And you're business partners? On Avalon King?'

Kingsley made a seesaw gesture. 'After a fashion. It's my

name on the deeds, but he's an active part of the business. You could say he does all right with it too.'

'Neil . . . Glennie.' Lomond checked the spelling. 'And did the houses come with the security features as standard, or did the buyers have to sort those themselves?'

'They were bespoke on most of the houses. We did them a good deal on a FiveBarGate system. Top of the range.'

'Oh, I've heard of them. Thought about going with them when I bought my house – passed out when they told me how much they wanted. Must have added a fair bit to the price, those systems.'

'A little. But I believe in the best, Inspector. And the people who buy my houses aren't the sort of people who pass out when they're given a bill.'

Lomond nodded graciously, allowing the barb to pass by. 'So if I was to ask for full blueprints and readouts of the houses, as well as the FiveBarGate system, you'd be able to provide that?'

'Sure.'

'For Myrtlewood Crescent, specifically?'

'Yes, to the absolute moment of installation, if you like. Can even tell you who put them in, testing data . . . Those houses aren't that old; it'll all be on file.'

'I'd be so grateful if you would do that.'

'The security cameras would have picked up whoever did it,' Kingsley said, staring at the place where red brick cut across blue sky on the nearest house. 'God. Imagine it. Someone creeping in. That poor woman.'

'Silly question – did you know her?'

'No. God. Once the plot was sold off, that was it. Everything else tended to be done through an estate agent, and in any case the Symes weren't the first buyers. I never met them.'

'You don't know anyone on that street?'

'Hmm . . . well.'

Lomond said nothing.

Kingsley continued: 'My ex-husband lives in one of the

houses.' She squirmed a little. 'It was part of the deal to get him off my case and out of my life.'

Lomond kept his voice neutral. 'Forgive me. I've spoken to some people on the street, but I had no idea . . . Can you give me his name?'

'Sure. Finch – Vincent Finch. Something about that name pissed me off. And it pissed him off that I didn't want to take it.'

'Yeah, I've spoken to Mr Finch. How's your relationship?'

'It's functional. Not through choice: we have a son, Shane. He's seventeen. We're civil enough. I have another kid, Cherie. She's six. Things are fine now. Vincent's happy enough with the house. It's all a bit Kramer versus Kramer. Or Godzilla versus Kong, if I'm honest.'

'I won't ask who was who.'

'Whichever one was the winner – that was me.' It was a simple declaration. No joke, no irony, no crease in the foundation on her cheeks.

'Was he involved in Avalon King?'

'Again, you could say he was an active partner. In a more legally binding sense than my current husband. I learned my lesson, you might say.'

'He cost you money, then?'

'He cost me a house. That's money. Moved his new piece in with him promptly. Still with her, to be fair. They've got a wee girl.'

'I met her too.' Lomond refrained from saying she was lovely.

'Yeah, it's worked out for him. Incredible money you can make, being a nerd. Computers and what have you. They'll make you some cash, but not as much as houses. At the end of the day, computers can go down overnight. We'll still need to live somewhere.'

'That's the truth.'

Kingsley smiled and cocked her head at Lomond – the flirtatiousness was quite startling to him. 'Fancy a spin around our showroom? See if something takes your eye.'

'I'm very tempted,' Lomond said, hoping that the lie would not show itself in his eyes. Nothing short of a missile landing on his house would persuade him to leave it, and even at that he might need a shove over the threshold. 'Maybe another time. They're beautiful homes. Got a good rep.'

'I should hope so. Well, I'll get the details sent to you this afternoon. Earlier than that, in fact – as soon as I get on the phone to head office.'

'That would be ideal. And please don't hesitate to call me if there's anything you think might help.'

She blinked. 'Like what?'

'Well . . . anything. At all. Any detail.'

She held his gaze for a long time. Lomond felt absurdly disconcerted – even with hostile witnesses, he rarely felt on the back foot. It was as if he was being scanned, or a helicopter searchlight had just scuttled over his bedroom wall and stopped. 'No, that's not it,' she said at last. 'I think you want something else. Why not just ask me?'

'Ask you what?'

'Whatever it is you want. Whatever it is you're looking for.'

'What I'm looking for is the person who killed a woman at a house your company built. And I'm also looking for someone who killed another person and dumped the body at a set of flats your company is going to demolish then rebuild.'

Kingsley laughed in open mockery. 'Do you know how many sites we have across Glasgow alone? Taking every point on the map into consideration, there's not a murder in this town that we won't be connected to.'

'I'm guessing you won't put that in your brochure?'

Her smile faded. 'Brochures are very last century, Inspector.'

A call from Slater saved him from any more awkwardness. 'Got time for a time out, gaffer?'

'What's the score, Malcolm?'

'CCTV from near Hazell Court shows that someone drove in late at night, week after Christmas. White van. Delivery driver. We checked the plates. Turns out it was driven by a Mr Daniel Laybourn.'

'Hmm. How you fixed for a wee day trip then, Malcolm?'

'On it. My car or yours?'

25

Slater had thankfully ditched the zebra-in-a-blender jacket. He was chewing gum, gaunt jaw pistoning. 'Buckle your seatbelt, gaffer,' he said as Lomond got into the car.

'Whereabouts is he?' Lomond marvelled at the cleanliness of the car: the dangling air freshener, the lack of dust on the dashboard.

'Apparently he's out delivering stuff in Yorkhill, Dumbarton Road, Great Western Road and the good old West End. Scheduled drops starting in somewhere called Regent Moray Street, near the Art Galleries.'

'Odds that someone's tipped him off?'

'Not bad, I suppose. Though when we rang up, we got routed through a call centre. Had to spell the name repeatedly. Guessing they don't all sit among each other in the canteen.'

'Mechanised,' Lomond said, then pondered awhile.

Slater's complexion was Scottish pale. Sunshine didn't suit him. In the pictures Lomond had seen of Slater and Meghan on holiday, he looked as if he should be wearing a hazmat suit rather than sunnies and flip-flops. But while he was lean, skinny and whiter than a plain loaf, he had never looked quite so tired.

'Feels like we've not really spoken for a bit,' Lomond said.

'Eh? It's been a day, or something. Last time we spoke to this character, in fact.'

'How've you been taking it?'

'Taking what?' The eyes narrowed; he glanced over at Lomond.

'This case. We're going to get busier. Worst one since the Ferryman.'

'Well, y'know. We know the form. How'd you get on with the guy at Avalon King?'

'The woman. The "King" bit comes from Nicole Kingsley. Raglan's daughter.'

Slater snorted. 'Christ. And how was she?'

'Charming. A bit frosty, but nothing like her da. Or anyone connected with him. Impression you get: successful business-woman, all the trimmings. Dresses well, polite. Wouldn't have thought she was from the bad end of Blackhill.'

'If she agreed to speak to a polis, that's a bit of a change of gear for the Kingsleys. Her dad's meant to be the guy who crucified that boy in Possil. Full crucifixion job down to the crown of thorns. Everything apart from the rising from the dead bit.'

'Aye. Legend has it. He's currently in retirement somewhere leafy. Old dears doing their crochet, making jam or whatever, and he's sitting there in the corner.'

'They probably say "What a nice man he is". Bit like that one horrible kid in school who all the mums thought was lovely.'

'I thought you might have been that one kid, Malcolm.'

'Cheers for that. What are we thinking, Laybourn our man?'

'Well, he was out and about on the day Kath Symes died. And he knew the woods; that's his own admission.'

'You doubt it though, eh?'

'I'll see what's what. No gut feelings or anything. Bit that doesn't really stick is how the guy got in, because we can't square that. No trace evidence either. Nothing. And Daniel Laybourn didn't strike me as a meticulous sort of guy.'

'He is mental, though. Ghosts?'

'Nah, it was the Finch girl who talked about ghosts. He was the UFOs guy.'

'Course he was. Definite space cadet.'

'Let's see what he has to say for himself. He's linked to both sites, plus . . . I pulled out his record. Former soldier. Para reg. Maybe something else that isn't on the books.'

'Christ. He one of those SAS guys who can't tell you he's in the SAS?'

'Nah, he's not one of those guys.'

'How do you know?'

'He didn't tell us he was in the SAS.'

'Which might mean he actually *was* in the SAS.'

Lomond drummed his fingers on the door frame. 'I'll get it out of him. Anyway, when you go into those regiments, they tend to tell you how to kill people. Sneaking up on them, that kind of thing. Bit like our guy.'

'Well, if he was SAS he's put those skills into good use, driving a van.'

'Makes you think, that. About how your job will get swallowed up. Happens to everyone eventually.'

'Won't happen to us, though. Robots? Robocop, and that?'

'Could do. If they work out how to police people with drones and AI, they'll do it. Same with every other job.'

'Nah, doubt it – where are they going to get the charm from?' Slater grinned mirthlessly. 'That'll keep us in a job.'

'There's probably a better reason than that.'

'What's that, then?'

'We're cheaper than robots.'

'But harder to get spare parts for. Mind you, Tait's ready to replace the lot of us. Hang on . . . is that a delivery van I see before me?'

'Blue, white door?'

Slater squinted. 'Blue, yes . . . not sure about white door.' Kelvingrove Art Galleries appeared to the left, all red sandstone under the blue, an illuminated manuscript brought to life. Slater sped up, skirting round the traffic in front as it came to a halt at a set of lights. On the other side of the road, angry faces behind glass, raised palms. Slater gave a wolfish grin and waved.

'Bit naughty, Malcolm,' Lomond said.

'We're in hot pursuit, gaffer! It's allowed.'

'It isn't.'

'C'mon, it's a car chase! I did the advanced driving. It'll be a laugh.'

'It is not a car chase.'

'But that is a white door, right there.'

Lomond triggered the button for his window. There, in the driver's seat of the van next to him, framed with no little distinction by the dirty glass in the white spare-parts door, was Daniel Laybourn. He turned an expression of mildly stoned interest, no sense of surprise, to the car cutting into the opposite lane at the bottom of Argyle Street.

'Pull over,' Lomond said. 'Police. Remember me? We want to talk to you.'

Then the eyes flared, and Laybourn shot through the red light.

'Oh, you absolutely have to be joking,' Lomond said, head dropping into his hands.

'Right!' Slater growled. 'We're on!'

There were some near misses, red lights cut, brakes slammed on, and Lomond's heart kicked into a very high gear.

'Should get some lights on the go,' Slater said conversationally as Charing Cross blurred past, the Mitchell Library shoved behind them with almost indecent speed. 'Fancy sticking your head out the window and going nee-naw?'

'This is not a car chase, Malcolm,' Lomond said sternly. 'We are not in a film.'

'It is a car chase, though, gaffer. He is definitely trying to get away from us, and we're chasing him. That's the facts, and that's the criteria. Full marks. C'mon, let's claim it.'

'For God's sake, there's a bunch of school kids up there! Stop!'

Slater did – and so did Laybourn. Both vehicles idled as a crocodile of children all wearing hi-vis were led across the road by smiling teachers and classroom assistants. A couple of them waved. Lomond waved back.

'Right, we've got him now.'

They hadn't. Heavy traffic and lights cut them off. The van was close a few times, distant at others. Fortunately, that strange, off-bluey-purple colour gave it away every time. Lomond wanted to say it was cobalt, but he'd have to check online to be sure. He even resorted to ringing Laybourn's mobile.

'Now, stop being silly,' he said, dredging up an earnest yet stern primary school teacher voice that Slater had never heard before. 'Give yourself up, stop the van and we'll have a wee chat. There's no point to this. Don't make us get the roadblocks out.'

'Roadblocks!' Slater shrieked, once Lomond hung up, face reddening. 'How about a helicopter? Honest to God, I'll never get over this.'

It was a while before they finally caught up with the van, parked near some ancient Anderson shelters beside the allotments out near Blairdardie. A solid wall blocked off the allotments, every inch of it covered in graffiti tags.

'Where the hell is he?' Slater said.

'Now it gets interesting,' Lomond remarked, getting out of the car.

'Yeah. You should've let me cut him off on Great Western Road, I told you . . . now we need to find him on foot.'

Lomond stopped short. 'Oh, for the love of God.'

Around the corner, Daniel Laybourn stood facing the wall. His piss was cutting furrows in the remaining patches of snow at his feet. He turned his head, and removed one hand to wave at the two policemen.

'Sorry, gents,' he said, 'this is my usual spot for a nature break. Nice and quiet, just the way I like it . . . There we go. Now, what can I do for you?'

26

'Thing is, there are some vibrations that get intense, you know? Like there's something off. I get it a lot. I mean, it doesn't happen all the time. This old dear, I had to deliver a tea set – she was giving everything away before she died – she wanted me to post it to her pal, or a cousin or something. She'd wrapped it up in all these bits of paper, and I'll tell you something – one of the cups came undone a wee bit, so I was rewrapping it, and you know what year it was on the bit of newspaper she'd torn out? Nineteen ninety-one. That long ago. Talk about Ravenscraig. So I got good vibrations off that. It had history. When I'm delivering stuff for the big shops – you know, video games or that, anything made of plastic – I get nothing off it. No life to it. It's just poured into a mould.'

Sitting on the opposite side of the table, Slater looked as if he was the one being questioned. He leaned forward, his chin on his hand. 'Can you tell us what kind of vibes you got with the dead guy in the fridge in the back of your van, Dan?'

Laybourn sighed. 'I was coming to that.'

'Can you come to it a wee bit faster?'

'Obviously it gave off bad vibes. Obviously. Weird job, but that's just looking back on it, isn't it? In hindsight. In retrospect.' He pronounced this last word as if he'd imparted a great secret. 'But then I get all kinds of jobs. I'm in employment.'

Lomond said, 'Tell us about your employment. You work full-time with the big shops?'

'I don't work for that company that winds its way through South America.' He twirled his two forefingers in the air, tracing the bows and elbows of a waterway. 'I work for myself.

Sometimes there's things going for some of the bigger companies. They always need people. If I don't have a job to do in my own right, then I'll see what they've got going. They know me. I'm reliable.'

'So it's a zero-hours contract?'

'That's a new name for it. Aye. I phone up, see what they've got. If there's a shift on and I'm available, I do it. Decent money, weekends and evenings.'

'And tell us about your other work,' Lomond said. 'How does that come about?'

'Old-fashioned way – I advertise. Notice boards. Church halls. Newsagent windows. Council offices. Everywhere. These wee news-sheets that double up as parish leaflets; I advertise there. Pays for itself, you'd be surprised. My rates are good. I do house clearances, trips to the council tip, you name it.' Laybourn grew animated as he said this. It was a business pitch. His eyes seemed to flicker under the interview-room lights.

'And what can you tell us about the job with the fridge?' Slater asked.

'I get the phone call. Can you come and pick something up? A storage unit. To go from a lock-up garage to Hazell Court. I says to him at the time, "Hazell Court's empty, son, you sure about that?" Says he's sure. Hazell Court, he says. Special delivery. Cash up front.'

'You said "he",' Lomond said. 'Can you tell me about the voice?'

'Just a guy,' Laybourn said. 'Maybe a wee bit rough, but I couldn't be sure. Just a guy.'

'Young? Old?'

'Neither, or both. Hard to say. I can say he was local. Glasgow. That's for definite.'

'How did he get the money over to you?'

'Posted it – cash in an envelope.'

Slater laughed. 'Seriously?'

'Seriously. We don't all live in the world of bank transfers and direct debits, son. I take my wages when I can get them.'

Lomond said, 'Do you still have the envelope?'

'I doubt it. I'll look.'

'Did he leave any instructions with you? Anything written down, a printout? Voicemail messages?'

Laybourn shook his head. 'All by phone. I wrote it down, got it all straight. Bit weird, like, but they can be. I moved caged birds one time – that was mental. You know that kind o' pigeony smell you get on the underground lower level? It was a bit like that.'

'Speaking of which,' Lomond said, 'did you smell anything unusual in your load that night?'

'No, nothing unusual.'

'Tell us about how you picked it up.'

'This is the thing – I thought I was going to meet someone at the lock-up when I picked it up. But there's no one there. Bear in mind I've already had a hundred and fifty pounds in an envelope through my door just to show up. The lock-up was in Carnwadric, down a wee lane. The fridge had just been left there. I wondered if I was going to get jumped. Quite a lonely place, you know? After dark, as well. Anyway, there's this fridge. Wheels on it. Sealed, fibreglass. Kind of thing you see in big storage units, with a keypad on. But there's no keypad, just a big padlock. He was lucky it never got tanned. Looked new, you know?'

'And then what?'

'It took a bit of time to pull it onto the ramp and I nearly put my back out, but I'm used to that kind of work. Got one of these motorised numbers in the van – it took the weight, and I got it in. Then over to Hazell Court. I had to go there for eleven p.m. It was specific. Had to be that time. I was just after the deadline.'

Slater sat back in his seat, hands behind his head. 'No one challenged you?'

'There was security. I was expecting it. But the guy on the line told me to get the thing up to the second floor and leave it there. There was an opening in the fence. I took the fridge through.'

'How did you get it up the stairs?'

'I took the lift.'

'You couldn't have,' Slater said. 'The lifts were out of order. Power was cut weeks before.'

'Ah, see, that's what I was told as well. But there's another lift shaft, left of the ground floor. Taped off, but there's still juice going through it. Or there was that night.'

Lomond made a note. 'Go on.'

'So I got it to the second floor, dumped it near the door. Swear to Christ, I don't scare easy, right? Lonely places, I'm drawn to them, like I told you before. Wanderer, me. I follow the ley lines. I take the overgrown path. I go where the trees are thick. But I didn't like that place. Bad vibes all round, man. Smelled a bit – like there were rats. I know that smell. Old warehouses. People had been there too. All sorts of mess and wreckage. I didn't hang about.'

'And then what?'

'Couple of days after that, the rest of the cash arrives. Job done. I forgot about it.'

'Do you have any receipts?' Lomond asked.

'Nah. Just what's on the chit.'

'The what?' Slater barked.

'Chit,' Laybourn said. 'The docket. The document. The one I make out. My own records, my own files. I'm not that disorganised. I take notes of my jobs. I'm diligent, me.' He coughed. 'I could murder a cup of tea, boys. This isn't going to be much longer, is it?'

Lomond shook his head. 'No, you can go soon.'

'I'm not lifted or anything, am I?'

'Just taking a statement, Dan,' Lomond said soberly.

'So I won't need a lawyer? I'm glad about that. Don't have good vibes about lawyers. I mean, just be straight with people, that's the deal, isn't it?'

'You're probably right,' Lomond said. He tapped his notepad with a pen. 'Mind if I ask you one more thing?'

'Ask me anything, brother. This is brilliant, in fact. Most I've nattered in ages!'

'What sort of service did you have in the army?'

Laybourn's smile never faltered, but his eyes did, for a second or two. Then he said, 'That's classified, I'm afraid.'

27

Lomond liked Lorna McGill. She reminded him of someone, but he wasn't sure who. Maybe from his schooldays. The common cruelty had it that she could defeat Popeye at arm-wrestling, but her smile transformed her face, and transformed yours in turn. She had kind brown eyes. Lomond knew that this was bias, a weakness, something that would leave him vulnerable at some point. He had to remind himself at times that he wasn't there to make pals. But he knew too that McGill got people to open up. He also knew that Slater felt the same way about her as he did.

Lomond collared her without ceremony in the canteen over coffee. 'How'd you get on today?'

'How d'you mean, sir?'

'With Slater. How was he, out on the road?'

'Fine.' She took a sip of coffee. Her nails were the kind of purple that worked best with velvet. 'Well, maybe not his usual self. But his usual self can be kind of unbearable. I mean that in a nice way.'

Lomond smiled. 'I know what you mean.'

'He was a bit distracted. Messing with his phone.'

'He didn't mention anything to you about that?'

'Not exactly. I did sort of ask, said he looked tired.'

'And?'

'He just said he had a lot on at home.'

'Right,' Lomond said. 'Sure it'll sort itself out.'

'What's your thinking, sir?'

'About?'

'The case. The deaths.'

'William Ross was a first shot, I think. Maybe a practice. Looks like Ross was living rough – toxicology results will be interesting. Hard to build a picture. Looks as if he dropped off the radar just about everywhere. No friends. No family.' Lomond shivered a little, trying to imagine the alienation, the hopelessness. 'Where it gets interesting is, our man then pulls the same thing with Kathryn Symes. I get the impression that was well planned. But, don't worry, he'll have made a mistake.'

'Laybourn?'

'Not ruling him out. He dumped Ross's body. We're taking his van apart as we speak.'

'Maybe he was just a courier. They don't really ask questions, do they?'

'Or maybe that's what he wants us to think.'

McGill drank up. 'I'll see if we can dig out his service record. Oh, one other thing. The paperwork you were looking for from Avalon King came through.'

'I saw that,' Lomond said. 'Not had time to check it out yet.'

'Strange thing . . . the title deeds on the Symes' house . . . they weren't the first people to buy it. Isn't that what Nicole Kingsley said?'

Lomond frowned. 'That's right.'

'The first name on the title deeds was the same as that comedian. The one who got punched on the American talk show the other month. Benny Kettles. Can't be too many Benny Kettles out there.

'Oh, and there's some dodgy stuff he's been saying online that you'll definitely want to check out . . .'

*

Slater scratched his head. 'This song, gaffer. Again?'

Lomond's gaze had drifted out of the window as they drove along the Broomielaw. Another cold one. More frost was forecast tonight. He scratched his neck. 'What's wrong with it?'

'What's right with it?'

'I think you're being a bit of a snob there, Malcolm.'

'C'mon. You're not that old.'

'The song's not that old.'

'It kind of is. I was still at school when it came out.'

'And it was a big hit. You still hear it on TV shows, adverts . . .'

'The Lighthouse Family? Honestly?'

Lomond tapped his fingers on the steering wheel as the chorus came in again. 'Look, I like it. I'm sorry if it's not cool enough for you. What are you into, like?'

'Arctic Monkeys.'

'Whoa, cutting edge.'

'Well, you asked, I told you. I like them. And they're cooler than the Lighthouse Family. That's scientific fact.'

'It bloody isn't. I like it. Reminds me of when me and Maureen got married.'

'Wasn't your first dance, was it?'

'Nah. That was Bryan Adams.'

'The Robin Hood one? The one that was number one for ever?'

'The very one.'

'Bet everybody groaned when that came on.'

'Ach, not really. I had a bow and arrow, shot an apple off her head. This was a few years after the Robin Hood one. But it still felt current, you know?'

'Away you go.' There was more weariness than mirth in Slater's comment. For a moment, Lomond thought he was going to switch the MP3 player off. 'Hell is it you've got here, anyway? This is a fairly new motor. Surely you've got a streaming service you can use?'

'Nah, I like the old MP3. Got just about every album I've got loaded on it.'

'And every single one is the Lighthouse Family, right? Cos this is the second time you've played that song while I've been in the car. Is it on repeat or something?'

'Nah, it's on random. Algorithms. Maybe it's listening to us.'

'Maybe your sound system is haunted.'

'Maybe it is. Anyway, I'm not interested in your sniffy opinions – it's my motor, and that's all there is to it.'

Slater raised his hands. 'So are we sure Kettles is going to be here?'

'According to the message board, yes. He's got some adoring fans in the department; they confirmed it. No answer at his house. Apparently, no mobile phone either.'

'So Smythe and Tait said. Apparently he bust their chops a bit.'

'That what he does to folk?'

'Oh aye.' Slater grinned. 'One of those guys, you know his routine cos your mates send you the clips. Gets punched a lot.'

'I've never seen him on the telly.'

'Think he gets invited once, then never again.'

'I'll try to get a word in before he starts,' Lomond said, indicating to pull in.

28

'This going to turn into a hiding?' Kettles seemed genuinely gleeful. Lomond and Slater couldn't see them, of course, but his legs were swinging under the table, back and forth, like a kid on a swing. 'Is it cameras off, "right, lads, into him"? Like *The Sweeney*?'

Lomond was utterly determined, set in stone, that he'd play a straight bat. 'Of course it isn't, Benny.'

'There's been a murrrder. I heard the *Taggart* theme, there. You can't help it, can you?' He began to rasp out Maggie Bell's theme tune to the old TV show.

'We were asking you about what you said online,' Lomond said. His hands were perfectly still, laid flat on the table.

'So dramatic.' Kettles smirked.

'You're under suspicion of committing a crime, Benny,' Lomond said, not blinking. 'That means we lift you.'

'I didn't murder anyone. I've killed a couple of careers, maybe. Definitely died a few times, though that's more a suicide.'

'Your patter's murder,' Slater remarked.

Kettles' face froze. Then he laughed uproariously. 'That's going into my show. You're a comedian, mate.'

'Benny,' Lomond said, 'you made reference online to a case you knew of. Would you like to repeat, for the record, what you said?'

'I can't remember exactly.'

Lomond checked his notes. 'You made reference to someone who had been pulled out of the bath and smothered, and a potential second victim.'

'Did I?'

Kettles' lawyer was a woman of maybe thirty or so who looked terrified of both her client and the situation. 'My client has no need to answer that,' she said.

'No, it's fine,' Kettles said. 'Yeah, we'll talk about it, if you like. I was writing about Kath. That's what happened to Kath. Wasn't it?'

'How did you come to that understanding?'

'Does it matter?' Kettles cackled. 'It's true, isn't it?'

'You revealed certain details which we have kept back from the general public for operational reasons,' Lomond said. 'They could only be known by someone who had inside knowledge of the case.'

'Sure. Or who was just passing on what they heard.'

'So where did you hear it, Benny?'

'I can't name my source. But let's say, in my career, I get to know people who work in journalism. The papers that still exist. Websites, news agencies, the telly . . . there's a lot of talk. Especially if I ask them about it. Especially if it was my best friend who got killed.'

Benny began to shiver. It was alarming, the sudden tremor. Lomond fought several competing urges – to comfort him, to reach out, or to shiver in his own right, as if a draught had passed through the room, or a ghost.

'So are you suggesting to us that you were told this specific information by a journalist?'

'I'm not suggesting it,' Benny said, 'I'm telling you. It's true. But I'm not telling you who it is. And, obviously, I can't comment on how your special privileged information leaked out. How many people you got working on the case? Uniforms, crime-scene folk, hero cops?'

'Thing about that is, Benny, even if we mention it off the record, we make sure it isn't actually available to the public. Do you know why that is, Benny?'

Kettles shrugged. 'This an interview, or a quiz show?'

'The reason is to weed out troublemakers. Cranks. Delusional people, who think they have actually done it, or people who are so desperate to help that they phone in tips that are totally untrue, even though they believe them. So that's one problem. The other one, and I know this one's important to you . . . Kathryn has a daughter, Beatrice. And a husband.'

Kettles said nothing.

'It's something for you to bear in mind, next time you go mouthing off online about the killing of your best friend. It's not great if you're hearing for the first time exactly how your mum died on the internet.'

'Fair point,' Kettles said. 'Thing is, I want the same thing you do.'

'Another thing,' Slater said. 'About some business dealings you have.'

'Business dealings,' Kettles intoned. He was chewing his lower lip, digesting what Slater had said.

'You've made an investment with Avalon King, on a new property outside Bellmhor. Former plastics factory, brownfield site.'

Kettles scratched his chin. 'I've got a few irons in the fire here and there, sure.'

'How well do you know Nicole Kingsley?'

'I see her knocking around. I understand her dad's a bit dodgy. Old-style gangster. Razor blades for fingers, that kind of thing. Why d'you ask?'

'We'll ask you whatever we like,' Slater said.

'I wouldn't walk past Nicole in the street, or anything, and we might have sat round a table a couple of times. I'm an investor.'

'That's a hell of a look for a stand-up,' Slater scoffed.

'What do you mean?'

'Property baron. That's the credentials up in smoke, is it not?' Slater smirked. '"I'm all edgy, look at my portfolio. Here's my business card."'

'What credentials are these?' Kettles said, puzzled. 'I make a point of not believing anything or professing any admiration at all. For anything. Because everyone gets it, off me. Everyone. And everyone deserves it.'

'Oh, a cynic. Tell me all about it.'

'Hmm, that's kind of condescending. Next you'll tell me about all the bodies you've seen. Well, I've seen one myself. No one gives a fuck about your war stories.'

'I think we're done here,' his lawyer interjected.

'And what about you?' Kettles turned to Slater. 'What do you look like? Your voice is all strained and a wee bit try-hard. I'd say you're not that rough, really. Graduate, decent house with stairs in it. Not like your boss here; he's as rough as arse-holes, I'll give you that. He's the polar opposite, in fact. Trying to sound refined. But you, you're a wind-up merchant, aren't you? You'd have been better suited as a teacher or a minister.'

It was a jibe Slater had heard many times, and he bit back at it. 'Well, at least I don't look like a big baby. Or sound like one.'

Kettles clapped his hands, delighted. 'Hey, I'll sign a DVD for you. You look like a guy that still has DVDs.'

Lomond interjected. 'We'll want to know your movements, late October. Do you have a tour diary, receipts, that kind of thing?'

'Sure. I can prove that, probably. Right, I think we're done. I'll leave you geniuses to find someone else to fit up for it. Or some women to harass.'

'Don't overstep the mark, son.' Slater said.

'Thing is, you polis have a horrendous problem with battering your wives, don't you? Bit like the old racism and the funny handshakes: it's bloody rife in the polis. Something like ten per cent of you, maybe even more. That's before you get to the real psychos, and there's plenty of them in the force. I mean, some people actively want to be polis. It isn't just a job. Got something missing, those boys. I wonder what side of the psycho percentage you fall on, big man? You've got the eyes, that's for sure. Like to swing for me, wouldn't you?'

'Get that a lot, do you?'

'Now and again. Sometimes it even hurts. Last time I saw Ed Symes . . .'

'Wrap it up here,' Lomond said. 'You're free to go, Benny, but we will be calling on you later to check where you've been.'

'I'm already out the door, Inspector. I know my rights. Toodle-oo!'

Kettles leaned over to Slater and waved, inches from his nose. Lomond tensed, wondering first if the pudgy man was going to tweak Slater's nose, and second if Slater really was going to punch him for it. On camera, in the interview room. Instead, Slater smiled, his grin matching the comedian's, and said, 'That concludes our interview.'

29

Lomond had seen the expression on Slater's face before, and on his daughter, certain wee dogs, and people he'd lifted when he was in uniform.

'Want to talk me through it, Malcolm?'

'Nothing to talk through, gaffer.'

'You sure? I could have sworn you were going to actually swing for him. If it turns out he did it, that's probably the end of the case, right there. Not to mention your job.'

'Just as well I didn't, then, eh? Don't worry. I wasn't going to hit him. I mean, I wanted to. You wanted to. But I'm not daft. Sir.' The last word was as good as a jab.

'What's going on, Malcolm? Your dials are off, son.'

'You're not the first person to ask me that. Been sending out your wee spies, eh?'

'I want to know what's going on.'

'Nothing's going on. We're trying to catch a lunatic. And I don't know if you've spotted it, but Kettles' leak has been noticed. It'll be out and about on the websites and in the bloody papers.'

Lomond sighed. 'Maybe we should take a breather.' He checked his phone.

'Let me guess. Super's been on?'

Lomond nodded. He wondered if he now had that expression on his face. 'Sullivan. One slice of carpet coming up.' He dialled a number.

'Save some for me, gaffer. I'll check out Laybourn's movements.'

Annette Sullivan didn't bother with any acknowledgement.

The Chief Super had both bite and bark, often vying for supremacy in the same breath. Lomond could almost feel that breath, artfully blended with spittle meteors, on his cheek. 'Mind telling me why the press office is fielding calls from every twat on every news desk?'

'I suspect it's something to do with Benny Kettles.'

'You suspect right. What's going on with that?'

Lomond felt his cheeks burning. 'Benny Kettles knew details about Kathryn Symes. Ones we kept back.'

'Well, every bugger knows now. What in God's name has happened here?'

Lomond braced, held fast, while Sullivan vented. It went on for some time. There was someone else in the room, Lomond was sure. The Super liked an audience. She would have been good in the army, he thought.

Finally Lomond said, 'He mentioned another body, ma'am. That information is going to be out there now. We might have to break cover. Minchin and Khavari reckon it's the same man. We'll have to confirm it.'

'Excellent. Another true crime podcast for us all to enjoy.' Sullivan sighed. 'Right. We'll do the press this time. Don't go near it. I'll ask the obvious question – anyone in the frame for it?'

Lomond hesitated. 'Not yet. There's nothing from forensics, nothing from the security camera. But there'll be something. I'm going to go over the Symes' house again.'

'Suspects?'

'Laybourn's a possibility but there's nothing to pin it on him with. The word is there's nothing in the van.'

'And that's it?'

'Kettles knew a bit too much for my liking. That's why I lifted him.'

'But nothing.'

'Nothing we can charge him with. He's keeping his mouth shut about sources.'

'Christ. OK. Keep on it, Lomie.' Sullivan hung up.

Lomond tightened his jaw. Slater had disappeared down the corridor towards the office space. For a moment, Lomond was alone in the corridor, reflected in the glass fronts of the offices on both sides, where venetian blinds twitched occasionally. He tutted, checked his watch, then dialled Smythe's number.

'Sir?'

'How'd it go with Symes?'

'Well.'

Lomond liked the tone. He smiled.

30

There had been a time when Smythe had wondered, with the semi-detached focus of a scientist in the field trying to keep still while something small and rare creeps past, if Myles Tait found her attractive.

He certainly fancied himself. He had come pre-packaged with a certain reputation among the women on the force, and there was no doubt he was a good-looking man. His attempts at humour between them had been simultaneously brash and clumsy, which had tripped Smythe's early warning system, but gradually this had given way to an easier relationship. Witness: the fact that Tait was singing in the car, in a comically rich baritone, as unselfconscious as if he was in the shower.

Finally he noticed Smythe's lopsided grin. 'What?'

'That's the song he's into, apparently. The gaffer.'

Tait shrugged. 'Lighthouse Family? It must have got into his head.' He considered this a moment. 'Jeez. It got into *my* head.'

'It's a good song,' Smythe said.

Tait sniffed.

'I'm serious!' Smythe spluttered. 'There's nothing wrong with it.'

'Inspiring montages at the Olympics, that kind of thing.' Tait smiled. 'I need to clear the earworm.'

'"Baker Street"?'

'Eh?'

'I heard that if you start to sing the sax part of "Baker Street", it automatically clears any earworm.'

'OK, but how do you deal with "Baker Street", after that?'

'I honestly don't know,' Smythe said, after a pause. 'Well. Instead we could talk about how we're going to approach this.'

'He's not a suspect,' Tait observed.

'That makes it harder. Us turning up will make him think he is.'

'What's the thinking? That it's Kettles? That's what the gaffer wants us to probe here, isn't it? Benny Kettles? He a suspect?'

'Got to be. Knows way too much.'

'Shouldn't have lifted him though,' Tait said. 'Big mistake. Tipped our hand, a bit.'

'I don't think it's him,' Smythe said.

'What, cos he was crying?' Tait sniffed. 'That could be guilt. It gets to them. Even the reptiles. Something breaks inside. Some part of them knows they're wrong 'uns. They freak out. It's like a chemical reaction, instead of an emotion.'

'Maybe.'

Tait parked outside a detached house in the tree-lined hinterlands of the Southside. Handsome was the word – and not a new-build in sight. Red brick houses, whitewashed bungalows, and no bangers parked out on the streets to give the place a showing-up. It was chilly, the January nights seemingly never-ending. They walked on old footprints up the drive, facing a red sandstone villa that wouldn't have got you much change out of a couple of million, Smythe guessed.

'Some place,' Tait said, whistling. The last of the snow still clung to ornate stonework hemming in a large patio, the glazing immense, empty planters like icing on a cheap bun. Beyond, bay windows were curtained off, emitting just enough warm light to be inviting. Smythe had an utterly unreasonable vision of a prissy aunt, prone to opinions and disdain. She almost lost her composure when someone fitting that description answered the door, two seconds after she pressed the doorbell.

The woman was well into her sixties, slim running to gaunt, with permed grey hair and a mouth you'd have tucked into your back pocket for a street fight. Her arms were tightly folded, a throw draped over her shoulders, completing a somewhat imperious vision.

'This is some time of night to be disturbing people. What's your business?' Two sentences, with not much of a gap in between.

Smythe did the talking. 'Mrs Symes? I'm Detective Sergeant Smythe; this is my colleague Detective Sergeant Tait, Police Scotland.'

The woman said nothing.

'We spoke on the phone earlier? I realise it's a little bit later than we'd hoped, but we'd like to come in and speak to your son, if that's convenient.'

'ID,' Mrs Symes said, arms still folded. She did not take them, nor did she incline her head towards them as the cards were presented. 'OK,' she said curtly before turning on her heel. Smythe and Tait glanced at one another warily before following her in.

*

It was a comfortable, well-lit home, recently decorated, belying the somewhat austere exterior. It needed some heating going, though, Smythe thought, watching her breath cloud in the hallway.

Mrs Symes barred the way before allowing them any further in. 'Now this is on the understanding that there's nothing formal going on here?'

'Nothing at all,' Smythe said. She tried to sound reassuring, but Mrs Symes was someone whose manner seemed to forbid that, inviting conflict. 'We need to ask your son a couple of questions to get one or two things straight.'

'Whatever helps. I'll say one thing to you – your care of Edward since this happened has been sorely lacking. And as for the rumours, well . . .'

'What rumours are those?' Tait asked.

'That another body has been found. That my daughter-in-law wasn't the only victim of this . . . person.'

'The investigation is at an early stage,' Smythe said. 'Please believe me, we're working as hard as we can on this case.'

'All your fancy tricks and forensics and cameras, and you haven't made an arrest yet?' The woman sneered. 'Not sure what they teach you people these days.'

'Is it through here, Mrs Symes?' Tait asked, nodding towards a door, edged in bright light.

'It is,' she said. 'I'll give you ten minutes. Edward's . . . well, you can imagine. And keep the noise down, if you would. My granddaughter is upstairs, sleeping. Today's the first day it's sunk in for her.'

'We'll do our best,' Tait said. 'We promise.'

They were shown into a kitchen that had all the right utensils hung in the right places and nothing at all to indicate that food might ever have been prepared there. It was also missing a table, though a breakfast bar stuck out of one wall, an awkward peninsula. Huge conifers blocked out all the remaining daylight beyond latticed windows that Smythe didn't like at all.

Ed Symes got up from his seat and closed the gap between himself and the two police officers at an alarming speed. It was almost like an attack, but at the last moment he extended a hand, first to Tait, then to Smythe. He was twitchy, and Smythe thought he'd lost weight since she'd seen him, very briefly, a couple of days beforehand. That might have been more to do with the harsh lighting, which made depths out of hollows and turned bone structure into scaffolding.

'We're sorry to intrude,' she said, taking one of the seats opposite Symes.

'Is it true?' he asked them. 'About another body?'

'This is a very sensitive investigation, Mr Symes.'

'Another woman, then? That's two of them.' His voice caught. 'Another maniac, targeting women. I can't stop thinking about it, you know. Her last moments. She loved a bath. We'll never set foot in that house again, if I can help it. If it wasn't for the police, I'd torch the place.'

A silence descended for a moment or two. Tait said, 'We can tell you that we did find another body yesterday, but it wasn't a woman's.'

Symes' shoulders relaxed. 'Oh. An equal-opportunities maniac, then. Smashing.' He laughed awkwardly, covering his mouth as if he'd coughed.

'We don't want to take up too much of your time,' Tait said. 'Really we want to talk to you about Benny Kettles.'

'Favourite topic.' Symes smiled thinly, and in that moment he closely resembled his mother. 'Favourite person. Sure. What do you want to know?'

Tait flipped open his notebook. 'I understand you had a tense relationship with Mr Kettles?'

'That's one way of putting it. I hated him. Always trying to involve Kath in business deals, investments, property he was into. Trying to buy plots of land. Brownfield sites. I used to joke that he was just trying to get hold of my money before Kath divorced me. But . . . that wasn't funny, I suppose.'

'And you had a row recently?'

'Aye. Well. You ever seen him live?'

'I have. Not really my thing,' Tait ventured.

Symes nodded. 'Everyone I speak to says the same. Can't stand him. The man's a sicko.'

'Have you ever got on with him?' Tait was leaning closer to Symes. Smythe noticed the dead woman's husband responding more to the male presence, and backed off a little, pretending to take detailed notes.

'I'll be honest, no.'

'How long have you known him?'

'As long as I knew Kath. He was always there and thereabouts. Social gatherings, you know?'

'They were close?' Tait said.

Symes smiled ruefully. 'Leading question, eh? Am I a jealous husband, that's the question, eh?'

Tait said nothing.

'The answer to your question is . . . yes. They were close. Too close for my liking. I make no apologies for that. The thinking is that Benny Kettles is gay and I shouldn't feel jealous about him, but you know what? I only ever saw him with women on his arm, never men. If he was gay, he went about his business behind closed doors. It was too much, you know? Always touchy-feely. He knew it bothered me, but he kept going. Because that's who he is. You know, if I find out he was involved in what happened to Kath in any way, I . . .' He blinked. 'I don't know what I'll do.'

'You don't think they were ever together?' Tait asked. 'Boyfriend and girlfriend?'

'Well, no, I had no cause to think that. But he's one of those people who gives you the doubt. They had a thing. I don't know what the thing was, but it was there. A closeness. I didn't like it. You've asked, I've told you. Were they ever lovers? I can't say. Only he would know that. And Kath.'

'Did you and she have any mutual friends?' Smythe asked.

'Nah, it was strictly her tribe and mine – mostly mine, as time went on. She had friends from uni, but they all fell away as the years went by. The only cling-on was Kettles.'

'How often did you see him?'

'Him and Kath met up a lot. Lunch, nights out.' Symes' jaw tensed.

Smythe could see him, sitting at home, staring at his phone, alone, waiting for her to come back in. She felt an odd chill at the vision. 'Once a month? Every couple of months?'

Symes nodded.

'They ever go away together?'

'A couple of times. Not recently.'

'And how about the last time you met? The argument?'

'He was . . .' Symes took a deep breath. 'Wouldn't give it up, you know? Talked about this investment he was making. Big money, he said. Got a site. Working with Avalon King, the builder. I heard that Nicole Kingsley was involved in that – I mean, that's a red flag right there. Dodgy by default. He mentioned how much money he was going to make, how much of a money-spinner it was. I remember Beatrice was getting excited, even. Kath was totally taken in by it. And you know that way, when you know what's coming? You're braced for it? Sure enough, the bastard says, hundred grand outlay, you could double your money in a matter of weeks. These houses will just fly away, he says. Off-the-peg. Oven-ready. And it sickened me, you know? He could say anything, she'd listen to him, hanging on his every word. This muppet's practically signing away our savings, and her tongue's hanging out.' The strain told on his voice. It strangled him. 'I told him in front of her, in front of everyone. Fuck off. No more. Take your investment somewhere else.'

'How did he take that?' Tait asked, eyebrow cocked.

'The usual. Clowning around. Did his handstand thing, you seen that? Belly hanging out. I told him, "I'll put you the right way up, then launch you." He tried to walk out the front door on his hands, but he fell over. Kath thought I'd hit him, but I didn't lay a finger on the guy. Beatrice was crying. So was Kath. Terrible scene, and I was the bad guy, as well.'

'Did Kath ever see him again?'

'Nah. That was after new year, so not long before . . . you know.'

'Do you have any details about the plot?' Smythe asked.

'You know, he left a prospectus. I meant to throw it out, but Kath and I had a row that night, and I forgot all about it. I don't think I saw it in the recycling. It might still be around.'

Smythe got up and crossed the kitchen, light on her feet. Before anyone could ask what she was doing, she had opened the door.

There was the little girl, in her pyjamas, an oversized dolly in her arms.

'I heard someone say my name,' she said, in a quivering voice.

31

Smythe ignored the looming presence of Mrs Symes, and allowed the little girl to lead her into the front room. It was the kind of room that would have suited a grand Christmas tree and all the trimmings; the grandmother looked as if she was the kind that might grudge it. *Same way she grudges the heating. Nice big radiators, there. You'd need them for a place this size.*

Smythe had a niece she doted on who was just about to cross the threshold from primary to secondary school. This wee one was a bit younger. The detective went with her instinct, and decided to ignore the great big horrible thing.

The girl tweaked open the curtains. 'Granny's got lots of space out here. But you can't see it now.'

'I love these windows,' Smythe said. 'Must look amazing in the snow.'

'It does,' Beatrice said. 'I wish it would snow again. We didn't have enough for a snowman when it snowed at the start of the week.'

She didn't take after her father so much; maybe a suggestion of his brow and his lips, but nothing else. She had the same hair and features as her mother. Pretty little thing. It was hard not to feel for her; it was also hard to plug in to what she was saying, to lead her a little. No amount of training could set you up for this.

'They say it might snow again at the end of the week.'

'Even in February?'

'Oh aye – I remember it snowed in April once. A right thick one, as well. I went out sledging.'

'What? Here in Scotland?'

'Oh yeah. You get snow all year round sometimes, on some of the mountain-tops.'

'I'd like to go skiing.'

'Must be cracking to have a big garden to play in.'

'Do you not have a garden?'

Smythe shook her head. She caught sight of her own reflection, then, in the bay window. The grandmother, arms folded, haunted a space over her shoulder, near the door. Smythe hadn't heard her move. 'I've never lived in a house, you know. Stayed in some nice flats. Never had a garden. Once I had a room underneath a garden – in a basement. That wasn't too bad.'

'I liked our garden,' Beatrice said.

'How about the woods? They're pretty cool.'

'Woods?' The girl frowned at her. She still clutched the dolly, who glared disconcertingly at Smythe from the crook of her elbow. 'There's only a couple of trees.'

'No, I mean the woods back at your house.'

'Yeah. I like them.'

'If I'd had woods, I'd have played in them all the time.'

'I play out a bit. In the summer. When it's light.'

'I'd have gone off on all kinds of adventures. In my head, I mean. I'd have made up castles and unicorns.'

The girl's eyes widened a little. She saw something outside, past the darkness, beyond the pollution of the lights. 'We did that as well. We used to have a place that was like a drawbridge. To a castle.'

Smythe picked up on it right away, but she didn't dive in. 'Was it like a bridge you could move?'

'No, silly. It was more like an old fence, or a gate. It was made of wood. You could move bits of it over the puddles. Some of the puddles were deep.'

'Ah, I see. Well then, technically, if it was over a moat, then it was actually a drawbridge. That's how I see it.'

'You're right. That's what I said, in fact. Like we didn't have to pretend.'

'And do you and your pals go back to it? Is it still there?'

'Oh yeah. I could show you. We . . . I know the woods really well.'

Smythe nodded. She turned towards the grandmother. 'Could I ask a favour? I'm really thirsty. Do you mind if I get a glass of water?'

Mrs Symes tutted. 'This is the height of cheek, this.'

'I wouldn't ask, but my throat's really dry. We've been out on the road most of the day. I'm awfully sorry.'

'I'd like a glass of water too,' Beatrice said. 'Please, Granny.'

'We're *grieving*,' the woman said, but she strode away from the door. Fast on her feet, as well as quiet, Smythe thought. She should work with us.

'I bet you've got lots of pals at school,' she said.

'Some. Lia, and Muna, and Grainne.'

'And do they come round to play?'

Beatrice shook her head. Then she leaned in close and whispered excitedly, 'Can I tell you a secret?'

'Absolutely. My favourite things.' Smythe grinned.

'I don't know. It's a real cross-your-heart-hope-to-die secret.'

'I can keep them. And I'll tell you what. You tell me one, I'll tell you one.'

Beatrice brightened. 'OK. Well, I have a pal in my street I'm not supposed to see.'

'Oh, right.'

'Yeah. I was told not to play with them, but I do.'

'I think everyone has a friend like that. Boy or girl?'

'Girl.' The child's voice had shrunk below a whisper. Perhaps knowing Granny well, she peered over her shoulder as if the besom was still there, poised behind the door.

'And do you play with her in your garden, as well as the woods?'

'No. Dad doesn't like her.'

'What age is she? Can I guess?'

The girl coloured. 'Bet you can't.'

'I would say she's . . .' Smythe's gaze went towards the distant ceiling. 'Fourteen.'

'Ha! Miles out.'

'Eleven?'

'Warmer.'

Smythe clicked her fingers. 'Eight!'

'Oh, cold! Miles out.'

'Umm . . . ten?'

'Yes.'

'Now I'm going to try and guess her name.'

'You'll never guess. And I don't think I can tell you, anyway. That's a definite.'

'Ah, I'm good at guessing, though. Hold tight. I think her name is . . .' Smythe had a moment of doubt. Surely that was the name? Nothing else for it . . . she heard footsteps outside, rattling the china behind the glass on the wall unit . . . 'Kay. I'm going to guess she's called Kay.'

'You're a cheater,' Beatrice declared, thrusting her chin upwards.

'Hah! It was a good guess. I think it's great that you've got pals in your street. It's a good thing to have mates outside school. Some of my best friends were at different schools, you know. You can even have some best friends in your job.'

'Kay's been on a pony,' Beatrice confided. 'I'm not sure I believe her, though, and anyway, I would beat her. I've been on a proper horse.'

Smythe smiled. 'Sometimes a best friend ends up being competition. How it goes, I guess.'

'What?'

'Nothing. So you play quite a lot with Kay?'

'Just when it's light.'

'Anyone else?'

'Well . . . that's a double secret. I'm definitely, definitely not allowed to tell you.'

'Oh. I'll tell you two secrets if you will.'

'Hmm. Well, I can tell you it's a boy. Or I think it's a boy.'

'That's funny. How can you not be sure?'

'I can't see his face. He talks to us, though. He hides.'

Smythe and Beatrice both leapt when Granny Symes said, close enough to bite, 'Here's your water, love. But your voice seems fine, detective. Still thirsty?'

'I'm going to have to ask you to step outside, Granny, if you wouldn't mind.'

The woman's chin dropped. 'I beg your pardon?'

'I was talking secrets with Beatrice. I'd much rather do it here, where we're both comfortable, rather than somewhere like an interview room.'

'What? Are you serious?'

Smythe kept her tone light. 'Oh yeah. Thanks for the water. Just what I need.' She took the glass. 'Two minutes, Mrs Symes. Please.'

Beatrice's eyes shone with admiration as the dragon stomped off, slamming the door behind her like a scolded teen. 'Wow,' she said.

'You have to keep some secrets from Granny,' Smythe said. 'So tell me about this invisible boy, then.'

'You promise not to tell anyone?'

Smythe hesitated. 'I promise you won't get into any trouble.'

Beatrice's eyes narrowed. 'That's not what I asked you to promise.'

Smythe considered a moment. 'How would you like to be the kid who catches a baddie?'

The sparkle came back. 'Properly? Like, in court?'

'Maybe. Would you be up for that?'

'Sounds scary.'

'It's something only big girls get to do,' Smythe said soberly. 'I wouldn't trust the assignment to anyone but you.'

'Not even Kay?'

'I think you'd be *much* better in court than Kay.'

'The baddie. Is he the one that killed my mum?'

Smythe didn't hesitate, though her voice cracked a little. 'It could be.'

'Well. The invisible boy seems quite nice. He told us he's there to make sure there are no wolves in the woods.'

'Wolves?'

'It's just a silly story,' Beatrice said knowingly. 'You know. Red Riding Hood, that kind of thing. He doesn't mention her, though. But he said there are wolves, and we had to be careful out there. He told us not to speak to any strangers.'

'And you've no idea what he looks like?'

She shook her head. 'He was hiding in the trees.'

'How about height?'

'Hard to say.'

'How old?'

'Well, he might be a bit older than a boy – a young man. I'm not sure.'

'Did he remind you of anyone?'

'No. No one we'd seen around here before.'

'Very mysterious,' Smythe said. 'Tell me more.'

32

Lomond braced the spaghetti in the tongs, enjoying the moment of tension like a fly fisherman making his lure dance. The steam, the starch, that indefinable alteration in the composition of the atmosphere, delighted him. He was in his thirties before he realised that he loved spaghetti Bolognese. He would have it with mushrooms, he would have it with meatballs, he would have it with mince (reduced-fat steak mince, though – he was adamant about that). He would make it on a Thursday night, then head out to an Italian place on a Friday after pay day, have it again and be roundly slagged for it. He would make sure never to wear white and tear into it. He layered on the mince and the sauce, growling faintly in the back of his throat without realising it, enjoying the colour, the glistening surface. Just the right amount of puree; tomatoes subdivided perfectly; not too chunky but not too smooth. This was important. He liked texture.

Despite himself, despite having seen the place, Siobhan's flat closed in around him. A residue of guilt lingered, with all the heavy lifting having been carried out by hands other than his. He had prepared dinner for the three of them. There was a sense of ritual and propriety. Plates were laid at the tiny table, place mats in triumvirate. Won't be the three of us for much longer, Lomond thought, and felt a twinge of sadness. The Santa-isn't-real sadness. ('Santa is real,' Lomond had said, in fact, when challenged years ago by Siobhan, with utter conviction. 'You're looking at him. You believe me?') He laid down the grater and a chunk of Parmesan, cracked the peppermill without asking, sat down before Maureen and Siobhan, and failed to eat.

'Want to take it home?' Siobhan asked.

'Nah. You can use it to christen your new freezer.'

'What's the score – did you already have a roll or something on the way back?' Maureen asked, coiling some pasta and sauce into her spoon.

'No, I did not,' Lomond said, nettled at the idea. 'I was busy today.'

'Saw your picture on the telly,' Siobhan said. 'Couple of the other teachers and TAs were asking if we were related.'

'What'd you do, deny me outright?'

His daughter smiled. 'Nah, they were amazed. Tell you something else – they remember you. "That's the guy who caught the Ferryman," they said.'

'Jeez, you didn't tell them about you?' Lomond regretted the tone of this immediately.

'No. I tend to leave that bit out.'

'Anyway,' Maureen said. 'You want to talk about it? Or are you just going to play with that pasta all night?'

'We're no nearer. Thought we had a delivery driver, but it turns out he was just a delivery driver. And now everyone knows about the second body. Let's talk about it another time.'

His phone shook him, crudely. Lomond excused himself. It was Smythe.

'Got something,' she said. 'You know the Symes' wee girl?'

'Beatrice. Aye?'

'Well. You know how Vincent Finch said he had fallen out with the Symes? And his wee girl was the same age, but they didn't get on at all?'

'They're the best of pals, right?'

'That's right. Did you know?'

'Ach, no, just a guess.'

'Well, it turns out they've got another friend. A secret one.'

Lomond shut the door on Siobhan's kitchen. The hallway was enclosed, not even a window at the oak-framed door onto the communal landing. He was in total darkness. 'Tell me more.'

'It seems that the secret friend actually interacts with them.'

'Does it have a name?'

'No name, no face. But they think it's a boy, Beatrice said.'

'Boy?'

'So she said at first, but later she said he might be older.'

'And what does he talk to them about?'

'She wouldn't really say. She said he told them a story about a king and a princess trapped somewhere, and warned them to watch out for wolves. That shook me a little bit, I'll be honest. Nothing else.'

Lomond fished out a notebook and wrote by the light of the phone, set into the crook of his neck. 'How many times did they meet this guy?'

'Three times, she said. She couldn't give the dates, but said the first time was on a week day, when it was still light outside, during the summer holidays. After that it was on a Sunday, when it was getting darker, after they were back at school. Last time was just before Christmas.'

'And how often do Beatrice and the Finch lassie get together?'

'Whenever they're sent out to play.'

'The parents must have known about that,' Lomond said scornfully.

'The mothers would have. A working dad, away from home – like Symes – wouldn't have noticed at all.'

'True. Or maybe just on another planet, like Finch. I'll talk to the Finches tomorrow.'

Lomond hung up. He glanced at the door. The only luminescence was a single lime-green light on the alarm system. Brand new, like the rest of the place. Hard to get into, he thought. Nothing to worry about.

He rejoined Siobhan and Maureen. The latter had a resigned look about her. 'You're not charging off to a murder scene, are you?'

'Nah, not yet. Business will go on.'

Siobhan sipped at a glass of red. 'You can stay over in my spare room, tonight, if you like. Have a glass of wine. Drink to the new flat.'

'Best not, darling.'

Lomond's dinner remained in disarray, uneaten and still steaming.

'It's horrible thinking people like that are out there. Maybe having dinner right now,' Siobhan said. 'Doing normal stuff. Eating with their families.'

'What are you saying?' Maureen spluttered, trying not to choke on her mouthful of pasta.

Lomond made no comment. Siobhan was right. They were out there, and the horrible thing was they weren't all like this guy either. Sometimes the guys Lomond arrested weren't anything like monsters. They woke up one day, and when they next slept their status, and their lives, had changed. Lomond remembered collaring a guy who had beaten his girlfriend to death – he struggled to recall what the alleged reason was; it seemed to have been nothing, a nothing row. Too much Parmesan on the Bolognese, maybe. An accumulation of small explosive events, words spoken out of turn, hot tempers. He was an office worker, well groomed, and he had strangled her. He had gone beyond barking or even lashing out, way beyond. He had been young and muscular, and he had strangled her. You couldn't imagine the expression on his face, but Lomond had seen the one on his girlfriend's. The boy must have stared into that face, those eyes, have heard the sounds she'd made, and he had tightened his grip, and kept going, beyond obvious distress into desperation and grim quietude. Minchin said his grip could have lasted two or three minutes: insensate rage. He'd been bulky, spent all his time in the gym, and had also taken steroids, which had been spoken of in depth at his trial. He'd pleaded provocation. The jury had rightly ignored it. I must check if he's out yet, Lomond thought. Every chance he will be by now.

'Good security system you've got,' he remarked.

'Yeah, it's an Avalon King house,' Siobhan said. 'Everything's tight as you can get, really. Security locks, alarm system, sensors . . . no messing.'

Lomond considered a moment. Then he took up his fork and tried again.

*

At that moment, Smythe was easing herself into a deep bath, in water that was just a little too hot. A moment of infernal immersion, then it devolved into heat, and from there relaxation. A smart speaker played Radio 4, something of an affectation she'd inherited from her father, who preferred polite conversation as background noise rather than loud music. Smythe opened her eyes and stared up into the steam, which was shot through with flickering candlelight. The news came on, including the story about the second body recently found in Glasgow. 'The two cases are thought to be connected' was the key phrase. The dread of being in the papers in the morning was upon her. Probably the opposite of what the killer felt.

She was about to close her eyes again when she remembered Mrs Symes. And how she had encountered her killer. A ghastly fantasy played in her mind's eye. She envisioned a shadow stealing through the illumined steam. It might be a bit like a dark liquid creeping in. Amorphous, sinister patches and pools, shifting fast, ready to close over her.

Smythe's eyes snapped open. Nothing, of course, just her mind playing tricks. Occupational hazard.

All the same, she got out of the water and tiptoed over the rug to the door, just to be sure she'd locked it.

33

They both had a day off, and it was a lazy one. The morning had drifted away with the mid-morning DJ they had disliked at first but eventually taken a shine to. Steady pulse of aquamarine lighting on the digital radio, a cafetière filled and then refilled – rinsing it out could wait – and then revolving off into their own hobbies and activities once the phones had been laid aside for a bit and the lunchtime news had come on. Rowan Beattie had been left in the kitchen, perched on his bashed office chair, his comical headphones clamped to his ears, the hiss of the vinyl records mercifully removed but the graceful revolutions remaining, a silken spiral caught just so in the watery light from outside. Behind Rowan was the garden, the one Drew Gough had put together over most of the previous year, the one Rowan hated but tolerated. No lawn, no potted plants, lots of stone and terracotta. Yes, Rowan had to admit, this meant no clutter, and it was low-maintenance, sure. But the lack of plant life was alienating.

Drew tipped up his training top and secured his sweat bands. He didn't care how silly he looked, and weathered the jibes well. Drew had times to run, every single day, and lunchtime was his favourite. He liked the level path that ran along the canal, liked the lack of dogs, children and maniacs at that time of day.

'Don't say maniacs,' Rowan had told him. 'Too many of them about.'

Rowan had been joking, but all the same, as he cinched up his trainers, Drew had said, 'Make sure that patio door's locked anyway.'

Rowan fished out a Curtis Mayfield album, with the man himself on the front cover doing some sort of warm-down pose, resplendent in beige or perhaps even peach slacks. Drew remembered thinking it took some man to wear that gear, deliberately, and yet still be admired and envied fifty years later. He didn't get the chance to say it to Rowan, who had already fitted the album onto the turntable and dropped the needle on it, and was now sitting back down, eyes closed, head back. He had drifted into whatever zone he went to with those headphones on. Not even a wave of the hand.

Drew ran for fifty minutes, gaining a distance that might have taken a county-class runner twice as long to achieve. He was tall and spindly – not broad, but the type of runner you knew to get out of the way of. Focused. He listened to music, but not the same way Rowan did. Techno, long mixes, not household names, not something you'd ask for in a club. Frenzied, hardcore mixes that'd make you cringe if you heard them dopplering out of a car window. The odd thing was, the music in no way matched Drew's steady rhythm, his superb control and fitness. Drew ran in events all over Scotland; Drew had won medals.

He was running along the canal bank, giving dogs a wide berth – they didn't know to keep out of his way, and had been responsible for all the injuries he'd sustained since school, if you didn't count the time he'd been jumped on the way home one night, well before he met Rowan. They barked at him in blessed silence, thanks to his top-of-the-range wireless ear-buds, with one woman in cosy grey fleecy bottoms struggling to keep an alarmingly muscular Bully-type thing out of his path. Drew smiled and put on the pace. He was going too fast to worry about the frost, which wasn't as bad as it had been first thing. Too fast to worry about the icy puddles, some of them punched through into shark's-mouth shards.

Drew lapped the woman with the Bully just after he made his customary turn at the bollard where the canal bank gave onto a forked path with a grocer's at the end. It was an ancient place that had once been an ice cream emporium but now sold booze right up until midnight, if you were feeling brave enough to go there after dark, which Drew occasionally was. He was too fast for the Bully to go for him, but the woman didn't half get a fright, lurching all over the place. He smiled and ran past them, *the bullet*, he thought to himself, pulse up. The sweat, cooling fast too. Drew felt it freeze on his face, the moisture chill at his armpits, his neck, his groin. He was looking forward to his shower.

Back around to the cul-de-sac, the detached houses, the whitewashed cladding bright in the January sun and the pepperoni roof tiles, blowing steam here and there as the boilers kept the heating going.

He slowed to a walk on the drive – the warm-down would come on the exercise mat, a full half-hour of stretching, in the bowling-lane-style hallway that led into the utility room where the washing machine, boiler and spare freezer lived. The door was closed fast, which was the first sign Drew had that something was a bit off. The corridor needed as much light as it could get, and Drew kept the utility room clean and minimalist – that door was rarely shut.

And so to the terrible thing. Into the kitchen, and again, each door firmly closed, as if each adjoining room had split off from an argument, disgusted with each other. Into the kitchen where Rowan had been left listening to his records, leaning back on the bashed old leather seat, its lustre now the colour of dried blood. Something requisitioned from an old office on Bath Street where, rumour had it, Rowan's old man had died in it. One of those guys who'd refused to retire, Rowan had said of him.

The chair was on its back, brass castors pointed towards the door. Albums were scattered across the floor, but not untidily, which was another thing that Drew would remember with absolute clarity. The albums were all face up, titles showing. R&B, soul. Sly Stone, Howlin' Wolf and Curtis, of course.

No Rowan, at least not that you could see. But the storage box, leather-upholstered, long as a canoe against one wall, had been pulled ninety degrees out of position, facing the kitchen door directly as you came in. A confrontation, and notably clean, shiny and slick, like the skin of a newly beached whale. And trailing from the whale's mouth, only a little askew from its lower jaw, just enough to suggest an opening, was the wire from the headphones, with the headphones placed neatly on the floor.

Drew pressed pause on his phone, stopping the music.

Sixteen seconds later they heard the screaming two doors away as the dog on the canal path paused, ears pricked, at the terrible sound that its owner couldn't hear.

34

It took a lot, Lomond reflected, to draw the breath out of you. The man stuffed into the bean bag did it. He'd seen bodies dredged from water, some in terrible states. He'd seen faces, hands, ghastly rudiments of people and personality; joints and sockets articulated by earth, by animals, by insects. Glistening carnivals of maggots. You had to forget about them as best you could, and carry on. Death was just life repackaged. But when Lomond saw the young man's blue face appearing from the upholstery, the white polystyrene stuffing spilling across the floor and pouring from the open mouth, that did it.

'Christ's sake,' he said.

Over his shoulder, Slater coughed.

Anita Khavari turned to Lomond, concern showing in her eyes. 'OK?'

'Sure.' Lomond forced himself to face it. Somewhere in his mind he could still hear the man's partner screaming. He'd found it. He'd seen the face first – vanguard of a body folded in on itself as usual, forced into a crouch. Even more sickening, it had been stuffed into the bean bag that had lived in the corner, close to the patio door, and then stuck in the storage box with the tell-tale headphones cable trailing from the closed lid.

Rowan's face had protruded from the zip, a blue petal preparing to bud between the corduroy fabric.

'This has to be the same guy,' Lomond said.

Khavari nodded. 'I'd put the house on it. And yours.'

'Your money looks safe. And mine.'

'Smothered again – probably with the bean bag. Looks like whoever it was came through the patio door. The stereo was still connected but had been switched off. Maybe he sneaked right up to him when he had the music on, then jumped on him with the bean bag, smothered him with it. Fingernails look like they have the same material underneath as the bean bag, and there's some blood, but we'll firm that up later.'

'Three,' Lomond muttered. 'Lone woman. Homeless guy. Young gay man.'

'Not the usual victim profile,' Khavari ventured.

'Not at all. And no obvious link.'

Lomond winced as flashbulbs went off in the garden. Beneath the tent, every single bit of it was being photographed. Slater joined him.

'Looks closed off,' Slater said.

'They're not overlooked. End terrace. House next door's empty,' Lomond said. 'We'll have to go over that too, make sure he wasn't hiding there.'

'He's targeting them, gaffer. Surely. Watching the houses.'

'That's a definite. Woods and the water at the back. Broad daylight.' Lomond bit back the urge to kick out at the stuffing that was floating over the hardwood floor like dandelion seeds. 'Surely someone saw him.'

'There's a security camera at the patio,' Slater said.

'Aye,' Lomond said. 'Same make as the Symes'.'

'I thought I recognised it,' Khavari said.

'Same builder too,' Lomond said. 'Avalon King.' He took one last look at the boy. Suffocated. Little chance to put up a fight.

'Strong bastard, eh?' Slater said.

'Yep. Bloody gorilla.' You tried not to think of it, of course. The pure shock. Presumably pressure on the chest, knocked right off the seat, then the crude intrusion of the fibres and the pressure, the air snuffed out, the struggle for life rather than the struggle to fight off the attacker, and all too soon the lights, the darkness, and whatever came next.

'We'd better talk to him, the partner,' Lomond said. 'Got to do it fast.'

'Good luck,' Khavari said, in a tone that suggested there was none to be had.

*

The portable incident room was an oasis of sorts in the darkness. The glare from the lights cut out the rest of the street. Only the police tape was prominent, laser-blast bright around the perimeter.

Drew Gough had changed out of his running gear. They'd had to take samples and test his clothes, of course. He'd understood. He'd been co-operative.

Lorna McGill had taken the lead on it. She'd held his hand and sat close to him; Lomond had felt reassured himself by her warm tone and smile.

'Thing is,' Drew said, 'I absolutely hated that bean bag. I hated it sitting in the kitchen, you know? We had the big dining table, tons of room, and that's fine. Rowan had his music and his record player and the headphones, you know, and that was all fine too. He liked to sit there when it was dark. See the stars, he said. He actually wanted a conservatory. We were saving that for our forever house.'

He began to shake. Lorna placed her other hand over his free one. He tried to drink some of the tea she had made, but spilled it en route to his mouth.

'So he had that bloody bean bag in the corner. Slumped in it, you know? I've got strong legs and I can't even stand up from it. I told him that . . . told him . . .'

'How long have you had the house?' Lomond asked.

'Eighteen, nineteen months?'

'Had bother with the neighbours?'

'No . . . well, one or two comments from the people who used to be next door. Nothing nasty, but people do say stuff and can get a bit weird. But nothing that would make them do . . . nothing . . .' He swallowed and focused in the distance.

They'd found him screaming in the street. Off his head, apparently. Not making a bit of sense. He couldn't be made to go back in the house, and someone had the presence of mind to call the police. Lomond had been on the scene in half an hour.

'Was anyone ever threatening or unpleasant? Say anything dodgy?'

'No, everyone was lovely, I have to say. Even those old neighbours. Presents at Christmas, invited for drinks. But Rowan was the chatty one. He got on with folk. He could talk anyone round. The wives on the street loved him. Better-looking than me. Not hard, mind you.' He laughed bitterly.

'So no bother at all?'

'I think one night there was a drone out. Just before Christmas. Early December?'

'Did you see it?'

'Just the lights. Two wee green lights, up in the sky. And that buzzing. I actually tried to chase it. Nosy bastards. I remember looking for chippy stones to throw. Rowan was laughing his head off.'

'How many times did this happen?'

'Just the once.'

'And no sign of an intruder or anything?'

'Nah. Just some teenagers during the summer, drinking in the woods at the back, but that was it. That was it . . .' He scratched his chin, staring into the distance. Gone, Lomond thought. And not coming back for a while.

35

They walked around the house, front and back. They ignored the neighbours; Lomond in particular tuned out the tumult that was surely growing. It wouldn't take this news long to travel at all. In fact, Anita Khavari had already had to tell a young woman to sling her hook. Turned out she was a reporter. They'd scaled back Lomond's media appearances since the Ferryman case, but he was still in charge of the investigation, still on the hook.

'He's escalating,' Lomond said.

'Mmm,' Slater said. 'He must have messed up somehow, though, eh? He's no ghost.'

'That's what I thought last time.' Lomond paused. He took in the corner of the house, the camera at the front, the closed windows and the curtained upper rooms with quick movements. 'Same deal with the Symes woman. Security system active, set to come on when someone enters the garden. It comes on. It takes a recording. But there's nothing there. How's he doing it?'

'He's re-recording the footage. What we're seeing is a recording.'

Lomond nodded. 'Possible. We can match the times and the movement of the sun on the back lawn.'

'Didn't have a lawn,' Slater said.

'You're right . . . they had that fake crap. Same as the Symes woman. Remember the plastic greenery all over her back fence? Same stuff.'

'No sign of footprints anywhere. Possible he crept over the rock garden. Nothing in the house, though.' Slater stifled a yawn. 'Sorry,' he said, face reddening.

'So how's he getting in? Locked back door, locked front door, both times. Symes' mother-in-law unlocks the door to get in. She's sure of it. And the daughter sees her taking out her keys. This man – his partner's adamant he locked the front and back doors when he left. He's the more clued-in, and he takes no chances. The doors are locked.'

'Going to ask the question, gaffer . . . is it Drew Gough?'

'What, all three? Doubt it.'

'Maybe a cover-up. Killed his partner, made it look like a jack-in-the-box . . . Sorry. I know you hate the daft names.' Slater winced at his own mistake.

'Never mind,' Lomond muttered.

'So let's say Gough kills his man, but makes it look like the other guy out there?'

'Too many similarities, too many coincidences, and too much inside knowledge if he did that. Plus there's the dog walker and the drivers who placed him on the canal. No, this is someone who sneaked in, did the deed, made sure they left no trace whatsoever and got back out again. Came and went through the woods at the back of the house yet dodged the security system, front and back. How did he get in? That's the key. How does he do it?'

'Houses were both Avalon King. The homeless guy's body was dumped at a place where Avalon King's going to develop some flats. Obvious link there, gaffer.'

'Laybourn's involved in the first two. Plus we found him loitering in the woods behind the Symes house. But he's got alibis.'

'Not fitting, for me,' Slater said. 'I know that counts for nothing, and I know we've been wrong about hunches before. But I just don't see it.'

'I agree with you.' Lomond kicked a loose stone back into the slated siding of the driveway and scratched his chin. He needed a shave. 'There's something we've overlooked. Something in both houses.'

'It would show up in the blueprints, wouldn't it? The plans?'

'I'll speak to the architect. He's bound to know.'

'What about the invisible boy? The guy the two wee lassies spoke to?'

'If they're telling the truth – and their stories do tie up – then I think he's the killer. But we've got nothing to identify him, except that he's male. That's as much as they can say.'

'UFOs . . . ghosts . . . invisible boys . . .' Slater laughed bitterly. 'Vampires and witches next, maybe? Is Nessie our killer?'

'I'll stake my career on the fact that Nessie didn't kill anyone.'

'Not according to St Columba, way back in the day.'

Lomond shifted his shoulders like a boxer spotting his opponent at the weigh-in. 'I'd like to see his evidence.'

'No witnesses, no one spotted going in or out. Where do we go from here?'

'It's got to be the houses,' Lomond said, nodding to himself. 'I'm sure of it. It's tied to Avalon King.'

'What's the motive, though?'

'I don't know. But the houses are the key.'

'So what's next, gaffer?'

'Rip them apart.'

'We can do that?'

'Too bloody right we can do that.' Lomond fished for a number, then sent a message. 'Get it started as soon as the forensics are wrapped up here. Both houses. There's another way in. If they aren't getting in by either door, and they're bypassing the security cameras, there's no question in my mind: we have to look at the blueprints. I'll talk to the techies.'

'He's stalking them too,' Slater said, pointing to the stunted fingers of the trees on the near horizon. 'Through the woods. That's the link to both houses.'

'Has to be. Drew mentioned green lights. Laybourn's UFOs.'

'And Laybourn.' Slater had his own phone out. It burred in his hands. 'What is it?' he said into the handset, turning away.

'Aye . . . I did mention this. I'm going to be busy on a case. All night, maybe. No, I can't pick up dinner for your mum. You'll have to do it. Well, we all have to work, don't we? Look, I'll call you later.'

Slater's voice had risen by the end of the call.

'How's it going?' Lomond said.

'Cracking,' Slater replied, slightly irked.

'That Meghan?'

Slater nodded.

'It's tough being out on a case,' Lomond ventured. Slater said nothing. 'Everything OK at home?'

'Peachy. Let's go and see about wrecking these houses, gaffer.'

36

'Now, here's the roundabout again.' The instructor coughed to mask his rumbling stomach and leaned back in his seat. 'Easy peasy. All you do is watch for traffic coming from the right. OK? That includes traffic coming all the way round. So anything from twelve o'clock through to three o'clock. You know, on the dial. OK?'

'OK,' Shane said. He was a tall, handsome lad of seventeen, with long delicate fingers which he wiped on his thighs, one hand after the other, as the roundabout approached. It was busy, and the streetlights were on.

'Now, you're watching, eh?' the instructor said. 'Here it comes, right? From the right? Got it?'

'Got it,' Shane said.

'Try not to grip the wheel too tight. You know . . . relax, Shane.'

'All right,' Shane said. He slowed up, a little heavy on the brakes.

'Right. Look to the right. Wee quick looks,' the instructor said. 'Can you go? Can you?'

The car edged forward. Shane's right foot trembled on the accelerator. A car swept around from the right, another one, then it looked clear.

'Can you? No, you can't!'

The instructor hit the clutch and brake on his dual unit, hard. The car came to a rough stop. Shane gasped, almost swallowing his chewing gum. From the right – though from nine o'clock, initially – a black 4x4 swung round. The driver had no intention of braking and was moving fast, though there was time to take in the finger tapped against the temple, the shake of the head. 'Bampot,' he said, quite clearly.

'That's quite rude,' Shane said.

'Ignoramus. You'll meet a few of them on the road – and elsewhere. Right, you need to restart the engine, Shane. That means turn the key. Then brake, clutch, into gear . . .' The instructor sighed.

'Sorry,' Shane said.

'One more time. Now we're looking to the right. We're watching for a gap. And we're relaxing, aren't we? Taking a deep breath.'

'OK,' Shane said. He swallowed. The car bunnyhopped a little, and there was a moment when it seemed they might stall, but the car eventually found its way round.

'You got there,' the instructor said, in neutral. 'Right. We're straight along here, then a left at the next roundabout and we're on the home straight. Think you can get us home, OK?'

'Sure,' Shane said.

'OK.' The instructor leaned back and checked his phone, but kept his feet poised on the dual control pedals. This was not his first rodeo, after all, nor his five hundredth.

Eventually the car came to a smooth stop at the bottom of the gated estate. Shane's mother was waiting by the twelve-foot brick wall that surrounded the big house. You knew the house was there, but there was no way of actually seeing it unless you stopped to look through the wrought-iron security gates, or, heaven forbid, were invited in. Great arrowhead conifers poked high over the top of the wall, and there was a hint of a huge garden. The instructor remembered once driving past and smiling to himself when he saw bubble-style graffiti and other spiky bombings spray-painted along the red brick exterior. When he'd driven by later that day, he had been slightly less amused to see a team of men in hi-vis vests scrubbing it all off with high-pressure washers.

'You're coming along well,' the instructor said. 'You're getting into gear, I'd say.'

Shane nodded. Then he laughed, a genuine laugh that lit up an anxious face. 'I'm not really.'

The instructor didn't contradict him. 'It's all about practice; it eventually becomes automatic. One day everything slots into place, and it'll be as normal as putting your shoes on and going for a walk. You'll get there, I promise.'

'Not any time soon, I reckon.'

'Confidence, Shane. The name of the game. Think of it this way: you remember the idiot in the 4x4?'

'The one on the roundabout?'

'Yes. The bampot guy. Forced his way through in his gas-guzzler. He was ignorant and rude about a learner. That guy has a driving licence.'

Shane smiled as the instructor paused, letting it sink in. 'That is kind of reassuring.'

'You'll do fine, son . . . Uh-oh, here's trouble.'

The instructor sat up straight as Shane's mother walked towards them. She had a long woollen coat on, smoky grey, and her hair was loose. Her lipstick was crimson.

'I'll head out then,' Shane said quickly, unbuckling his seatbelt. 'Thanks for today. I'm enjoying it now.'

'That's great. Next week, then?'

'I think there's another lesson booked in for the end of this week, actually.'

'Oh, you might be right,' the instructor said. He reached for a folder behind him on the back seat, but the teenager had already left the car and closed the door. He didn't appear to say anything to his mother in passing, simply fitted some earbuds and carried on up the driveway. His mother walked round behind the car and knocked on the passenger's window. The instructor opened it quickly, and Nicole Kingsley leaned down to look in at him.

'Hey, hello,' he said. 'How's it going?'

'You're fifteen minutes late.'

'Sorry, Ms Kingsley. Going out at this time . . . the traffic gets a bit heavier. It's good practice for him.'

'How much do I owe you?'

'For what?'

'For your time. Fifteen minutes extra. That means money, doesn't it?'

He waved a hand. 'No trouble at all. Don't worry about it.'

'Very reasonable of you. So how's he getting on? Shite?'

He was almost too astonished to laugh, but did so. 'He's as good as any other seventeen-year-old. He'll do just fine.'

'That's not really what I asked you.' He didn't think she'd blinked once since she bent down to the window. She had leaned nearer to him, an extreme close-up, an imposition. Her perfume was reaching him now. 'I asked you how he was getting on. And is he still shite?'

'He needs practice, that's all.'

'And he's getting it. He's been doing these lessons for a while.'

'Yeah, a few weeks.'

'I want him driving before his exams. They're coming up fast.'

'I'll do my absolute best. Well . . . he'll do his absolute best.'

She tapped the window frame. Her fingernails were dark purple, with a strange spattering of tiny glitter stars. 'You know, my dad was really great when he put us through our driving, back in the day. Every single one of us passed first time.'

'You must have been cracking drivers.'

'Some things run in families. My dad was a great driver. Raglan Kingsley. Started out in haulage. Something to think about. Anyway, I'll send the money through for the next lesson. Thursday, please. Let's get him up to speed.'

The instructor's heart was beating hard now. He averted his eyes from the tanned skin beneath her unbuttoned shirt. 'Absolutely, Ms Kingsley. Look forward to it. He's a great kid.'

'Course he is.' She drew back and he closed the window, sighing as he did so.

She was still watching him as he moved to the driver's seat and pulled away, with a glance in the mirror. He shook his head, but not so you'd notice from another vehicle, or on a security camera.

★

Shane barely heard her move up the driveway at his back. As he turned to close the door, there she was. He removed the earbuds and hung up his coat.

'How's the driving going, then?' she asked. She removed her coat and did up the top two buttons of her shirt.

Shane looked away, embarrassed.

'Fine. Just about there, I think.'

'I saw you on the roundabout at Kelliesburn Toll.'

'You followed me?'

'I said I saw you. I was coming back from the office, smart-arse.' He said nothing. 'You went around it like an old lady.'

'Old ladies are careful.'

'Old ladies crash.' She kicked off her shoes. 'I want you getting that licence before your exams. Speaking of which – your prelim results in yet?'

'Think it's tomorrow.'

'That's a weird one. Because I spoke to Orla Kemp's mother when I was getting petrol. She said the results are in.'

'Maybe she phoned the school? Orla's mum is a hysteric.'

'Or maybe you're not telling me.'

Shane knew his marks were good, but chose not to tell his mother. The barb, the spear, was always ready to be jabbed home, whether he performed well or not. This was not Shane's first rodeo either. He was an old stager. 'I'm sure you'll find out in good time.'

'I'm sure I will. Tea's in the oven, if your stepfather's done what I asked him to.'

'Yeah, I can smell the burning from here.'

Nicole Kingsley barged past her son – literally shouldering him out of the way. He watched her go, flicking on the downstairs bathroom light with some savagery as she went, then disappearing inside.

He entered the kitchen. On the Aga beside the huge farmhouse-style window a casserole steamed and bubbled. To be fair, it wasn't too burnt. Shane sniffed at it, and stirred the pot, watching the tinned tomatoes float to the surface. A creak at his back startled him, but he did not turn. 'Out you come, pardner,' he said.

The cupboard door creaked again, opening a little further. A dark sliver appeared, and something that might have been the gleam of an eye.

'Don't take all day. I know you're there.'

The door swung open. 'Boo!' Shane's half-brother leapt out, over-balancing before pulling a superhero pratfall on the tiled floor. Jared was the antithesis of Shane: blond curls, big blue eyes. But the boy never smiled. Even in play he was half looking over Shane's shoulder.

'Where've you been?' he said, in his squeaky mouse voice.

'Out driving.'

'Dad says you're rubbish at driving.'

'He's got nine points on his licence, kiddo; he should know all about it.'

'Dad says you're going to stay with your real dad soon.'

'Yeah. I might just do that over the weekend.'

Jared checked over his shoulder, then whispered, 'Can I come too?'

Before Shane could answer, his stepfather stormed into the kitchen. He still wore his work gear, though he'd ditched the tie some time before he came in. He ran his hands through his hair, gurning at his stepson. 'Get some of that down you, quick,' he said. 'And put some out for Jared while you're at it.'

'There's no potatoes. Want me to cook some?'

'No, I bloody don't. Just stay in here and eat it. Both of you.'

'OK. Keep your hair on.'

'Don't be cheeky, Shane,' Neil Glennie said, in what Shane thought of as his glinty-eyed tone. 'Not today. Some people are coming round to talk to us. It doesn't really concern you, but they might come in to say hello. They might ask some questions. It's very important you don't say anything stupid.'

'Who is it, exactly? The Feds?'

'Almost. The police, in fact.'

37

'That Nicole Kingsley?' Slater nodded towards the beast of a 4x4 as it rumbled down the road. There was a suggestion of blonde hair in the passenger seat, someone sitting high with their chin up, like royalty.

'Aye. Spoke to her already.'

'Anyone would think she saw us coming.'

'Enough bloody security cameras – maybe she did.'

'Wee bit dodgy.'

'Perhaps she's shy. If I'm honest, it's a result. I don't want her around when we talk to his nibs.'

'Those cameras – reckon it's the same make as the other places, gaffer?'

Lomond's keen eyes narrowed as he took in the brass plate on the gate. *FiveBarGate*, it said: one word, three capitals. 'Aye. That's it. Not exactly a ringing endorsement for their products if it wasn't.'

'Got to ask them about security flaws. Re-recording, hacking, that kind of carry-on.'

'We're already on it. Camera company laughed at us, but we'll look into it. Techies will take it apart. Tait's dealing with all that.'

'Lucky Tait.'

Lomond drove up the long driveway. The house was less than twenty years old, according to a quick search, but it looked much older. A real lawn, too, not especially well kept, with patches of water in dips, and overgrown bushes along the eastern wall. Lomond thought the conifers were a little bit tall, as well. There was private and secluded, and then there was oppressive. Smoke rose from a chimney, and there was a scent of burning logs through the vent of Lomond's car.

'Heard about this job that's coming up, then?' Lomond asked.

Slater sighed. 'Aye, gaffer. And, no, I'm not going for it.'

Lomond raised his eyebrows. 'Be a good fit for you.'

'So would long johns, but I'm not going for them either.' Slater frowned. 'Unless you're saying I should?'

Lomond hesitated as he engaged the handbrake, and the stone-chipped driveway cleared its throat beneath the car. 'I'm not saying you should go for it as in . . . "You should go for that, hint hint", you know? But, all the same, you should go for it.'

'This is taking a turn for the surreal, gaffer.'

'It usually does when we talk to a squillionaire.'

'Gangster, though. Getting together with, what, an architect?'

'She's a gangster's daughter, actually. Bit of a difference.'

Slater snorted. 'Doubt it.'

'Legitimate businesswoman.'

'We sure about that?'

'All legit.'

'She's in bloody property. How legit can she be?'

'I have the right to remain silent,' Lomond offered. He unbuckled his seatbelt.

*

As they were led through the hallway, Lomond and Slater passed a doorway through which the view was dominated by a desktop computer. It took a while for Lomond to realise that's what he was looking at – the thing was shelled in black mesh and dull metal, with slow-blinking lights denoting that it was at peace.

'Hell is that?' Slater asked, doing a double take before the door. 'Not a computer, is it?'

'It is,' Neil Glennie said archly. 'High-end, high-spec. You could edit a movie on that. Special effects, the lot.'

'Sounds complicated,' Lomond said.

'You bet it's complicated.'

'Use it for work?'

'Nah, it's Shane's. He's the tech guy. He codes, helps me with the website, the lot.'

Slater frowned. 'You know what it reminds me of? You ever seen that film *War Games*?'

'Was that the one with Johnny Five? The robot? Had a laser on his, eh . . .' He tapped his shoulder.

'Nah, you're thinking of *Short Circuit*. *War Games* has this massive computer, Whopper – W-O-P-R. They nearly launch World War Three.'

Glennie laughed. 'Well, that sounds like a job for Shane. It's his build. I should really find out what he's got on there, one of these days . . . Anyway. Kitchen. Here we are.'

*

'Sorry, I'm running late here, Inspector . . . Inspectors,' Glennie corrected himself. He was perched on a seat that seemed a little too high for him, at the end of a breakfast alcove. Lomond had a flashback to being taken to a barber's by his father, long ago, and suffering something of a humiliation in having to sit on the extension slat across the chair. Legs dangling.

Glennie was over fifty but looked a decade younger. Well-groomed and thick-haired, there was nonetheless something in him that reminded Lomond of Vincent Finch, though he would never have said so to the guy's face. Glennie was muscle-bound, while Finch's look was strictly nouveau-jakey, but there was definitely something there.

'We won't take up much of your time. We've had a quick look at the documents and blueprints you sent through after we spoke to your wife. Very comprehensive.'

'Least I could do,' Glennie said. He leaned back, his legs splayed wide. 'Terrible thing. I'm happy to help in any way I can.'

'The house in Myrtlewood Crescent that's similar to the one in Craigan Walk is also one of yours, I think.'

'Almost identical,' Glennie agreed. 'I designed both streets.' He folded his arms.

'Almost?'

'Sometimes there are modifications. A client can come in at the design stage and request specific features.'

'Christ,' Slater said suddenly, his foot slipping off the rail of his stool. 'Mind if I stand up? I feel like a singer on an old chat show.'

Glennie cocked his head. He sounded a little annoyed as he said, 'Ergonomics not suiting you?'

'Just general physics, I think.' Slater studied his notebook. 'Feel like my plums are on show. Anyway . . . these extra features you're talking about? Would these include things that might not have been on the initial blueprints?'

Glennie chewed the side of his mouth and studied the spotlights on the kitchen ceiling. 'Maybe not the initial ones, but I'm sure you got all the modifications and final plans. I was quite meticulous about it.'

'You were,' Lomond agreed.

'So what sort of modifications did you have in mind? Helicopter pad, sex dungeon, that sort of stuff? Aw, don't look at me like that.' Glennie chuckled. It was a jarringly insincere sound, as fake as the antique-effect radio, silenced in the corner. 'I have designed all of those things for clients.'

'Now that you mention it, I was thinking more like panic rooms. Hidden passages, escape hatches – anything of that nature.' Lomond kept his tone and his expression neutral.

'I don't think so, not on either of those homes. As I said, any modifications will show up on the blueprints I sent you. I've left nothing out.'

'Just checking.' Lomond smiled. 'Because we're going to rip both those houses apart.'

Glennie blinked. 'What?'

Lomond considered a moment. 'Let's say someone asked you how to break into a house you designed, with a security system you specified in partnership with FiveBarGate. You're the expert of all experts, right?'

'I suppose.'

'How would you do it?'

'Well . . . I'd take out the security system. Then maybe I'd have a key to the door. I don't know. That is a hell of a thing to ask . . .'

'It's expertise I'm after,' Lomond said. 'How could it be done?'

'This guy . . . the one they're talking about on the telly . . . this is what he's doing?'

'Two people have been killed in houses you designed,' Slater said. 'You've got a few estates dotted about the city and the wee posh armpits here and there, but your stuff isn't, like, everywhere. So it's a bit of a coincidence, we think.'

'Nothing to do with me. Or my designs.'

'Someone's breaking into the houses and leaving no trace, Mr Glennie,' Lomond said. 'There's nothing on CCTV. There's no sign of forced entry – no broken windows, or pits in the garden – and he hasn't teleported so far as we know. But he's getting in. How would he do it?'

'Hiding,' Glennie said, snapping his fingers. 'He might be hiding. In the loft. Somewhere in the house.'

Lomond pulled his stool closer – and, like Slater, almost slipped off. 'Now we're talking,' he said. 'How would he hide? What's the best place?'

'I designed big walk-in cupboards . . . it's possible. Did either of the houses have CCTV inside?'

'Nope, just at the front and back doors.'

'Maybe he's sneaking in and waiting. Holing out in the attic, or maybe a spare bedroom – did they have spare bedrooms?'

'They did,' Slater said, 'both of them.'

'So that's possible. Maybe he sneaks in . . . it's not difficult to do when someone's come home and switched off the cameras and the systems. Maybe when a pizza's been delivered, or a parcel – that kind of thing. Window cleaner's come round.'

Lomond and Slater shared a look.

'That's a decent idea,' Lomond said. 'But they'd have left a trace, wouldn't they? And this person hasn't left a trace. We've been up in the loft, looked through the cupboards . . . All we can be sure of is that they sneaked in, and sneaked back out. The back doors were locked.'

'Sorry,' Glennie said. 'You've stumped me. And scared me, a bit.' He glanced at his own back door, looking out onto the garden. Dark, now, with the trees leaning in a sharp wind.

'Amen to that,' Slater said.

A door behind them creaked. All three leapt. It was the kitchen cupboard. A tiny face, grinning with some glee, emerged from the crack in the door. For a moment Lomond was reminded of a ghastlier face he'd seen, not so long ago. Born again, he thought.

'Jared!' Glennie said, face reddening. 'That's rude. I've told you not to hide in there.'

'Keek!' the boy said.

Lomond laughed, as much to break the tension as anything else. 'Keek yourself! How you doing, my man?'

'Fine.' The boy sniffed.

'Shows you how easily it's done,' Slater mumbled. He fidgeted with his coat cuffs, nervous tension from the fright needing to drain somewhere.

'Go to your room,' Glennie said.

The boy pouted and walked out of the room slowly, head held in mock shame. 'Sorry,' he said.

'Six-year-olds,' Glennie said, face pinched in anger. 'Nature's wee comedians.'

'Ach, no harm done,' Lomond said. 'When my lassie was six

she decided to make a cake when we thought she was playing in the garden. Used a full bag of flour and every egg we had. When we went in the kitchen–'

'I'm sort of busy, gentlemen.' Glennie patted the table with an impatient little rhythm. 'Was there anything else I can help you with?'

'What are your thoughts on Vincent Finch?'

Glennie's percussion solo ended. 'Finch.'

'That's right. He's your . . . stepson's father, is that right? Forgive me,' Lomond said, genuinely embarrassed.

'Well . . .' Glennie lowered his voice, one eye on the door lest another member of his household should spring forth, 'Vincent is a pain in the arse. That's my honest opinion.'

'Any adult reason behind that?' Slater asked brusquely.

'As a matter of fact, yes. He never really got over the divorce. He's remarried, and we're all very civil at the birthdays and the other life events that everyone has to go to . . . and he pays attention to Shane. He's not hands-off. Not like some get. But he got a bit nasty during the divorce. Not nasty enough to wind up Nicole's brothers . . . You know who Raglan Kingsley is?'

'That name's familiar,' Lomond replied before Slater could.

'Then you'll know why he didn't get too silly. But he's playing daft wee games, you see. With the property business. He got the Myrtlewood Crescent house out of it, and another set of flats that he'd paid into years ago. Quite canny with his deals. Sold and reinvested at the right time. He's trying to put his own wee empire together. Game of Monopoly, for real, with new-build houses and some city centre property. He keeps making deals ahead of Nicole. Ahead of Avalon King. Not sure how he's doing it, apart from undercutting. Or how he's finding out about the best plots. Nicole's fuming, but she won't do anything about it. Guess it's best not to let it get too nasty, for Shane's sake.'

The front door closed. Jared reappeared, carrying a box

that was a bit too big for him. 'Daddy, there was a parcel at the front door.'

Glennie frowned. 'I didn't hear anyone knock.'

'I saw a van,' the boy said. He lurched and stumbled. Lomond instinctively caught an end of the box, to stop him dropping it. That's when he noticed the red scarf trailing from the lid, tickling the floor, threatening to tangle in the boy's legs. Then he saw the red writing on the top of the box. What was written there was not an address.

Lomond snatched the box from the boy, who looked up at the policeman with fear. 'That's good,' Lomond said, with a note of forced jollity. 'Tell you what, wee man, why don't you head outside and play?'

'What? It's freezing.' He looked at his dad, confused.

'What's going on?' Glennie said, getting out of his seat.

'Get Jared out of the house. Right now. Tell him to go to the end of the garden. Is his big brother in?'

'Yes—'

'Jared, go knock on your brother's door and tell him you're both to get out of the house. Right now.' Lomond's eyes were hard. The box quivered in his hands. The red scarf dangled like a spent party streamer.

Glennie's face changed. He'd read the writing too. 'Jared? Do what the man tells you.'

'Dad . . .'

'Jared! Now!' Glennie practically screamed it.

Startled, the boy turned and fled.

'Gaffer,' Slater said, voice scratchy, 'tell me this is a joke.'

'Here's hoping,' Lomond said.

On the top of the box, six inches from his chin, slashed in red ink on white printer paper, was a stark message. DEAR HOUSEHOLDERS AND GUESTS. IT WILL GO OFF IF YOU TRY TO LEAVE. YES, IT IS WHAT YOU THINK IT IS.

38

Lomond took the weight of the box in one hand. He flipped the paper over.

On the other side: OPEN THE BOX. OR ELSE. CALL NO ONE.

Lomond crossed to the kitchen table.

'Gaffer . . .' Slater began, bracing himself.

'What do we do?' Glennie croaked. 'Call bomb disposal?'

'Never mind that. We get out of here,' Slater countered. 'Grab the boys and run.'

'Just a wee minute,' Lomond said, surprised at how level and reasonable his voice was. 'The suggestion is, we're being watched.'

'So?'

'So if it's a bomb and we don't run for it, he might get in touch.'

'This is a gamble, gaffer. I wouldn't trust him an inch.'

'He,' Glennie said. 'You know who this is?'

'Yeah, fairly sure. Just a few details to work out.'

'It's him,' Glennie said, his hands braced on the back of a stool. 'This guy they're calling Jack-in-the-Box. Isn't it?'

'I need you to be calm, Mr Glennie.' Lomond placed the piece of paper on the kitchen worktop, holding one corner very delicately between thumb and forefinger. Then he placed his fingers on the edges of the box lid.

'I think we should do nothing,' Slater said. His face twitched. Lomond felt sweat prick his armpits and spine. He peered at the sliver of sky above the treeline beyond the window. A single red light blinked, silently, above them.

He flipped open the box lid. Slater let out his breath in a slow sigh, like a surfacing diver releasing the air in his lungs.

The red scarf dropped in languid coils to the floor.

Nothing else happened.

Lomond peered inside. At the bottom, a laptop computer – vintage, by the look of it, maybe a decade past its prime – was opened up at ninety degrees. Next to it was a block of greyish material, rectangular, regularly cut. Wires and crocodile clips, a card and an elderly digital alarm clock, with red LCD characters showing four zeros, flashing impatiently. The card read, GO AHEAD, SWITCH IT ON.

Lomond reached into his pocket and withdrew a sealed pack of rubber gloves. 'Never leave home without them,' he quipped weakly. He struggled to fit them, his hands sweating. One finger hovered over the slow-pulsing *on* button on the laptop.

'We need to get out of here,' Glennie protested. 'This is madness. This is–'.

'Just wait a minute,' Lomond said. 'Both of you, get behind the breakfast bar.'

'Gaffer, if that's what he says it is, it doesn't matter if we stand behind a tank in the street,' Slater said. 'Your man here's spot on. We shouldn't touch it.'

Lomond paused. He kept one eye on the trees. A green light flickered. Then he pressed the button.

*

White text on black, scrolling across the black screen. THANK YOU FOR CHOOSING THE SLOW DEATH. HAD YOU AVOIDED THE BUTTON, IT WAS THE FAST ONE. Lomond waited. The cursor blinked, then the screen went blank. A new message appeared. THIS IS A MESSAGE TO LANDOWNERS, GRIFTERS, THIEVES, ROBBER BARONS AND EVERY OTHER GREEDY CAPITALIST. I AM OUT THERE. I AM AMONG YOU. AND I WILL DO MY WORK.

Lomond felt a sense of relief, but he said nothing to the other two men. Glennie had done as requested, and was crouching behind the bar. He even had his hands over his ears.

The cursor blinked and the screen wiped again. More text came down. IF YOU RUN OR ARE DISTURBED, I'LL KNOW. IF YOU SEND THE PIG OUT, I'LL KNOW. IF YOU MAKE THE PIGLETS RUN, I'LL KNOW. AND I WILL PRESS A BUTTON.

'What do you want, then?' Lomond said. He had enough awareness left to feel ridiculous.

The screen continued. I WANT YOU TO BEAR WITNESS. I WANT YOU TO TAKE A MESSAGE TO YOUR SUPERIORS AND THE MEDIA. I CAN BE AMONG YOU IN PERSON, OR AT A DISTANCE. I CAN PRESS A BUTTON OR SQUEEZE THE LIFE OUT OF YOU. I CAN TAKE YOUR WIVES AND DAUGHTERS, I CAN BEST YOUR SONS AND FATHERS. YOU WILL ALL GO THE SAME WAY. I CANNOT BE CAUGHT OR STOPPED. I'M JACK.

'Sure you are,' Lomond said.

The door creaked. All three men flinched.

'What are you doing?' Glennie cried.

Shane, the older boy, stood in the doorway, frozen in the act of removing his ear pods. 'What's the score?' he asked, grinning at first, then sensing that all was not well.

'Get out of here,' Glennie said. 'For God's sake – where's Jared?'

'He gibbered something about having pizza delivered, then he ran out into the garden. Why? It's not a bomb, is it?' He blanched when a sudden silence and tense expressions answered the question.

'Just get out!' Glennie hissed, flinging an arm out. 'Run!'

But Shane took a step closer. 'A bomb – what, seriously?'

'Yes, seriously,' Lomond said. 'Or as serious as we can be.'

'That's not a bomb,' the boy scoffed. 'It's a wind-up, isn't it?'

Lomond peered out the window. Another reddish pulse. 'Can't be sure,' he said. 'Best we treat it as if it is.'

'Then what're you all standing here for?'

'The person who sent it might be watching us,' Glennie said. 'Now don't make me tell you again. Get out – now.'

Slater raised a hand, standing between Shane and the box. 'No, don't do that. We were warned not to let the . . . to let anyone leave.'

'Piglets,' Glennie sneered. 'Sounds personal. He's watching, is he? Knows us, does he?'

'Can we all just calm down?' Shane said. 'It's not a bomb.'

'What makes you say that?' Lomond asked.

'Well, it looks like plasticine to me.'

'That's why they call it plastic explosive.'

'Yeah, but it's not plastic explosive, it's plasticine. New plasticine, by the look of it. You can still see the furrows.'

'Furrows?'

'That's what it looks like when it comes out the pack. See?' The boy moved closer.

Slater shoved him aside. 'Don't get smart. You don't know what it is.'

The boy shrugged. 'I do. I know what the wiring and stuff is, as well.'

'And what's that?' Lomond asked.

'Well, the alarm clock's got a battery compartment, and those wires are just crocodile clips. And the timer's not been set. Pull the wires out and nothing will happen. It's a wind-up.'

TOY WITH ME AND YOU'LL ALL GO, the scrolling message continued. Shane giggled. 'What's this, *The Phantom Menace*? Guy's winding you up with an old BBC Micro screen. Here.' He bent forward and pulled one of the clips, a second before Lomond and Slater grabbed him. The alarm clock began to buzz.

Then the door creaked again, and Jared gasped at the sight of the two men struggling with his brother. 'Daddy?' he said, eyes brimming.

Glennie crossed the kitchen faster than anyone would have thought possible, grabbed the boy and darted out of the door with him, the soles of his son's tiny training shoes pinwheeling on his thighs.

A loud pop sounded inside the box.

Slater flung himself to the floor. Shane dived under the table, hands over his head. Lomond merely blinked, as the air filled with golden confetti.

REMEMBER WHAT I SAID, the computer text added. Then there was another pop, this time a genuine explosion, and a steady flame rose from the laptop keyboard.

39

Tait actually put his tongue in his cheek, and said, 'That's some fancy make-up, sir.'

Lomond brushed at his lapels and shoulders, the way you might if you felt a cobweb trailing over your face. Gold dust sparkled in the fading afternoon light. 'Thanks,' he said drily. 'I was thinking of glamming up. Changing my style.'

'Suits you.'

'And you too, pal,' Lomond told him.

'Report's in. It was what the boy said – a bunch of wires, plasticine and an old digital alarm clock. Hard drive effectively burnt out. Techies are seeing if anything's retrievable, but they told me to offer up prayers to St Jude. I presume that's some sort of in-joke.'

'Well. Hang on to St Jude's number. We might need it before the week's out.'

They were standing at the bottom of the driveway. Nicole Kingsley was remonstrating with the uniformed officers guarding the front door. Lomond had tried to keep out of her way, but she had managed to chew Slater's ear for a full five minutes while the DI waited in the trees. It wasn't often you saw Slater cowed, Lomond had reflected. That's where Tait had caught up with him.

'Mind if I ask what we're doing out here, sir?' Tait asked mildly.

'Nice spot for a pee . . . That's a joke, Myles.'

'Sir.'

'Actually I'm trying to get an angle on the kitchen.'

'Sir?'

Lomond was ebullient. This wasn't usually the case after he'd thought his life was in danger. It was the case, though, when he'd had a decent idea. 'Look towards the kitchen. You can just about see it through the conifers.'

'Can't see much from here, sir. Some lights . . . looks like the SOCOs passing the big windows.'

'That's just it. From ground level you can't see much. From above the treeline you can probably see right into the room.'

Tait glanced skyward. 'Say again, sir?'

'We need to think drones. I saw one. And I think I know what it was looking at. Besides us. In the kitchen.'

'Drones?'

'Aye. Let's go a bit closer.'

Tait followed Lomond towards the stone pathway. On catching sight of movement beyond their own reflections in the dark, the masked SOCOs glanced up from the bright kitchen space.

'Now what do you see?' Lomond asked.

Tait, irritable at the best of times when he was put on the spot, said, 'I dunno. Flowery wallpaper? That coming back in again? Bit too busy for a kitchen, in my opinion.'

'I'd agree, Myles. But keep looking at the wallpaper. What's there?'

Tait sighed and closed his eyes. He didn't feel like playing. Then he opened them and scanned the room. 'Clock . . . bad art, I presume by the younger kid . . . and a calendar.'

'That's right. But not just a calendar, a big old organiser. Detailed too. Mainly filled in by Nicole Kingsley, to judge by the neat handwriting.'

'The drone was checking out their schedule?'

'Among other things. And, look . . . it's the sort of thing that doesn't seem important straight off, but there's a photo of an inside wall facing a window at Myrtlewood Crescent, where Kathryn was killed.'

Tait zoomed in on the image Lomond presented on his phone, and smiled wryly.

'OK. Now, you want to bet what those boys had on their wall at Craigan Walk?'

'I'm guessing a calendar you could see from the garden.'

'Spot on,' Lomond said. 'And I saw a drone out here. Daniel Laybourn talked about UFOs – there's your drone. That's the link. I want you to trace it, any way you can. Talk to neighbours, see if anyone saw anything. Check the register, see who owns one around here. It had a red light – that's about all I could make out, but it must have a camera on it. He's spying on them, Myles. I know it. That's how he knows when they're going to be alone.'

'They weren't alone in the house today.'

'No, but then I don't think our guy was trying to kill anyone today. He was trying to wind us up.' Lomond picked at the golden specks in the crook of his elbow. 'Successfully, I might add.'

'But how'd he know you'd be here? Following you from a distance?'

'Clever what they can do with these drones, if you've got good enough gear. If you're smart with it.'

Tait nodded. 'I'll get on to it.' Then, seeing Slater approach, he walked off in the opposite direction.

Slater's face was grey. 'I see you managed to duck your way out of the chat with the homeowner, gaffer. Now I know how you got promoted.'

'I'm putting the case together, Malcolm,' Lomond said neutrally. 'What did she say?'

'She said something about suing us into the afterlife if we damage her house in any way. Those exact words.'

'All happy about her kids being OK, was she?'

'Barely mentioned them.' Slater sucked at his teeth. 'She mentioned she's got an oak floor. She ever say that to you?'

'Guess that means she won't be burying anyone under it.'

'Wouldn't have stopped her dad.'

'Allegedly, Malcolm.'

'Allegedly. So definitely a wind-up?'

'Seems like it, though the SOCOs will check out the gear. Plasticine's awful handy for trapping hairs and fingerprints. Could be our man has made a mistake. And we've a fair idea he's using drones, as well.'

'So what next, gaffer?'

'We're going to find out if Daniel Laybourn's van was around here anywhere.'

'Bomb deliveries, now?'

'Worth a shot. Then we're going to talk to Vincent Finch.'

'Kingsley's ex?'

'Yep.'

'If it's him, he just threatened his son. The older boy.'

'With a dud bomb. Be decent cover, wouldn't it? If you were trying to cover your tracks.'

'What's that based on?'

'Got a report from Laybourn himself, would you believe,' Lomond said. 'Apparently he's seen Finch cutting about the woods.'

'Maybe he's out looking for ghosties and UFOs as well?'

'Maybe he is.'

40

Lorna McGill had insisted on picking up Smythe, but Smythe rather regretted accepting the offer when she saw the car. Half of McGill was visible backing out of the front passenger side of a black Renault that was no stranger to a sore face, going by the meteor-shower scrapings along the wheel arches. Smythe was reminded of an auntie struggling to move child seats from the back of a car to make room for relatives at a funeral.

Finally, panting, McGill heaved out a bashed black case, out of all proportion to its handler. She almost backed into Smythe as the latter darted forward to help.

'What the hell is that?' Smythe said, helping her right the thing on the back seat.

'Euphonium.'

Smythe blinked. 'I believe it.'

'It actually is.' McGill's plump cheeks coloured. 'I play it. But it's bloody awkward getting it in the back; it's better in the front. Sorry.'

Smythe laughed. 'Christ almighty, Lorna, it's bigger than you!'

'Heightist! It's my thing. I squeezed in a quick practice with the band. I don't get much time to do it, not as much as I'd like.' She shrugged. 'The job.'

'I wish I had a thing. I keep trying to have things.'

'What, like *hobbies*?' McGill said the word as if it were her darkest fear.

'No, not exactly . . . interests, you know? Stuff with a skill. Exactly like your euphonium. I thought I could do art, then the Ferryman thing happened, so I gave that up. Then

I thought I'd try birdwatching. But I got bored of pigeons and I'm terrified of seagulls.'

'Ah, keep looking. You're still young enough to find your thing.' They got into the car. It might have been bashed on the outside, but inside it smelled of cherry cola, pleasingly so.

'Right. I'll stick Myrtlewood Crescent into the satnav, gimme a second . . .'

*

'You going for it, then?' McGill whispered as they wandered along the path.

'Going for what?'

'The job that came up on the intranet.'

'Oh, right.' Smythe paused. 'I'm not sure. Maybe.'

'Tailor-made for you, surely.' McGill's voice was very low.

'It definitely isn't.'

'So you're not going for it? Detective Inspector Smythe? I can see you getting it, if I'm honest.'

'I'm flattered. But, well, I doubt it.'

'You should give it a go. I'm going to.'

'Good luck to you' was all Smythe could think to say.

'I mean, I'm two minutes in the door, I get that. But show willing, and all that.'

'Slater will get it.'

'The tall baldy guy, like Nosferatu's handsome wee brother?'

Smythe grinned, tickled at the description. 'That's him.'

'Lomond's boy, is he?'

'Nah, Lomond doesn't work that way. Doesn't get on with the high-heid yins. They probably can't wait to put him out to pasture. But Slater would be good in an interview scenario. And he's not even close to as stupid as he comes across.'

'Kind of depressing if he gets it, though.'

'Kind of. We'll see.'

'I'm not sure why we're whispering,' McGill said, after a pause.

'Me neither. You started it.'

'Scary woods, I suppose.' McGill sighed. 'Why's Lomond so keen for us to talk to Finch again?'

'We need to find out about his hobbies.' Smythe cupped her hand over her phone, so that the light wouldn't carry between the trees. 'The path through to the street's just here.'

'I don't know why we came this way,' McGill said, kicking dead branches. 'We could just've parked nearby.'

'Then they'd have known we were coming.'

'So? Are they suspects?'

'Aye. So I want to keep an eye out, just in case, for the thing we've missed.'

'There's always a thing,' McGill said, whispering again.

*

Belinda Finch was an imposing figure. Arms folded, framed by bright light, she was full-figured, blonde, unsmiling. She wore a tasselled black shawl that aged her, like a Spanish widow, thought Smythe.

'He's out,' she declared.

'We were told he would be here,' Smythe said. 'We came here specifically to talk to him.'

'And I said he's out.'

'Out where?' Smythe said, summoning her patience.

'He's out the back, looking for clues.'

'Come again?'

'Doing his Scooby-Doo thing.'

'It was more Velma who looked for the clues, not Scooby-Doo,' McGill ventured.

There was a silence then, lasting a beat too long, in which the three women's breaths fogged up.

'Can we come in and wait for him?' Smythe asked.

'Can I be honest? No,' Mrs Finch said.

Another silence.

'I guess we'll wait here for him, then,' Smythe said.

'Did you want to talk to me?'

'Not at all,' Smythe said. 'We're totally satisfied as to your movements the past week or so. Unless you can shed any light on your husband's? Something we've all missed?'

That threw her the tiniest bit, but not for long. 'I'm not sure I like your tone, or your accusations.'

'I haven't made any accusations,' Smythe said. 'My tone's calm and neutral, but it shouldn't be. Because we called you and said we'd come round to speak to your husband, and he isn't here. So someone has wasted our time.'

'He's not a prisoner,' Mrs Finch said. 'Though the amount of times he's had to speak to the police this past week . . . because of something that happened in this street, God rest her soul. You're barking up the wrong tree.'

'We'll come back shortly,' Smythe said curtly. 'Call us if he gets back and we've missed him.'

'You'll find him out in the trees,' Mrs Finch said before closing the door. Even the security light blinked off on Smythe and McGill.

'Well, back into the scary woods we go,' McGill said.

'Aye, our own little fairy tale.'

'She's a cracker, eh?'

Smythe nodded. 'I bet she writes letters to the paper.'

'Bet she's got a Neighbourhood Watch sign, and means it.'

Smythe shook her head. 'Lost my patience there. You won't tell the interview panel, will you?'

'I'd tell them you were a saint. I was so pissed off, I wanted to practise the fucking euphonium in front of her.'

'I was so angry, I'd have listened to it.'

'So how are we searching? Split up? Actually, no, that's a terrible idea.'

'Never works out in *Scooby-Doo*.'

'Or anywhere else.'

'Let's just keep going and keep an eye out. If we have to go back to that house and wait until he arrives, or answers us, we will.'

'You reckon he was in the house? Stalling us?'

'It's odd, whatever's going on. I spoke to him earlier, and he said he'd meet us.'

McGill triggered the torch on her phone, and shone its milky beam through a faint mist among the trees.

'What's up?' Smythe asked.

'Thought I saw something.'

'Don't be doing the whole *Scooby-Doo* thing.'

'You started it.'

'No, you started it,' Smythe said.

'Wait . . . there, there it is.' McGill's torch rose. A red light blinked. There was a sound like fishing line reeling out, fast – a panicky sound.

'Yep. That's a drone.'

'So is Finch a registered drone owner?'

'Aye. And the gaffer reckons the victims are being tracked by drone.'

'It's on his doorstep, though,' McGill said. 'Bit much, eh?'

'If I'm honest, it's all we've got right now. Hey, that's not him, is it?'

It was. Vincent Finch was thrashing his way through some bushes in the lee of the birch trees. He looked up, startled, too late to make any reasonably explicable attempt to escape. He hid his face from McGill's torchlight. He wore a knee-length woollen coat, unbuttoned, and his green wellies were a little too big for him. His crazy-professor hair wasn't out of place among the curled, brittle fingers of the winter branches.

'What's going on?' he said. 'Switch that off!'

McGill aimed the light away from his face. 'Sorry,' she said. 'Just making sure it was you.'

'And who do you think I am?'

'Vincent Finch. I'm DS McGill, and this is DS Smythe. We're here to talk to you about your drones.'

'You've found it?' He took a step closer.

'Found what?' McGill asked warily.

'My drone, for goodness' sake! The one I'm looking for.'

He held a controller in his hand, lit by a landing strip of green LCD lights. He made no effort to conceal it, though there were deep side pockets on the woollen. He had a long stick, maybe a walking stick or a mop handle, in his other hand.

'When did you lose it?'

'I had two out tonight . . . one's gone missing. It's happened before.'

'We saw a drone,' McGill said. 'It was flying over us when we came out on the path. Not too far away.'

'Signal went off, camera went off . . . It's annoying. They're not cheap.'

'What were you using them for, if you don't mind my asking?' Smythe peered closely at the patch of bushes Finch was still thrashing.

He paused. 'I've had some trouble,' he said. 'With some of my properties.'

'You still in that game?' McGill asked.

Finch raised his head, glaring at her. 'It's not a game. It's my living.'

'What kind of trouble?'

'Biblical plagues, would you believe. Rats. Cockroaches. Fly infestation, the other week. Middle of bloody winter! All mysteriously breaking out in properties I'm trying to develop.'

'How long has this been happening?'

'On and off, for about a year and a half.'

'How do the drones come into it?'

'I fly them to keep an eye on the properties after they've been finished.'

'You've not got security?'

'Sometimes. They get past it. Whoever they are.'

'So you think someone's messing with your houses?' Smythe frowned. 'Who would do something like that.'

'No idea. Incidentally, have you met my ex-wife?' He laughed bitterly.

'You think she's got something to do with it?'

'I have the right to remain silent.' He continued thrashing. 'I've pinpointed the place I lost contact . . . Around about here.'

'And why were you out here, particularly?'

'Because one of my sites is over the brow of the hill, over there. New flats, just up. They've been wired and finished. Then, would you believe it, some rats got found a couple of days ago. On the one site I'd had a problem with staffing on the security side of things. Bloody filthy. Here's one for fact fans – I was bidding against Avalon King for that one.'

Smythe considered this for a moment. 'You share a son with Nicole, is that right?'

'That's right. He lives at the Ponderosa . . . He'll be off like a shot soon as he gets into uni. Far away from her. He wanted to stay with me, you know? But he didn't want to upset his mum. No one wants to upset his mum.'

McGill cleared her throat. 'So you don't have a good relationship with Nicole Kingsley, then?'

His laughter was infectious. 'You met Nicole?' he said. 'You know who she is? Where she came from? I honestly believe that if it wasn't for Shane I'd be in with the foundations on a nice plot of family homes by now.'

'Christ,' McGill said. 'How did you meet her? I mean, I don't want to be weird, or anything, but you two . . .' She tilted her hands in parallel.

'Yeah. I ask myself the same question. The answer is, I had money and contacts. She just had money. Wanted to take old Raglan's cash and make it legitimate. Succeeded, as well. Once she got started she didn't need me.'

'Sounds like money-laundering to me,' Smythe said.

'Sounds like, yes, but isn't. Nicole's not daft.'

'Avalon King's doing well,' Smythe said. 'That means Nicole's doing well. So why would she want to put you out of business?'

'Spite, and the fact that I'm still competition. She's got what they call reputational damage, owing to her charming background. People would rather go with me than her. Plus, she likes stepping on toes. Mine, mostly, but just about anyone else's too. They say she's got more of Raglan in her than her three brothers, and I think they're right about that. Raglan was mental, but he wasn't daft. The brothers . . . let's say they came out of the shallower end of the gene pool.'

'You ever get bother from them?'

'Nah. Nicole wears the trousers.'

McGill asked, 'Still doesn't explain why you got together. I mean, you said you had money – an inheritance, was it?'

He cocked his head at her. 'You been spying on me?'

'Aye,' McGill said coyly. Smythe was discomfited to see her flirting quite so openly, but let it run.

'Well, she has the body of an angel, I'll give her that. And she can give you patter. I met her at the Piano Bar one night. Had no idea who she was until our third or fourth date. I wondered why people acted all tense whenever she showed up. I thought it was because she was beautiful. One of the doormen at some club or other put me right. It ended in a complete farce. I was glad to be shot of her, really.'

'Know what else I found out? When I was spying on you?' McGill asked. 'I found out that drone owners have to be registered . . . and you are. Expensive hobby, no?'

'I can afford my toys,' he said simply. 'Second childhood. Always wanted to be a pilot. Might take lessons in that too.'

'Do you take films with your drones?'

'I have done. Western Isles, Campsie Fells, Loch Lomond, you name it.'

'Could we see them? Would that be cool?' McGill asked.

'Sure. I've got them all somewhere. You'll want to see the

ones of these woods, eh?'

McGill brightened. 'Now you mention it, that would be very cool.'

Smythe cut in. 'What do you think has happened to the drones you lost? Tech problem, maybe?'

'Not one of these,' Finch said firmly. 'Best in the market. Top of the range.'

'What's your theory?'

'I think another drone has taken it out.' He sighed. 'Let's head back to the house. Belinda will be delighted to see you.'

'She already has been,' Smythe commented drily.

'Yeah, she told me you were coming, but not till later. Sorry about that. Anyway, I've got the videos all backed up on the cloud, and a few memory sticks as well.'

'It would be great to see those,' McGill said. 'Maybe give me a wee shot with one too?'

'I can do that,' Finch said brightly. 'You can climb into my cockpit – I've got one in the loft.'

Dear God, Smythe thought. Horny dads. Spare us.

'You know,' Finch went on, 'I've absolutely nothing to hide. Whatever you're looking for from me, there's nothing to tell you. Honestly. But I guess there might be a wee clue somewhere.'

'I'll get you a medal if there is,' McGill said.

41

Tait knuckle-rapped the window, driver's side, which irritated Slater. He stabbed at the button, but kept his face neutral as the window lowered. 'I'm sorry, sir, but I've just had my car washed. Why don't you try the local welfare office?'

Tait frowned. 'I think I'd be more worried about what's on the inside if I was you.'

'You only kept me waiting five minutes,' Slater said. 'You're slipping, boy.'

'It's Myles, by the way,' Tait said, walking round the car to open the passenger door. He had stacked two takeaway coffee cups in one hand, and had to angle his body awkwardly as he got in to avoid spilling them. 'Or Mr Tait. Or DS Tait.'

'DI Tait soon. Am I right?' Slater locked eyes with him, still smiling.

Tait didn't respond. But he didn't flush or flinch either. 'Here. You want to clear the crap out of your holders so I can set one of these down?'

'It's all clear. You go for it.'

'And you're welcome, by the way.'

Slater pulled away before Tait could secure the seatbelt. 'Thanks. Why'd you choose the Kiosk? I could have picked you up.'

'I'm happy to meet you halfway.'

'It isn't halfway, though, is it? I could have got you from your house . . . but you don't want me to meet you at your house, for some reason.'

'You'd take the look off the place.'

'Quite a nice house, all the same,' Slater said. 'Nice big bedrooms.'

'You what?'

'I mean, I had a look when you put it on the market. Took it off sharp enough, though. Change your mind? Nobody biting?'

'The wind-ups and carry-on . . . you know, they're going to get you killed one day.'

'Keep fantasising about it. One day you might get your wish.'

Tait tried to blow air down the sip-hole in the polystyrene lid. 'If you must know, I was at the office. Tying up some loose ends. Following tips, ruling folk out.'

'Mention that to the interview panel.'

'They'll know it already. How about you? Turn anything up?'

'Not really. Following the gaffer's hunches.'

'Any of them worth anything?'

Slater shrugged. 'You know the gaffer. His hunches have a funny wee habit of turning out right.'

'Except when they don't.'

'Well, we're a team. What're your thoughts, then? Any suspects?'

'I think the guy's a ghost.'

'The guy we're going to talk to can tell us a bit about that.'

Tait ventured a drink of coffee. 'I meant – he's no one. In the background. We haven't spoken to him yet. He's not on our radar. Probably never been in bother before. And he's going to do it again. Papers are gasping for it, anyway. If there's anyone in the frame at the minute, it's Laybourn.'

'Weird guy. Ex-army, and you would think it to look at him, but, speaking to him, you'd think he was more likely a cult leader or something.'

'Yeah, I can see that being Mr Jack-in-the-Box.'

'Fucking papers,' Slater said.

'Whoever spilled the details is at fault there.'

'Definitely victim one's mother,' Slater said. 'I don't think you'd stop her talking with a gag. Anyway, best we get through the tunnel.'

'He heading south?'

'He was picked up going through Paisley.'

'Could we not have stopped him leaving in the first place? And don't we have his van in storage anyway?'

'He's hired another one. Guy's got to work. And we've got nothing to charge him with. Besides, I want to know what he's up to.'

'Doesn't he work for a distribution company?'

'Sometimes. And sometimes he works for himself. Leaves wee adverts in shops, local guides you get through the door, message boards and social media. That's how he got hired for the Hazell Court drop-off. Wonder if he gets much business through that, in fact?'

'Nice,' Tait muttered.

They drove in silence, taking the tunnel at Anniesland. Slater was going to joke about seeing who could hold their breath longest, but, studying Tait's narrowed eyes, he thought, no. No jokes. What's the point?

'Is Lomond still going ahead with his mad scheme?' Tait asked suddenly.

'Yep. Not to be deflected. He reckons that's the key.'

'What's he looking for? Secret tunnels?'

'Exactly that.'

'He'll be believing the UFOs and ghostie theory next.'

'The guy's getting into the houses somehow, and we don't know how. No witnesses, no fingerprints, no hair, no blood, no footprints, even. So there's something we've missed.'

'Could end up with his jotters on this one. He almost got taken off the Ferryman case.'

'He's caught a few dafties. They'd be mental to sack him.' Slater kept his tone neutral. Partly to suppress anger, partly to see how wide this muppet would open his mouth.

'He's taking his time on this one. People will end up dead.'

'How would you go about lifting our guy, then? Share your theories.'

'I don't think he's anything to do with property companies or anything like that. There's no motive. No link between the victims. He's just a sicko.'

'Avalon King houses both times.'

'Not the homeless guy – who we still don't know anything about.'

'We know enough about how he lived; a couple of snouts came in. Off the grid, on the gear, desperate, about as vulnerable as a grown man can get. Gaffer reckons he was practice. So give me some more of your theories.'

'I'll keep them to myself. And I'll wait and see what our guy Laybourn is up to.'

'Think it's him, don't you?'

'He's the only clear link, isn't he? We know he dumped a body. That'd be good enough to charge him, for me.'

'Except for the stuff that clears him. But' – and Slater raised a hand to cut off any protest – 'he's as close as we get, I'll give you that one.'

'We're heading into the sticks here.' Tait frowned at the houses, growing grander but more sparse as the city limits receded.

'Satnav says he's about half a mile ahead. Turned off at . . . hey, a quarry. Senses twitching yet, mate?'

Tait gulped down the last of his coffee. 'They're rarely wrong.'

42

Tait shook his head and made a kissing sound with his teeth. 'He can't be for real, this guy.'

Slater sighed. 'How'd you mean?'

'He's under investigation for murder . . . I mean, whether he knows it or not, it must have registered somewhere that we're interested in what he's up to. And he drives out into the boonies, doing Christ knows what.'

Slater scratched his scalp. 'I dunno. As I said, guy's got to work.'

'He's up to something. I know it. Here we go . . . Where the hell is this? Satnav doesn't know.'

Slater said nothing, concentrating on keeping a fair distance from Daniel Laybourn's Transit van. It was a brand new rental, and nippy with it. Tait had chided Slater for letting the white blob get so far ahead of them. They were heading out into the Renfrewshire hills now, and a fine mist appeared as the two vehicles dropped into a dell. This would seem spooky, Slater thought, if it was a film. Right now, it was just a pain in the arse.

'If he does anything daft like switch off his lights and turn off somewhere, we won't see him,' Tait said.

'Got a good reason to lift him then, don't we?'

'He's slowing up . . . Christ, get the brakes on, eh?' Tait said. He gripped the handle of the passenger door, and Slater briefly entertained the idea that he might leap out, action-movie style, and perform a forward roll on the roadside.

'Calm yourself,' he said, though he kept a close eye on the rear-view mirror as he braked, for fear someone would clobber them from behind.

'He's turning.'

'I can see that, Columbo.'

The mist had thickened, and the red lights ahead took a sharp left into a side road concealed by tall trees whose nude branches reached out to each other across a hollow. Slater's eyes widened; there was no sign of the van. He put on some speed, the car lurching over the uneven surface before he spotted a group of squat shapes in a clearing.

'There he is,' Tait pointed. Catching Slater's look, he added, 'Just in case you missed it. Don't get tetchy.'

The van was parked in the centre of a ring of shipping containers, blue and white and yellow. Slater braked to a halt and killed the lights as the van door opened and Laybourn got out.

'What the hell is he wearing?' Tait asked. 'Looks like a hazmat suit.'

'That's exactly what it is. Or a boiler suit, maybe . . . looks like he's gone back to 1989 for a rave.'

They sat in silence for a while, watching him pull on a pair of gloves. For a second or two, he seemed to stare straight at Slater and Tait in the car, his hooded eyes unblinking. Then he fitted a surgical-style mask over his face and opened up the back of the van.

'What the hell?' Tait said, leaning forward to peer over the dashboard.

'Something he doesn't want to be touching, by the looks of it,' Slater said, watching the white-clad figure with the black gloves struggling to lift out a box and then allowing it to crash to the ground. Laybourn pulled out a carpet knife from a zip pocket and cut the seals on the box, then tipped it up and stepped back fast.

'Can't see it,' Tait said, nose almost touching the windscreen. 'What do you reckon?'

'Hard to say cos of the mist. You'd think it was lava the way he jumped back.'

'He's going for another one.'

Laybourn heaved a much larger box from the back of the van, and subjected it to the same rough treatment. This time, it was clear what was inside.

Both men flinched as if Laybourn had indeed poured a torrent of lava from the reinforced cardboard. Tait actually lifted his feet from the floor.

Slater unbuckled his seatbelt. 'I think it's about time we had another wee chat.'

As they walked towards the site, Laybourn spotted them, dropped a third box and ran.

The lava stream of rats – tails, feet, moving fast – diverted around the detectives like water torrenting past rocks in a burn. Slater leapt aside, surprising himself with his reflexes. Tait foundered for a while, arms aloft like a high-wire act. Then Slater spotted some of the rodents scampering around their new playground, investigating the shipping containers, and cleared his throat. 'When I used to go to my uncle's house he had all these ancient paperbacks, you know? I was always trying to find dirty bits. Anyway, one of them had this big rat on the front, with horrible teeth, and the book was about rats eating people.'

Tait's head swivelled slowly. 'That wouldn't have been *The Rats*, would it?'

'That's the one. Anyway, just came to mind.'

'Right. So you don't really mind rats.'

A dropped heartbeat. 'What makes you say that?'

Tait nodded at Slater's feet, and there was something in the seriousness – it was close to actual concern – that made Slater lurch even before he spotted the rat an inch away from his toe. He kicked it, with a near-perfect form and connection that would have had him purring had he done it at the five-a-sides. There was a clear impression of the rat in silhouette, its horrible human-like paws outstretched, tail slightly curving in the air, against the grey sky.

Slater cupped his hands around his mouth and called out, 'Dan! Do us a favour, mate. We're going to find you. Now show yourself, mate.'

There was a silence, apart from the bustle of tiny limbs, then a muffled voice said, 'Nah.'

'C'mon, mate,' Slater said. 'We need to talk. You can help us nail this Jack-in-the-Box character. I know it's not you' – Tait frowned but said nothing – 'but maybe you know who it is. C'mon, it's getting cold out here. We won't bite.'

A head appeared above one of the shipping containers. It had a disembodied quality to it that made Slater laugh. Hysteria, he supposed.

'Should I get hold of a lawyer?'

Slater gestured to the rats still scurrying over the ground. 'Take your pick, pal.'

43

Tait drummed his fingers on the desktop in interview room one. 'OK. Let's start with an easy one. Explain the rats to us.'

Since they'd brought him in to give a formal statement, Laybourn's demeanour had changed. He sat with his arms folded, but this was the only defensive thing about him. He seemed calm, relaxed, as he leaned back in his seat. 'Not sure I want to talk about that, really.'

'We were there,' Tait snapped. 'It looked to us as if you were tipping boxes filled with rats out on waste ground. That's what it looked like.'

'It can look like whatever you want it to,' Laybourn said. He had a twinkle in his eye – not the kind the hash-heads got, in Slater's experience, though you'd have bet your life on the man being one. It was the glint of the flyman, the guy who knows something and wants you to know he knows something, but won't give it up without a wee carry-on first. Slater had a headache. He took a deep breath and pinched the bridge of his nose.

'I dunno, Dan . . . you look a bit like the Pied Piper.'

Laybourn sniggered. 'Aye, I do need a haircut.'

'Suits you, mind. You know that actor Sam Elliott? *Tombstone*? You look a bit like him.'

'Don't know the guy, but I'll take it as a compliment.'

'C'mon, Dan. You've committed a crime – animal cruelty, for a start. The SSPCA are very interested in what you're up to. Maybe more interested than we are.'

Laybourn's shoulders came up. 'Cruelty?'

Slater nodded. 'Animal cruelty. They've got rights. You're not cruel to animals, are you, Dan?'

'Exact opposite, mate. Tell you that now.'

'So tell us,' Slater said. 'Help us, we'll help you.'

'You feel a connection with living things. *I* feel a connection with living things, rather. Even if I'm just walking through the trees. Even if it's only pollen in the air. Won't be long before the light changes and we get the pollen, you know.'

The silence that followed was so unbearable that Laybourn's lawyer looked as if he wanted to break it; he was practically bouncing on his seat.

'Anyway, I was given this job,' Laybourn went on. 'Deliver some boxes. Bit like the dead guy. I don't ask too many questions. I was asked to take these boxes to a house before it went up for sale. Or out for rent. Same difference. I let these cockroaches out. I knew it was dodgy, but the money was good.'

'When was this?' Tait asked.

'Tail end of last year – October maybe.'

'What was the house?'

'New block of flats. Tanner Close, it was. Out Blairdardie way.'

'I think I know where you are.' Tait scribbled a note.

'No security?' Slater asked.

'Not on that occasion. It was cockroaches, man . . . by the time I'd done what I was told I felt terrible.'

'You didn't try to sort it out?' Tait asked.

Laybourn laughed. 'Yeah, you try herding a couple of hundred cockroaches. Let me know how you get on.'

Tait's scribbling sped up. 'I meant, with the person who hired you.'

'I don't know who it was. Cash-in-hand job.'

'Same as the body in the fridge?' Slater asked.

'I don't think it was the same number or name . . . John, he called himself. Seemed like the same deal, though.'

'And it was the same guy who hired you to pick up the rats?'

'No, that was someone called Noel.'

'You get a lot of these cash-in-hand jobs,' Tait remarked.

'I'm a small businessman.'

'Doesn't mean you should just take any job going though, does it?'

'I'm a very cheap small businessman.'

'So when did this Noel hire you?'

'Two days ago. Just before you took my van off me. It's costing me to hire one, you know. I can get mate's rates at the plant hire place, but I need my van back.'

'Your van's connected to a murder – I wouldn't bet on you getting it back any time soon,' Tait said. 'If you want it back at all, you need to start being honest with us.'

'I am being honest with you,' Laybourn sighed. 'This is the thing I don't like about the polis, if I can keep being honest with you. Implications. Insinuations. It's like being back at school. They just want to keep you on your toes. You want to keep me on *my* toes.'

'Where did you pick up the rats?' Slater asked.

'Same place I dropped them off. Those old shipping containers. Christ knows how they got there, or what was in them. I picked up the trailer. That was the job.'

Tait frowned. 'So . . . you picked up the rats and went where?'

'Well, I was due to drop them off at Killen House.'

Slater nodded, catching Tait's eye. 'New-build flats. Clydebank. I know where you are.'

'That's it. Well, I stopped off for a pee. As one does.'

Tait raised his eyebrows. Said nothing.

'And when I was coming back to the van and passed the trailer, I heard the noise.'

'You didn't hear anything when you picked the trailer up?'

'Nope. But when I'd stopped . . . well, it was obviously rats in the boxes. Lots of them. So I took a decision. I contacted the Noel guy. Said that I had got there, and the boxes were empty. Made it sound as if they'd got out, like. Then I drove back and let the rats go. Not sure what else to do with them.'

'You could have called the SSPCA.'

'I could have,' Laybourn agreed. 'Also, I'm not as daft as I look. Think I want the jail? Look, I didn't want to transport the cockroaches. I did what I was told. I'm not proud of that. I took the money. I took the container to the flats. You know about that. But the rats . . . I drew the line at the rats. I mean, it was someone trying to infest the new flats, wasn't it? I don't know, though. Not for sure. Whatever they were meant for, I didn't want anything to do with it. So I stiffed the guy.'

'Have you been in contact with him again?'

'Text message, aye. I think he said he was off to check it out.'

Slater got to his feet a second before Tait. He excused himself from the interview room to make a call. When he got back a few minutes later, he tried to appear at ease, with his usual lack of success.

'Let's talk about when you met Vincent Finch out on your walk.'

'Aye . . . well,' Laybourn said. 'It was a bit weird. He was out bushwhacking, you know? Jungle warfare stuff. He didn't like the look of me, told me to my face, as well. He's seen me about. I walk the woods. You know that.'

'You said he was looking for his drone.'

'That's what he said. Said someone had got his drones. Expensive ones. He blamed me – was questioning me, asking what I knew. I said I'd seen UFOs out here, but they weren't like a drone. These were big ones. Actual UFOs, maybe. Who knows?'

'You called it in,' Slater said. 'That's weird.'

'Weird how?'

'Well, you're not a grass. You didn't grass anyone up for the cockroaches and rats. Why grass up Vincent Finch?'

Laybourn shrugged. 'It was dodgy. Wasn't it? About the lassie. I'm thinking of the lassie. What happened to her. That's why I called you.'

44

Lomond took the underground. It was a little treat to himself. In terms of stations, he had no favourites, but he did feel a yearning whenever Hillhead zipped past the windows. It spoke to him of the West End, Kelvingrove Art Galleries and, on extremely rare occasions, beery summer Sunday nights in Ashton Lane. To admit to these things was of course to submit to ridicule, even among his own family. 'Ashton Lane, is it?' Slater had once brayed. 'Tapas? Wee fancy coffees? You're an epicurean, you.'

But Slater wasn't here. Hardly anyone was here, in fact, as Lomond let the escalators take him down at forty-five degrees to St Enoch station, the biting cold of January suddenly changing as if enveloped in gentle hands.

The trains were new and beautiful, granted. But Lomond missed the colours of the old service. Bright orange was not normally something he gravitated to, for more than one reason, but down here its brash tones were muted. The seating in the old carriages had been brown and beige, like the flooring, and this had granted a sense of comfort. Now, the panelling on the walls was stark white, as was much of the décor. Yet there was still that cocooned feeling as you sat down. Taller people had to look lively, and some had to crouch: it was easy to bang your head if you stood up too fast. The adverts bore images of smiling, peach-complexioned young people promoting university courses and the promise of a folk festival at Kelvingrove bandstand, which Lomond thought sounded quite good, until he noticed that the poster was five months out of date.

Another reason Lomond liked the underground was that no one could phone him there. Signals were cut out. This was something he had come to recognise as a rare guilty pleasure, and also a brief dereliction of duty. They could wait until he got to Govan. Whatever turned up. A quick spin on the underground allowed him to drift, to think of nothing.

The train moved off with a mechanical shriek. A lightning flare of blue in the dark. Just Lomond, alone. In the dark tunnels he caught sight of himself in the window opposite. He looked depressed. He supposed he usually did.

Lomond thought of Kelvingrove and bright spring leaves, of a nice bitey pint out of Brel, dinner somewhere overpriced, maybe a film at the Grosvenor. It was sunny in his head, dark and cold and misty above. Once the stop came round – he had some company by this point: a couple of workmen and a few older ladies – he snapped out of it. Today was the day. Today Lomond would put it all together. He was sure of it.

*

Lomond arrived at Myrtlewood Crescent. He caught up on the phone calls he'd missed, with one particularly excited one from Slater about Daniel Laybourn, something about rats. This triggered a deep percussive sound in Lomond's mind, but he only made a note and filed it away.

The crew came in. Heavy boots and overalls, gloves and hats. The site foreman, James, a man with husky-blue eyes and a brow like an ice shelf on the verge of collapse, seemed incredulous.

'Everything?'

'That's what I said. Start with the patio. I want it all dug up. The walls pulled apart.'

'You've not told us what we're looking for.'

'Anywhere there's a space. Even if it doesn't seem likely someone can squeeze in. I want access to the roof checked.

Anywhere that doesn't fit with the plans, that looks off the grid.'

The blue eyes widened. 'The entire house? Seriously?'

Lomond met that stare, held it. 'I'm in charge here, James. I want it done. What I need to know is how someone could creep into the house without unlocking the back door. There has to be a way. Down to the level of a tunnel. Some way of climbing up the walls like a lizard. Anything like that.'

The foreman sniffed. 'This the place where the lassie was done in, eh?'

'This is the place where the woman was murdered, yes.'

'Hey, maybe he got delivered in the post? That's his name, eh? Jack-in-the-Box?'

The man's expression was so open, almost innocent, that Lomond quelled the impulse he had to butt it. 'You trying to be funny?'

'Seriously, that's a better bet than anyone tunnelling in. I mean, Christ–'

'Do what I'm asking you to do – and do it fast. There's something not adding up.'

He watched them file in, listened to the sounds of industry. Curiously comforting. Just as he had on the tube, Lomond felt a wave of nostalgia. Proustian, that was the word. Lomond hadn't read a word of the man's books, but he knew the meaning of this one. He'd grown up near a yard. He'd heard chippies at work, hammering, sawing, singing, swearing. He'd heard timber fall, with no forest nearby. This was the same, except the work was destruction. Sledgehammers. Falling plaster. Meticulously painted sideboards, cracked and splintered. Shouts of warning, or merriment. Crumbling brickwork. And then, a blessed pause.

The foreman came out, on his face the greasepaint glow of white plaster in the places where he didn't sweat. 'Might be something,' he mumbled.

Lomond followed him into the ruin. Chaos: holes in the wall, floorboards uprooted. Nothing unusual in the guts, but the guts were a mark of shame. He felt the dead woman's presence. She'd been houseproud. She'd worked hard; the place had been spotless. This was a new desecration, insult upon injury. All Lomond's fault.

'Here,' the foreman said. He indicated the space beneath the bed.

'What am I looking at?' Lomond said, irritated.

'Think it's a safe or something,' the foreman said. 'Not combi-locked, or anything. You might want to take a look . . .'

Lomond felt fear – imagining sexual paraphernalia, vintage porno, perhaps the black casing of hard drives, more sinister than any bright pink hues in magazines. But it was worse than that. Boxes of keepsakes. Precious things. A teddy bear reduced to a stump with button eyes and the stitching on the mouth pulled loose, maybe through too much kissing. A child's white-bound leather bible and prayerbook. Birthday cards. Love letters bundled and squeezed tight by elastic bands. Framed pictures of parents and grandparents. All these things, these relics, that had outlived her.

Anger swelled in him. Rare, slow to rise, but unstoppable. He placed the teddy back on top. 'That's just a cupboard, basically. I'm looking for a way in and out. A tunnel. A hatch. A teleport system. An escape pod . . . an actual panic room. Somewhere someone can hide. Somewhere he could creep in without being seen.'

The foreman took a more conciliatory tone. 'There was a good CCTV set-up here.'

'It shows nothing. The guy got in; he killed a woman, then he got out. We don't know how. *I* don't know how.' Lomond sounded desperate. He'd wasted the morning. He'd grown cold, and so had whatever leads they had. Even the ersatz bomb had turned up nothing significant. Lomond needed to sit down. The canvas cover spread across the bed was frosted with dust, chips of plaster. The carpets were stripped, rolled up.

And nothing. All day, nothing. The crew were only hired for so long. Lomond went outside and rested on a covered garden bench. He gazed across the fake grass, now rolled up to expose the hard-packed frigid earth. Nothing. He got up and trailed a hand along the moss-effect covering on the fence. Nothing behind there either: no conjuror's trick.

Slater called, 'How's it going?'

Lomond placed his thumb and his ring finger on his temples. He squeezed. 'Nothing,' he said. 'Nothing's turned up. No tunnels. No hatches. They've torn the place apart.'

'How can there be nothing?'

'I don't know! I'll be happy to ask the guy responsible when the time comes!' Lomond took a breath. 'Sorry. What turned up with Laybourn?'

'Rats.'

'Say that again?'

'Aye. Rats. Remember the exterminators we saw at Myrtlewood? He's been hired to plant rats and cockroaches, would you believe it? We caught him dumping boxes full of rodents in the middle of nowhere. Had an attack of conscience, disobeyed orders. He made it sound like it was a big deal. Oh, and the background checks came back. Guess how many men Laybourn killed twenty years ago?'

'Don't mess about, Malcolm. I'm tired.'

'Four. Four people.'

'Smother any of them?'

'Nah. Guns and, on one occasion, his bare hands. Worked with early drone warfare, apparently, at the end of his time in the forces. No mention if he shot anyone by remote control. He was in demand as a private contractor when he left the army. Decided to wander the forests like Gandalf, shifting gear in his van. Still a suspect, gaffer. A big one. And there's one other thing. We had a wee poke about the shipping containers where Laybourn dumped his furry friends. It turns out someone was living there.'

Lomond watched the workmen file out of the house. Ruined, he thought. All on account of him. He'd been so sure.

'Let's follow it up. I need something to chew on.'

45

One thing Shane had liked about his grandfather: the name. Raglan. It was like a character from an ancient Icelandic saga. A berserker, arms spread wide, a chest you measured in feet, not inches. Shoulders that made goalposts feel insecure. The reality may actually have tallied with this, in fact.

Although his mother and father never spoke about it, Shane had heard the rumours. People disappearing. People encased in the foundations of his property empire. Which Shane's mother had expanded. But Raglan was something else. A link to an unimaginable past. It wasn't true to say Raglan had risen from nothing – no one ever did, really. His dad had owned some bookies, then some pubs, and then there was Raglan. Shane's uncles, Struan, Tosh and Ranald. Hard names, tending to the north, hanging a right past Orkney.

Shane had been mortally afraid of him. Now, even in his decrepitude, there was still something frightening about Raglan. Shane was maybe an inch or two taller already, but the breadth and bearing of the old man was still there, dressmaker's lines you could put through the shoulders and hips and elbows, even if the head had sunk. He still had his hair – Shane was sure he'd inherited it, looking at the old photos of the black-haired, scowling man that adorned too many walls in the family home. Now it was white, but thick and untidy as if it had been cut by someone with a sense of humour. Below, the jaw jutted comically – at one time it had been imposing, but now it looked as if something had come unhinged. The muscle was still there, though, filling out the stained grey jumper and joggie bottoms as he stood with his back to them, looking out of the window. The rest of his room in the nursing home was cosy, and far too warm. He had a view of the grounds, and beyond that the lights of Glasgow.

The face swung around, disconcertingly fast, to take in his grandson. The old man looked him up and down. 'Where's Tosh?' he said. Tosh was the middle son, the de facto head of the clan, and, everyone thought, the hardest. If you didn't count Nicole.

'Tosh is looking after his business affairs,' Shane said. He had learned not to make sudden moves in front of the old man. Even taking off his headphones had been akin to a gunfighter unlooping his belt, very, very slowly.

'Fuck are you?' Raglan asked, tilting his head to that dangerous angle. Shuffling his feet.

'I'm Struan.'

Confusion. It was said that Shane took after Struan – might have been his son. Apart from one detail. 'Eh? Struan? Struan's a ginger.'

Large hands, closing over the forearms. Still looked as if he worked out. Been a swimming star as a kid, had Raglan. Something terrible had happened to him since the days of the muscleman poses of the 1960s, the black bathing suits.

'It's just Shane trying to be funny, Dad,' Nicole said. 'And failing.'

'Shane?' The confusion remained. That could be a precursor to a wild swing. Nicole had been in the way of one of those, a long time ago. She had borne the black eye and burst nose with commendable chill. Patiently explained what had happened. Raglan hadn't hit her – it had been The Condition. It was Understandable. Shane had never been given one, though he supposed his number would come up eventually.

'Shane's my son,' Nicole said. 'With Vincent.'

'You're not still with that wanker, are you?' Raglan huffed.

'I'm not,' Nicole said, with a winsome smile.

'Good. Always thought he was a poof.' The old man stared at his grandson with a renewed curiosity. 'Shane, eh? What kind of name is that? You bent?'

'Well, it's better than a big jumble of consonants,' Shane said. He met his grandfather's gaze coolly.

'I've ripped somebody's jaw off their head,' the old man said, in a matter-of-fact tone. 'Oh aye, you should've seen that. Nobody made any smart remarks after that.'

'Especially not the guy who got his jaw ripped off.'

The old man cackled. 'Some mouth on him!'

'Yeah, he takes after his father,' Nicole said. 'We're going to have to go now, Dad. Been lovely to see you.' She kissed his cheek. The old man opened and closed his mouth, seemingly astonished at the gesture of affection.

'Got my papers?' he said.

'You got them this morning,' Nicole said. She guided him, subtly but firmly, towards his chair, his tartan blanket and the remote control.

'Shame about Eddie.'

'It is. Crying shame.'

'I'm going to his funeral.'

'Of course you are. It'll be nice to say cheerio.'

'Aye. He was old, right enough. Rickety.'

'It's a shame when they get that way.'

'I won't keep you,' the old man said, sinking into the chair. 'Mind and leave a window open for me, now.'

'The last time that happened, you squeezed out, Dad,' Nicole said.

'Not my fault if they can't lock their bloody windows! When am I getting home?'

'Soon as you're better.' The winsome smile again. Then Nicole nodded to Shane. He read the gesture and backed off.

'Bye, Granda,' he said.

'Bye, Glenda,' the old man said, and grinned, showing a gap in his front teeth big enough to admit a shotgun barrel.

In the corridor they nodded politely at the nurses, and squeezed past a resident inching forward on a walking frame. He was struggling a bit; Shane instinctively took him by the elbow. 'Want me to get a nurse?' he asked.

'You're fine, son,' the white-haired gentleman said. 'Room's at the end. Nearly there. Got to keep moving, you know. Old Eddie didn't.'

'Yeah, shame about Eddie,' Shane said. 'Take it easy now.'

Nicole watched this exchange without blinking. Once they were past the security doors and out into the cold air, she said, 'It's good that you can look after old people like that.'

Shane shrugged. 'We'll all be there one day.' Nicole said nothing. 'Can you drop me off at the top of the hill before we get back?'

'Sure. Any reason?'

Shane shrugged. 'Meeting someone.'

Nicole hid a smile. 'Oh, I see.'

'Just a pal.'

'You don't need to hide things from me, son. I've lived.'

'Haven't you just,' Shane muttered.

Nicole let that go. They strode down the tree-lined pathway towards the main road. 'I wanted to bring you out here to have a chat with you, in fact. It's been hard to catch up with you.'

'Sure. What's on your mind?'

'I know the police being in the house is weird. They have to do their work.'

Shane grinned. 'I notice you didn't mention that to Granda.'

'No. Granda doesn't like the police. Anyway, we have to let the police do their work. But I wanted to say . . . I'm proud of you.'

The boy cleared his throat. 'It was obviously a fake. Obviously.'

'The police didn't think so. They reckon you were a bit daft.'

'I was right, though,' he said, a surly tone now.

'You were. No denying it. And you sorted the situation out.

They could still be standing there in the kitchen now, waiting for the bomb squad to defuse it.'

'Had to defuse it anyway.'

Nicole pursed her lips. 'I gather your stepfather wasn't too happy.'

'Is he ever?'

'He cares. He thought he was going to die.'

'He dived for his son. Brave, I guess.'

'Well, instinct kicks in. His was to dive for Jared. Yours was to defuse a bomb.'

'There was no bomb,' said Shane. 'It was a wind-up.'

'That brings me to the next point.' They had reached the bottom of the hill, close to the public park where Nicole had parked the car. 'Any reason you can think of that someone would target us with a fake bomb?'

'Nothing to do with me.'

'You sure about that? I wonder what you're up to sometimes. All that time spent on your computer.'

'I can tell you one thing I'm not doing – making pals with bomb hoaxers.'

'No, I know. But it does make me wonder – who's targeting us?'

'It's a bit weird, the box.'

She frowned at him. 'What do you mean?'

'There was a scarf or something, stuck in the lid.'

'So?'

'So . . . don't you go on the internet?'

She looked at him blankly. 'Sweetheart, I can't remember the last time I sat down to watch the telly. So what's the thing with the box?'

'It's to do with Jack-in-the-Box. Same with the guy who turned up dead in the old fridge at Hazell Court.'

'Well, maybe, maybe not. No one's breaking into our house though; I can guarantee you that.'

'Nah, he'd be mad to do that. Makes you think, though.

It must be something to do with us, or he's targeting us. Or something.' The boy shivered. 'Maybe we're suspects.'

'Maybe we are. But the police'll catch him, sooner or later. Right now, we're going somewhere else.'

Shane gave a lopsided smile. 'Taking me to McDonald's?'

'Oh, better than that.' She looped an arm through his. 'I'm taking you to the sale.'

'Sorry?'

'Eddie's sale. There's an auction of his stuff.'

'Who's Eddie?'

'You heard your granda – old man, lived down the block from him. Died the other week. No close relatives. He had a few antiques and first-edition books. Stuff's gone to auction. For an absolute song.'

'Right,' Shane said uncertainly.

'C'mon. We'll get a bargain then put it on a proper auction site. I've had some of the stuff assessed. Hey,' she whispered, coming close, her perfume strong in his nostrils, 'I'll split the money with you. It'll be our secret.'

'Sounds good to me. I'll defer to your judgement.'

She glared at him with something like passion, something certain and fixed. 'It's a skill to master, son, because let me tell you, you've got to learn one thing in life, and that's profit. Your granda, whether he was ripping people's jaws off or not, he knew it, and he taught us all that. You do more damage making deals than you do with your bare hands. Know why? Because you never get caught. You need to have an eye for a deal. You need to see it through. And you always make sure you get paid out.'

Shane took a long, slow breath. His eyes were wet. 'Why are you telling me this? Auctions? It's weird. It's not right.'

'Right and wrong doesn't come into it. You've got a good life. You've got a decent brain. You're good-looking. And you've got a name. Lots of things going for you. But if I was to die first, you might have a problem. You won't inherit everything. But, eventually, your brother might. Half-brother, I should say.'

'Brother,' Shane said sharply.

'You follow my meaning. So we're going to the auction. You're going to make some deals. You're going to get used to it. And soon you can go into business with me.'

'That'll be brilliant.'

'Won't it? Right?'

She crushed him with her embrace. This was as close as Nicole got to hugging her son. It was a curiously aggressive gesture. He wanted to shrink away. Instead he said, 'I'll let you start the bidding.'

46

The IT guy had put himself forward as liaison, and Lomond couldn't work out why. He was ponderously slow. There seemed something insolent in his slouch and his let's-see-that-again demeanour – either that or a carefully masked anxiety disorder. The drab, baggy clothes hung off his frame as if they couldn't wait for the blessed release of the washing machine. His name was Fahey and, he said, he'd been with the police for years.

'So, uh, I didn't catch your name?' Fahey said as he opened up a triptych of computer screens in a curtained room several fathoms down in Govan HQ.

'Inspector Lomond.'

'Right. I'll take you through the drone footage we got off Mr Finch.'

After a brief bumble through log-in screens and asterisked-off password fields, Fahey found the files. 'He keeps quite good records. All dated and filed.'

'He didn't initially strike me as that sort of guy,' Lomond confided. 'Hobbyists, though, eh? Some guys don't take anything as seriously as their wee pastimes.'

'Amen.' Fahey pursed his lips. 'Right, this is the first one. Whee, off we go!'

The first film was startlingly professional-looking, credit where it was due. Summer grass, gilded by what Lomond knew instinctively to be evening light – something in the red, not yellow or white, a base tone. 'Crepuscular, that's the word,' he said out loud. Fahey turned his head very slowly to gaze at him, but said nothing.

The picture rose, sci-fi fast, taking in a panoramic view of woodland. Lomond recognised it right away. 'That's the back of Myrtlewood Crescent.'

'Yeah. The woods. All totally verified, triangulated and pinpointed. Can give you the day, as well. This was in August. About five fifteen p.m.'

The drone rose vertically, no deviation, just a straight line up into the pale blue. Then it banked to the left, and skimmed the treetops. Birds – Lomond recognised a jay's blue and brown plumage – rose and arced away at the drone's progress.

'Big enough to scare the natives,' Lomond commented.

'Aye, that's a big drone. Hi-spec model. Now, this is a good bit of flying.'

A thrilling plunge through the trees, a Hollywood swoop. Lomond felt butterflies in his tummy at the illusion of velocity, of perspective, as green leaves and warm wood spread out before the drone. Surely it would crash, he thought. But, no, it followed a sure path through the interstitial spaces between the leaves on the canopy.

'He knows the trail,' he said.

'Aye. Now. Here's the houses.'

Fences came into view, one of them stained burgundy – that was Finch's own house. Then came the house of the dead woman, with its back fence overhung with the astroturf drapery.

'Weird stuff, that,' Fahey said. 'The fake grass. Not for me. Bad enough on the lawn, eh? She's got it hanging up.'

'Not for me either,' Lomond said. 'But I guess it keeps. No mess. Low maintenance.'

'Suppose there's that.'

'I hate it. I'm a gardener.'

'I've got a flat,' Fahey said, almost wistfully.

'Wouldn't have it on a windowbox, either.'

After another long pause, Fahey said, 'Heh.'

Before it reached the house next door the drone had

veered away, sharply, as if it had taken fright. 'Hold it there,' Lomond said. 'Can you spool the video back a bit?'

'Sure.' A couple of clicks, and the footage ran back slowly.

'There.' Lomond pointed. 'Freeze it there, please.'

A split-second was a cliché, but that's precisely what it was. 'Yep. There's a woman in the window,' Fahey said.

Lomond peered closely at the figure. The definition was excellent, and for a chilly moment Lomond wondered if she was clad all in white, like a shroud, or something from an adaptation of a novel by a Brontë. Then he realised she seemed to be wearing a hoodie, some sort of novelty animal pattern, like a sheep, or a llama. She had dark hair, a coffee cup in her right hand, and she appeared to be peering up into the sky, right at the drone.

'That the victim?' Fahey asked softly.

'Aye.'

'Christ. You must have seen it. The body. For real. You know, some folk ask me how I can do this job. I say I've got it easy compared to some.'

'I won't disagree with you.'

'OK to move on?'

Lomond paused a second on the woman in white, then nodded. 'OK. Let's run it on.'

There were six videos in total, lengthy pieces that swooped over Ben Lomond, that Appalachian blue on a rare hot day in July, trails of hillwalkers like dropped sweetie wrappers on the path and a boat trailing a billowing saltire across the water. Geese on the wing, thrillingly, drew close to the drone in another film. Then there was a trail across white sands as the tide drew in on one of the islands as the sun rose – an image so lovely and mesmerising that neither man spoke until it ended with a woman struggling to control a black dog in the surf.

'He's got an eye, has Mr Finch,' said Fahey.

'Yeah, these are all excellent. Hey . . . see that?'

Fahey frowned at the new image. 'That kid?'

'It's his son. Shane.'

On screen, a tall, broad-shouldered boy peered up at the drone, frowning slightly. A backpack was looped over one shoulder, and he was moving along the crescent, framed by a gap in the trees for an instant before the drone swooped away as if spooked.

'Bit weird, eh?' Fahey ventured. 'Spying on your son? Looks like an accident, maybe.'

'Maybe. Are there offcuts?'

'Oh aye – plenty of them. But they're all footage shot indoors, in his garage. Lots of false starts and crashes. Some only last seconds.'

Lomond nodded. Where once he had butterflies, now there was a sinking feeling. 'I'm going to have to go through them all. One by one.'

'I was afraid you'd say that,' Fahey said, folding his arms. 'Afraid, but prepared. Got them all lined up. Coffee?'

'Good man. Milk, no sugar, please.'

Once the coffee was placed on the edge of the desk – on top of an AC/DC coaster, Lomond noted with a smile – he asked, 'How about the security camera images?'

'I had those ready. Two seconds . . .' He brought up the images. 'This one's Myrtlewood Crescent, day of the murder. Recorded before, during and after. Weird of them to keep the camera running, but there it is.'

Lomond studied the image. 'Can you speed it up for me?' he asked. 'Not too fast – just enough so that I can make everything out.'

'Easy done.' Fahey worked his magic again, and the images moved quickly. A slow dawn breaking through thick night. Lomond sensed the pinkening of the snow clouds, knowing this was an illusion. The shot kept changing, a wide angle taking in every expanse of the garden in a fish-eye style. It moved from wall to wall, sweeping back and forth, as the light poured into one end of the garden then distilled across to the other side before it was interrupted by the old lady's frightened face. Even in the silence of the image, he thought he could hear her speaking, her flailing voice. Even at high speed, her mouth didn't look out of sync with her normal tempo.

'What's going on?' Fahey asked. 'She speaking through the door?'

'Maybe. I think she's shouting past the fence to the kid in the car. Maybe just shouting. I'm not sure. No audio, is there?'

'Nah, switched off.'

'Manually?'

'I checked that,' Fahey said, offhand. 'It had been switched off for weeks.'

'Strange one.'

'Yeah. It's customisable, as part of the system. I thought it was weird, but it goes back as far as their residency.'

'No chance it could have been turned off manually and deleted?'

'It doesn't look possible to do that and then re-upload the material to the server.'

'So it's more likely they just had it switched off.'

'Guess so. Loud noise can trigger the alarm. Maybe they argued a lot. Maybe they didn't want it recorded.'

Lomond pondered this for a moment as the footage spooled on. 'Let's go back to the time of death,' he said.

'Got it bookmarked,' Fahey replied grimly. The dead woman's mother receded, a plump, jerky marionette, creeping backwards, her hysterical face turning merely agitated, then becoming just concerned, before exiting stage left. 'Here it is. One-sixteen p.m.'

'Take it back maybe fifteen minutes before.' Lomond sighed as he watched the image return to its familiar sweep.

'Fast-forward again?'

'No. Now we watch. Keep our eyes peeled.'

Back and forth went the camera. The decking, with its thin crust of snow, broken only by crows' feet. The bird feeders, white-bearded sentinels. The lawn, its stiff green fronds breaking through the snow. By the wall to the left, beyond a row of white stones and the black soil, the hanging garden of the fake vine.

'Bloody ridiculous, that,' Fahey muttered.

'What is?'

'That plastic stuff.'

'The lawn?'

'Not just that. I mean, there's an idea behind it all, a kind of aesthetic. Know what I mean?'

'Kind of.'

'I mean the stuff at the back. The vines. Look at it. All fake.'

'You're right. And there's something else as well.' Lomond pointed.

'What – the hanging lamp?'

'It's off,' Lomond said.

Fahey shrugged. 'It is the daytime. Middle of winter, but it's daytime.'

'Then how come the ones in the opposite corner are on?'

'Good point.'

'They've not been on today. Make a note of this. We'll check back to see when they went out. For now, let's keep our eyes peeled.'

'You've checked for other ways in? Windows, hole in the fence . . . Christ, a tunnel?'

'Aye,' Lomond said, with a tone close to disgust. 'We've checked for that stuff. Early payday for the workies. And probably my P45.'

This would have been the time, Lomond thought. If he sneaked in, this is probably when he did it. Through the door and in. Right past the camera. But how? 'Possible to run past?' he speculated, the tip of his pen tracing the sweep of the camera.

'It's not out of the question. But running from where? He'd need to be behind the shed. Then he'd need to run full pelt up the path, without leaving any footprints. He might have reached the side of the decking, where the edge of that vine stuff cuts out the snowfall . . .' Fahey tugged at his chin, a curious reproof. 'I don't buy it, though. The angle changes, but not enough to totally shield someone running, what, twenty-five feet?'

'Twenty-eight and a quarter.'

'Then there's the snow. He'd have to have been a ballet dancer moving at the speed of light to get down those rocks, probably on his tiptoes, and the camera not pick him up.'

'That's true.'

They watched as the camera moved. One sixteen p.m. – round about the time Minchin had estimated Kath had been attacked.

The camera paused in its sweep. Just a flicker.

'See that?' Lomond said.

'Aye.'

'That's unusual.'

'It doesn't look like it's happened any other time,' Fahey agreed. 'But it doesn't actually pick up anything.'

'Is the camera motion-sensitive?'

'There is a motion sensor, but it's not that sensitive. Otherwise it'd pick up every squirrel and sparrow that passed through the garden; alarms'd be going off all the time.'

Lomond sighed. A curious sense of panic cinched his guts tight. An awful sense of helplessness, as if they could rescue the doomed woman at the press of a button.

Then there was a flare of light. 'That's triggered by the sensor,' Fahey said. He shifted his seat so he could peer more closely at the screen. 'But there's nothing.'

'Something moved there,' Lomond said suddenly.

'Where?'

'The vine. See it?'

Fahey paused and moved the image back two, three seconds, then ran it again, in slow-motion. 'What're we looking at?'

'Here.' Lomond indicated the leaves, a blanket of

unseasonably bright green. Bloody eyesore, Lomond thought again. 'You see that stirring?'

'Could be wind.'

'Could be, but it doesn't correspond with the background. Look again.'

'I kind of see what you're getting at . . . but it could be nothing.'

'It's not nothing. It's like a smudge, a smooth part appearing on a rough surface. And look – that stone, dead centre in the row.' Lomond indicated the white humpbacks breaking the dark sea of soil, unmarked by the snow. 'See that slight trail of light?'

'Not sure what you mean, to be honest with you.'

'There. See it? That sudden line of light.'

'It is a bit weird. Could be interference. Could be the wind.'

'There's something there.'

'We've watched it twice now. There's nothing there.'

The figure appearing by the side of the bath. Lomond thought of it, a waking nightmare, a night terror siphoned from the darkest depths of your mind. It was scary enough for a grown man, a copper – for anyone. Naked in the bath, nice and warm – the water temperature had still been tepid when forensics had arrived. Still cosy. Thinking of a cup of tea. Plenty of time before school collection time. Then this figure, rudely conjured. What face did the devil have? Did he grin? Was he expressionless? Was he masked? Maybe utterly lost in whatever compulsion he served. No longer a human face. No longer a human being.

Lomond's head snapped up. 'These images can be messed with, can't they?'

'How d'you mean?'

'Digital stuff. Hacking. These images can be hacked?'

'We've run all the diagnostic tests there are. The image hasn't been altered or uploaded. It would show on the metadata – be recorded on the system somewhere. No one's been into that system. All the logs show is it being armed when they're going out, or on full-time when the husband's away. It's a good system – high-spec.'

'It's here,' Lomond said. 'I know it. We're looking at it. It's here.'

Fahey said nothing. He sat awkwardly, cramped in on himself as the fatal minutes ticked away. There was no more stirring. No slickness on the stones lined up on the left.

'OK,' Lomond said. 'Now the young lad. The house where he was murdered. We're going to go through it all. I want to see it.'

47

No advance, no progress, nothing in Lomond's mind but the after-images from Fahey's screens. Nature's screenburn, the pistol flares of the snow, the skies, the sweep of the camera, the thin creep of the winter sun. These reconstructions were a sluggish windscreen wiper every time he blinked: Lomond wanted to keep his eyes closed, despite this mental interference.

'Hey.' Slater tapped him roughly. 'Not meditating or something, are you?'

'Meditating?' Lomond straightened up in his seat. 'Don't be daft. We don't have time for any thinking round here.'

'Fancy a roll and sausage?' Slater held out a grease-stained paper bag.

Had he the talent, Lomond would have wanted to paint the beautiful image. He sighed. 'Already had one.'

'That's not what I asked you.'

With the furtiveness of an addict pocketing his deal, the bag was in Lomond's hands before Slater saw him move.

'Chief been on the phone?'

Lomond nodded, taking in half of the roll in a single bite. 'I gather you heard?'

'Yeah, literally, from the other end of the office. Threaten you with your P45? Giving you twenty-four hours? Asking for results?'

'He'd like to do all of that and more. But after a couple of lines of screaming he went really quiet. Like he was reading out a prepared statement with a gun at his head. That's what threw me. Scared me, a bit, to be honest.'

Slater leaned on the edge of Lomond's desk, arms folded.

'You're not going to get taken off the case, gaffer. It's all he's got to threaten you with.'

'I know that. But he's got to save face. And Sullivan will want to mutually assent him to death. I heard they don't get on.'

'Big deal.' Slater looked exhausted, with lines etched on his already brutally thin features that Lomond hadn't noticed before. He also seemed to have sprouted some impressive late-onset acne at one corner of his mouth, perhaps a reflection of the fuel he was taking in from the canteen. But this was a stage in the investigation where you couldn't really judge anyone. Well, maybe Smythe could – she only ever moved a notch or two off immaculate, even on her worst days. 'It's a downer. But it looks like we're chasing a ghost.'

'Maybe we are.' Lomond became alert at that. He finished the roll, scrunched up the bag and lobbed it casually into a wastepaper bin an impressive distance away. 'What did you turn up at the shipping containers?'

'Looks like that's where fridge man was living,' Slater said. 'His personal effects were found in one of the containers. Edge of a life, gaffer. Grim. You seen a junkie's flat lately?'

'Not lately. Seen a few, though. Pre- and post-mortem.'

'Like that, but worse. Looked like he was sharing his living space with every kind of creature you can think of.'

'You lifted Laybourn?'

Slater nodded. 'Talking to him. He's on remand and saying nothing now. One was enough. He has solid alibis for the other two. But here's another thing. He was delivering near Nicole Kingsley's house when the kid-on bomb arrived. Made a drop six miles away, twenty minutes before, then nothing until two hours later after he went back to the depot. No sign of him on CCTV. Claims he pulled into a lane and had a sleep.'

'At least it wasn't another high-risk pee.' Lomond drummed his fingers. 'You're not sure about him, are you?'

'Nah. I think he's been used. Even if he did deliver the dodgy computer.'

'Any of his sacred receipts telling us anything?'

'Nah, nothing about a job to the Kingsleys' house. And he's not saying anything about one.'

'I don't think he's our Jack,' Lomond said. 'But I have to admit he's the closest we've got to drawing a line between all three cases.'

'Doubt he'll say a word to us now, though. "No comment", that's all we got. Want a crack at him?'

Lomond shook his head. 'Nah. Tait can have it. Or you, if you want.'

'I was thinking Tait is welcome to it.'

'Tait is looking forward to it,' said Tait, as he entered the room. He had an imperious air to him, Lomond thought, but then he usually did, despite being as crumpled as the rest of them. Swanning in. Leading with the chin. 'I think he's the guy.'

'He's a fit for the first victim, maybe. The rest . . . I don't see it,' Lomond said. 'Work on him, though. Hard.'

'You weren't expecting me to do anything else, sir?'

'He might spill a detail he forgot. This is a guy who was ordered to deliver boxes of rats and creepy-crawlies to new flat developments, thought about it, and decided to dump the live cargo back where he found them. If I'd murdered someone out there, I think the last thing I'd do would be to go back. In fact, I'm amazed he hasn't torched it. Who owns the place? Do we know?'

Tait gave a twisted grin. 'Would you believe it's part of Vincent Finch Enterprises?'

Lomond frowned. 'Seriously? This is getting tangled now.'

'Aye, he owns the land, and he owned the shipping containers, though no one's quite sure why. Apparently, he was planning to turn it into an out-of-city storage depot. Plans submitted to clear the woodwork and level it out, perimeter fence, security guards, the lot.'

'Enterprising boy,' Lomond remarked.

'The dead guy lived there. Lot of empty tins stacked up. Might have been on a survivalist trip.'

'I would have thought that was more Laybourn's thing.'

'Maybe so. We'll find out.'

Smythe appeared, with a giant refillable coffee mug, and nodded to all three. She was pale, and some of her hair had come loose.

'Hiya, Cara – how've things been?' Lomond asked.

Smythe laid her cup down, cleared her throat and counted off her fingers. 'I've eliminated the window cleaner, the guy wandering around with the dog lead but no dog, the private-hire driver who parked near Myrtlewood, and the guy who was reported for being a prowler. That was a good one – he was a school lollipop man just changing out of his uniform in a side street.'

'Lollipop not a giveaway?' Slater asked.

'Apparently not. So that was my day.'

'Good work,' Lomond said. 'He'll turn up soon.'

The other three stared at their shoes and said nothing, until Tait asked, 'Nothing from Myrtlewood Crescent?'

'No,' Lomond told him simply.

'Even, like, a panic room or something?'

'I said no.'

There was another silence.

Lomond crossed over to the whiteboard near his desk and wiped a space clean. 'I just wanted to tell you what I think happened.' Next to the whiteboard was a corkboard, with printouts attached. 'This is an analysis of the back windows. Now, Kath Symes had an appointment calendar on the wall opposite the kitchen window. Big boxes, big letters. Easy to read if you fly a drone overhead. We know for a fact that Vincent Finch flew drones over the gardens. He claims his machines got taken out of the air by another one.'

'Maybe it was a hawk?' Tait said. After a moment of astonishment, he went on: 'That's how you can take out a drone – fly a hawk. They do it at airports. Saves a fortune on counter-drone technology. Train a bird to recognise them, they sort the thing out, pronto.' He insisted: 'I'm telling you. Look it up.'

Slater clicked his fingers. 'What's that thing where you wear the big leather glove, and it's like in *Kes*, and you train falcons? What's that again?'

'That would be falconry,' Tait said slowly.

'Not bad,' Lomond said, scribbling a note. 'Bear it in mind. But Finch could be havering. That's the simplest answer: he's stalking people with his drones, people living in houses he sold to them. Nicole Kingsley's been targeted, and she's his ex-wife – that's a line to draw. Now there's this stuff with the rats and cockroaches. Someone up to no good. Trying to affect property prices? Any other reason?'

'Seems the obvious one,' Smythe said. The others nodded agreement.

'So he's on the list. He's using the drones to check calendars. Our second victim, they had a very similar wall calendar, easy to see from the top of the garden fence. The partner went for timed runs at specific times of the day – he was a keen runner, very precise, got his spare time for running almost down to the second. Did Celtman, fell-running, that kind of thing. So this guy stalked them with a drone, maybe to check their habits, but also to check when they would be alone.' Lomond noted this all down; the others followed suit. 'Next. What's the score with the killer? How's he getting around unnoticed?'

Smythe tapped her pen on the pad. 'I think there's something in what the two wee girls said. That they had a friend who was a ghost. Someone who spoke to them from the trees. They thought it was funny.'

'Good chance that's him,' Lomond said. 'It stood up?'

'Apparently. Both said the same thing. Backed each other up. Think their friendship caused a bit of a stooshie in both houses, which is an awful shame.'

'No description, though?'

'No. But I'm thinking Laybourn. His record. Para reg, possibly SAS. Trained in jungle warfare.'

Tait nodded. 'Yes. Spot on. Which one's the trained killer – him or Vincent Finch?'

'I don't know about trained,' Slater said, 'but if you believe the hype, and I do, the Kingsleys are practised killers. This rats and roaches carry-on affected both Finch and Kingsley's properties – there's some kind of turf war going on. Maybe it extends to dumping bodies.'

Tait's mouth twisted as it formed a retort, but he paused before uttering it. 'That's not the worst shout. One other thing about Laybourn – he's for hire. Maybe for serious dirty work. A lot of former special forces guys make a living like that abroad. Mercenaries, assassins. So, yeah, that ties in with Laybourn. As everything does, eventually. Regarding his alibis, all people have seen is a van, and parcels and packages delivered from a depot. Laybourn might have got a ringer in and hidden out in the woods. There are trees at the back of both houses.'

Lomond was scribbling everything down. 'This all makes sense, but the thing that's driving me mental is: how's he getting in? I thought there must be some flaw in the houses, something in the designs to exploit, but there's nothing. Ideas?'

To Lomond's dismay, there were none. They were reluctant students posed a tricky and possibly embarrassing question. Slater didn't even have a stupid comment for the rest to parry. Smythe came close to one, though seeing as it was Smythe no one took it that way. 'It's like he's the invisible man. Apart from the two wee girls, no one saw him get in, no one saw him get out.'

'And the security cameras weren't tampered with,' Lomond said. 'Front and back of the house. Full gardens. Nothing. If he managed to sneak in during a split second when the camera was turned away from the fences, then we are talking the supernatural. Or science fiction. It just doesn't look possible.'

The silence grew too heavy.

'Best we knock off for a bit. Tait, you're holding the fort. Let me know if forensics pick up anything we can use from the shipping containers. I'll be on call. I'd better check I've still got a wife.' Lomond reached for his coat.

48

He was pacing up and down the garden. Listening to the grass fracture, the coolest green under frost. It was close to midnight, and Lomond was cold and fed up. He used his own footsteps as a guide, his own Wenceslas path, so as not to ruin any more of his lawn.

Maureen coughed from the patio door, trying not to startle him. 'It's freezing out here,' she said.

'Aye. Maybe it'll kick my brain up a gear.'

'*I'll* kick your brain up a gear, love,' she said kindly. 'Please come back in. I'm a bit worried about your welfare, but, more importantly you're doing my nut in.'

Lomond paced on. The trees at the back of the garden had long lost their plumage, knotted against the back of the shed as if for comfort, or protection. Beyond the treeline, a streetlight cast an orange glow through the cage of tight branches.

'Say you had to sneak into someone's house,' he said, his back to his wife.

'That what he's doing?'

'Let's say aye, for talking's sake. He's getting in somehow, and there's a good security system. We check – system hasn't been re-recorded or had anything deleted. It's picked up nothing. No sign of him getting in or out. Doesn't make sense. So how's he doing it?'

'Not being daft – or maybe I am – but is he being delivered? In a box?'

Lomond spun on the ball of one foot, surprisingly athletic. 'You know, I did think about that. How does a jack-in-the-box get in the house? He gets his box delivered, with him inside it. We did look into it, but door cameras from the other houses would have picked up on it. Delivery drivers coming in and out. Some folk set up their cameras just to catch delivery drivers out; complain about them reversing out the estate too fast, that kind of thing. But that's not what happened.'

'Maybe he was there for a while? Hiding? Like, days before?'

'Thought about that too, but nothing in either house makes it look as if he was hiding out anywhere. And I should know – I had both of them pulled apart, down to the bloody nails in the carpet.' Lomond had a peculiarly haunted look at that moment. That was a defeat. Something else for him to chew on. It drew her towards him, unconsciously. 'That's how they'll probably bin me, you know. Going over the score on budget. Throwing money away. Workies were delighted, having to rip a place apart and not have to put it back together again. But the owners will want it put back together again. Better than before. They'll want compensation, those people. No wonder.'

'They'll not sack you. And you're trying to help those people. Get a murderer off the streets. Find out who did it.'

'Not how they'll see it. Imagine it. Trying to put together a funeral. Trying to deal with it. With everything. And then on top of that, some clown blunders in and turns your house into a cowp. That clown was me.' He blinked, then snapped himself out of it. 'But anyway . . . he hasn't been posted. He hasn't been hiding in the attic all that time. He's sneaking past the cameras, through the back gardens, but it doesn't make sense. Images of the gardens show nothing. We've used geolocation, we've looked at all the time stamps and signatures, metadata, the way the sun moves across the scene – everything tallies. There's just no sign of the creep.'

'OK, next daft question. Is he using a tunnel? Underground? In through the basement?'

'No. It's as good an idea as any, but he isn't tunnelling in. There's no basement in either house.'

'Do they know him? Familiar face? Someone they'd just let in?'

'Well, there's not much of a connection between the victims. Different people, different circles. The connection is the bloody houses. All Avalon King.'

Maureen's voice dropped, just a little. 'Was the woman having an affair? Did she manage to switch off the door cameras? Reprogramme them?'

'No sign of it. Been through her phone, her apps, social media . . . nothing like that. Not even a flirtation. Mother knew nothing, cos if she did she'd have bloody told us, all right. She's high energy, high volume. And if she was having an affair, and he did kill her, what about the other two? You've got three completely different victims, three different profiles. It doesn't fit. Psychology people will be going off their nut with this one. They like patterns, and there isn't a pattern.'

'Maybe there's a personal motive?'

'There's nothing obvious. It's not, strictly speaking, random, either. What is it about the houses? What's with the bloody boxes? Why the bomb hoax?'

Detecting something in the rising pitch of his voice, Maureen steered him towards the back door, the rectangle of light. 'I suggest bed. No more pacing. Even if you can't sleep, just close your eyes. Let it all close down. All right?'

'All right,' he said. 'I can sleep. That's the thing. Could sleep in two minutes, if I wanted. I just can't afford to. I can't afford to have it happen again . . .'

Maureen cut him off. 'He won't try it again, love. Not tonight.'

49

April worked as a doctors' receptionist, the kind who had time for the people worth bothering about. The old dears, the men who took a while to ease themselves into chairs in the waiting room, rusty knives in need of a whetstone. She knew some of them needed pastoral care. She'd reached the age where she hoped some would see sense and join a church group. By her own admission, April had been doing the job too long.

But that day she had a day in lieu, and she took pleasure in doing nothing. January was not a great time to work at a doctors' surgery, but then, she reflected, in Glasgow January wasn't a good time to be doing anything.

The flat was always tidy, a sorry contrast to her ex's place. April had been in the building once, when she'd been picking up their daughter, Alice, just before Christmas. The smell of old grease wafting through George's doorway had taken April back to a time she thought she'd forgotten. Tenement stairways, chip pans, pulleys in kitchens, cigarette smoke. George had always disgusted April – even when she'd agreed to marry him – and she took a cat's-eye pleasure in seeing him living in relative squalor, to the far north of the city. George hadn't come out to see her while she waited on the landing, staring out onto a back court that looked as if it had been hit by a ballistic missile – tin cans, burst bin bags, chromium sheen of takeaway trays. The latter were probably George's, she'd reflected. She wondered if there was a problem with rats out there. She could hear George grunting as Alice zipped up her hold-all and bid him farewell.

'He keeping well?' she'd asked.

Alice shrugged. 'Seems happy enough. Still working on the taxis.'

'So I heard.'

And that was that for George. That was that for Alice too. She was in Edinburgh now, sharing a flat – paying a fortune for it – but she had a decent job in accountancy. She visited less and less. April made plans to go through to meet her for lunch, a nice afternoon's shopping on Princes Street. She'd even talked about doing the festival one August, and her daughter's slightly embarrassed look at this statement continued to haunt her.

Still. A day off was not to be sniffed at. April had started hers with coffee and BBC Sounds. She looked out onto her patio, her own little nook among the concrete boxes. No one else seemed to like it, but it suited April just fine. Her sometime partner, a butcher called Tommy who had been coming around less and less recently and had been telling anyone who would listen he was thinking of converting to veganism, had said he didn't like it at all – it was an ivitation to burgle the house. But April was a fan of the green awning, the leaf-effect coverings along the side of the staircase and the fake grass that covered the balcony. Alice had actually shouted at her for this, bemoaning the environment, microplastics, the dearth of bees and tiny wee birdies and God knew what else. April just liked things to be clean, sheltered and, above, all her own. The balcony was even nice to look at. Otherwise, she was looking at the arse end of a takeaway and a tanning salon. Who wanted to look at that, even in the height of summer? Plus, it would take a major effort to get over the wall, open the gate, then creep up the stairs – especially with the security camera and light she'd had installed. Anyone breaking in, she reasoned, would have to be some kind of ninja.

After coffee and a not entirely serious attempt at yoga, April got dressed. A trip to the post office to send off her cousin Angus's birthday card, first of all – the only living relative on her own side, really, at least in that family tier. A relationship that she clung to for pathetic reasons. They would never meet again. He lived in Gloucester, somewhere like that. The pictures he posted on Facebook always looked nice and leafy. She sometimes fantasised about being invited down, meeting his wife and their young daughter. She'd be about secondary school age, April reckoned. Still, the cards arrived for Christmas and birthdays. It was something.

The snow from earlier in the week had turned into a bitter wind, and the puddles were frozen in the gutter as she made her way to the shops. Wrapped up tight in a big coat, hat and scarf, boots on, April's get-up made her look like a blundering dinosaur crashing through the streets, she thought. She kind of liked that. In the post office, she made a point of buying herself a newspaper. She had an aversion to online media, due to sitting in front of screens and trying to book online appointments and prescriptions all day. She'd had enough of it, although one of the girls in the office did have a fruitful time of it with the online dating. Should Tommy's drift towards mycoprotein sausage rolls and ersatz chicken nuggets take a step further beyond comedy and into full ridicule, well, why not? She was fifty-three. Fifty-three was nothing these days.

'Some carry-on, that,' said Mrs Fahed, behind the reinforced glass, nodding towards the paper April had folded up and laid on the counter. April agreed. Truth be told, she had a ghoulish interest in these things, and often frightened herself into the early hours watching documentaries about serial killers. She did not know why she did this. She would lie awake at night. Don't think about the murderers. Don't think about the murderers. Listening for creaks, cracks and coughs in the night.

She read about the murders, read the opinion columns having a go at the police – felt a sympathetic pang there, seeing public servants openly and brutally criticised. Not their fault. Doing their best, most likely. Like at the surgery. People wanted bloody miracles. They thought they owned you.

Not today, April thought.

She rounded off her outing with a coffee at the Filling Station, a dodgy car-wash place that had been raided, or abandoned, a few months ago. Someone had taken over the premises with a nice but slightly expensive coffee shack, with home-made brownies. The coffee was good and strong, and April enjoyed her moments perched on a high stool, watching the world go by, away from the wind. She never felt lonely at these times. It never occurred to her.

Strange that whoever it was had murdered first a woman, then a young man, and what looked like a junkie before that. Weird mix. Seemed like a few murderers in one, there. Coming to a digital channel near you at half eleven at night. For those of you who live alone . . .

Back at the flat she watched the light fade on her little Eden, the black wicker table and chairs tucked into a corner, awaiting the spring. There was no question of seeing a sunset out there, on the world's silliest balcony space, but you gained an impression of another winter day giving way to darkness.

The security light blinked on, startling her as she was washing up that morning's breakfast things. It happened. Once, she'd been startled by a fox up there, and birds were sometimes visitors to the unlushness of the green carpeting. But no wild creatures could be seen. She had a quick glance at the garden space outside. The leafy wall hanging, the minty green carpeting, still beaded here and there with the odd yellow leaf. There was nothing. She checked the video monitor, with its minimalist framing of the austere space and the stairway. Nothing. No one.

She double-checked the patio door. To get through, you'd need to smash the glass, and that double glazing could take a volley of grapeshot. April turned away from the kitchen and returned to the living room. Although she had a decent music system – it was modern but took cassettes, which she loved, having hoarded them from when she was younger – April usually listened to the radio through the TV, taking comfort in the voices and jingles.

She'd picked up the remote when she heard the patio door open and close with a firm click.

She automatically shut down the thought that someone had opened it. No, she thought. Then she sobered herself up. Gave herself a talking to. I know what I heard. She got up to check, heart thudding, but resolute.

The sight of the shape standing in the hall punched the breath out of her. Just standing there. A nightmare. It yelped, like an animal, and sprinted forward with its fingers curled into claws.

April sank to one knee; something clicked inside it, and she had a weird out-of-body sensation that she'd torn something in there, something important. Indeed, her whole leg was in revolt, staging a protest as she got up, breath wheezing in something like a scream, but she was in her bedroom with the door slammed shut before the figure could reach her.

Laughing at her, outside the door, 'I'm coming, coming, coming for you!' April reached the en-suite, turned the lock and sat there, pissing herself, sagging against the basin, while he laughed outside.

All it took was a coin to turn the lock. You could even do it with a fingernail. Whatever he used he was doing it now. She had a grip of the brass lock with both hands, fingers white, but he was turning it effortlessly, giggling, and it slithered out of her hands and she turned to grab something from the shelf – the mirror, her deodorant, toothpaste, anything. It all fell from her grasp and landed on the floor as he yanked the door open.

She screamed. 'Oh, Christ, help me! It's him, it's Jack-in-the-Box! Help me!'

Still giggling, the figure – the nightmare – leaned forward, placed a gloved finger against where she supposed its mouth was, and said, 'Shh!'

50

That bloody song came on again when he started the car. This time, Slater hit the pause button a split second before Lomond did.

'Not in the mood, Malcolm?'

Slater said nothing. They eased through the gloom and the low-lying mist. The blue lights going outside the flats lit up the fog like a distant thunderstorm. A hint of muffled panic.

'Bloody circus, is it?' Lomond said. It was as close to a snarl as he ever got. He was beyond nerves now. Everything taut. Jaws working. He paused as he unclipped the seatbelt. Take it down a notch. Deep breath. And down another notch . . .

He was shown to the front of the house, on the main road, and through to the communal entranceway. 'I want the back,' Lomond said to the PC, who smarted at the order.

'It's kind of closed off,' he stammered.

'Course it is,' Lomond said. He took another one of those deep breaths and laid a hand on the lad's shoulder – and he was a lad, no more than twenty-odd. 'You're doing fine, by the way. Good work keeping the ghouls away.'

Lomond saw a couple of people on the other side of the road. One of them had a handheld camera, filming the scene. The other was a woman Lomond was sure he recognised from press conferences, with delicate ankles underneath a padded coat that was much too big for her. Even through the mist, Lomond was sure he could make out her dark eyes. She was speaking into a tripod-mounted video camera. Lomond could tell by her eyebrows what tone of voice she was using, even if he couldn't actually hear her. A man, standing apart from the other two, with a tie burst open at the throat, was scribbling intently in his notebook. Lomond patted his pockets to check for his own as he was shown into the back court.

It was fenced off, concreted over, shabby, with a row of filthy wheelie bins. Other buildings were visible over the top of the fence. Turning back, Lomond gazed up at the block of flats. Every light was ablaze in the windows.

April's flat was second-top.

Smythe was there. She looked relieved to see him, which wasn't like Smythe at all.

'What's that over the fence?' Lomond asked, after a cursory greeting.

'Chinese takeaway and bookies. Tanning salon. No CCTV anywhere, before you ask.'

'Gate for the binmen?'

'It's open. Push the latch and you're in. Been like that for a while. Complaints to the council, complaints to the landlords – bugger all done.'

'Reminds me of my daughter's flats,' Lomond mused. He blinked rapidly. 'Not as nice, though. This isn't an Avalon King building, is it?.'

Smythe shook her head. 'Different developer, slightly older build – maybe twenty-five to thirty years old.'

'It's got that look about it – wee bit past its best.' He whispered this, on the off-chance one of the silhouettes framed in light above might have heard him say something disrespectful. He felt like a tenement kid, in fear of being checked by the lunging presence of an old dear at the windows.

'Solid enough. Security door,' Smythe said.

'Don't tell me – no one saw anything?'

'You've got it, sir.'

'How do you get onto the fire escape? Someone must have seen or heard someone going up it.'

'No one. Nothing. It's quite secluded. I've been up and down it. If you're light on your feet . . . say, if you were wearing trainers . . . I'll show you, sir.'

Lomond was reassured by Smythe's presence. Something relaxed in his shoulders. Slater could be a tonic. Slater pushed him on. Slater went places Lomond wouldn't go in the interview room, and Lomond fed from it. But sometimes it was better to have a calmer, more grounded presence. Lomond had a recurrence of an old, melancholy premonition: that Smythe would not be working with him for much longer.

The fire escape creaked underfoot, but then it always creaked in the wind, according to some of the neighbours. Not so you'd think there was something wrong. It zig-zagged up one side of the building, and Lomond knew that there was another fire escape on the other side. Running across the back of the rows of flats, separated by leaping distance, Lomond supposed, was a series of mostly well-kept balconies, some of which had tables and chairs, pot plants, clothes drying even at this time of year. One or two were an explosion, a vent of personality. One resident had covered the balcony railings and every other available space with butterflies: glass butterflies, brass butterflies, glowing butterflies, neon butterflies, and even paper butterflies, veterans of more than one season, ragged-edged and fluttering. One garden was a jungle: April's balcony. Vivid green, even in the shade, at the far corner of the building next to the fire escape, and seeing that shade of green was when Lomond knew. He got it. Something clicked into place; some component that had been thrown out of sync was now back in its proper slot and functioning well. The cloud that had enveloped him for days was suddenly gone. In the mist, moving up the fire escape behind Smythe, taking care not to touch the iron railings, Lomond grinned.

'Aye,' he said.

'Sorry, sir?' Smythe glanced at him over her shoulder.

'Sorry, fine. That's good. You were saying?'

'No one heard anything. Bottom line.'

'How about the roof? Silly question?'

'See for yourself.' She pointed.

Lomond squinted at the black tiles. He could only imagine the moss. No obvious way into a loft area. 'Spider-Man would have a job climbing down that. It'd certainly be one way to get yourself noticed.'

'Looks like a non-starter. We'll check it, though,' Smythe said.

They stared at the green enclosure. About chest-height, with no obvious means of ingress other than the one that had clearly been used.

'See how the green canopy has come away from the railing, sir?'

'Aye. That's it. He leaps across. Not much of a jump – make a mistake and he's had it, mind you. Be a good way to round the case off. Find him twitching in the gutter. That'd be a good one. Then he just pushes his way over the fence, with the canvas above and in front of him, makes his way to the edge of the canopy, and forces his way through. Then he's at the back door.'

'Looks like it. Couple of problems, though.'

'The back door's locked, and there's a security camera,' Lomond said.

'How did you know that?' A slight frown on Smythe's face. Lomond felt a shameful satisfaction at this. Smythe was good, one of the best, but she hadn't quite put it together yet, and Lomond had. He knew it was only a matter of time now. Things were looking up. Sort of.

'Educated guess. I'll tell you on the way back. We need to get in and see her.'

Smythe's face was grim. 'Yes. It's not good, I have to say. She's in some mess.'

Maybe, thought Lomond, but I bet you anything I've seen worse. He did not say it, however. He fought that surging glee, the knowledge that very soon he would have this wrapped up.

'Weird that she should close herself in like this,' Smythe said. 'Like a jungle, almost. Leaves, vines . . .'

‘I don’t blame her at all.’ He pointed over his shoulder. ‘Not much of a view, is it? Not much sunlight either, I bet. Imagine planning your new life in a flat with a balcony, and that’s what you’re looking at. Why not have your own jungle? Why not have outer space? Surface of Mars? Anything but a grotty alleyway and the arse end of a bookies.’

‘Not forgetting the takeaway. Cash only.’

‘Sometimes they’re the best.’ Lomond suppressed a smile – and a sudden rumble in his stomach.

*

The neighbour, Mrs Hanley, was a short, thick-set individual who seemed to be in perpetual motion as she looked from one face to the other.

‘April was always on the go – worked at the doctors’. Probably had a good phone voice. Not sure if I ever got her on the line, though. I thought she’d be good for getting you in for an appointment . . .’

Lomond nodded, taking notes out of politeness. ‘Did she have many visitors?’

‘Well, she had a man come over . . . sometimes stayed over, you know? Tall, good head of hair, totally grey. She split up with her husband. Nasty divorce, I think. Sometimes there was a daughter. Grown up.’

‘How long have you lived next to her?’

‘As long as she’s been here. Four years?’

‘What did you reckon to her garden?’

‘Garden?’ The woman spluttered. ‘I wouldn’t go that far. More like a tent, a windbreak on the beach. God knows what she was thinking with that. Absolute eyesore. Is this important?’

‘Absolutely. Did you ever see anyone hanging about the back court, or on the fire escape?’

‘Nah, never. I think some folk wanted it taken down, you know? It’s a bit old and rickety. But no one used it to break into the houses. You'd need to jump across, and even if you could, you'd need to get the gear down the back steps . . . it's all locked up tight. Never had any problems like that, no prowlers or peeping toms, nothing . . .' Then it occurred to her. 'That how he got in? Through the fire escape? My God.'

'There's nothing for you to worry about, Mrs Hanley. I don't think anyone will try to break in here again.'

'Was it him? That's what she said, you know. When she started screaming. That's when I called the polis. I said, I don't think she's kidding on, but my Alan said it was probably a wind-up. He went through when she screamed again and battered her door.'

'You've been a great help, Mrs Hanley. And please don't worry,' Lomond said, as Smythe caught his eye.

*

Now in white overalls, masked and using the stepping plates to avoid contamination, they went into the flat itself. Lomond scanned the kitchen: the table barely big enough for one, the mug and teaspoon in the drainer at the sink, and, beyond that, the jungle.

'Security system is FiveBarGate,' he said.

Smythe peered at the unit on the wall, the tiny screen still showing the balcony. 'Looks like it. How did you know?'

'Same as the other ones.' Lomond narrowed his eyes, taking in the jungle outside. Like a windbreak at the beach, Mrs Hanley had said, and she was absolutely right. It looked daft, but totally understandable. Why have a blank wall when you could put a nice picture up? Why have a wall at all if you couldn't decorate it? He felt a sadness for April Burgess's life, her tiny flat, the twists and turns that might have led her here, to her seat down at the doctor's surgery, fielding angry calls all day.

He swallowed it. 'Where's the box?'

'Next door.'

It was placed on the dressing table. Cardboard box, no obvious markings. Unblemished and unbashed, a box that might have been mailed within another box. Well packaged, everything slotting together perfectly.

The box was flipped over. A red scarf trailed out of the lid, a tongue, from a mouth above which were two cartoon eyeballs drawn on by marker. Crazy pupils, pointing at weird angles. Lomond looked for some significance in the drawing, some angle. A clue from someone who maybe wanted to be caught. At their core, so many of them did, even the really bad ones. But this bore no coordinates, no cryptography.

'Can't see inside it yet,' Lomond said – a remark, not a question. Smythe did not respond. 'Let's go and see her.'

*

The lights were too bright, but Lomond was not minded to extinguish them. The curtains were drawn. The room was warm, the heating put on especially. The bed had several layers of thin blankets, with fancy stitching round the sides. Very old bedding, perhaps second-hand, the sort an older lady might have. The kind of place they might be found dead one day, arms folded, posed as April Burgess was posed. Even down to the folded hands, lying on top of the bedclothes.

She was on her back, bloodshot eyes staring, face a mottled grey. Lomond nodded to the two uniformed officers, who left quietly.

He pulled out the padded seat from underneath the dressing table and sat down gently, giving Smythe loads of space. Smythe crouched down, and reached out for one of the hands. They'd be cold, Lomond knew. The heat and the blood rushing to where it needed to go. In extremity. In shock.

April's eyes shifted left, taking in Smythe. Then they shifted right, and took in Lomond. He expected a scream.

'It's OK, April,' Smythe said, leaning close. She put her

other hand over April's. They clutched her tight. 'It's absolutely fine. We're here to help. Just take your time.'

But she emerged quickly, faster than Lomond had supposed. He knew to say nothing. He knew that just a man's voice would be disastrous. But he had to hear what she said.

'He said I was a warning,' April told them, her voice gurgling on the end of each sentence. 'He said I was to sit and wait. He put the box over my head. He said not to move or I'd be like the rest. I thought I was going to be like the rest. I'd locked the door. I had the camera on. He wasn't on it. He's invisible. He said I was to tell you. Warn you. Said I was to tell you he's the devil and he's going to keep going. He kept me alive. He kept me alive so people would know. So people would know he can get in and out anywhere. He said you had to know.'

51

'Nice interview room this, by the way. I heard the two-way glass and stuff is a myth, though? Is it?'

Lomond placed his hands on the table top. 'Benny, I'm trying to catch the guy who killed Kath Symes. Do you want to help me or not?'

Benny Kettles hadn't lost any teeth or broken any bones, but it must have hurt to talk. Lomond shivered on his behalf every time that stitched mouth opened.

'Aye,' Kettles said. 'Stupid question, if I'm honest.'

'Good. You can help us catch the guy who killed your pal. I know it wasn't you. OK?'

Kettles began to twitch. Lomond was almost braced for him to leap forward onto his hands, legs flailing. But 'OK' was all he said, eyes filling up.

'It's clear to me that you were very close to Kath Symes and, my God, son, I'm sorry. Someone did an appalling thing. Absolutely terrible. Totally senseless. What you tell us could be very, very important. I want to know why you got in a scrap with Vincent Finch.'

'It's not vital to the investigation, but I'd like to know,' Slater said.

'Well.' Kettles folded his arms and leaned back in the chair. Tears spilled from his eyes. He made no effort to wipe them away. 'Thing is, Vincent Finch is a prick. And I can prove it.'

'Tell me about it,' Lomond said earnestly. 'Everything.'

'Well. I found out that Vincent Finch and his ex-wife, Mrs Gangstery-McGangster, whatever her name is, have been trying to mess me around.'

Lomond and Slater said nothing.

'What I mean by that is, they've been dumping vermin at my sites.'

'You mean your property? That side of your business?'

'It's only business,' Kettles said, a little hurriedly.

'How do you know this?'

'Well. The first time I had a biblical plague of cockroaches, I thought, damn, that's an inconvenience. Like dodgy plumbing. You accept it's something that'll happen. I paid a pest controller. He sorted it, but he told me a weird thing: there were no signs that cockroaches had ever been on the site. He said it looked like a load of them had been dumped. So I was suspicious when I bought another site out in Paisley, built a few flats and, all of a sudden, I had a rat problem.'

'And what made you think Vincent Finch was behind it?'

'I carried out enquiries. I made like a maverick policeman who plays chess and quotes philosophy, and I caught the bastard.'

'That's our job,' Slater said.

'Oh, right enough. Yeah, like that'll work. I call up my local friendly police station and tell them my half-baked theories. Think they'll be interested?'

'What kind of enquiries did you carry out?'

'Well, I put a wee bit of cheddar into a trap, sat back and waited. I had a new site, out near Temple in Anniesland, and I set up a camera system. Had a drone ready. Something set it off. You know what it was?'

'A UFO?' Slater offered.

'Correct. Until I identified it as another drone. Someone was carrying out surveillance on my site. So I used my drone to spy on their drone. Got a model number too. There's a register of them. And let's just say I've got sources. I traced the drone to Vincent Finch. Sure enough, a week or two after this, a big load of rats got dumped at the same site in Temple. So you tell me – was I right or wrong?'

'What was your next step?' Lomond asked.

'Well, first I knocked his stupid drone out the sky. Thought he might get the message. Then a load of cockroaches appeared at a cottage I was renovating. That's when I went to speak to him.'

In a tone that would have turned a glass of milk, Slater said, 'And having gone through all that, how do you feel about being beaten up by Vincent Finch?'

'How do I feel? About this?' Kettles pulled back his top lip, revealing the ugly line of tiny knots and threads. 'I couldn't care less. I got a reaction out of him. Flying drones, dumping pests on my projects – the guy's a menace. A gangster. He didn't marry Nicole Kingsley because he's a soft touch; you need to be seriously out of your mind to be part of that family. I took him on.'

'You've given us some very helpful information,' Lomond said. 'Do you have footage you can give us to back it up?'

'Suppose so,' Kettles mumbled.

'Great. Please take care of yourself, Mr Kettles. The after-effects of an assault can creep up on you.'

Slater said, 'What is it that makes an anti-establishment comedy guy go into the property business? I mean, you're a bit political, aren't you? Police and government, authorities, you don't like them. But developers and landlords, they're all part of the system, and that means you. I don't get it.'

Kettles spread his hands and exhaled. 'It's . . . a job. I don't like it. Who does? Do you like your job, Inspector?'

'Love it,' Lomond said.

'I believe you. I don't think I could do it . . . sorry, I mean I don't think I would do it. Though in fairness I probably deal with more criminals than you.'

Lomond sighed. 'Interview is terminated.'

As Kettles got up and pushed his seat back under the table, he looked Lomond straight in the eye and said, 'You'd better catch that bastard – and catch him soon.'

52

Vincent Finch's hair had a halo effect under the interview-room lighting. It seemed to crackle like lightning as he moved his head wildly to and fro. Lomond wondered if he was hallucinating. Maybe he was just tired.

'Thanks for agreeing to see me,' Finch said, and that's when Lomond lost patience.

'Not very funny, Mr Finch.'

Finch gestured helplessly. Aware of the scrutiny, aware he was being recorded, he folded his arms and shrank into a tight ball.

'Can you explain what happened with Mr Kettles?'

'I'm not sure I should say anything about that.'

'I'd like to know the general scenario. Someone else can look into the fight scenes.'

'Well, he's a prick. Isn't he?'

Lomond shot a warning glance at Slater. 'How do you know him?'

'Just here and there, knocking around . . . property development. He's got his fingers in a few pies. He wants to see himself as my rival. If it's an auction or bidding for a site, sure, no problem, let's have a competition. But it's never a fight. Never a war. This guy, when he opens his mouth . . . did you know he's a comedian?'

Slater laughed, a genuine guffaw. These had been too few of late; it was so startling, he had to apologise, hand raised. 'Aye,' he managed, when he could speak. 'We're familiar with his work.'

'Don't know why he bothers. He does OK with the property stuff . . . Why would you do stand-up if you were good at business and made a few quid out of it? Beats me. Unless he likes the hassle. Heckling. Into getting his ticket punched.' Finch realised what he was saying and closed his trap.

Lomond let the silence brew for a few seconds. 'When did you first come into contact with Mr Kettles?'

'I think I was still married to Nicole, so we're talking more than ten years ago. He was a trust-fund kid, Daddy's money, you know. Glasgow Academy boy.' Finch brushed the sleeves of his tweed coat. 'He was cheeky as sin. Knew who Nicole was – everybody did. Called her the Gangster's Moll. You can imagine.'

'I can,' Slater said.

'Were you friendly with him at one point?' Lomond said.

'Me personally? No, but Nicole was. She actually liked the cheek, a bit of banter. I thought he was disrespectful and unfunny.'

'So you were jealous,' Slater suggested.

'Not at all. He's clearly gay.'

'Did you clash over property deals? That kind of thing?'

'All the time. He actually wrote graffiti on a sign outside a block of flats we had built out in Royston. Couldn't believe it. He'd scrubbed out "applicants" and written in "dickheads". Then he wrote "Come to Kettles instead", with an email address and phone number and a website. It was him. Went viral. Nicole just laughed, but you don't want to be associated with a person like that. Even as a rival or an opponent – puts you on the same level as him, like there's an equivalence. I don't like that.'

'You think he's beneath you, like?' Slater asked.

'Yeah, by miles.'

'Maybe you don't like competition, mate? That's the vibe I'm getting here.'

Finch glanced around himself, as if tracing the flight path of a bluebottle. 'Look, I came here, under my own steam, to answer your questions about the . . . the altercation with Benny Kettles. I didn't come here to be insulted.'

'Mr Finch,' Lomond said, 'Benny Kettles has accused you of stalking him, using your drones. He claims to have video evidence of this from his own drones.'

Finch's face went slack, then tightened in consternation. 'It was him. That bastard. He was the one attacking my equipment. That settles it.' Then a smirk of his own played across his lips. 'Well, he got what he was asking for. He won't forget that in a hurry.'

'Mr Finch, you have also been accused of releasing pests at building and renovation sites owned by Mr Kettles. Rats and cockroaches. We've discovered the source of several of these outbreaks – a delivery driver who's not sure who hired him. Are you the person responsible for that?'

Finch gawped at the two detectives. 'But that's what happened to me! That exact same thing. Rats, when we'd begun work on the foundations of a site out past Drumchapel. Came out of nowhere. I'm sure Nicole mentioned it too. I thought she was fishing for information, maybe thought I'd done it myself.'

'So, to be clear, Mr Finch, you weren't responsible?'

'Course I wasn't. I spent a fortune cleaning up the site and having them killed. There was a chance it was going to turn into a permanent problem. Rats everywhere, when you're trying to sell flats? Disgusting. So you're saying Benny Kettles did it?'

'No,' said Lomond. 'We're saying he reported the same complaint.'

'Stumps me. And as for the drones – it's a hobby. I've already explained it. I've given you every bit of footage I have. I can't help you any more than that.'

Slater tapped at the tablet in front of him and turned it round for Finch to view. The footage showed a drone making a sharp turn over some trees, then surging towards a flashing green light. The two images collided, and the screen went blank. 'Weird one here, mate,' Slater said, exaggerating an air of puzzlement. 'You did pass us the footage. We've checked all the dates and times, and this image shows one of your drones, registered to you, out on a flight. But the times don't tally with any of the ones stamped on the footage you sent us.'

'What?' Finch sat forward, pushing his glasses up his nose. 'Show me again.'

Slater rewound the footage, pausing it at certain points. 'There . . . look at the serial number on the drone. It's registered to you. Benny Kettles hunted it down.'

'That's one of the drones that went missing, sure. But I've no idea . . . I mean, nothing . . .' He flushed. 'I've told you all I know. If that flight doesn't match any of the data I have, it wasn't flown by me. I'm saying nothing else, by the way. Nothing.' He leant back and folded his arms.

Lomond smiled. 'It's OK, Mr Finch. That's your right, but for the record I believe you.'

'Right. I'll be off then. And I'll be contacting a lawyer, by the by.'

'You'll need one anyway, for panelling your mate Benny,' Slater said agreeably. He reached out a hand, and Finch took it, surprised. Slater gave him a firm handshake. 'Well done, and thank you, mate. I mean that.'

Finch stared at his hand as Slater withdrew his grip.

'And another thing,' Lomond said soberly. 'How do you fancy an early Christmas present?'

53

Smythe had time to dry and style her hair, enjoying the ritual and rhythm of the straighteners, letting the metal follow the curves and swells of her hair. She hated her hair. She loved her hair. It was worth the effort, either way. But she didn't have time to do her make-up as well. Driving into the office for Lomond's meeting – seven a.m., for God's sake, please let this be a breakthrough – she recalled a friend who would do her make-up while driving down the motorway in rush hour, staring in the rear-view mirror and switching between implements one-handed with an impressive dexterity.

Smythe was no longer friends with that person, and her memories of her were not good ones. She thought of the high-speed make-up artiste often, though, and sometimes smiled, then thought about it some more and stopped smiling. Smythe had told the woman about some of the things she had seen at accident scenes. Having to unwrap a sixteen-year-old from around a steering column after a car had overturned on a rural road was one of the worst – forever closed up in a big box and shut inside an even bigger box somewhere in her head.

In the toilets, with a spare ten minutes before she was due to sit down with Lomond in the IT suite, Smythe was applying concealer to an alarming red patch which had begun to form beneath her cheekbones when she realised that the person who had come into the toilets was a man. At first the sense of familiarity had overridden any sense of surprise. Then she gazed at the newcomer frankly in the huge, brightly lit mirror, hand poised mid-air.

'Malcolm.'

'Oh. Hello.' He nodded, then continued pacing back and forth in a state of agitation. If you saw it in a zoo, in an enclosure, you'd question your excuse for being there, or deplore the place's very existence. Stress, it seemed, did weird things to people, even Malcolm Slater.

'Either I've made a mistake, which I definitely haven't, or you have. Or something else is wrong.' She kept her tone even.

He stopped. Double-take. Eyes widening, then he actually flinched. 'Oh, Jesus. No urinals. I'm not usually down this level. Just following my feet. Sorry.'

'Want me to pee standing up or something? Make it less weird for you.' She grinned, but it faded as he marched back to the door. She saw him check both ways, furtive as a shoplifter, before exiting fast. To see Slater fazed was a sign Smythe didn't like. Goosepimples rose on her arms; she could feel them beneath the material of her shirt. She made a mental note to revisit this encounter, and not for laughs.

In the IT suite downstairs, she was comforted by something lovely in the air: jasmine, maybe fresh cotton, something that could have come from a fancy candle. The lighting was low, but not low enough to induce squinting or discomfort, and the space was orderly and clean. There was something of a church-between-services vibe about Fahey's room, the IT guru. The man himself was seated at his machine, in the far corner, close to the window. But Lomond presided over the scene. If Slater had become alarmingly twitchy, Lomond seemed to have gone the opposite way, genial and plump in his winter coat. The low lighting flattered him in a way that he might have disliked were it pointed out. It made him cuddly, and Smythe supposed the whole team needed a cuddle.

'Thanks for getting here early. Particularly the IT people.' Lomond nodded to a couple of Fahey's assistants who hung back in the shadows. 'To get the good news out the way, we've had a breakthrough, and I think we can demonstrate it before we get down to business at the briefing for the rest of the team.'

A sharp, musky scent was tainting the spa-day candle aroma to Smythe's left. She knew it was Tait before she saw him. He gulped down water, acknowledging Smythe with a nod, but he and Slater did not acknowledge each other.

'OK,' Lomond said, 'we'll start with Myrtlewood Crescent. We'll call it site A. Kathryn Symes' murder. Go for it, Niall.'

Fahey launched a screen which dominated the back wall. The scene began to unfold, so familiar to Smythe now that it held the dread of a recurring nightmare. The sweeping camera. The security light coming on. The countdown, the numbers reaching the time when they knew – they had proved – that Kathryn Symes had been dragged out of her bath, smothered with a towel, then shoved into a box.

'Now – the common denominator in the two killings and the incident involving April Burgess yesterday, anyone?'

'Security camera system,' Smythe said.

'The lighting,' Tait ventured.

'Shit garden,' said Slater. There were one or two titters from the IT team. 'Seriously, the fake grass stuff. Hate it. No one likes it. That's got to be it.'

'You're all spot on,' Lomond said. 'Or near enough. The camera system is the same. The houses weren't all built by Avalon King, which was kind of a red herring. But the system is the same. FiveBarGate. All one word. That's the company who installs the cameras and the security lighting, provides the software for the builder. They're good. But like any computer system, it seems it's got vulnerabilities. Now, Malcolm pointed out the fake lawn, and, yes, I wouldn't have it in my garden, but what's the positive thing? The thing hardly anyone mentions when they have a go at it?'

'It's tidy,' Tait said.

'You don't have to cut it,' added Smythe.

'Again, spot on. But the important thing for the killer is that it's uniform. It's still not the most important part of the whole scene, though.'

'They've all got that crap fake jungle thing at the back. Looks like camou–' Slater looked up suddenly. So did everyone else. An electric current passed through everyone in the room, eventually lighting up Lomond's face with a faint, kindly smile. 'Camouflage,' Slater finished, for the benefit of everyone else.

'Exactly,' Lomond said. 'That's the key point. Look at Mrs Symes' garden at Myrtlewood. Now, Niall, if you would . . . on to Craigan Walk, where Rowan Beattie lived. And, finally, on to Gourlay Dyke, where Mrs Burgess lived.'

'It's all enclosed,' Smythe said, indicating the green wall coverings, the green carpeting, close to baize in the sudden lights where the security sensors had done their job.

'But we can't see anyone,' Tait said. 'The security light comes on at Myrtlewood and Craigan Walk – that ties in with when the killer gets into the house. The light comes on. But there's no one there. You told us that the image hadn't been messed with or reprogrammed or overwritten in any way. Are you saying that's now not the case?'

'No – the image is just as you see it. It was recorded like that, at the time when the killer got into the three properties. It also records when they left. The security light comes on – Niall, you mentioned the lighting, and it's important.' Lomond nodded towards Fahey.

The static images showed the greenery, the white light flaring on. The tones of the green mixed with the white light all appeared identical.

'All the same,' Lomond said. 'Not an accident. Myrtlewood, Craigan, Gourlay. You see it? Right. Here's where we get it. I got Niall to run the images through a special filter. It lets us flip the image we see here.'

'There's still nothing there,' Tait said. 'The only part of any image we have is that sudden appearance on the cameras at Myrtlewood. It could just be a drop of rain, a bird dropping . . . that's it. No one's there. Unless it's a camera trick.'

'It is a camera trick. You're right. Very cleverly done. Just lights and colour. Niall?'

Fahey clicked the mouse. The sweeping footage from Myrtlewood appeared. Then the colour and the gradient changed to something akin to an eighties music video. The word that appeared unbidden in Smythe's mind was chroma-key, and it may have been right. The greens flipped to cerise, the backgrounds nuclear. It might have been nuclear purple, gamma rays, something out of sci-fi. She didn't ask.

Someone gasped.

'There's our killer,' Lomond said.

54

The invisible man – the jack-in-the-box – crept along the wall, unhurried, unfurtive, then stood up straight. Entirely confident that he wouldn't get caught. That he wouldn't be seen. Around six feet tall, covered in some kind of sheet or military poncho, like a cartoon ghost. The figure was hooded. Only a ghostly impression of eyeballs remained, like a rapist in a ski mask but bleached of colour, identity, basic human features. The figure stood at the bottom of the vine-covered canopy, walking along the greenery. Leaving no footprint.

Smythe shuddered.

'You see how the canopy links to the false lawn?' Lomond said. 'Now, watch the stone, where the mark appears.'

'He slips,' Tait said. 'It was a footprint, after all. My God. He made himself invisible.'

'Green screen?' Smythe said.

Lomond pointed at her. 'Absolutely right. A very old camera trick. Kids can do it these days with felt sheets and play cameras. That's basically what happened here. He made himself invisible. The camera system was rigged so that anyone it captured would be invisible. The sensor picks up the person and the light comes on. The light is crucial – it floods the scene, and the only thing that catches it is the exact same hue as the background and foreground. The light filters out any details that would make him stand out. Had it been raining, or snowing hard at the time, it might have given a bit of texture and we'd have seen it. But in every case, the space is enclosed. A canopy along the side of the shed, in Mrs Symes' case. It seems they installed it to avoid attention from neighbours on the other side. With Rowan Beattie and Mrs Burgess, there was enclosure from above. Next shot, Niall, at Craigan Walk . . . there we are . . . we can see he's crouching, making sure he doesn't appear against any background where he might stand out, to the naked eye or the camera. It looks like a full body covering, probably camouflage effect, like the fake vines. So if he should be spotted or disturbed, by someone coming out of the back door, say, all he has to do is stand still. Even if he's moving, I'll bet that in the dark you might not spot him. You'd be used to the security light coming on – happens all the time in my garden. It gets so that it doesn't spook you when maybe it should. I know people who switch them off or dismantle them. Not in these cases.' Lomond nodded to Fahey, who switched to the same acid house image, showing the figure, crouching low, appearing through the gap in the balcony fence at Gourlay Dyke, lunging towards the camera.

'Jesus,' Slater muttered. 'There goes sleep.'

'What's sleep?' Tait asked mirthlessly.

'Don't think it's Benny Kettles,' Smythe said, peering at the screen. 'Hard to say . . . but I think he's taller.'

'Benny Kettles is taller than you think,' Lomond said. 'He's baby-faced and fairly stocky, and that can throw you. I want to discount him, but I can't. Plus, he's bendy . . . *very* flexible, for a guy his size. Look at the way the killer's crouching there, at Gourlay Dyke, on Mrs Burgess's balcony. We've seen the contortions on stage, the hand springs and whatever. I want to say we're not looking at Kettles, but I can't be sure.'

'I don't think it's him,' Slater said, but he didn't sound sure. He bit the side of his mouth distractedly.

'Could be Laybourn,' Tait said.

'It could,' Lomond said quietly.

'Might be Finch. Finch is about six foot. How about Symes? We ruled him out?'

'He couldn't possibly have done it, unless he did something very weird with a body double, or something,' Lomond said, 'something a bit Agatha Christie. We've mapped out that one.'

He nodded towards Slater. 'But as usual we rule nothing out until we definitely rule it out.'

'Surely not Symes,' Smythe said.

'He was stalking them,' Tait said. 'How? Drones?'

'Yep,' Lomond said.

'That points to Finch,' Slater said. 'Or Kettles. Both of them used drones.'

'We're overlooking the one person we know for a fact has actually killed people. Laybourn,' Tait said sharply. 'Part of his redacted career before he started delivering parcels was being attached to a unit that flew unmanned drones to take out terrorists in the Middle East. And we know he personally handled a corpse connected to this case. He's all over it.'

Lomond raised a hand, cutting off Slater's twisted-face riposte. 'Laybourn is probably top of the list on that evidence. But there're too many things that count him out. Alibis, mainly.'

Smythe frowned. 'So he's using drones to scope out his victims and finding out when they're going to be home alone – right?'

'Too much of a coincidence to be luck.'

'There's something that really jars, though.' Smythe counted on her fingers. 'One – a woman on her own. Good-looking, looked after herself. But no sign of sexual contact. No semen, no indication she was touched or violated that we know of. If there was something paraphilic, it's not obvious. I mean, he got off on it, that's what creeps do. But not obviously. Then we have victim two – gay guy, young, strong. Again, no sign of any sexual assault. Three – another woman, early middle age, survived. And then we go back to the original victim, if he actually was a victim. Homeless guy, drifting around. All the signs point to him being a trial run, but we can't know for sure. Let's assume he was, and we've got three people dead and one left alive to mess with her head . . . and ours. What's the connection? There's no victim profile here. We've got a method, fair enough, and we've got a shape, at least. There's a person there. Apart from that, I don't get it. This looks so bloody *random*, but it can't be, can it?'

'No,' Lomond said. 'In terms of the victims, I'm tempted to say it doesn't matter. Could be anyone – all that matters is the location, the times, the setting, the circumstances, every element but the face. If Mrs Burgess hadn't told us about what he said to her, then I'd be tempted to say he backed out of killing her, that something spooked him, or there was a detail he didn't like, so he aborted whatever mission he has in his head. But he left her alive deliberately. On top of that, there's the bomb scare at Nicole Kingsley's.' Lomond began to pace up and down, touching the empty seat backs as he went. 'So we know that, as well as being very organised, he's a games-player. Likes to mess with us. I wouldn't be surprised if his next attempt to spook us involved an actual bomb.'

'I agree,' Tait said. 'We have to look at stepping up security. It was confident, for a hoax.'

'He's a confident guy,' Slater said. 'First victim, the homeless guy . . . God knows, he could have been out his mind on smack, but he wasn't a shrinking violet. Then there's Rowan Beattie – he worked out, he was fit, it's not like he was drunk or anything. He had headphones on when Drew left, so he'd have been surprised. Our jack-in-the-box was taking a big chance with him. Even Mrs Symes did boxing training, worked out with a heavy bag; she was physically fit. He's got away with it so far. So he's strong and he's cocky.'

'Don't want to do the bias thing,' Tait said, 'but I'm saying Laybourn, all the way.'

'It does fit,' Lomond said. 'But I'm open to other ideas.' He nodded towards Fahey. 'Niall, thanks. We're going to head into our briefing room. I need to talk it over with the team.'

'You've got a plan? Catch him at it?'

'Oh aye. He's escalating. He'll do it again, and soon.' Lomond looked grave for a moment. 'But we know what he's about. And I've got a wee idea.'

55

Kelly Martin was forty-one, weathering well. Park run every Saturday, spin class on a Thursday, and swimming every other week. She was at home in the water, but pool etiquette killed her. Always some bloody Tarzan zooming past. Not that Kelly wasn't fast, but it was such a luxury to swim at your leisure, a very human thing. Animals always got hunted. Survival was at the heart of everything they did. Enjoy your swim too much, you forget about the crocodiles, the sharks – the humans.

Kelly was doing an online yoga thing – not live, pre-recorded, part of the deal she had with her fitness tracker that probably knew the day you were going to die, but didn't tell you. Kelly could have done with that sort of forecasting when Louis had left her six years ago. Louis had wanted kids; Kelly had not. They should probably have sorted that out before they married. Now Kelly was seeing a guy she had matched with in Loughborough. Lovely, own house, toilet-trained, knew how to wear his clothes, might even be trusted to buy some for Kelly, as he had done on her last birthday – an upgrade on Louis, that was certain. A decision might have to be made, but not any time soon. She enjoyed the travel, the time away, her own space. There was a sense that she owed nothing, and no one owed her. Kelly hadn't ever imagined what forty-one would be like, but if you'd asked her even ten years ago she would never have told you it would be . . . all right. There were things to look forward to, places to go, people to meet. Nothing harsh, nothing uneasy.

She lived in the end-terrace house on Killenmuir Close, an unexpected but welcome legacy from a great-aunt in Australia who had met Kelly twice when she was little and adored her. That had come at the right time, make no mistake – Louis fired out the door, then the legacy waltzing in, a gift from the gods. It was cold tonight, everything in Kelly's garden frosted over – even the imitation lawn (and, yes, she did like it, thank you very much – the bloody bees and butterflies had other places to go, she was sure). Hoarfrost.

On the calendar was a date in two weeks' time: down to Loughborough to meet Drew, with his crinkly Irish eyes, blue and so sparkly there seemed to be a bit of sunlight trapped in there. Drew. There it was, in black and white on the calendar, with the train time and a starburst around it for good measure. She'd even written *Early night* before it. Who else would do that?

★

She drank a hot chocolate in the kitchen. There was a dash of blue in the sky that night, and she watched the darkness chase it away, enjoying the conifers' swaying in the window, jagged black on indigo. At one point a single red eye had blinked somewhere in front of the conifers, enough to catch her eye. But it was soon gone, whatever it was. Weird how the mind played tricks.

She had a cosy evening, listening to the radio turned down low. She was clearly visible through the back windows, but the garden was secluded and the vine-effect hanging she'd left by the far wall meant that anyone who wanted to peer in at her would have to be very determined indeed.

She made sure the door was locked. She made sure to take the key out. She set up the video camera and made sure the security light was armed. She kicked off her slippers and got underneath the covers. It was a big, thick duvet, the best, and the sheets were fresh on that day. The quilt swallowed her up. She was cosy as cosy could be.

Kelly closed her eyes.

Beyond the curtains, the security light came on, an intrusion even through the thick velvet curtains. A razor's-edge white flare visible through a crack in the material.

56

The trick is to keep breathing. Gets you calm and focused, any therapist will tell you. He'd even said as much to the bitch in the bath. 'Just slow down your breathing . . . slow . . . slow it down . . .'

On came his spotlight. He should have loved it. Should have taken a bow – it wasn't like anyone would see it but him – but certain things in the mind told you it wasn't the right thing to do, even wearing your Sunday best. Part of you wanted to freeze, like an arrow-branded convict in a cartoon. But he knew the science behind it, knew this was part of the plan, knew he'd get away with it. You just had to follow the steps, like mirror, signal, manoeuvre.

A quick hop, skip and a jump, and one of those nasty seconds when the key jingled. This was the moment, now. If they'd taken one simple wee precaution, then the mission was over. It had happened once: that woman up in Bearsden. Next door's dog had been a problem there as well – simply hadn't shown up in any previous recces. Usually the four-legged friends barked their heads off at the UFOs, but no dice with that one. It had stayed quiet until he'd appeared on the decking. Had to get out of there fast.

Excitement was kicking up a notch. Several notches.

Clanking key – that would get the bedroom window shoved open. There she was, fast asleep.

This one was to show he was serious. Deadly serious. Do a guy next time, for balance. So they didn't think he was a pervert. Not an obvious pervert, anyway.

A satisfying click. A well-oiled mechanism, doing what it

was supposed to do. No alarm triggered, of course – who did that? Even with dangerous characters roaming around? No one would arm an alarm while they were in the house. And yet it might have saved them. You could isolate it just for the back door. Ironic.

Close the door, carefully now. Wait until the light clicks off in the garden. Naked eye, that was the trouble. All bets are off then. Polis would be over soon if he was spotted, and he couldn't silence her straight away. Some of them were handy; went to self-defence. You couldn't be too careful there. Treat them the same way you would some meathead. Cover the face. It would happen fast tonight. She'd see. Or, rather, she wouldn't. They never saw him if he could help it. They might not even hear his heavy breathing, his excited mutterings. But they'd know, just before the lights went out, who was in their house, snuffing them.

Be funny if he did one of the polis. That baldy pipecleaner one would be good. Give them all something to think about.

Right. Focus. Kitchen. Clean. Tidy. Saw his own shadow on the wall. Scary in silhouette, the hood, the bulky figure. Have to go light on your feet. Don't want to stand on a cracker she left on the tiles. Don't want to slip on a puddle of spilled wine or something, and definitely, *definitely* don't want to leave any footprints. Time enough to wipe up anything afterwards. He usually did a thorough clean. You could get paranoid about it though. *Oh no, I've used kitchen towels, but have I contaminated the roll? Left a hair somewhere?* That was how they got you. How they'd probably get him. But, whatever, that was fine.

Imagine opening the door and – boom – she's there, unexpected, having wandered down half asleep to get a glass of water. Imagine the face framed in moonlight, then the eyes widening – you'd be in the game then. You'd need to move fast. You'd have your work cut out.

But he was ready for that, if it happened, and of course it didn't. Opening out onto the hallway. Jesus, this place was tiny.

He'd heard of compact, but this was ridiculous. Guess it was cosy in a way. Made you feel safe and protected, like in the womb. Well, she'd be wrapped up tight soon, right enough. Flip the cover over her, pile some cushions on top, and his body weight would do the rest. Wait till the spasms had stopped . . . they could play dead. You had to be sure.

No creaky stairs – they made these places solid, hats off to Avalon King. The queen bitch didn't stand for any incompetence, no stupid behaviour, no bottles of piss walled up anywhere. Any hint of any of these things and you got your cards. And you only messed with the queen bitch once.

The anticipation, the jangling nerves as he took the steps, so very slowly. Good thick carpet. Warm in here. Kept the heat in well. Hopefully the sound too. Just in case she got a scream out.

Bathroom, spare room, ninety-degree turn, and there it was. He paused, collecting himself. Breathing. That was the thing. He focused. Everything was throbbing, his head and his entire perception pulsing, like when the waves come in when you're stoned. Collapsing in on yourself: a dark star, a black hole, where not even light escapes.

No light for this bitch now.

The green-gloved hand quivered slightly as he reached out, and here was the biggest violation yet: into the bedroom. First time he'd done it in the bedroom. Made it special. It had bothered him, a little, that he'd had that Symes bitch all to himself, slick and wet out the bath, and . . . but no. No time for that. What did they think he was, some kind of pervert?

He almost burst out laughing.

No stirring on the bed. One step, two. Then he paused. Felt like she might be watching him. Like when you know there's a television on in a room, before you've gone all the way through the door, even though you can't hear anything or see any change in the light. There's a vibration, echolocation, proprioce-ption, something like that. You know, you sense it. She awake?

She wasn't. Soft, quiet breathing, head turned to one side.

Big wardrobe with mirrored doors. One not enough for her, obviously. Vain. Might let her see herself. Uncover her eyes, just long enough so she can see herself. That could be done.

Another step forward.

The mirror on the left-hand side swung wide.

'Boo!' Lomond cried.

57

The bedside light clicked on.

To say he roared would not quite cover it. It was a peal of astonishment, like a church bell cut free from its moorings. Lomond advanced on the ghost, the invisible man, this green swamp creature from a nightmare. It wore a poncho that left the arms free. They were green too, covered in a different material but the same colour. The face was hooded, a vague dimpling in the material where Lomond supposed the eyes were.

The ghost stumbled backwards.

The woman in the bed had kicked back the covers and was approaching from the other side. Not the woman the ghost had been watching: someone equally diminutive but muscular, with black hair swept back across the scalp and intense brown eyes.

'Stay where you are,' Lorna McGill said tersely.

Lomond stepped forward, fast.

The ghost backpedalled, collided with a bedpost and fell heavily. With a rebound technique available only to the very supple or very drunk, he was back on his feet almost instantly, diving for the door.

Smythe blocked the way. She locked his hands and kicked away his legs and threw him to the floor. Lomond placed a knee on the small of his back and had the handcuffs over his wrists as if he'd waved a wand. The ghost bucked, writhed and screeched at an unearthly pitch. He dislodged Lomond, got to one knee, then up straight, just in time to aim a brutal kick at Smythe, which she could not dodge. She grunted, taking it high on the hip. The ghost, hands fastened behind his back, leapt for the gap in the door. Lomond extended a leg, and he tripped headlong into Slater, who blocked the doorframe.

Slater finished it with a single meaty punch – a piledriver below the ribs that folded the ghost in half. The sight of it stole the breath from Lomond. The ghost landed on its face with an unmistakable finality, wheezing.

'Enough of that,' Lomond said, raising a hand to Slater.

'Bastard,' was all Slater said, glaring at the green shape at his feet.

Lomond planted a knee on the hooded figure's back for the second time. His hands probed all the usual nooks and crannies, where shiny, sharp things were usually kept: nothing.

'I don't like doing this, son, and we'd rather not hurt you. Don't try anything. We'll let you get your breath back, then we're heading down to the station. I'll do the formal thing, first. Shane Kingsley, I'm arresting you for murder. You have the right to remain silent, but anything you do say may be taken down in evidence and used against you. Do you understand what I'm saying to you?'

The prone figure's left foot came up, a lazy gesture reminiscent of a whale's fluke breaching. Then it fell.

'You can nod if you like, Shane,' Lomond said. 'Can't hear you. Do you understand what we're saying, son?'

Smythe, still wincing, lunged forward. Lomond was sure she was going to hit the captive. Instead, she snatched off his hood, biting her lip in compressed fury.

Sure enough, it was just a boy on the floor. Tall, rangy, muscular, but still a boy, eyes liquescent in the soft lighting. He was still struggling to breathe.

'It would have been funny if we'd got it wrong, you have to admit,' Slater said, with a wry smile. 'Like if it turned out to be the butler after all. Worse if it was Laybourn. Tait would have been unbearable.'

The boy on the floor forced some words out. His eyes were wide open, staring at nothing.

‘Come again, son?’ Lomond said.

‘I said,’ Shane Kingsley whispered, drooling, ‘don’t call me son.’

‘OK, Shane, joint enterprise here: we’re going to get you downstairs, then after a wee drive, we’ll get a doctor to look you over, then we’ll all have a nice cup of tea and a biscuit. Could be a long night.’

58

They headed for Lomond's car. Blue lights washed the scene, with the SOCOs just arriving. Soon there'd be the tents, the lights, but no body, and – the inspector smiled at the thought – no Lomond.

Shane Kingsley was penned in between him and Slater, his arms gripped firmly. The boy didn't resist, and it was a short walk, but a chill had come down and the street was icy. 'Mind your step,' Lomond said. 'Looks a bit slippy out the front.'

Having recovered his breath, and a little of his moxie, Shane said, 'Yeah, someone could come to grief out here if they're not careful. Maybe we could find some stairs for me to fall down?'

Slater jerked his head into Shane's eyeline. 'Don't joke about it, wee man,' he growled.

Lomond chose two of the bulkiest PCs to flank the boy in the back of his car, leaving Smythe to get checked over by the doctor they'd had on stand-by. He put McGill in charge of the crime scene until Tait arrived.

'Bit sexist of you,' Shane sneered, as the two officers squeezed him into the middle of the seat. 'Picking the big boys. Not wanting me to chat up your bitches?'

'All above board,' Lomond said benignly, signalling to the officer guarding the bottom of the street before pulling out. 'But, yeah, if I'm honest, I don't like you kicking my colleagues.'

'Especially if it's a lassie,' Slater said, turning in the passenger seat to glare at the young man. 'Brave guy you are, going after women like that.'

'I'll do anybody,' Shane said, chin up. 'Anybody at all. Doesn't matter who they are. Men, women, whatever. I'll do them.'

'Not any more, son,' Lomond said.

'I told you not to call me that.'

'Touchy about that, eh?' Slater remarked. 'Maybe a daddy issue there? Keep having to remind myself who your da actually is. It's the nutty professor, isn't it? Vincent Finch? No need to remind me who your ma is, like. Or your granda.'

'One for the psychologists,' Lomond said dismissively, indicating to join the main road. 'And folk who're into that kind of thing. Not for us.'

'Is it my turn now?' Shane said brightly. His eyes locked with Slater's in the mirror. 'OK. You're some kind of fitness freak who decided to be a cop because there was nothing else out there for you. Your hair's never coming back and you're never going to be promoted. It looks like you're second fiddle to Inspector Chocolate Labrador here, and, honestly, I think most people would rather be unemployed. Your big old dome makes you look years older than you are, and I can't see anyone ever taking you seriously.' He sat back, pleased with himself.

Lomond drew breath to riposte, but Slater saved him the bother by laughing out loud. 'You say all that, but we caught you.'

'Probably cutting corners, relying on technology, some CCTV or something,' Shane scoffed. 'Forgive me if I don't think I'm dealing with two street philosopher geniuses here.'

'It doesn't take geniuses,' Lomond said. 'You put your hands all over that fake bomb. Like a cat marking out its territory. Strange thing to do with a thing that could blow you to hell. Almost like you wanted to make sure you got your DNA on it. To deliberately contaminate it. That's what it suggested to me.'

'Wowee,' Shane said, pretending to yawn. 'Call Mensa. My lawyer will demolish you in court. So, yeah, be ready for that. I am.'

Slater turned to Lomond and exhaled loudly. 'Looks like he's got us right where he wants us, gaffer. In control of the situation.'

Shane sighed. 'Proper double act, the pair of you. Comedians. You tried doing a podcast?'

'We might,' Slater said, brightening. '*How to Catch a Perv.* You'll be in it – for maybe half an episode.'

'Honest?' A new note crept into Shane's voice. He cocked his head as he eyeballed Slater in the mirror. 'I think I'm worth more than that. And there'll be plenty of podcasts about me.'

'I wonder if there'll be a TV drama,' Slater mused. 'They'll have to find some gawky wee virgin to play you. Always a poisoned chalice for an actor, isn't it? Could end up typecast, if you're not careful. Anthony Perkins was a cracking actor, but . . . Anthony Perkins, gaffer. First film you think of? Go.'

'*The Black Hole*,' Lomond said, without a pause.

There was a silence for a beat or two.

'I like the way you're thinking here,' Shane said. 'I like the way it's going. It's all sitting nicely, isn't it? They'll be reading about this all across the planet. Hey, they even gave me a name. Exactly the one I wanted. Planned it that way. Boxes and such.'

'You didn't plan on getting caught,' Slater said.

'No, but I knew I would. Luck runs out eventually.'

'It wasn't luck, son. We just caught you,' Lomond said.

'Nah, I just slipped up,' Shane said, reduced to a petulant teenager. 'I knew I would get caught. See, when it comes to doing people in, I like it. And when I like something, I like a lot of it. It's like when some guys who take to the bevvy . . . You on the bevvy, Inspector Roundarse?'

'Nope,' Lomond said cheerfully.

'Nope? Boring. Anyway, some guys get on the bevvy, some guys get on the drugs. You know what my hit is?'

'Being a creepy wee pervert?' Slater said.

'The answer to that question is no, you don't know what my hit is. Not really. That's what fascinates people, isn't it? They don't know. They *can't*. Anyway, you can bet on this – I'll get out. I'll do it again.'

'You do have the right to remain silent, you know,' Lomond reminded him. 'And I wouldn't bet too much on getting out.'

'Fresh air might be as good as it gets. But only if you're good,' Slater said. 'Only if you play nice with the big boys. They're going to love you in there, pal. Hey, I just thought – what's your motive again? The stuff you wrote in your wee manifesto with the laptop you sent to your dad? You don't like houses? That it? Property? The stuff that puts a roof over your head? Well, here's the good news: you're going to move into a really big house soon. With lots of other boys in it. Big boys.'

'I'll be separated from the apes, don't worry about that,' Shane said. His face morphed into a pathetic mask, eyebrows steepled in the middle. 'Oh, please, please, my mental health . . . those boys are making me do things! I might kill myself!'

'You'll feel great about doing that,' Slater said. 'Alpha behaviour. Real manly stuff.'

'Clever, actually. And don't forget who my granda is. Mum too.'

Slater's tone grew dark. 'She's going to be very, very disappointed in you, young man. Very disappointed indeed.'

'She won't. She'll just move on. We're two of a kind. She'll turn it to her advantage. She might even hire a cracking lawyer and get me a good deal. Who knows . . . I might be out and about at some point. Back on the streets. Same streets that you're on. Same streets as your families.'

'Cling on to your dreams,' Slater said, in a lounge singer's half-croon. 'Never let them go . . . Reach for the stars . . .'

'You married, guys? Got kids?' Shane glanced at Lomond. 'Even if I don't get out, there's more of me out there. There are ways round your CCTV and bully-boy surveillance. Technology's not everything. And it's a cert you catching me isn't down to your genius. You've got some IT nerd to thank for this.'

'We do,' Lomond agreed. 'And he's not a nerd; he's a very nice guy. A grafter. He was a massive help. Wanted you caught as much as the rest of us. You'll probably see him in court, if you're daft enough to go for a trial. He can tell you all about it then.'

'Whatever.' Shane yawned. 'End of the day, I did it. You couldn't stop me. Three down . . . or are there more? Did I do some others? Easy to get a dosser on a hook, you know. That first idiot, I got him a sixty pence tin of beans. He ate it cold. He was so grateful. I was talking about the economics of the situation before I snuffed him.'

He laughed uproariously. His mirth went on far too long. It was a slap. The PCs on either side of him tightened their jaws and tried to keep their faces still, their eyes forward.

'And that Symes bitch, God, I wish I'd taken my time there. Made a mess of her. I wanted to, if you're wondering. Could have had her all ways. But had the old forensics to think about. You didn't have a clue back then, did you? I could have done one a night if I'd wanted. Then the wee guy listening to his albums. Stronger than he looked, him. But not stronger than me. I improvised with the bean bag – inspired! Then that barrel of a woman. You should have heard her squeal – she thought she was for it. I'm surprised she lived! She'll be in a loony bin soon. What a cracker. If I'd told her she could just jump head-first out the window and save me the effort, she would have! It was in the palm of my hand. I was in control. It was easy, always. Slip in, slip out. Maybe I'll do it in prison, if my lawyer doesn't get me off? Anyone dies unexpectedly? Unexplained fatalities? Happens in the jail, eh? Some lifer dangling from a bedsheet in the cell next to mine. You'll wonder if it was me, but you'll never know. I'm good at this. I won't stop. I can't be stopped. Prison's nothing, mate. Just another box to go into, and I'll get out, I promise.'

He leaned forward in his seat, teeth bared. Lomond felt his body heat, spittle misting the back of his neck. He reached forward to trigger the stand-by switch on the MP3 player resting in front of the gear stick.

The Lighthouse Family blared out, and Lomond sang along at the top of his voice. '*We could be lifted . . .*'

Shane stopped talking. He frowned.

The two PCs' eyes widened in surprise. Slater threw back his head and laughed, then joined in with Lomond. '*Lifted* . . .'

'Shut up!' Shane said.

The PC to Shane's left swayed, barging into the boy and roaring, '*Lifted!*' in a powerful baritone.

'*Lifted!*' all the officers sang, a capella.

Slater spun around and conducted the line with a finger barged into the teenager's face.

'Shut up,' Shane whined as all four roared their laughter at him. He slumped back, chin trembling slightly, eyes watering.

'*Liiifted!*'

The car disappeared into the mist, the throbbing music and the raised voices a faint pulse fading into the gloom.

59

Lomond pulled his seat in, smoothed down the front of his second-best working jacket, tucked in his tie, straightened his cuffs, and folded his hands on the table of interview room one.

'Shane, first of all I'd like to talk about William Ross. Do you know William Ross?'

Shane Kingsley – or Shane Finch, as he sometimes admitted to – stared directly at Slater. The harsh lighting of the room bred hard shadows, and he leaned into those. He was flanked by a designated adult, a woman who had set out her stall early as no-nonsense, but was quiet when the interview began, and a solicitor, a woman in her late twenties, beautifully turned out for this time of night, in a bright red jacket that it hurt to look at under the lights.

'Do you know William Ross?' Lomond repeated.

'No comment,' Shane said.

'Did you lure William Ross out to the Heights, Shane? Did you promise him money? Did you give him food?'

'No comment.'

'Shane, a young man answering your description was seen talking to William Ross in Garnethill, back of Sauchiehall Street, at least four times just before he went missing. Did you speak to William Ross in Glasgow around that time? He had a pitch in the street where he would ask people for money. Wore a baby-blue knitted bobble hat, you might recall.'

'No comment.'

'Shane, did you smother William Ross with a bin bag in a shipping container at the Heights?'

'No comment.'

'Shane, did you tie a ligature round his neck to finish him off? To be sure?'

'No comment.'

'Shane, did you store his body in a fridge and then hire Daniel Laybourn to take the fridge to the high-rise flats?'

'*Pas de comment.*'

'Did you find out about Daniel Laybourn through your mother or your father's contacts?'

'No . . . comment.'

'Did you hire him for cash, using a burner phone and a fake address?'

'Not fast learners, are you? No comment.'

'We've got a lot more questions,' Lomond said. 'And we'll be asking them if you don't mind.'

'No comment to that, either.'

'Did you steal and hack into your father Vincent Finch's drones?'

'I don't want to answer your questions.'

'Did you stalk Kathryn Symes using your father Vincent Finch's drones?'

'No comment. Heh. That was it, wasn't it? Dad's new drone. You were tracking it. You found something. Bravo.'

'Did you use the drones to physically disable parts of the security systems on the houses – collisions, that kind of thing?'

'Maybe I did, maybe I didn't.'

'Did you know Mrs Symes from business discussions with her husband with regard to a property deal?'

'No comment.'

'Were you responsible for sending pests to various sites to sow discord between your mother, your father and Benny Kettles?'

'No comment.'

'Did you hack into the FiveBarGate database to target people?'

'I really can't say.'

'Did you use a drone to pinpoint a date to kill Mrs Symes and Rowan Beattie?'

'No comment.'

'Did you use the drones to zoom in on their wall calendars and trace their movements?'

Shane grinned. 'I'll let your imaginations fill the next couple of seconds of silence. Now, imagine what my response is.'

'Did you use your driving lessons to help you stake out their neighbourhoods?'

The eyes widened a little at that, then he said, 'No comment.'

'Did you use your mother and father and stepfather's business records to select targets, using the garden coverings and flooring as a green screen?'

'That's a very fancy accusation. I have no comment to make.'

'Did you tamper with the materials and the security systems on the new-build homes to set up a system where you could get into and out of properties without the cameras picking you up?'

'Nah, no comment.'

'Did you enter your mother's business premises to access a skeleton key to get into and out of the back doors of those properties?'

'Ask her. No, on second thought, seriously, I wouldn't. Don't ask her anything. No comment.'

'Did you hack into your father's drone to use it to stalk another customer connected to your family and stepfamily through FiveBarGate – Kelly Martin?'

Shane tapped his lips. 'Give you credit for that one. Fancy move, that. God knows how you swapped her for the little piglet. They call it a Texas switch in the movies, you know.'

'Did you use your father's new drone to stalk her?'

'You kind of told me already – you must have had it tracked. Planted. And you must have picked her out the way I picked her out, with a database. I didn't expect that. Just shows, you can't plan for everything. Well played.'

'Don't make any more comments,' his lawyer said sternly.

'I mean, no comment,' Shane said. He licked his palms and slicked down his fringe, a mimicry of Bart Simpson smartened up for church.

'Did you have seven more targets lined up?' Lomond asked.

'No comment. Obviously.'

Slater looked up. He had not blinked since Shane had tried to stare him out, and he didn't blink now as he said, 'Think your mother is impressed with you?'

'Deep down?' He grinned. 'Yeah.'

'Is there anything you'd like to say to us, Shane?' Lomond asked.

'It's all in the eyes.' He pulled back the skin of one eyelid, displaying one bloodshot, glassy lower eyeball.

'How about to the friends and families of the people you killed, and the one you frightened half to death?'

'It's all good. That's my only comment. All is as it should be. The world's wrong. Isn't it?' He turned his full attention to Lomond. 'That's a question for you.'

'No comment,' Lomond said. 'I'm now terminating this interview. You'll be held in custody. We'll talk again soon, if you like. I'll see you again before you're in court, and you can answer a few questions for us in detail.' He stood up.

Slater scribbled something on a notepad and sat back to show Shane, fingers flattening the page. He had drawn a reasonable sketch of a box with a big padlock on it. Then, without a word, he closed the notepad and left the room in Lomond's wake.

60

It wasn't particularly warm in the interview room, but Nicole Kingsley had chosen to take her coat off. She looked around in vain for somewhere to hang it, before reluctantly draping it over the back of her chair. The trailing hem on the faded beige carpet somehow got on Lomond's nerves; he almost wanted to help her look for a suitable place to put it.

In a plain silk ivory shirt, she looked more fragile than Lomond remembered. She folded her hands and said, 'There's a reason you don't have a coat stand or hangers in an interview room, I guess.'

'Probably for the best,' Lomond replied.

'For the eyes, right?'

'I'm sorry? The eyes?'

'Yeah.' She stiffened a thumb and jabbed it towards her eye. 'Hook on a rack, coat hanger . . . could cause you a problem with the eyes. If you were in here with a wrong 'un, I mean. Wouldn't it?'

'I suppose it would.' Lomond turned to the second person on the other side of the table. 'Would you care to sit down, Mr Finch?'

'I think I'd prefer to stand,' Finch said. His hair had been doused in a sudden heavy shower on the way over. Lomond had been caught in it too; his own overcoat sagged, sodden, on the back of his chair. While Nicole Kingsley was flat calm except for a slight fluttering at the nostrils, Vincent Finch was a constant pulse of anxiety.

'Dear, the inspector's being polite,' Kingsley said, looking up at her ex-husband. 'He means you should stop pacing up and down.'

'And I said I preferred to stand, *dear.*' The last word was filed into a jagged edge.

'If you wouldn't mind taking a seat, Mr Finch, it would be a lot less awkward for all of us,' Lomond said agreeably.

Finch shrugged and sat down heavily. More of a teenager than his son, Lomond reflected. Side by side – the first time Lomond had seen them together – their incongruence was almost comical.

'I'm having trouble believing this,' Finch said, scraping his fingers through his damp hair. 'I mean, there's bad and there's bad–'

'Shut up,' Kingsley said.

'You keep your trap shut and speak to me with courtesy,' Finch said through gritted teeth. A rasping edge of real rage was audible in his voice.

Lomond tensed.

'You say nothing,' Kingsley said simply, 'because you know nothing. Like I know nothing.'

'This isn't a formal interview,' Lomond interjected. 'You're not under caution. We've already taken the statements from you. I just want to talk to you about what's happening with your son and what the next steps will be. He's with a specially trained adult who will help him through the process, and of course we'll–'

'And his lawyer,' Kingsley said.

'Obviously, he'll have a lawyer too.'

'Don't forget it.' Kingsley smiled icily. 'Speaking for myself and my family here, we're finding it all a bit hard to swallow. You think a teenage boy managed to kill . . . how many people, was it?'

'I can't go into details about the investigation. I'm sure you can understand.'

'Oh, I understand about the police. I'm very well versed.'

'We'll update you throughout the process. Shane's going to be in court tomorrow morning, and I expect him to be remanded in custody from there.'

'Shane was a good boy,' Finch said, hands clenched tight. 'I don't believe it. Quiet. Clever. No edge to him. Never any bother.'

Kingsley closed her eyes. 'Please, Vincent. Stop talking. For once, just stop.'

Finch ignored her. 'He had the best of everything. Everything we built was for him.'

'There's every chance we'll find out he didn't do any of it,' Kingsley said. 'That's the way I'm approaching it. For the record. That's how the police and the courts operate in this country.'

'It'll be for the jury to decide,' Lomond said. 'If you have anything to tell us about your son's whereabouts on key dates, then that would be useful.'

'I might just do that,' she said. 'Wouldn't be good for your case if I did, would it?'

'So long as you're happy to say it in court, under oath. You know about the courts, so I won't need to remind you about something called perjury, Mrs Kingsley. If you're found guilty of that, judges tend to throw the book at you for it.'

A grin transformed Kingsley's face into something close to outright glee. The expression was close to the one Lomond had not long before seen, and disliked, on the face of her son, after he'd reached the obvious conclusion that he'd been caught, that he was in trouble and that pretence was useless. Simultaneous mirth and contempt. Lomond shivered at the resemblance.

'A threat!' she spluttered. 'Wow. That was a threat, wasn't it?'

'Absolutely not. Just a statement of fact. We're all about the facts here. It's our job.'

'Is it, though?' Finch said quietly. 'Is it really?'

'I'm sorry, Mr Finch?'

'All about the facts, I mean.' He shook his head. 'Not, like, the stuff you find out, places and dates and all that. I've been racking my brains. Just this past hour, waiting to come in here. You go through things . . .'

'Vincent, please,' Kingsley said.

'And you blame yourself a bit, of course you do. What is it they say? Sad, bad or mad? Which one is he? All of them? And is it my . . . is it *our* fault?'

'For Christ's sake, Vincent,' Kingsley snapped. 'You won't be happy till they've banged you up as well. Dimwit.'

'Genetic? Born that way? Take after his grandad? Or something we did? Something we didn't do? God knows he wasn't *abused* . . . or I don't think he was. What would make someone do something like that? Grow up that way? What was missing?' Finch looked helpless and scared, and Lomond almost wanted to comfort him. Almost.

'We'll find out in time,' Lomond said.

'If I can speak to him . . . if I can talk it through with him . . . whatever was going on in his head . . . I'm his dad. I can reach him.' He looked to Lomond for . . . what? Guidance? Reassurance? Absolution?

Lomond could provide Vincent Finch with none of these. In another place, in other circumstances, Lomond would have given way to his instincts – his reflexes. He would have been on his feet, a hand placed on the man's shoulder. Hey, c'mon, he might have said. It's not your fault. It can't be your fault. You weren't involved. It wasn't anything you did or didn't do. That was the thing you did with someone in distress. Only, even in those circumstances, Lomond wouldn't have believed himself. There were times in life you had to tell white lies. But Lomond couldn't have done it, just then, in any circumstances. So all he said was, 'We'll be in touch, Mr Finch. Mrs Kingsley.'

'No, you'll be in touch with our lawyers,' Kingsley said. 'My lawyers, specifically. Understand?'

'Perfectly. And I look forward to it, Mrs Kingsley.'

'And I've told you before – it's *Ms* Kingsley.'

She glared at Lomond, unblinking, as he got up from his seat and pulled on his damp overcoat. He looked right back. As a flashbulb moment, examined on its own by a stranger, his expression might have seemed pitiless.

61

Finch's hair was shorter, his jaw chiselled and his expression lethal. He paced up and down the tiled kitchen floor in his bare feet. The slapping sound might have put an ordinary person's teeth on edge. It did no such thing for the boy, staring at his father through the crack.

'He just sits there. Won't do his ABC, won't do his numbers, won't paint a picture, won't colour in with his crayons, even. Nothing!' Finch's voice was high and raspy.

He speaks about me like I'm not here, thought the boy. Am I not here?

'Something's wrong with him. Is he doing it to wind me up? The little bastard!' The face loomed closer to the crack. The boy felt something wet, just underneath his eye. He did not blink. It was a trick he had learned, though he could not remember when.

The boy had seen millipedes on the television and that one time at school when they'd had a display. The girl with the nice smile, handling beetles and spiders and even a snake. His mother moved the same way as the millipede. It seemed effortless. Like she had a thousand tiny invisible legs working overtime beneath her feet. She slipped across the floor now, pausing before the crack with her hands on her hips.

'So this is your idea of discipline?'

'I'm out of ideas!' Finch shrieked. 'I said I'd take his toys away from him for a week, and he just shrugged. He doesn't care. This happy-clappy stuff doesn't work. So I decided to put him in there. Maybe that'll shake him out of it. I'm well past the nicey-nice stage, Nicole. The boy's a freak!'

'That seems harsh, Vincent. Maybe you should leave it to me.'

Finch bent over and stared through the crack. Then his expression went blank. His lip trembled. The boy knew what this portended, but he was prepared.

The crack become the whole of the kitchen, and hands gripped him by the scruff of the neck and under an armpit. No effort at all, he was on his feet. Whee!

'You laughing at me?' Finch screamed. 'You laughing? You're going to catch it, I swear to Christ. I swear to almighty Christ!'

The boy hadn't realised he'd been smiling, until that moment. He let his face relax, and much more besides.

'Now look! He's pissing himself! In the name of God . . .'

The boy was dropped. He fell to his knees. He felt wetness seep through there too.

'Vincent.' His mother's voice was firm now, the voice that almost always won out. 'I think we should leave this, OK? Just go and do your thing. Go back to your computer, whatever you were doing. You've got emails to catch up on, don't you?'

'Don't take this away from him,' Finch said, jabbing a finger at the boy. 'Don't. We've got to knock it out of him. Whatever it is that's wrong. Whatever means that he can't function.'

'It's fine,' she said, closing the door behind him. She spun on her heels, drew a breath and looked down to the floor. 'Now what seems to be the trouble, young man?' she said.

The boy made no reply. He could think of several at once, but he knew it was best not to express them. Especially with her.

'Did you do that deliberately? Or accidentally?' She pointed at his wet trousers. 'Never mind. The outcome's the same. Mummy will clean it, won't she? Mummy cleans all messes. That's what mummies do.'

Then she took him by the scruff of the neck and the armpit. Once again. Whee!

He was back inside, shoved into place. His knees and hips hurt. She was strong, he knew that. Stronger than she looked. Her fingers on his neck, not hard enough to bruise, but impossible to resist. She forced him down.

'You know, your dad may be onto something. But don't tell him I said that. While I'm mopping the floor, you can stay in there. You might get a chill, but that's on you, son. You might not learn anything,

but I'll punish you. It'll make me feel better, because Mummy's had a hard day.'

She looked at him, not with contempt, not with anger, not with sorrow or remorse or any of these things – or, in fact, anything at all.

'You didn't cry,' she said tonelessly. 'Mummy's proud of you. Now don't you move a muscle or make a sound. It's quiet time now. Got it?' She dropped the lid of the toybox, hard, expunging all light. 'There's a good boy.'

62

Smythe was still limping. The slow blush of bruising from her pubic bone to the top of her hip had turned to something of fascination rather than horror as the colours shifted from mauve to black to cerise to yellow.

She eschewed the canteen for a chilled sandwich from the vending machine, then found a quiet corner to sit down and catch up on a bit of personal admin on her phone. There was an email in from HR. She ignored it for the moment, sipping at a coffee and waiting for the sandwich to warm up. Then McGill appeared, and her corner was quiet no longer.

'All right?' McGill asked.

Smythe felt a sting of irritation at the children's TV-presenter demeanour. 'Hiya, Lorna. Were you off yesterday?'

'Aye, a half-day. I spent most of it chasing that spiker in the new pop-up club in town.'

'Heard about that. Sounded like a weirdo rather than anything too sinister.'

'Aye. Bouncers dealt with it fast.' She sighed. 'Anyway, I brought in a spare couple of Specials. Want one?' She grinned and held up a cardboard box. Slightly greasy but the kind of grease you didn't mind at all, knowing it portended good things.

'What's a Special?'

'I *made* them.' McGill enunciated the word as if imparting a great secret. 'Want to see?' She flipped the box open without waiting for an answer.

'Wow – proper Danish pastries!'

'Cinnamon swirls, but I'll take Danish pastries.' McGill smiled. 'This one's for you.'

'Really? That's kind. You one of those *Bake Off* bakey people?'

'Aye,' she said proudly. 'C'mon, have it while your coffee's warm.'

'I will.'

McGill sat down as Smythe munched on the end of the swirl. It was lovely, Smythe thought. Crumbly, but not annoyingly so. Bit of crunch to it. Sweet and spicy, perfect filling. 'This is superb. You been baking long?'

McGill looked abashed. 'Och, not really. I used to help out my auntie. She had a baker's out in Pollok.'

'Honest?' A flare of recognition. 'McGill's Bakers? That you? Or your family? I used to go in there a lot. I had a Saturday job in Pollok, when I was at school. Worked in a newsagent's for a few months, and I'd go into McGill's for a sausage roll and a pineapple cake when the queues weren't too long. And they used to be too long a lot of the time.' Now Smythe recalled a woman about the same height as Lorna, but plump, and very good-looking with it, who had blue-overalled men and twitchy teens and building-site boys on the end of a hook with one smile. Almost the same face Smythe was looking at now. 'How's your auntie doing?'

'Oh, she died,' McGill said, with not even a hint of a reduction in her grin. 'Anyway, I just thought you might like one. I think I saw you at the interview the other day.'

Smythe was on her guard. 'Oh aye. I went in for it. Did you?'

'Course I did. Remember we spoke about it? Worth a shot. You might miss this time, but you won't miss the next time.'

Smythe nodded. The email. McGill wasn't looking for information, or currying favour. 'Well, best of luck with it, eh? For what it's worth, I hope you get it.'

'I didn't.'

'Oh.'

'I'm commiserating, really.'

Before Smythe could say 'What have you heard?' someone

pulled out the spare seat and sat down. Myles Tait had a relaxed, even graceful expression as he bowed his head. 'Ladies,' he said.

'Oh, hey!' McGill said. 'Congratulations!'

'News travels fast.' Tait grinned. 'I want to say that I'm looking forward to carrying on working with you same as before, with the same results.'

'What team are you assigned to?'

'Not sure yet. Won't be going over to Edinburgh for a while. But I wish it was with you two, if I'm honest. I think we work well together.'

'Myles, congratulations,' Smythe said, offering a handshake.

'Cheers. No hard feelings, eh?'

'Course not. Best man won.' Smythe was seized by an irresistible desire to cough – a stray flake of pastry had clung to the inside of her throat. Maybe it was embedded there, like a splinter.

'It's not true, but nice of you to say so. Well, best be off – got some paperwork to sort out. And I need to wind Slater up.' He smiled and got back to his feet.

Slater passed by, with a steaming cup of coffee. 'Myles,' he said stiffly, 'I understand some congratulations are in order.'

'Nice of you to say so,' Tait said.

Slater turned to McGill. 'Lorna, congratulations on your Oscar nomination. Show's on in a couple of weeks, eh? I'll be watching.'

Tait looked briefly as if he'd just realised he'd left the house without his wallet. 'I'm going to miss you, Malcolm. Hopefully you aren't charged with police brutality while I'm away. Heard the Kingsley boy complained about you lifting your hands. I laughed about that, I tell you. Malcolm Slater couldn't punch his way out a wet paper bag, I said.'

'Well, you know. Justice calls for a firm hand. A bit like . . . och, what's the name of that guy? Him that batters the baddies? You know . . . wears a costume? Like a bat? What's that man's name?'

'That would be Batman,' Tait responded, turning on his heels and walking away.

'Works every time,' Slater said, when the laughter died down.

'He'll miss you, really,' Smythe said.

'He'll miss something. Anyway, Cara – I'm sorry that eejit got your job. It was yours, the way I see it. I was shocked you didn't get it.'

McGill broke the silence by fishing out another pastry from the box. 'Compliments of the chef,' she said.

'Ooh!' Slater brightened up, accepting the pastry.

McGill waited until he was gone. 'Yeah, I didn't bake one for Myles,' she said sweetly. Turning to Smythe, she said, 'That was gracious of you. Couldn't have been easy. That was your job, and everyone knows it. Sorry.'

'Ach, it's not as bad as a kick in the fanny,' Smythe reflected.

They laughed for a good while. Smythe didn't wince quite as much as she wanted to.

*

He let himself sink into the sofa, all elbows and knees, a spider poised to spring. It wasn't his best look, but he enjoyed the coffee all the same. He liked the coffee shop, liked that it wasn't a big chain, liked that they went to an effort, baking their own cakes and biscuits ('cookies', they called them – that irritated him).

On the table in front of him, he'd spread out the newspaper to show pages four and five, covering the Jack-in-the-Box case. Lots of pictures. They even included a web link – as if you'd type one of those into your device after seeing it in a paper! – and a QR code for 'bonus content'. Probably a nightmare of pop-ups, sign-up prompts and all the usual irritating nonsense. Dying, he thought to himself. It's a dying industry. That, and all the news that goes with it. A shame, in a way.

'Terrible, isn't it?' said one of the other customers as she passed by with a milkshake and a brownie as thick as a kerbstone. She had cropped white hair and big, thick glasses.

He nodded. Half tutted, half sighed, all lament. 'It's shocking. Glad they got him, though. Can't have folk like that running about.'

'I heard he was just seventeen years old,' the woman said, scandalised.

'Unbelievable, isn't it? Seem to be starting younger and younger.' He grinned. He had noticed years ago that when he did that, people smiled back, and they still did, even at his age. It was true what they'd said at school. It was amazing the things you could go on to do – the things you could talk people into – when you had a nice smile.

If any of them had survived, that's what they'd have told the police. *A lovely smile, he had. Just drew you in.* Something like that.

'Hope they throw away the key. I know what I'd do with him.'

'Ach, violence solves nothing, really,' said the man.

The woman behind the counter, who had listened to this exchange closely, waiting for a moment to leap in, said, 'I wonder if they'll ever catch that Flick character?'

The white-haired woman clutched her milkshake and brownie to her bosom. 'Oh my God, you forget he's still out there. Him and Bible John.'

'And Jack the Ripper,' said Flick, grinning.

63

Lomond stared at the doll. Straw-yellow hair, made of delicate strands of wool that would come right out if you pulled too hard. Siobhan had done this once or twice before she understood that the hair wouldn't grow back and couldn't be combed any more, or put in bunches. She had left it alone after that. Staring up at Lomond from the box, the doll seemed melancholic – though it always had done; it wasn't just his mood. Not just that.

If I ever see this doll again, Lomond thought, it'll be when I'm helping Siobhan move house. Or if I ever have to clear *her* house out for any reason.

He stared at the sad eyes, with their radial Aunt Sally eyelashes, sparsely stitched around each wide blue orb, then placed her back in the box on top of the rest of the precious childhood toys. He closed the box. Jojo – that was the doll's name. He didn't hear Maureen padding into the room – she was good at that when she wanted to be – and leapt when she said, 'Having second thoughts?'

'What d'you mean?'

'Well, you're as sentimental as they come,' Maureen said frankly, opening the box. 'You used to get just as wrapped up in the games as she did. When she thought she'd lost Jojo you tore the house apart looking for her.'

'Found her, as well,' Lomond said. 'Left underneath an empty plant pot in the garden. A game of hide and seek. We declared her the winner.'

'I remember.'

'Just as well Daddy's a detective, eh?'

'You've been in sorting out this box for an hour and a half.'

'Have I?' He checked his watch. 'Jeezo. Just looking through them. The memories in every one. Christmas. Birthdays. Wee presents we gave her, just cos she had a good day at school. Just cos it was Friday, sometimes.'

'Wee presents *you* gave her, mostly.' She nudged his hip. 'You know, we don't have to take these over to her now. Her flat's not small, but it's not that big. Maybe wait until she's got a bigger place. One with a loft. Then she can stuff her own space with her old toys and free up some room for us.'

'I suppose. We've got plenty of space now she's definitely away.'

'Well, until the next crisis.'

He looked up at his wife sharply. 'What d'you mean?'

'Well, you know. Stuff happens in life. People find partners. They break up. They need hotel mum and dad as well as banco di mum and dad.'

'True. Never happened to us, though.'

'There's time yet.' Maureen combed her fingers through Jojo's woollen hair, smoothing back the remaining strands. 'Museum piece, this.'

'Your mum knitted it for her before she was born.'

'True enough. She loved it, all the same. One of her oldest wee pals.'

They gazed at the doll and the jumble of teddies, Barbies and other toys around it. Most of the childhood stuff had been given away, and Siobhan's treasured companions had dwindled to this hard core. Not to be given away, not to be donated to charity shops, and absolutely not to be thrown out. Relics beyond price. There was a whole universe of childhood games in here, often shared with Mum and Dad, willing participants and observers of their daughter's theatre. Often it took the form of a school, with Siobhan as teacher, and sometimes it became a sleepover or a school disco or, alarmingly often, a skirmish between the girls over which boy they liked, before puberty brought an abrupt end to these exchanges, at least among the toys.

'Hard to let go, isn't it?' Lomond said.

'Well, don't let go. Stick them up on the shelves. They can be ornaments. They can stand guard. Say hello to them when you go past. I bet you will, as well.'

'I might. Treat it as a live investigation. Ask them searching questions.'

'So long as you don't strip-search them, honey.'

'They'll need a dedicated female officer for that,' Lomond said soberly. 'Might bring Smythe round for it. She didn't get the job, you know.'

'Oh,' was all Maureen said.

'Aye. That was my reaction. Can't say anything. Couldn't even tell her it was nothing to do with me, which happens to be the truth.'

'Who got it, then? Oh, don't tell me.'

'The guy you're thinking – that guy. Presuming you're not thinking about Slater, cos it wasn't him.'

'Tait. Ach.'

'He's a decent copper, to be fair. Just not as decent as Smythe. But there we go.'

'Sounds like pish.'

'It is. But at least she stays with us for a bit longer. I'll miss Tait, for what it's worth. He boots Slater's arse for him, so I don't have to.'

'Why don't you finish up what you're doing and we'll open a bottle of wine, get the fire on, and watch an old comedy?'

Lomond grinned. 'What are you thinking?'

'*One Foot in the Grave*.'

'Perfect. Lead on.' Lomond shut the box and pulled out a length of sticky tape from the roll. But an instant before he sealed down the lid, he thought better of it. He wound back the tape as best he could, and put the roll on the bare dressing table. Then he pulled out the doll and sat it on the shelf where

Siobhan had kept all her perfume bottles, feet dangling, gingham dress draped demurely just below the knees. 'Welcome back, Jojo,' he said. Then he shut the box and slid it under the bed.

'Back of the net!' Maureen cried, clapping her hands. 'Now, how about you eat something?'

'Nah . . . guts are iffy.'

'Something you ate?'

'Just thinking about stuff.' He shrugged. She came closer, feeding an arm around his waist and tucking a strand of hair over his ear. He swallowed.

'Go on then,' she said gently.

'Just the usual. It's another couple of faces to zip up, put in a box and put in the ground. But they stay in here.' Lomond tapped his temple. 'That's a price to pay. I'll pay it, like your tax and NI, fees for the union - no problem. No complaint. Has to be done. But there's always more. When I stop – when you stick me in a box – it'll go on. There'll be more creeps and perverts. I was just thinking about that. But . . . no work tomorrow. Let's have some wine and watch a bit of Victor and Margaret.'

Maureen sighed. 'There'll always be baddies out there, love - but think of the ones you stopped. And think of the ones who weren't zipped up in a bag. They're still out and about now, walking the streets, living their lives. The ones you protected. The ones you kept out of a box. Siobhan's one of them. Some very bad people are in their own box as well, because of what you did. One with bars on the window. Some of them won't ever get out of it. That's the thing to remember. That's the thing that keeps everything going.'

'C'mon, then, we're done here,' Lomond said. They left the room and turned the lights out on Jojo. The doll who never smiled and never blinked sat there silently in the dark. Beyond the door, the warm voices carried on.

Acknowledgements

Thanks to Alison Rae, Ellen Cranston and everyone at team Birlinn for all their help, support and guidance. Special thanks go to Nancy Webber, copy-editor extraordinaire. I've got a brilliant team behind me and am grateful for the opportunity and all the help they've given me. As ever, thanks to Justin and Kate and all the utter heroes at the Kate Nash Literary Agency. Apologies for the over-running Zoom calls, but I do love a blether, and the less on-topic and more irrelevant it is, the better.

For the technical stuff, I want to thank Colin Taylor, a pint-after-work hero and a friendly face across the hallway from my days at Anderston Quay. A former office, all shiny and new at the millennium, now gone to dust thanks to the bulldozers. Hard to believe it doesn't exist any more . . . but nothing's for ever. Anyway, Colin is the guy who told me that It Could Be Done.

Thanks again to Dr Stephen Docherty for the medical stuff, and to my brother James for all the help with the police procedure as it happens in the real world, to real people. These folk know what they're doing, and they are good at it. Any errors, discrepancies or omissions are entirely down to me.

The idea for this book came from a chat with the neighbours, Jonny and Michelle, about a strange event in our street. There had been talk of people appearing at odd times and, seemingly, scoping out houses and cars. They had crime in mind, we were sure. The lightning-bolt moment for me came when I viewed the doorbell-cam footage on my phone. At first, I couldn't see anyone, but someone *was* there. Loitering beside a wooden fence. Not exactly camouflaged, but hard to notice with the change of texture in the background. Calm and cool as you like, looking from one door to the next, from one window to the other. It still makes me shiver. And, as I type, I realise it's getting late and I should really check all the doors are locked . . .

Eternal thanks, as ever, to Claire and the kids, and to all the family. All my love.

A shout-out to Bob McDevitt and the gang at Bloody Scotland – thanks so much for the opportunity and second-to-none hospitality during an unforgettable weekend in Stirling. Thanks also to the awesome Rob Parker and Brian Meechan for being absolute heroes when they were landed with me on my first-ever author panel. I hope we can bellow at an unsuspecting public again someday.

I want to thank Kelly, Dwayne and Kevin – aka Love Books Tours, Dunfermline Reads and The First Eleven Minutes – as seen on social media. They were the first book bloggers I met in person at the Bloody Scotland launch, and they put me at ease. I cannot overstate the importance of such a kind, welcoming and enthusiastic community.

And, finally, my sincere thanks to you for reading this book, and to the lovely people who came to see me at Bloody Scotland. I'll be out and about again before long. (This sounds like I'm in jail. I am categorically not in jail.) I hope we can meet again soon. Until then, all the best!

Polygon

AN IMPRINT OF BIRLINN LIMITED

Head over to our website to find more Birlinn books across fiction, non-fiction, sport, poetry, children's books and academic history.

You can also sign up to our newsletter. Keep up to date with all our new publications, launch events, author interviews, special offers and much more.

http://birlinn.co.uk/birlinn-newsletter/

Follow the link or scan the QR Code below:

Explore Scotland with our app, Scotland-by-the-Book, a new tool for readers at home and around the globe with an interest in Scotland. Find out more on our website.

https://birlinn.co.uk/scotland-by-the-book/

Follow the link or scan the QR Code below: